Symphony of Soul

An aging Black in the deep South learns the price and the pride of being a man . . . a Black girl from New York comes to terms with her racial sexual hang-ups in the West Indies . . . a Black Muslim is torn between his fervent faith and his stubborn love for his white mother . . . a Black college student is forced step-by-step from conservatism to revolutionary consciousness . . . a great Black entertainer struggles to escape the prison of his own celebrity . . . a group of young Blacks intensely debate the choices that lie before them . . .

Each of the stories in this volume stands by itself as a finely wrought individual expression of one Black writer's experience, talent, and vision. Together they combine and blend to give the reader an unparalleled panoramic view of Black writing as for the first time it has truly come into its own.

MENTOR and SIGNET Books of Related Interest

BLACK
SHORT STORY
ANTHOLOGY

Edited by
Woodie King

A SIGNET BOOK from
NEW AMERICAN LIBRARY
TIMES MIRROR

Library of Congress Catalog Card Number: 72-77398

Acknowledgments

"The Smoking Sixties," by John Oliver Killens. Copyright © 1972 by John Oliver Killens. Reprinted by permission of the author.

"A Revolutionary Tale," by Nikki Giovanni. From *Black World*, June 1968. Reprinted by permission of the author.

"Frankie Mae," by Jean Wheeler Smith. From *Black World*, June 1968. Reprinted by permission of the author.

"Harlem Transfer," by E. K. Walker. From *Black World*, May 1970. Reprinted by permission of the author.

"Dandy, or Astride the Funky Finger of Lust," by Ed Bullins. From *The Hungered One*. Copyright © 1971 by William Morrow. Reprinted by permission of the author.

"Sonny's Not Blue," by Sam Greenlee. Copyright © 1972 by Sam Greenlee.

"Testimonial," by Paula Hankins. Copyright © 1972 by Paula Hankins.

"The Ray" and "The Flogging," by Ron Milner. Copyright © 1972.

"A Good Season," by John A. Williams. From *Urbanite*, May 1961. Reprinted by permission of the author.

"The Alternative," by Imamu Amiri Baraka (LeRoi Jones). Copyright © 1967 by LeRoi Jones. From *Tales*. Reprinted by permission of the Sterling Lord Agency.

"Strong Horse Tea," by Alice Walker. Copyright © 1968 by Alice Walker. From *Black World*, June 1968. Reprinted by permission of the author.

"Love Song for Wing," by Charles H. Fuller, Jr. Copyright © 1972 by Charles H. Fuller, Jr., used with permission of the author and Ronald Hobbs Literary Agency.

"The Convert," by Lernone Bennett, Jr. Copyright © January 1963 by *Negro Digest*. Reprinted by permission of *Black World*.

"Not Your Singing, Dancing Spade," by Julia Fields. From *Black World*, February 1967. Reprinted by permission of the author and *Black World*.

"A Happening in Barbados," by Louise M. Meriwether. Reprinted from The *Antioch Review*, Vol. xxviii, No. 1, Spring 1968. Copyright 1968 by The Antioch Press. Reprinted by permission of the *Antioch Review* and the author.

"Early Autumn," by Langston Hughes. From *Something in Common and Other Stories*. Copyright © 1963 by Langston Hughes. Reprinted by permission of Hill and Wang, Inc., and Harold Ober Associates Incorporated.

"Just Like a Tree," by Ernest J. Gaines. Reprinted from *Bloodline* by Ernest J. Gaines. Copyright © 1963, 1964, 1968 by Ernest J. Gaines and used by permission of the publisher, The Dial Press, and Dorothea Oppenheimer.

"Not We Many," by Clarence L. Cooper, Jr. From his novel *Black!* Reprinted by permission of the author.

(The following page constitutes an extension of this copyright page.)

Second Printing
Third Printing
Fourth Printing
Fifth Printing
Sixth Printing
Seventh Printing
Eighth Printing
Ninth Printing
Tenth Printing

 SIGNETTE TRADEMARK REG. U.S. PAT. OFF. AND FOREIGN COUNTRIES
REGISTERED TRADEMARK—MARCA REGISTRADA
HECHO EN CHICAGO, U.S.A.

Signet, Signet Classics, Signette, Mentor and Plume Books
are published by The New American Library, Inc.,
1301 Avenue of the Americas, New York, New York 10019

First Printing, October, 1972

PRINTED IN THE UNITED STATES OF AMERICA

This book of short stories is dedicated to Hoyt W. Fuller. It was he who made me aware that the National Endowment of the Arts supports short-story anthologies that never include any Black authors. The white editors select most of the anthology stories from little magazines that never publish Black authors. The editors of the anthologies, the Federal Government who supports them, and the racist literary magazines perpetuate racism in publishing by ignoring Black writers and Black literary magazines. As if *Urbanite, Freedomways, Liberator, Black World, Black Dialog, Umbra, Journal of Black Poetry, Soulbook, Black Scholar,* and *c* never existed. And indeed as if Black short-story writers never existed. I felt it necessary to do what little I could to change this misconception.

Woodie King
Editor

CONTENTS

IT WAS A GREAT TIME. A crazy time. It was a hopeful time. At times it was a decade of despair and tremen-
dous desperation. It was an era of great Black courage. It
was Integration Time. Black Power and Black Nationalism.
Near the beginning of the decade the N.A.A.C.P. said opti-
mistically that we'd be *FREE IN '63*. There were moments
of Black unity; there were times of great confusion. Medgar, Malcolm, and Martin were with us. The students and
the masses were in motion. Weren't they? "Three little
words!" Brother Martin said, "We want it *ALL!* We want
it *HERE!* We want it *NOW!*"

I remember rather vividly a New Year's Eve party in
Park West Village. There were several Black writers present. We toasted in the sixties amidst a din of noisemakers
and horn-blowing in the house and down in the streets all
over New York town. If I remember correctly, there were
Loften Mitchell, Julian Mayfield, William Branch, and
John Killens. And others I do not recall. Perhaps it was the
booze. In any event, we were all in an optimistic mood. The
sixties, we agreed, would see a great change in the nation
and the Black man's situation. And we Black writers would
do our part to bring about the change. We would make a
witness for Black liberation. All hail to the glorious new
decade. Hurry midnight, see what the sixties bring.

What did the sixties bring? The sixties were a mixture
of triumphs and defeats. Sitins, Freedom Rides, Voter
Registration, Elijah Muhammad, Marches on Washington,
assassinations, rebellions in Watts, Newark, New York,
Nashville, Chicago, Detroit, the District of Columbia. Erup-
tions in the streets and on the college campuses. Some said,
"The brethren are getting it together!" Others proclaimed,
"It's Revolution Time!" It was a time when James Mere-
dith "integrated" Ol' Miss. A time when Brother Stokely
and Brother Willie Ricks shouted, "Black Power," on a
lonesome road in 'Sippi. We began to understand more
profoundly what Brothers DuBois and Robeson and Garvey
and Hughes had advocated long before: that the fate of our
brothers in Africa was linked with ours in North America.
In Central and South America, also, for that matter, and
the Islands of the Sea. There were many disquieting moments. This U.S.A. is a peculiar kind of a country. Sometimes we Blacks lost ground even as we struggled forward.
We lost Medgar, Malcolm, and Martin by the guns of hired
killers. We lost Patrice Lumumba, Ben Bella, and Nasser.
Modiba Keita of Mali and Nkrumah of Ghana were over-
thrown. Before our eyes Africa was being recolonized be-

fore she realized independence. The counterrevolution was everywhere, oftentimes before the revolution could gather up steam and get underway. The stakes were high, simply to win the world, that's all. And the Liberation Movement was faced with an opponent the most powerful and most sophisticated the world had ever known. But there were optimistic moments.

In the U.S.A., Black men were winning seats in the Southern legislatures and city councils for the first time since the era of Reconstruction. Blacks braved the wrath of Crackerdom and registered and voted in increasing numbers. We no longer sat on the back of the buses unless it pleased our dispositions. We won mayoralties in several Northern cities, and finally in Mississippi. We slept in Southern hotels and ate in Southern restaurants. Things were looking up, as we played seesaw over a bottomless pit. The sixties were a wonderful and terrible decade.

The stories in this anthology are a reflection of those times. Men and women will read this anthology and obtain a clearer picture of the sixties. They will read this anthology ten, twenty, thirty years from now and understand the times they live in more profoundly. Moreover, this anthology gives a vivid picture of all those roads down which Black folk traveled in the turbulent sixties. And every road was Freedom Road, supposedly. Just as we have learned from the Harlem Renaissance of the twenties, folk of future generations will learn from the Black Renaissance of the sixties. There are similarities between the twenties and the sixties. In both periods the South for the most part was relegated by the writers to unimportance and oblivion. Most Black writers seemed to think that the only thing worth writing about was the happenings in the Northern urban areas—New York, Chicago, Watts, Detroit—even as many of the same Black writers proclaimed that it was "Nation Time." Surely they (we) must have understood that Black Power, Pan-Africanism, and National Liberation at their roots meant land, earth, soil. Dirt. Black dirt. Our own dirt. To taste. To dig our Black hands into. To plant our own crops, to watch them grow, to create. Black dirt to mold Black images. And there certainly was no dirt available in the crowded Northern cities except the filth of urban pavement and earth of cemeteries. One of the strong points of this anthology is that it reflects the Black condition North and South.

What became clearer than ever during the sixties was that the U.S.A. was essentially a Southern country, from

Maine to the Florida Keys, from the State of Washington all the way to San Diego, and all those amber waves of grain in between, from sea to shining sea, polluted air, poisoned waters and all. In 1964, I wrote that Georgia, where I was born, was downSouth and New York, to which I escaped, was upSouth, and that the only basic difference was the degrees of sophistication. It is difficult for an upSouth Black to accept this truth, but the brothers in slavery time knew it in their very bones. When they escaped the old plantation, more often than not they did not stop running till they crossed over into Canada. And even then they lived uneasily. Men like Frederick Douglass and Denmark Vesey understood that no Black man would ever be free anywhere in these United States until slavery was destroyed. The same is true today.

The sixties saw a blossoming of the Black arts. Some hailed it as the New Renaissance. Others called it a cultural revolution. One thing was very clear. Something new was being added. Black writers were proclaiming their Blackness. Very seldom did you hear a writer say, "I'm not a Black writer. I'm a writer who happens to be Black." We began to understand that no writer was born hunting and pecking on a typewriter, but that every Afro-American writer was born Black in a white racist society. The sixties saw many changes in the Black writers' attitudes. Most of them were no longer concerned in leaping willy-nilly into the so-called mainstream of American writing, which, after all was said and done, was a rather stagnant stream at that. Most of us no longer went for the ruse that to write about what it was to be Black in white America was to deprive ourselves of "universality." We came to understand that we *are* the universal men, the First World people (not the "Third"). We are the human race, the exploited, the colonized, the colored peoples of the earth. When the white man uses such catchwords as "mainstream" and "universality," he is speaking of a white mainstream, a European Anglo-Saxon universality.

Many Black writers decided to tell their stories in the idiom and nuances and rhythms of the Black experience. Too long had our writers, like the rest of us, looked at our Black selves through the eyes of white America. The sixties saw a cultural movement back to Blackness similar to the movement of the twenties, but with differences, one of which was that most Black artists of the latter period made their statements *specifically* to Black people and generally to the world at large. We moved from the posture of Richard Wright's *White Man Listen!* to one of *Black Man Speaks* to Black people in particular but for humanity to listen.

Now it must be said that not all of our writers made the entire journey to our Blackness. It is a long and tortuous journey. The road is lonesome and white and full of land mines and obstructions. It is not easy to throw off centuries of white brainwashing. The highway to our Blackness is like an army obstacle course, full of twists and turns and forks in the road heading sometimes into nothingness, full of ditches and hurdles and sand traps and illusion and mirages. Some of our writers, like some of our people, still regard themselves through Anglo-Saxon eyes, still insist, and militantly, on looking upon themselves as "niggers." But most of us are trying. Lord and/or Allah know, the brothers and sisters are trying to throw off the shackles of "niggerdom."

Imamu Amiri Baraka (né LeRoi Jones) moved during the sixties from the integrated hippy sickness of Greenwich Village to Black Harlem and from Harlem to Black Newark. The New Lafayette Theatre opened in Harlem as did the Negro Ensemble Company in the East Village. Harlem gave birth to the Black Magicians, the New Heritage Theatre, the Langston Hughes House of Kuumba, the National Black Theatre. OBACI got the Black writers together in Chicago. Painters from OBACI constructed the great Wall of Respect on the Southside of Chicago. As the seventies began, the *Negro Digest* under the leadership of Hoyt Fuller became the *Black World*. It had been heading in that direction all during the last decade. Nathan Hare published the *Black Scholar*. Black poets all over the nation were speaking as they had not spoken since the twenties. Askia Muhammad Toure (né Roland Snellings), the Last Poets, Nikki Giovanni, Carol Clemmons, Donald Graham, Sonia Sanchez, Carol Rodgers, Mari Evans, Don Lee, Quincy Troupe. Many many more. And they were speaking to Black audiences.

Of all the Black voices, one of the most important was the resonant voice of Lerone Bennett. While some voices were screaming and screeching, he was steadily taking care of business, making sense, telling it not only like it is but where it is and what it is; telling it not only like it is but like it *was,* knowing full well that a people ignorant of their history are condemned to repeat their history. Lerone Bennett writes history in the service of the people. Like all historians he has an ax to grind, and his ax is Black Liberation. His essay in the August 1971 issue of *Ebony* magazine is an example of his countless contributions to our understanding of ourselves in relation to our history and in relation to the real world, not the world of fantasy. In this essay he warns us not to mistake surface revolutions for the real thing. He warns us that if we do not keep our eyes on the ball, we might very well go through another so-called "Reconstruction" in the dear old Southland, and that if we haven't learned from our previous history, the present "Reconstruction" might be just as transitory and as phony as the other one.

The name of the game is still *Power*. Political, economic, social power. Communications power. The power to change men's basic situations, to change men's ways of life, to change men's minds. "Speak truth to the people," says Mari Evans. Warm Southern white hearts and liberal-minded Northern white hearts have nothing to do with anything. This world is not run by the grace of God or Allah or men's hearts, but by power. Whoever controls the sources of power controls the nations and the world. Witness how helpless was New York City in 1965 when the power was shut off. Power can be used for the good of people, power can be used for evil against the people. But power is essential. Self-determination means the power to chart your own destiny. A people without power is a helpless people, a desperate people, who will eventually become beggars. The problems facing Black people have never had anything to do with love or fair play or acceptability or invisibility. Our problem as Black people in this country is that we have been and are still without power. Years ago some of our leaders thought that if we cleaned ourselves up and got an education and were courteous, that if we proved to the white man that we were human beings, he would graciously accept us into the human race. Remember that a few years ago that great liberal writer from Mississippi, that unreconstructed plantation owner, William Faulkner, gave the Black movement those profound and revolutionary slogans that would bring all things to pass. "Patience! Courtesy! Cleanliness!"

The great Frederick Douglass saw through this ruse more than a hundred years ago. Listen to him speaking in Rochester, New York, July 5, 1852:

Must I undertake to prove that the slave is a man? That point is conceded already. Nobody doubts it. The slaveholders themselves acknowledge it in the enactment of laws for their government . . . There are seventy-two crimes in the State of Virginia which, if committed by a black man (no matter how ignorant he be), subject him to the punishment of death; while only two of the same crimes will subject a white man to the like punishment What is this but the acknowledgment that the slave is a moral, intellectual, and responsible being? The manhood of the slave is conceded. It is admitted in the fact that Southern statute books are covered with enactments forbidding, under severe fines and penalties, the teaching of slaves to read or to write. When you can point to any such laws in reference to the beasts of the field, then I may consent to argue the manhood of the slave.

Of course, the sixties continued to hear the voices of James Baldwin, the historic and Pan-African voice of John Henrik Clarke, the voices of John Williams, Loften Mitchell, William Demby. And likewise the new voices of William Melvin Kelly, Ernest Gaines, Ishmael Reed, Sam Greenlee, Cecil Browne, Ronald Milner, Ronald Fair. Many many more. We waited with great expectations for the second novel of Ralph Ellison, author of the powerful *Invisible Man*.

Somewhere during the beginning of the fifties, an organization that was eventually called The Harlem Writers Guild got itself together. There were eight of us at that first meeting up above a storefront on 125th Street in Harlem. I believe that none of us were published except John Clarke, who had published a book of poetry. At that first meeting John Killens read (in a very trembly voice) the first chapter of a novel in progress that was published a few years later under the title of *Youngblood*. The brothers and sisters at that first session liked the chapter immensely, but the consensus of the group was: "It's great stuff, but ain't nobody gonna publish it." The H.W.G. became the proving ground for many Black writers. At least fourteen published novels have been given to the world by men and women who have had (some still have) an association with the Guild: eight books of nonfiction, eleven plays, three featured films. H.W.G. members and former members include writers like Paule Marshall, Rosa Guy, Sarah Wright, Julian Mayfield, Louise Meriweather, Maya Angelou, Charles Russell, Piri Thomas, Jean Bond, Lonne Elder, Douglas Turner Ward, Alice Childress, Irving Burgie, John Henrik Clarke, and John Oliver Killens. Ossie Davis read *Purlie Victorious* (in the rough) to the Guild workshop.

I don't know of any workshop in the country past or present that has the record of productivity and creativity that the Harlem Writers Guild has. The H.W.G. had its impact on the literature of the fifties and the sixties. It was not a screaming strident impact. Screaming and proclaiming was not the H.W.G.'s style. There were other groups that postured and strutted like peacocks. Sometimes there was more strutting than there was producing. The Guild emphasized production. Its members did not proclaim that they were prophets or soothsayers. We did not lay claim to some unearthly power or that God had kissed our hands or spoken to us. We sought to create no cults. We said that we were Black writers and that we would speak to Black people and the world about the Black experience. We would reflect and interpret. Some of us saw the writer as a hunter and this civilization as the man-made jungle. To stalk the truth in this jungle was to us the writer's mission. Not to kill truth when we cornered it but to hold it aloft as a torch to set men free. Truth. Tough truth. Relentless truth. Liberating truth.

Included in this anthology are so many truths that go to make up the Black experience. North, South, East, and West. Beautiful truths, Black truths, universal truths, humorous truths, terrible truths, magnificent truths, paradoxical truths, tragic truths. There is a beautiful story herein that re-enacts the history and the struggle and the heroism of the children of the late '50's and early '60's. There's a happening in Barbados. There's a story of love on a Southern plantation. Stories from Sam Greenlee, Ed Bullins, James Thompson, E. K. Walker, Woodie King, Clarence Cooper, Sam Anderson. The stories here reach various levels of artistic achievement. It is an anthology that will bring the reader to a profounder understanding of the Black Experience.

A Revolutionary Tale

Nikki Giovanni

Nikki Giovanni is the author of three books of poetry: Black Feeling, Black Thought; Black Judgment; *and* Re-Creation. *She is the editor of the anthology* Night Comes Softly *(Anthology of Black Female Voices), editor of the book of poems by the late Langston Hughes. Miss Giovanni teaches at Livingston College and Rutgers University. She has won awards from the Harlem Cultural Council and the National Endowment of the Arts.*

The whole damn thing is Bertha's fault. Bertha is my roommate and a very Black person, to put it mildly. She's a Revolutionary! I don't want to spend needless time discussing Bertha, but it's sort of important. Before I met her, I was Ayn Rand-Barry Goldwater all the way. Bertha kept asking how could Black people *be* conservative? What have they got to conserve? And after a while (realizing that I had absolutely nothing, period) I came around. But not as fast as she was moving. It wasn't enough that I learned to like the regular mass of colored people—as a whole, as it were, but she wanted me to like the individual colored people that we knew. I resisted that like hell but eventually came around. Bertha is the sort of Black person where eventually you come around. Now just be patient, you want to know why I'm late; don't you? So I got an Afro and began the conference beat and did all those Black things that we were supposed to do. I even gave up white men for The Movement . . . and that was no easy sacrifice. Not that they were that good—nobody comes down with a sister like a brother, but they were a major source of support for me. I agreed that they shouldn't be allowed to support The Movement, but I believe in income being passed around, and if anyone has income to spare, whiteys do. So I cut myself off from a very important love of mine—money—

19

and that presented a problem. No I'm not going round-robinhood'sbarn, this is a part of it. So when my income was terminated for ideological reasons, you'd think she'd say something like, "I'll take over the rent and your gas bill since you've sacrificed so much for The Movement." You'd really think that, wouldn't you? But no, she asked me about a job! A job, for Christ's sake! I didn't even know anybody who worked but her! And here she was talking 'bout a job! I calmly suggested that I would apply for relief. You see, I believe society owes all of its members certain things like food, clothing, shelter, and gas so I was going to apply to society since individual contributions were no longer acceptable. She laughed that cynical laugh of hers and offered to go down with me. No, says I, I can do it myself. So I went down at the end of the week.

Now I'm a firm believer in impressions. I think the first impression people make is very important, and since I would have to consider welfare my job from now on, for Bertha's sake at least, I got dressed up and went down. I'm sure you've applied for relief at least once, so you know the procedure. I went to Intake and met an old civil servant; the kind who's been on the job since Hayes set the system up. She asked me so many questions about my personal life I thought she was interviewing me for a possible spot in heaven. Then we got to my family. I told her Mommy was a supervisor in the Welfare Department and that Daddy was a social worker. She shook her head and looked disgusted—just plain disgusted with me—huffed up her flat chest, and said, "Young lady, you are not eligible for relief!" And stormed away! I started after her. "What the hell do you mean 'eligible'?" I asked. "I'll take somebody's job who really needs it. Somebody with skills or the ability to be trained, with a wife and kids, or maybe just an unwed mother will be put out of work! What kind of jive agency are you! You sure don't give a damn about people!" As she turned the corner, I had to run to keep up with her. "And who are you to decide what I need? You nothing but a jive petty bourgeoisie bullshit civil servant." Yes I did. I told her exactly that. I mean, that's what she is! "Going 'round deciding people's needs! You got needs yourself. Who decides how your needs gonna be filled? You ain't God or Mary or even the Holy Ghost—telling me what I'm eligible for," and I was laying her out. The nerve! I'd come all the way down there and didn't have on Levis or my miniskirt but looked nice! I mean really clean, and she says I'm not eligible. Really did piss me off. At the end of the corridor where she was hurrying to, I saw this figure. It looked real small and pitiful like. It was Mommy. I guess someone had recognized me and called her to come down. I went over to put my arms around her. "Don't cry, Mommy. It'll be all right." But she just cried and cried and kept saying, "Oh Kim. Why can't you be like other daughters?" I got so involved with soothing her that the servant got away. "Mom," I said as I walked her to her office, "there's going to be a Black Revolution all over the world, and we must prepare for it. We've got to determine our own standards of eligibility. That's all." She quit crying a little and just looked at me pitifully. Then she put her arms around me and said, "Oh Kim. I love you. But why can't you just get married and divorced and have babies and things like other daughters? Why do you have to disgrace us like this? I didn't mind when you got kicked out of school for drinking, and I even got used to all those men I didn't like. And remember the time you made the front page for doing that go-go dance at the Democratic Convention? I've been a democrat all my life! You know that. But I was proud that in the middle of Johnson's speech you jumped on the table, shoes and all, to dance your protest to the war in Vietnam. But this is my job! Your father and I have worked very hard to give you everything we could." "Mom," I cut her off, "I'm not against your job. I tried to explain it wasn't personal even when I had to throw that rock through your window that time. We didn't fire bomb, did we? 'No,' I told the group, 'don't fire bomb the welfare department.' And when we had to turn the director's car over, you noticed that he didn't get hurt? I told the group, 'Be sure not to hurt the director.' That's what I told them. But Mom, I'm broke now. All my savings are gone, and if I don't get on relief, I'll have to take a job. Oh Mommy, what will I do if I take a job? Locked up in a building with all those strangers for eight hours every day. And people saying, 'Good morning, Kim. How's it going?' or 'Hey Kim, what you doing after work?' I mean getting familiar with me and I don't even know them! How could I stand that?" Then for the first time in the twenty-three years I've known her she looked me dead in the eye—I mean exactly straight—and said, "You'll either have to work or go to grad school." It floored me. I mean she's never made a decision like that all the time I've known her. "Mom," I said, "you don't mean it. You've been talking to Bertha. You're angry with me for what I told that civil servant. I'll apologize. I'll make it up somehow. I swear! I'll get my hair done!" But she would not budge. "Kim, it's school or a job." "Mom, 'member when I went back and graduated from college? magna cum laude and all. 'Member how proud you and Daddy were that I had the guts to go back after all they did to me in college? 'Member what you said? 'Member how you said I had done ALL you wanted me to do? 'Member how you kept saying you wouldn't ask me for nothing else? 'Member, Mom? Mom? 'Member?" But she wouldn't budge. I tell you it's something when your own mother turns against you. She knew I was working for The Revolution. "What would happen to The Revolution if I quit to take a job? What would my people do?" I asked her. And she looked at me and said, rather coldly if I recall, "Your people need you to lead the way. Not just toward irresponsible acts but toward a true Revolution." "There's nothing irresponsible about chaos and anarchy. We must brush our teeth before eating a meal." "Kim, I've read everything you've written. I've heard on tape all your speeches. And what are you talking about now? Program. I've read Frantz Fanon and Stokely Carmichael. I especially enjoyed *Burn the Honky* by Rap Brown—he's got an amazing sense of humor. I've read Killens and Jones and Neal and Mc-Kissick. I've read most of the books on those lists you gave us. Haven't I always tried to understand you and sympathize with you? When I was going to get Mother a cook book, did I buy *La Gastronomique?* No! I bought the *Ebony Cook Book,* even though Mother has forgotten more than Frieda McKnight could ever have known. When your father and I went to the Social Work Convention in Detroit last year, did we stay with the other delegates at the Hilton? No! We stayed at the Rio Grande. I've done all I could for The Revolution, and I'll probably do more. But I'm not going to allow you this behavior. You will get a job, or you will go to school." "Aw Mom," I protested, "you just don't understand . . ." "Kim, that's all there is to it. I'll give you a surprise when you tell me something definite." I was crushed. Absolutely crushed. My own mother turned against me. I must have looked terribly hurt because she kissed me again and said, "Oh Kim. It's best—really it is. If I can read your people and try to understand your way, you can try mine." I called my father.

I asked him to take me to lunch. I think he knew. He didn't know when I called him, but by the time we met for lunch—he knew. 'Course being a social worker and relating to people and all for a living, he didn't just burst in and say, "I agree with your mother." No. He sat down and ordered me a drink. He doesn't drink anymore since he and his liver made an intellectual decision that Negroes shouldn't get high. That is his sacrifice for The Movement. Of course he quit five years ago when he was in the hospital; he considered it a religious-conversion thing. His own special sacrifice to Jesus. We used to ask about it, but he always just said Jesus had spoken to him through his liver. And nothing would shake him. He quit church after a couple of months, but he continued to tithe every month faithfully and never drank again. His tennis game improved, and he got to be a good swimmer again. He took up golf and to tell the truth had gotten so damned clean-cut-american Mommy began sneaking gin into his eggs every morning just to keep him from becoming a real bastard. He doesn't know that, however. So we sat down and I had a drink and we ordered lunch. "What's on your mind, chicken?" (He always calls me some sort of animal or inanimate object. I'm not sure what his message is.) I didn't want to throw it on him right away. "DADDY MOMMYSAYSI'VEGOTTAGOTOSCHOOLORTAKEA JOBANDIDON'TTHINKTHAT'SFAIR," I said. "Uhmm. Would you say that again in English . . . I mean American?" "Mommy says I have to go to school or get a job." "Good, lambie-pie. Which one is it?" "Daddy, you don't understand. I don't think it's fair." "Of course not, sugar lump. She shouldn't have said it like that. You just get yourself a nice job. You don't even have to consider school. I'll call up Harry White and see what he can do for you. 'Course you can get one on your own . . . you just let me know what you would like." "Oh Daddy," I said, "you're on her side, and she's been talking to Bertha, and nobody ever understands me." "I try to understand you, angel cake. I've read almost all those books on your lists and everything you've written, and I've heard all your speeches. I think you're doing fine work, but you must set an example, too. You just show your people that new systems can be created. If you want to destroy something, you must first learn how it works and what need its filling. After the—how you say 'Black Flame?'—encases the world, you'll want your people to work for The Black Nation. How can you encourage that if you have no idea of what you're asking of them? That's one thing I noticed about everyone from Nkrumah to Ben Bella to Brown. They don't really know what they're asking everyday people to do. Not that they don't work—and hard—but do they punch a time clock? Do they have a thirty-minute lunch hour? Do they dig ditches? Work in a mine? Not that they have to do every one of those; but have they labored? Have they punched a time clock? It's important that they do. And all the reading and writing in the world doesn't give a true understanding of time clocks. Maybe they'll do away with time clocks, but they must first understand what purpose they serve before they do."

"Oh, Daddy, not that many Black folks ever punch a clock!" "I'm not talking just about a clock, and you know it. I'm talking about going to work on time, eating lunch on time, getting off on time, going home on time. All those meetings, conferences, and rallies—even if they are on time—are scheduled to your and their convenience—not the people's. Get up at 6:30 or 7:00, go downtown, eat lunch with a couple of thousand people, relate to your supervisor, relate to your clients, relate to the people in your office or sewer, get off at 4:30 or 5:00, rush home, read your paper while your wife cooks dinner, talk to your children, listen to their troubles, put them to bed; talk to your wife, listen to her troubles, take her to bed; and in your spare time watch TV, say hello to your neighbor, run to the store, go to a rally, try to read a book. Try that and you might understand why The Revolution, as you call it, moves so slowly." "Oh Daddy, I didn't want a lecture. I just wanted you to be on my side." "Is that my name now? Ohdaddy? I am on your side, brown sugar. That's why I'm telling you this. Get yourself a job, then do all the things you're doing. You may readjust your methods." "I won't change! I won't let the bourgeoisie system get me!" "I didn't say your thinking, Kim. I didn't say you would readjust your thinking. I said you *may* change your methods." Lunch was ruined for me. I went home to type a résumé, and that wasn't easy. It had been that kind of a day.

I have this really neato pink IBM—it was a gift; though when I got it it was a down payment. It's always worked right. I've had it for two and a half years and never had a bit of trouble. Once a year I call the people and they clean and service it—that's it. It's a dream. But that day, of all days, it just wouldn't work right. The "s" was skipping, and the "a" was hitting twice, plus the magic margin wouldn't click in, and it was just a fucky day. I quit and stretched out on the floor. I fell sort of half asleep. I couldn't decide between school or an agency job, and it must have been on my mind 'cause I had this really terrible dream. There was this university chasing me down the streets. I turned the corner to get away from it and ran right into the mouth of an agency. It gobbled me up, but it couldn't digest me. When it tried to swallow me, I put up such a fight that it belched me back into life. As I hit the street, there was this university again, waiting for me like a big dyke that has run her prey into a corner, with a greasy smile on her lips. I woke up screaming. Both of them would destroy me! And furthermore, what did I need with a master's degree? As I brooded on my future, the image of educational institutions kept coming back. Going to school is like throwing the rabbit into a briar patch. There would be scores of students that I could convert. And because of "academic freedom" the school would have to accept and support me; or at least leave me alone unless I flunked out, drank a lot, or smoked in public. And if I applied in social work, both Mommy and Daddy would be pleased 'cause I'd get a degree and agency training and an inadequate paycheck to boot. So I sat down at my pink IBM to type a letter for an application blank. Surprisingly enough the typewriter was fixed. I mailed it immediately and sat back while others stronger and wiser than I would determine my fate.

Geeze you've got a one-track mind! I'm trying to get around to explaining about the delay. I was, you know, accepted in school. I thought everyone would be happy and leave me alone. That was February, and I had nine months of Freedom before enrollment day. And I fully intended to use them. I got my acceptance letter on a Tuesday. That was so upsetting that all I could do for a long time was just gnash and growl. It didn't bother Bertha a bit 'cause she just started running 'round the house singing "Kim's going to school . . ." You know, like she was happy. My mood wasn't too positive, so I told her, dead calmly, that if she didn't get the fuck out of my half of the apartment, I'd kill her. She laughed one of those grand "ha ha ha" type things, then spread her arms and pirouetted out the door. It was hard to take. After these years of freedom of choice and movement I was going back to school. I just cried and cried. Then I thought: What the hell! Hadn't I survived the time we were playing The Prince of Wales? Hadn't I survived the Wisconsin Sleeper? Hadn't I been to Harlem? Hadn't I refused to screw a white boy when we were in Mississippi on the big march? Why wouldn't I survive now? I was really talking it up to myself. Much worse things had happened to me, and here I was acting like a cry baby. Why wouldn't I survive, I asked myself bravely; boldly, perhaps—brazenly! Why would I not survive? BECAUSE!! came the answer, and I just cried and cried.

I've got to tell you this. No—don't be that way—listen, if ever something happens to you that makes you real unhappy, and you've just got to cry about it, don't cry in the same spot. Move around. That's what I learned. After I cried and cried, there was this shiny puddle around my feet, and there were these blood-red eyes looking up at me. I learned then, never cry in one spot. But I was cool with it. I never really became emotionally involved in it. I cleaned up the mess, took a shower, got dressed to a "T," then went out walking the streets. I stopped by this bar I know and had a drink. One of my brothers, soul brothers, bought me a drink, and we started discussing what would have to come down. He and I got into a real deep thing, and we talked until the bar closed. He kept wanting to kill toms, and I still think that's not who we have to kill. Toms, I told him, only have power if we let them have power. I mean, if a tom says get off the streets and you get off the streets, then that's your fault, not his. If, on the other hand, a tom tells you to get off the streets and you don't—well then the power structure has no use for him—plus if you can encourage him in a physical way to come on over to your side, then you've made a friend. I mean you can beat anyone or boycott them or something besides killing a brother to get him to either help you or get out the way. There are too few brothers on this shore already to be killing each other off. We need to get rid of whitey. I mean, if we can't kill a whitey, how can we ever justify killing a brother? That's a hell of a cop-out to me. Talking 'bout killing brothers—and sisters, too—and not being able to kill a whitey. The only way we can ever justify offing a brother is if we have already offed twenty whiteys—that's the ratio, I told him, for offing a brother. So we went to his place to talk further.

The next morning all my problems were solved, I thought. I had figured it all out. Now this much I knew about social work school—they will put up with anything at all except heterosexual relations—I mean anything at all. And the school where I was accepted was founded by two ladies who had adopted children. I just knew if I wrote them and explained that I had not only been screwing but had enjoyed it—well, I thought, they'd write a nice letter explaining the mistake in accepting me and that would be the end of that. So I jumped up and dashed home to compose a letter. Then I thought that won't get to them soon enough—I'd better send a wire—so I did.

TO THE SCHOOL OF SOCIAL WORK
DIRECTOR OF PLACEMENT
PLEASE BE ADVISED STOP I HAVE SCREWED
STOP IT WAS GOOD STOP SO THERE EXPLANA-
TION POINT

YOURS IN FREEDOM
KIM

I thought the minute they receive that they would really be sick of me. I got a long involved letter explaining how proud they were that I was so open to new things and that they were very pleased at my level of honesty. I tell you, I was pissed. That's the only way to describe it. And what the fuck did she mean "new things?" I'd been screwing since I was twelve, ten if you want to count the times before it was serious. And he wasn't new, anyway. I was truly indignant, but Bertha discouraged me from expressing my feeling to the school by just demoralizing my whole intellectual thing.

Well, yes, it was a calculated intellectual involvement. You see, I never act on my unabridged emotions. Emotions are to be controlled by the intellect. Even when I act in what could be considered an emotional manner, I have thought it out before and have *decided* this will be the way I act. So to have my whole intellectual bag blown sky high right before my eyes, well that was frightening. I started to give Bertha a quick punch in the gut, but my whole action-reaction syndrome began to reek of emotion, so I just cooled it a bit and dropped a half teaspoon Drano in her coffee later during the day.

Strange about that. I was only playing a little joke, and there was plenty of milk on hand, you see, to help offset the effects. So Bertha drank her coffee and went to the john and never once indicated that anything was wrong. Later, when I asked, she did say it had been awfully runny, but that was all. I'm a failure, I told myself—a failure. Oh goody! I'm a failure . . . I don't have to deal with it any-more. I dashed a telegram off to the director of placement:

PLEASE BE ADVISED STOP HAVE PUT DRANO
IN ROOMMATE'S COFFEE STOP SHE LIVES
STOP I AM A FAILURE YOU MUST REJECT ME
STOP

Those ridiculous people up there just considered it a bid for attention. I got a nice long letter explaining how they realized I hadn't received my placement yet, and they were sorry but that they had a lot of work and sometimes even the best of us get tied down, etc. Plus, if you can dig it, they think I have ingenious ways of letting them know my needs. I mean, really! Ingenious! Goddamnit, I am a failure. If I don't find a decent quick way out of this, why I'll end up in an institution—a part of an agency—being decent, responsible—all those ugly, sick things that I hate. I'd really have to think of a scheme.

It was way in the middle of April before it even dawned on me. I mean, it was so simple that I was overlooking the obvious. What is the one thing we know for damned sure about white people? I mean, you know, beside the fact that they hate Negroes, children, and sex. What is the one thing we know absolutely and positively about any honkie anywhere in the world? That he worships money. He's got such a case on money he's transferred it to anything green. That's why you see those goddamn KEEP OFF THE GRASS signs. Not that he cares about grass but that it's green. What's the quickest way to turn a honkie off? Ask him for money. He's as nice as he can be as long as he thinks he'll get your money—but the minute you ask him for some, well that's like asking a hippie for his pot or a Negro for his knife; I mean they get hostile. You don't believe it? Go into any bank and deposit five bucks. Then go back in a week and withdraw it. When you go to deposit it, they're all smiles. The V.P. will come out and shake your hand. The teller smiles and welcomes you to the family. And that's only five bucks I'm talking about. When you go to withdraw it, the first thing is the teller will say, "You realize this will close your account." Just like you didn't know that if you deposit five bucks and you withdraw five bucks that you were closing your account, and you just smile at him and say, "Yeah, groovy." He'll frown and say, "This will cost you one dollar." And you say, "Cool. Gimme my four bucks." Then he says, "This will take a minute." That's when you look at him very menacingly and say, "I should surely hope the hell not." Then he'll slam your money down and scream, "NEXT," or he'll slap the NEXT WINDOW PLEASE sign up and turn his back on you. And this is a Black teller I'm talking about. So knowing this I wrote the director of placement and told her I had no money; that I needed a stipend and a tuition grant. I just knew for whatever my charm or whatnot that they weren't going to pay me to go to their school. I mean as tight as they are they are not about to give me any money. I was as happy as a ten-year-old turkey the day before Thanksgiving—I knew I now had them by the ass—I was just naturally too tough to handle. I walked a little taller, breathed a little deeper, felt a little prouder. I was so happy that I went back to my Revolutionary Work. Not that I hadn't been working for Revolution all along—but I had really been hung up on this thing about a job.

We set up a Black Arts Festival, and I was working my you know what off. You may have heard about me being on the radio telling all the honkies not to come. I'm sure you heard about Lonnie going into the honkie neighborhood with his sign saying, YOU'RE NOT READY. It was great advertisement for us, and we were all really sorry about that kid. However, though the papers played it down after the first day it is not true that Lonnie tore his leg from the joint—he only fractured it. And contrary to first reports the kid will walk again. I personally tell all the brother Black Belts I know that they shouldn't provoke white kids, then beat on them. But, well, you're not always able to control Folk, even if they do take a lot of your advice. But that was the only incident that could be, in some quarters, considered unfortunate. It was a groovy set. The blue beasts foamed at the mouth, but it was our day! I say again, it was Revolutionary! Slavetown, U.S.A., was back in the movement 'cause the Kim was back into her thing.

I really forgot all that shit about school and jobs and do. I just put it out of my mind. Our underground press, yes it does have something to do with why I'm late. You see, we were putting out a magazine called *Love Black*. It was a group thing, you know, but it really belonged to all the people. We had learned the secret of why the folks don't read. C'mon, see do you know? You jive, they can too read. But nobody ever writes for them or writes anything they can relate to. So having figured that out through the very difficult process of stopping every brother we could on the corner one day asking them what they would enjoy reading, we went about getting *Love Black* out. See, most folks don't read, honkies especially, but people, too. You think they really read *GH* or *Time*? They look at the pictures and will scan any article they can see the end of. Most people like to read what they can see the end of. So we started a Black mag on 8½ x 11 with articles that ran a page or less. Also it doesn't run over twenty pages all toto. Therefore a brother can read the whole damned thing, which is a legit mag, and really do two things: learn something positive about himself and complete something he started. Now don't start breaking into my explanation. It may well be propaganda, but all pieces of paper with writing are propaganda, and if I have to deal in mind control, it's much better to be Black-Washed. I mean the honkie press and stuff just naturally fucks with any Black man's mind 'cause first it doesn't recognize that there is a Black mind. It does what it can to a Black mind—it whitewashes it—it flushes it out of his head—that's what it does. But we were giving the people something, and we were getting a lot. One issue we were late, and all kinds of soul stepped up and told me if I didn't get my thing together and get the mag out, well, they would look upon that with disfavor. And they also sent articles in. Like we'd get slightly used toilet tissue with an article on it or brown paper bags with short sayings or just a note to say they dig us. Some of it looked like our ancestral writing, Egyptian, and we really had to work at deciphering it, but when you saw how the man changed after he had "published," well it would really hit you. You see, the brother will read if he's writing it or if he knows people who are, and *Love Black* was strictly ours. It wasn't the prettiest thing in the world, and sometimes it wasn't too clear. I've always maintained that if we lose the Revolution it'll be because we don't know nothing about machinery—but it was ours. It talked about Slavetown and what the brother thought and felt, and the brother was digging it. You got to understand the whole concept of writing.

Like in the East everything is dishonest. They do a lot of things, but mostly it's three thousand per cent B. S. The people are so used to talking Black, buying Black, and thinking Black, they don't get shook no more. Every hustler (why is it a Black capitalist is called a hustler?) and every panhandler is Black, so Black don't mean nothing. It's taken for granted. And one Black thing is like another. They've been saturated with a program that has never come off. Between Garvey and Malcolm, Harlem should be owned lock, stock, and barrel by us—but we still trying to get rat control and jobs, and paying rent to circumcised honkies. In the Dupont plantation state they even passed a law that said if building codes aren't lived up to, you can deposit your money in one of the company banks and leave it there till the cat comes round. Ain't that the jivest shit you ever heard of? I mean, paternalism with a capital WHITE.

No, wait a minute. If you live in a house or apt. and something is wrong with it and you living there every day the good lord makes you Black, well you should fix that place up and what's left over from rent should go in your pocket. So the old witch from the Welfare Dept. comes down and tries to explain that she'll have to hold your check if you don't pay your rent to the rightful owner. And that's when you come out of your thing so righteously and whip it on her so beautifully. You just light up a joint and calmly explain, "Honkies have made women, bombs, and Kellogs corn flakes, but they have never made a piece of land. The land is one bitch that is everybody's woman, and I, being man and all, have got a right to a piece of her." You see, the honkies' whole sex thing is tied up to land. No lie. Land is their love. All land, except Germany, is female. The motherland, her, she—all land is woman. And they do anything to prove that they are worthy to be land's man. Only land don't give a shit about white people. See, land has this memory thing. Land remembers god stepped out on space and looked around and said, I'LL MAKE ME A MAN. God reached down into land, a woman, and formed this thing—you know, a man. Now land has always been Black. And you know god well enough to know that he goes first class. So god got the best land he could find, which had to be the Blackest land he could find. You just don't know about no white land. Snow, maybe, some white sand, maybe; but you just don't know about no white land. And land is hip to that. Land is very put out that we are making her prostitute herself for the beast. You didn't hear about no land being raped until the beast came along. We live in harmony with land because we are a part of land and we are out of land. The honkie came from sand and snow. Now what is that? That's nothing. It has a place on earth, but it's nothing. Snow freezes land, and sand dries her up; both destroy land and land wants to live and recreate. You run it on down to where you are going to free land so that she can go about woman's work of taking care of her children—the Black people of the earth. Now she'll send the law out, but that don't mean nothing, either. The law only means something if you think it does. So she'll send out the law to make you pay, and you smile sincerely and promise to get it in next week. After you're alone with your piece of land, you remove very carefully anything that cannot be replaced; like pictures of your first lay, your joints, etc., and you throw kerosene on everything else. You see, it's yours and if you can't enjoy it in freedom and peace, then land wants you to destroy it. You can't destroy land because it'll always be there, but you can destroy the rapist's claim stake. The only thing about that land that makes the beast think he owns it is the claim he's staked, a house, a building, a fence, so you destroy that. That's when you burn. You don't burn to get the thief to fix it up, you burn when you've staked your claim and they try to steal it from you. And I really believe that after you've fixed it up and made it yours, you'll kill for it.

That's the one thing we've got to understand. This Revolution isn't to show what we're willing to die for, Black people have been willing to die for damn near everything on earth, it's to show what we're willing to kill for. Yes it is! Do we love life enough to deal righteously with key honkies? We don't have to deal with King and Young and those other three or four if we don't want to. We have got to deal with the folk who send them up. Which means we have to control ourselves. I have got to control me, and you have got to control you. Like if I see something that needs to be done and you see something else, we don't got to argue about what to do. You do yours, and I'll do mine. It's like we're on a road that forks off, then comes back together. We just had different priorities, and that don't make one right or wrong, just different. But if I use the fact that you want to do something I don't want to do to keep from doing what I have to do, then I'm not together. I'm B.S.'ing, and I know it. See, you and I are never in a conflict situation 'cause we're after the same thing—we're after the same honkie, and however we get him is our business. All that jive about coordination and keeping people in line and Elites and shit don't really mean nothing. That's not Revolution—that's not anarchy! And anarchy is what we want. This country doesn't have anything that we can't build again if we need it. But to even try to think of taking over and preserving GM or something, what for? Nobody's trying to make the system Black, we're trying to make a system human so that Black folks can live in it. That means we're trying to destroy the system. It's not even a question of can Black folks run it better than white folks. We don't have to prove to whites that we can—and if we take over their system, that'll be the reason. We haven't got to prove nothing to honkies 'cause they are nobody's authority on nothing.

Look here, we take over their system, give Black folks jobs and property, and what'll we have? We'll still have troops in Asia, we'll still be raping Africa, we'll still be controlling and killing folks in South America 'cause that's what makes the system run. You can't rape Europe 'cause her legs are spread and her mouth is wet just waiting to suck in Black people. No, that's one whore we'd better avoid. She's not even good from what I heard. She wants to blow you, but that's nothing new 'cause America has been blowing your mind for half a century or more. And the latest reports from Hanoi do indicate to me that some folks' minds are hanging between their legs. We have got to rid ourselves of those needs.

But the whole damn thing I do blame on Bertha. 'Cause I was just as happy sitting at home twittering my toes and masturbating every now and then. I didn't even know that I was colored let alone anything about Blackness. But she kept bringing those beautiful Black people home, and they kept talking that talk to me, and as I moved, I moved toward Black Power, and I recognized the extent of white power, which is so pervasive that the American solution cannot be Black Power at all, though as a world solution it is a possibility, but must be Revolution—anarchy, total chaos—and this should not be so hard for us since we have worked so diligently in every other cause we can now work for our own. We have sacrificed our lives and interests for white power, and now we can save ourselves through Revolution—our baptism by fire. But as I worked this out, people kept calling me a hater, and really I'm a lover. No one knows how much I do love all that is lovable. Then Bertha chimed in to ask do I love Black folks enough to trust them to TCB, and do I trust Black people to do those things necessary by any means necessary, recognizing that the means is in fact the ends. She kept saying if they and I are one, then I should get out of the way and see where they would go without me. And since Revolution ages you so quickly, and having watched the summer I had to admit that I was old and tired and recognized that already we were moving beyond my vision, so maybe I should step aside and regroup.

So I packed and made arrangements to come to school, and everybody cheered and was really pleased with my decision, and I kept telling myself that it would be good and that I was dealing with the best the system had to offer and that if I couldn't relate meaningful enough to them for me to accept them, then I could easily go back to destroying it in a very real manner. So having made my decision, I decided to walk. I mean, it would have been much too easy to hop a flight or thumb a ride. And though physical pun-

Frankie Mae

Jean Wheeler Smith

Jean Wheeler Smith was born in Detroit. She now lives in Washington, D.C., where she teaches at Federal City College and at the Center for Black Education. She holds a B.S. in chemistry from Howard and an M.S. in Food Science from U. of Maryland. Her stories and articles have appeared in Negro Digest, Redbook, New Republic, Black Power Revolt, *and* Black Fire.

The sun had just started coming up when the men gathered at the gate of the White Plantation. They leaned on the fence, waiting. No one was nervous, though. They'd all been waiting a long time. A few more minutes couldn't make much difference. They surveyed the land that they were leaving, the land from which they had brought forth seas of cotton.

Old Man Brown twisted around so that he leaned sideways on the gate. Even though he was in his fifties, he was still a handsome man. Medium-sized, with reddish brown skin. His beard set him apart from the others; it was the same mixture of black and gray as his hair, but while his hair looked like wool, the strands of his beard were long and nearly straight. He was proud of it, and even when he wasn't able to take a bath, he kept his beard neatly cut and shaped into a V.

He closed his eyes. The sun was getting too bright; it made his headache worse. Damn, he thought, I sure wouldn't be out here this early on no Monday morning if it wasn't for what we got to do today. Whiskey'll sure kill you if you don't get some sleep long with it. I wasn't never just crazy 'bout doing this, anyway. Wonder what made me decide to go along?

Then he smiled to himself. 'Course. It was on account a Frankie Mae. She always getting me into something.

35

Frankie was his first child, born twenty-two years ago, during the war. When she was little, she had gone everywhere with him. He had a blue bicycle with a rusty wire basket in the front. He used to put Frankie Mae in the basket and ride her to town with him and to the café, and sometimes they'd go nowhere special, just riding. She'd sit sideways so that she could see what was on the road ahead and talk with him at the same time. She never bothered to hold onto the basket; she knew her daddy wouldn't let her fall. Frankie fitted so well into the basket that for a few years the Old Man thought that it was growing with her.

She was a black child, with huge green eyes that seemed to glow in the dark. From the age of four on she had a look of being full-grown. The look was in her muscular, well-defined limbs that seemed like they could do a woman's work and in her way of seeing everything around her. Most times she was alive and happy. The only thing wrong with her was that she got hurt so easy. The slightest rebuke sent her crying; the least hint of disapproval left her moody and depressed for hours. But on the other side of it was that she had a way of springing back from pain. No matter how hurt she had been, she would be her old self by the next day. The Old Man worried over her. He wanted most to cushion her life.

When Frankie reached six, she became too large to ride in the basket with him. Also he had four more children by then. So he bought a car for $40. Not long afterwards he became restless. He'd heard about how you could make a lot of money over in the delta. So he decided to go over there. He packed what he could carry in one load—the children, a few chickens, and a mattress—and slipped off one night.

Two days after they left the hills, they drove up to the White Plantation in Leflore County, Mississippi. They were given a two-room house that leaned to one side and five dollars to make some groceries with for the next month.

The Old Man and his wife, Mattie, worked hard that year. Up at four-thirty and out to the field. Frankie Mae stayed behind to nurse the other children and to watch the pot that was cooking for dinner. At sundown they came back home and got ready for the next day. They did a little sweeping, snapped some beans for dinner the next day, and washed for the baby. Then they sat on the porch together for maybe a half hour.

That was the time the Old Man liked best, the half hour before bed. He and Frankie talked about what had happened during the day, and he assured her that she had done a good job keeping up the house. Then he went on about how smart she was going to be when she started school. It would be in two years, when the oldest boy was big enough to take care of the others.

One evening on the porch Frankie said, "A man from town come by today looking for our stove. You know, the short one, the one ain't got no hair. Said we was three week behind and he was gonna take it. Had a truck to take it back in, too."

The Old Man lowered his head. He was ashamed that Frankie had had to face that man by herself. No telling what he said to her. And she took everything so serious. He'd have to start teaching her how to deal with folks like that.

"What did you tell him, baby?" he asked. "He didn't hurt you none, did he?"

"No, he didn't bother me, sides looking mean. I told him I just this morning seen some money come in the mail from Uncle Ed in Chicago. And I heard my daddy say he was gonna use it to pay off the stoveman. So he said 'Well, I give y'all one more week, one more.' And he left."

The Old Man pulled Frankie to him and hugged her. "You did 'zactly right, honey." She understood. She would be able to take care of herself.

The end of their first year in the delta the Old Man and Mattie went to settle up. It was just before Christmas. When their turn came, they were called by Mr. White Junior, a short fat man, with a big stomach, whose clothes were always too tight.

"Let me see, Johnnie," he said. "Here it is. You owe two hundred dollars."

The Old Man was surprised. Sounded just like he was back in the hills. He had expected things to be different over here. He had made a good crop. Should have cleared something. Well, no sense in arguing. The bossman counted out fifty dollars.

"Here's you some Christmas money," Mr. White Junior said. "Pay me when you settle up next year."

The Old Man took the money to town that same day and bought himself some barrels and some pipes and a bag of chopped corn. He had made whiskey in the hills, and

he could make it over here, too. You could always find
somebody to buy it. Wasn't no reason he should spend
all his time farming if he couldn't make nothing out of it.
He and Mattie put up their barrels in the trees down by
the river and set their mash to fermentate.

By spring Brown had a good business going. He sold to
the colored cafés and even to some of the white ones.
And folks knew they could always come to his house if
they ran out. He didn't keep the whiskey at the house,
though. Too dangerous. It was buried down by the water.
When folks came unexpected, it was up to Frankie and
her brother next to her to go get the bottles. Nobody
noticed children. The Old Man bought them a new red
wagon for their job.

He was able to pay off his stove and to give Mattie some
money every once in a while. And they ate a little better
now. But still they didn't have much more than before
because Brown wasn't the kind of man to save. Also he
had to do a lot of drinking himself to keep up his sales.
Folks didn't like to drink by themselves. When he'd start to
drinking, he usually spent up or gave away whatever he
had in his pocket. So they still had to work as hard as
ever for Mr. White Junior. Brown enjoyed selling the
whiskey, though, and Mattie could always go out and sell
a few bottles in case of some emergency like their lights
being cut off. So they kept the business going.

That spring Mr. White Junior decided to take them off
shares. He would pay $1.50 a day for chopping cotton,
and he'd pay by the hundred pound for picking. The hands
had no choice. They could work by the day or leave.
Actually, the Old Man liked it better working by the day.
Then he would have more time to see to his whiskey.

Also, Mr. White Junior made Brown the timekeeper
over the other hands. Everybody had drunk liquor with
him, and most folks liked him. He could probably keep
them working better than anybody else. He did fight too
much. But the hands knew that he always carried his
pistol. If anybody fought him, they'd have to be trying
to kill him, 'cause he'd be trying to kill them.

Brown was given a large, battered watch. So he'd know
what time to stop for dinner. His job was to see that the
hands made a full day in the field and that all the weeds
got chopped. The job was easier than getting out there
chopping, in all that sun. So Brown liked it. The only hard
part was in keeping after the women whose time was
about to come. He hated to see them dragging to the field,

their bellies about to burst. They were supposed to keep up with the others, which was impossible. Oftentimes Mr. White Junior slipped up on the work crew and found one of the big-bellied women lagging behind the others.

"Goddamit, Johnnie," he'd say, "I done told you to keep the hands together. Queenester is way behind. I don't pay good money for folks to be standing around. If she sick, she need to go home."

Sometimes the Old Man felt like defending the woman. She had done the best she could. But then he'd think, No, better leave things like they is.

"You sure right, Mr. White Junior. I was just 'bout to send her home myself. Some niggers too lazy to live."

He would walk slowly across the field to the woman. "I'm sorry, Queenester. The bossman done seen you. I told you all to be looking out for him! Now you got to go. You come back tomorrow, though. He won't hardly be back in this field so soon. I try and let you make two more days this week. I know you needs the little change."

The woman would take up her hoe and start walking home. Mr. White Junior didn't carry no hands except to eat dinner and to go home after the day had been made.

One day when he had carried the hands in from the field, Mr. White Junior stopped the Old Man as he was climbing down from the back of the pickup truck. While the bossman talked, Brown fingered his timekeeper's watch that hung on a chain from his belt.

"Johnnie," Mr. White Junior said, "it don't look right to me for you to leave a girl at home that could be working when I need all the hands I can get. And you the timekeeper, too. This cotton can't wait on you all to get ready to chop it. I want Frankie Mae out there tomorrow."

He had tried to resist. "But we getting along with what me and Mattie makes. Ain't got nothing, but we eating. I wants Frankie Mae to go to school. We can do without the few dollars she would make."

"I want my cotton chopped," White said, swinging his fat sweating body into the truck. "Get that girl down here tomorrow. Don't nobody stay in my house and don't work."

That night the Old Man dreaded the half hour on the porch. When Frankie had started school that year, she had already been two years late. And she had been so excited about going.

When the wood had been gathered and the children cleaned up, he followed Frankie onto the sloping porch.

She fell to telling him about the magnificent yellow bus in which she rode to school. He sat down next to her on the step.

"Frankie Mae, I'm going to tell you something."

"What's that, Daddy? Mamma say I been slow 'bout helping 'round the house since I been going to school? I do better. Guess I lost my head."

"No, baby. That ain't it at all. You been helping your Mama fine." He stood up to face her but could not bring his eyes to the level of her bright, happy face.

"Mr. White Junior stopped me today when I was getting off the truck. Say he want you to come to field till the chopping get done."

She found his eyes. "What did you say, Daddy?"

"Well, I told him you wanted to go to school, and we could do without your little money. But he say you got to go."

The child's eyes lost their brilliance. Her shoulders slumped, and she began to cry softly. Tired, the Old Man sat back down on the step. He took her hand and sat with her until long after Mattie and the other children had gone to bed.

The next morning Frankie was up first. She put on two blouses and a dress and some pants to keep off the sun and found herself a rag to tie around her head. Then she woke up her daddy and the others, scolding them for being so slow.

"We got to go get all that cotton chopped! And y'all laying round wasting good daylight. Come on."

Brown got up and threw some water on his face. He saw Frankie bustling around in her layers of clothes, looking like a little old woman, and he smiled. That's how Frankie Mae was. She'd feel real bad, terrible, for a few hours, but she always snapped back. She'd be all right now.

On the way to the field he said, "Baby, I'm gonna make you the water girl. All you got to do is carry water over to them that hollers for it and keep your bucket full. You don't have to chop none lest you see Mr. White Junior coming."

"No, Daddy, that's all right The other hands'll say you was letting me off easy 'cause I'm yours. Say you taking advantage of being timekeeper. I go on and chop with the rest"

He tried to argue with her, but she wouldn't let him give her the water bucket. Finally he put her next to Mattie so she could learn from her. As he watched over the field, he set himself not to think about his child inhaling the cotton dust and insecticide. When his eyes happened on her and Mattie, their backs bent way over, he quickly averted them. Once, when he jerked his eyes away, he found instead the bright yellow school bus bouncing along the road.

Frankie learned quickly how to chop the cotton, and sometimes she even seemed to enjoy herself. Often the choppers would go to the store to buy sardines and crackers and beans for their dinner instead of going home. At the store the Old Man would eat his beans from their jagged-edge can and watch with pride as Frankie laughed and talked with everyone and made dates with the ladies to attend church on the different plantations. Every Sunday Frankie had a service to go to. Sometimes, when his head wasn't bad from drinking, the Old Man went with her because he liked so much to see her enjoy herself. Those times he put a few gallons of his whiskey in the back of the car just in case somebody needed them. When he and Frankie went off to church like that, they didn't usually get back till late at night. They would be done sold all the whiskey and the Old Man would be talking loud about the wonderful sermon that the reverend had preached and all the souls that had come to Jesus.

That year they finished the chopping in June. It was too late to send Frankie back to school, and she couldn't go again until after the cotton had been picked. When she went back in November she had missed four months and found it hard to keep up with the children who'd been going all the time. Still, she went every day that she could. She stayed home only when she had to, when her mother was sick, or when, in the cold weather, she didn't have shoes to wear.

Whenever she learned that she couldn't go to school on a particular day, she withdrew into herself for about an hour. She had a chair near the stove where she sat, and the little children knew not to bother her. After the hour she'd push back her chair and go to stirring the cotton in the bed ticks or washing the greens for dinner.

If this was possible, the Old Man loved her still more now. He saw the children of the other workers and his own children, too, get discouraged and stop going to school. They said it was too confusing; they never knew what the teacher was talking about because they'd not been there the day before or the month before. And they

resented being left behind in classes with children half
their size. He saw the other children get so that they
wouldn't hold themselves up, wouldn't try to be clean and
make folks respect them. Yet every other day Frankie managed to put on a clean starched dress, and she kept at her
lessons.

By the time Frankie was thirteen she could figure as well
as the preacher, and she was made secretary of the church.

That same year she asked her daddy if she could keep
a record of what they made and what they spent.

"Sure, baby," he said. "I be proud for you to do it. We
might even come out a little better this year when we settle
up. I tell you what. If we get some money outta Mr. White
Junior this year, I'll buy you a dress for Christmas, a red
one."

Frankie bought a black-and-white-speckled notebook.
She put in it what they made and what they paid on their
bill. After chopping time she became excited. She figured
they had just about paid the bill out. What they made from
picking should be theirs. She and the Old Man would sit
on the porch and go over the figures and plan for Christmas. Sometimes they even talked about taking a drive up to
Chicago to see Uncle Ed. Every so often he would try
to hold down her excitement by reminding her that their
figures had to be checked against the bossman's. Actually,
he didn't expect to do much better than he'd done all the
other years. But she was so proud to be using what she had
learned, her numbers and all. He hated to discourage her.

Just before Christmas they went to settle up. When it
came to the Old Man's turn, he trembled a little. He knew
it was almost too much to hope for, that they would have
money coming to them. But some of Frankie's excitement
had rubbed off on him.

He motioned to her, and they went up to the table where
there were several stacks of ten and twenty dollar bills,
a big ledger, and a pistol. Mr. White Junior sat in a brown
chair, and his agent stood behind him. Brown took heart
from the absolute confidence with which Frankie Mae
walked next to him, and he controlled his trembling. Maybe
the child was right and they had something coming to them.

"Hey there, Johnnie," Mr. White Junior said, "see you
brought Frankie Mae along. Fine, fine. Good to start them
early. Here's you a seat."

The Old Man gave Frankie the one chair and stood
beside her. The bossman rifled his papers and came out

with a long narrow sheet. Brown recognized his name at
the top.

"Here you are, Johnnie, y'all come out pretty good this
year. Proud of you. Don't owe but $65. Since you done
so good, gonna let you have $100 for Christmas."

Frankie Mae spoke up. "I been keeping a book for my
daddy. And I got some different figures. Let me show you.'

The room was still. Everyone, while pretending not to
notice the girl, was listening intently to what she said.

Mr. White Junior looked surprised, but he recovered
quickly. "Why sure. Be glad to look at your figures. You
know it's easy to make a mistake. I'll show you what you
done wrong."

Brown clutched her shoulder to stop her from handing
over the book. But it was too late. Already she was leaning
over the table, comparing her figures with those in the
ledger.

"See, Mr. White Junior, when we was chopping last year
we made $576, and you took $320 of that to put on our
bill. There. There it is on your book. And we borrowed
$35 in July. There it is. . . ."

The man behind the table grew red. One of his fat hands
gripped the table while the other moved toward the pistol

Frankie Mae finished. "So you see, you owe us $180 for
the year."

The bossman stood up to gain the advantage of his
height. He seemed about to burst. His eyes flashed around
the room, and his hand clutched the pistol. He was just
raising it from the table when he caught hold of himself.
He took a deep breath and let go of the gun.

"Oh, yeah. I remember what happened now, Johnnie. It
was that slip I gave you to the doctor for Willie B. You
remember, last year, 'fore chopping time. I got the bill last
week. Ain't had time to put it in my book. It came to, let
me think. Yeah, that was $350."

The Old Man's tension fell away from him, and he resumed his normal manner. He knew exactly what the bossman was saying. It was as he had expected, as it had always
been.

"Let's go, baby," he said.

But Frankie didn't get up from the chair. For a moment
she looked puzzled. Then her face cleared. She said, "Willie
didn't have anything wrong with him but a broken arm
The doctor spent twenty minutes with him one time and
ten minutes the other. That couldn't a cost no $350!"

The bossman's hand found the pistol again and gripped it until the knuckles were white. Brown pulled Frankie to him and put his arm around her. With his free hand he fingered his own pistol, which he always carried in his pocket. He was not afraid. But he hated the thought of shooting the man; even if he just nicked him, it would be the end for himself. He drew a line: If Mr. White Junior touched him or Frankie, he would shoot. Short of that he would leave without a fight.

White spat thick, brown tobacco juice onto the floor, spattering it on the Old Man and the girl. "Nigger," he said, "I know you ain't disputing my word. Don't nobody live on my place and call me no liar. That bill was $350. You understand me?!" He stood tense, staring with hatred at the man and the girl. Everyone waited for Brown's answer. The Old Man felt Frankie's arms go 'round his waist.

"Tell him no, Daddy. We right, not him. I kept them figures all year, they got to be right." The gates of the state farm flashed through the Old Man's mind. He thought of Mattie, already sick from high blood, trying to make a living for eleven people. Frankie's arms tightened.

"Yessir," he said. "I understand."

The girl's arms dropped from him, and she started to the door. The other workers turned away to fiddle with a piece of rope to scold a child. Brown accepted the $50 that was thrown across the table to him. As he turned to follow Frankie, he heard Mr. White Junior's voice, low now and with a controlled violence. "Hey you, girl. You, Frankie Mae." She stopped at the door but didn't turn around.

"Long as you live, bitch, I'm gonna be right and you gonna be wrong. Now get your black ass outta here."

Frankie stumbled out to the car and crawled onto the back seat. She cried all the way home. Brown tried to quiet her. She could still have the red dress. They'd go down to the river tomorrow and start on a new batch of whiskey.

The next morning he laid in bed waiting to hear Frankie Mae moving around and fussing, waiting to know that she had snapped back to her old self. He laid there until everyone in the house had gotten up. Still he did not hear her. Finally he got up and went over to where she was balled up in the quilts.

He woke her. "Come on, baby. Time to get up. School bus be here soon."

"I ain't goin' today," she said, "got a stomach ache."

Brown sat out on the porch all day long, wishing that she would get up out the bed and struggling to understand what had happened. This time Frankie had not bounced back to her old bright-eyed self. The line that held her to this self had been stretched too taut. It had lost its tension and couldn't pull her back.

Frankie never again kept a book for her daddy. She lost interest in things such as numbers and reading. She went to school as an escape from chores but got so little of her lessons done that she was never promoted from the fourth grade to the fifth. When she was fifteen and in the fourth grade, she had her first child. After that there was no more thought of school. In the following four years she had three more children.

She sat around the house, eating and growing fat. When well enough, she went to the field with her daddy. Her dresses were seldom ironed now. Whatever she could find to wear would do.

Still there were a few times, maybe once every three or four months when she was lively and fresh. She'd get dressed and clean the children up and have her daddy drive them to church. On such days she'd be the first one up. She would have food on the stove before anybody else had a chance to dress. Brown would load up his trunk with his whiskey, and they'd stay all day.

It was for these isolated times that the Old Man waited. They kept him believing that she would get to be all right. Until she died, he woke up every morning listening for her laughter, waiting for her to pull the covers from his feet and scold him for being lazy.

She died giving birth to her fifth child. The midwife, Esther, was good enough, but she didn't know what to do when there were complications. Brown couldn't get up but $60 of the $100 cash that you had to deposit at the county hospital. So they wouldn't let Frankie in. She bled to death on the hundred-mile drive to the charity hospital in Vicksburg.

The Old Man squinted up at the fully risen sun. The bossman was late. Should have been at the gate by now. Well, it didn't matter. Just a few more minutes and they'd be through with the place forever.

His thoughts went back to the time when the civil rights workers had first come around and they had started their meetings up at the store. They'd talked about voting and about how plantation workers should be making enough to live off of. Brown and the other men had listened and talked and agreed. So they decided to ask Mr. White Junior

for a raise. They wanted nine dollars for their twelve-hour
day.

They had asked. And he had said, Hell no. Before he'd
raise them he'd lower them. So they agreed to ask him
again. And if he still said no, they would go on strike.

At first Brown hadn't understood himself why he agreed
to the strike. It was only this morning that he realized why:
It wasn't the wages or the house that was falling down
'round him and Mattie. It was that time when he went to
ask Mr. White Junior about the other $40 that he needed
to put Frankie in the hospital.

"Sorry, Johnnieboy," he'd said, patting Brown on the
back, "but me and Miz White having a garden party today
and I'm so busy. You know how women are. She want me
there every minute. See me tomorrow. I'll fix you up then."

A cloud of dust rose up in front of Brown. The bossman
was barreling down the road in his pickup truck. He was
mad. That was what he did when he got mad, drove his
truck up and down the road fast. Brown chuckled. When
they got through with him this morning, he might run that
truck into the river.

Mr. White Junior climbed down from the truck and
made his way over to the gate. He began to give the orders
for the day, who would drive the tractors, what fields
would be chopped. The twelve men moved away from the
fence, disdaining any support for what they were about
to do.

One of the younger ones, James Lee, spoke up. "Mr.
White Junior, we wants to know is you gonna raise us like
we asked."

"No, goddammit. Now go on, do what I told you."

"Then," James Lee continued, "we got to go on strike
from this place."

James Lee and the others left the gate and went to have
a strategy meeting up at the store about what to do next.

The Old Man was a little behind the rest because he had
something to give Mr. White Junior. He went over to the
sweat-drenched, cursing figure and handed him the scarred
timekeeper's watch, the watch that had ticked away Frankie
Mae's youth in the hot, endless rows of cotton.

Harlem Transfer

E. K. Walker

Evan K. Walker lives and works in New York. His full-length play, East of Jordan, *was produced by the Free Southern Theater. A one-act play,* The Message, *was produced by the Freedom Theater of Philadelphia and The Performing Arts Society of Los Angeles. Mr. Walker is currently working on a novel, a play, and an original screenplay with Larry Neal.*

He shot the Browning automatic rifle down into the crowded street, and the people did not move. The bullet slammed into the hood of a new lavender Eldorado cadillac dappled with snow, and not a soul moved. He shifted his position in the window and aimed the BAR at a hustler outlined against the dirty gray snow near the curb. The rifle was aimed at the center of the man's head, but before he fired, he raised it a click. The bullet tore a large hole in an overstuffed garbage can out of which scurried two large rats—one white, one black—and ran into the deserted house across the street. Then the people on the crowded street in the middle of Harlem moved, moved as if they had been jolted from a deep sleep, and found cover in the cellars, hallways, and stores.

As he saw the hustler crawl into the Lucky Dollar Bar and Grill, he smiled and moved back from the window. The smell of cordite stung the air in the small living room, and it made him think of the last time he had fired the BAR many years ago in a land he barely remembered. It flashed across his mind in pieces and fragments, fragments and pieces, of snow, of valleys, and of mountains, always mountains, seemingly strung out across the face of the earth. He looked at the BAR and rubbed his hand over the steel and wood, freshly oiled and cleaned, and it felt good.

Down on the street he could see that a few people had come out of their hiding places. He thought this strange but

47

passed it off as curiosity; anyway, they had nothing to fear from his rifle; Dap was not among them. But Dap would soon come out of the Lucky Dollar Bar and Grill. Of this he was sure. Several men had gathered around the lavender El D and were talking and pointing to the hole in the hood. From his sixth-floor window he could not hear what they were saying, nor did he care. He smiled. They probably think one of them rats ate that hole in that caddy, he thought. And he waited by the window, calmly, quietly, quietly as he had been trained to do light years ago, to wait in the snow in a land that was now only disjointed pieces and fragments reforming themselves into meaning in his mind.

He saw the Dapper Dude come out of the Lucky Dollar Bar and Grill, walk coolly over to his El D, and rub his hand over the wound in its hood. Dap took off his hat and scanned the buildings, his sleepy eyes bare slits against the blazing yellow sun. Then Dap kicked the dirty gray slush with his slick alligator shoes and bared his teeth toward some ungodly thing that he could not see and under his breath he said, "Some motherfucker done shot my El D."

Up on the sixth floor, he aimed carefully, breathing in and then breathing out as he squeezed the trigger, as he had been trained, and saw the top of Dap's head fly through the air and land on the wound in the hood of his lavender El D. The red and white blob did a little shake dance and then was still. He switched the BAR to automatic and ripped off a burst that plowed into Dap's heart and turned his yellow coat into a bright orange. The sun caught Dap for a second, and then he fell into the gray streets.

He left the smoking barrel of the BAR sticking out of the window until he was sure someone—it was, in fact, a junkie who had been strung out since Bird died—had seen where the shots came from. That ought to get a little action 'round here, he thought. That ought to bring ,Bull runnin'. But maybe the bastard's off threatenin' somewhere over on 125th Street for some money. Yeah, that be just like Captain Bull. I be givin' him a chance to be a hero, and he be off blackjackin' some hustlin' woman in the name of the law and the Christmas spirit. Well, one thing for damn sure, he got his last Christmas gift from Dap. Fact is, Dap ain't gon lay nothin' on nobody no more. Come on Bull, you bastard. Come on and see what a air-conditioned skull look like.

A shroud of silence lay stiflingly across the street below. Never during the eleven years that he and his family lived there had he seen such stillness. Silence. Not a hustler wrote a number; not a junkie nodded; not even James Brown wailed from the record shop. Silence. And he never felt so good as when he looked down on the Dapper Dude, not so dap now, and saw a white rat scurry away from what was left of his head. Even the rats, he thought, don't want his ass now.

He lit a cigarette and sat in his overstuffed chair and watched the silent, flickering images on the television set. A children's chorus was singing Christmas carols, songs praising the young lord who had come to deliver the people from eternal bondage. Even with the sound turned down, he knew the song they were singing. He had learned it from his mother as a child in Georgia, and he had taught it to Bobby, his only son. He remembered that the song never failed to bring tears to his eyes. He rose from the chair and turned up the sound, and the children's voices rang into the dark, close little room and seemed to shake the picture of the Christ child that hung behind the set. They sang about peace, love, and eternal deliverance from suffering. But this time no tears came to his eyes. He sat down in his chair and waited.

There was nothing to do but wait. The first part of his plan was completed. After seventeen years, the BAR worked perfectly; his eyesight, as he had feared, had not failed; his aim was as good as the day he qualified as a master marksman in advanced infantry school. The clips of bullets lay neatly spread out on the coffee table. The gas mask was on the floor near the window. He had made his choice, the time had come, and now he walked the lonely passage that men must take when their grief turns to anger and that to solitary action; when they can no longer depend on man or God for redress of their grievances. And he neither wanted nor expected the help of either. But most important of all, he was not afraid.

He had felt the absence of fear many times, especially when he was thousands of miles from home firing his BAR and taking the unending snow-capped mountains for reasons that he only vaguely understood. Once, it was after they had taken Mountain 999, he asked his young captain why they had taken the mountain, what was its strategic importance. The young veteran of more than two hundred campaigns around the globe—his white face was already beginning to wrinkle and was streaked with blue and red blotches, the result of, so the rumor went, locked bowels—

took off his helmet and narrowed his pale eyes, hitched up his pants, and said, "We are taking these mountains, boy, to rid the world of our enemies!"

Warming up to his subject, he went on. "In the course of human events, we and God have decreed that it is our moral right to make the world a fit place to live in. And, boy, when you got moral right in your heart and a gun in your hand, anything is possible. Anything. . . ." The young captain would have undoubtedly told him more, the very secret of the universe, but the order came from the general to take Mountain 1000, and the young captain led the troops down the mountain exhorting them to their moral duty: "Charge! Charge! Ye defenders of decency, charge!"

The young captain, a merciless commander, drove him up the next mountain, drove him to stalk the padded figures and silently slit their throats. "A slit for decency. Good show, my boy," he said. One of the figures pleaded for mercy, shot through the eye, begged to be spared. The young captain leaned into his ear and said, "Do your moral duty, boy. Your country demands it." And he laid down a heavy burst into the enemy's good eye with his BAR. As they marched across the endless mountains, the young captain gave him a bright green gas mask; and he was indifferent to the stench of death even among the severed arms and heads and legs freezing in the falling snow, soon to be forgotten, not even remembered by God who—wearing his dark shades and squinting from behind the sun—watched as the young captain whispered to him that he was the true king of the world and God was on his side. With this, God split for lunch.

Now, sitting in his thick overstuffed chair smoking a cigarette, he did not even feel the last traces of outrage; they had vanished after he and his wife Mae had gone, to no avail, to the police precinct for the tenth time and then finally, still hopeful, downtown to the hundredth-floor offices of N.E.G.R.O.—the Negro Enigmatic Grievance Research Organization. He and Mae stood before the chief of N.E.G.R.O., Pimpleton, who seemed to listen patiently, benignly, as they explained their grievances but was secretly looking past them and out of the window, wondering if the low clouds meant more snow and his flight to Miami Beach would be canceled. His attention vaguely drifted back to the couple before him.

". . . So you see that cop captain up there, he in on it, too," Mae said.

"Won't lift a finger. Talk to us like we ain't in our right minds," he added.

Pimpleton smiled benignly and said, "What proof have you of these accusations?"

"What more proof I need? Everybody in Harlem know it."

"But my dear sir, N.E.G.R.O. cannot, nor I as chief of N.E.G.R.O., move on such flimsy evidence." Pimpleton sucked on his pipe as if it were a warm sugar tit and went on. "I mean, my dear sir and madam, things simply are not done that way. The gravity of your charges beg to be substantiated by facts. Facts, not hearsay, are the only means by which N.E.G.R.O.—and I am N.E.G.R.O., to state it bluntly—can move. By the way, do you belong to N.E.G.R.O.?"

"I can't afford to belong to N.E.G.R.O."

"A pity."

He clenched his fist and looked at the little old negro seated in his large leather chair behind his ten-foot mahogany desk. What kinda game this joker think he tryin' to run on me, he asked himself. He wanted to strangle Pimpleton's wrinkled little chicken-skin neck.

But instead he said, "You got lawyers suppose to work for us; let 'em check it out. I'll show 'em where to look for facts, evidence as you call it."

"My dear sir, you can't expect N.E.G.R.O. to go off on a wild goose chase, as it were; we can't unleash our lawyers on speculation. We must have reasonable faith that we will be successful. Heavens to Betsy, what would our board of directors say? That is the foundation of N.E.G.R.O., success in the mainstream!"

"Bullshit."

"I beg your pardon."

"I said, bullshit!"

"Oh, oh, yes. But we must remember that everything has its time and place. We must not become impatient. Justice is certainly not blind; she is sometimes tardy but never blind."

He smiled as he looked at the shrunken little man, his Brooks suit about three sizes too large for him. He bared his big white uneven teeth and blood-red gums and thundered into Pimpleton's face, "Pimpleton, fuck justice. I think the bitch needs bifocals. Fuck her! Funny time dressin' slut. Fuck her!"

Pimpleton sprang up from his chair like a shot, his sunken little eyes jumped to attention and twitched in step, and he wiped the spit from his narrow little head with his spotless white handkerchief. He was shocked. Shocked! Shocked that there were still half-crazed niggers raving about their mythical grievances, niggers who were beyond redemption, beyond ever swimming in the mainstream to which he had devoted eighty years of his life. "Well, sir, Washington was not built in a day, neither was Calcutta for that matter. But we must persevere, mustn't we? Godspeed and goodday, sir."

And with that, Pimpleton did a quick shuffle from behind his desk and ushered them past rows of pictures of him shaking hands with presidents and out of his office. Pimpleton went back to his mahogany desk and with trembling hands poured himself his fifth shot of Chivas Regal that morning. He smacked his thin little lips and got back to plotting what he would say to the Concerned Citizens of Miami Beach in his everlasting quest for funds to research and eradicate grievances. He wondered about his accommodations; he would accept nothing but the best. The couple who had stood before him only seconds before were now faint shadows floating on the dark side of his mind.

The next morning Mae sat stiffly at the kitchen table. She had not touched her breakfast, and it lay limp and cold on her plate. She sipped some water and was careful to avoid looking at the empty chair to the right and her husband sitting opposite her. He lighted a cigarette, sipped his coffee, and watched the vein jump on the back of her small hand.

"I don't seem to have no appetite in the morning," she said, trying desperately to smile through the pain that seemed permanently engraved on her face.

To look at her like this, to see her red-rimmed eyes pleading for answers he could not give her, lashed his soul. But he managed to smile and say, "You got to eat something, baby. You ain't gettin' tired of your own cookin', good as it is, are you?"

She smiled weakly and picked at her food and noticed that he had eaten only half of his eggs. "There ain't," she said, calmly, evenly, "nothing we can do, is there?"

"Don't say that, Mae."

"It's like don't nobody care. Like we hangin' off on the edge of the world and everybody stompin' on our fingers."

"Don't say that, baby."

She forced herself to look at the empty chair and said,

"They took our hope away, and ain't nothin' we can do."

He held his right hand, hoping that she would not see it tremble.

"I wouldn't bring no more into this world; same thing happen to 'em—just like Bobby."

"Mae, Mae, baby . . . Don't say that."

"It's all fixed. Nothin' we can do."

"The hell there ain't."

"What can I, you, anybody do?"

"I'm gonna . . ." He caught himself. It was better that she know nothing of his plans.

"What we need," she said, her voice detached, seeming to come from outside her body, "is a god or somebody who got us in mind when he plannin' and plottin' the way things suspose to go down."

"Come on, baby. If I'm gonna drop you by Sara's 'fore I go to work, we better be makin' it."

She did not move. She just sat there looking through him, beyond him, her eyes angrily riveted on the picture of the Christian savior hanging above the television set in the living room.

"It'll be better for you at your sister's today. She'll be good company for you."

He took his wife down into the street. The wind, blasting from the west and across the river, blew the heavy snow into their faces; and for a moment they were blinded by it. But they wiped the snow from their eyes, leaned into the west wind, and walked up the street. On the corner, through the driving snow, they could see the lavender El D parked, its motor running, and through the windows they could see the two men seated inside: one a thin black blur dressed in yellow, a cigarette slanting from his thick lips; the other, a fat ghostly white dressed in dark blue. They walked on. They said nothing. She because she thought all hope was gone. For him words were no longer of any use.

In front of Mae's sister's house he kissed her, holding her closely and tightly to him. Mae felt the tightness of his grip and wondered why it had such urgency. She looked into his face, but it told her nothing. He gave her an envelope and told her not to open it until Christmas. She smiled, and he kissed her lovely face again. He watched her walk into the apartment house and to her sister. He turned and walked quickly home.

He butted the cigarette and noticed that the sun had

crossed the river and was dropping quickly behind the hills. He rose from the chair and slowly became aware of the noise coming from the street below. He was not surprised. It takes a little longer, he thought, when it ain't nothin' but a dead nigger laid out in the street. He crossed to the window and saw that the street was filled with people, many crowded around Dap's body, now that the police and ambulance had come. Four cops, wearing white riot helmets, bulletproof vests and carrying rifles and tear gas guns, had jammed a junkie up against the wall near the Lucky Dollar Bar and Grill. The junkie was talking slowly and pointing to a building near the end of the block. Bull was not among the cops. "Sonofabitch," he muttered to himself. Come on, let's get it on. Then he glanced down to the center of the block, in front of the record store, and saw a mobile television unit. Its crew was busy shooting the scene. One cameraman was moving in to shoot Dap's body as it was being loaded on a stretcher by two attendants from Harlem Hospital. Do it in color, man, do it in color. Maybe some of these other bastards get to thinkin' 'bout how they messin' with they own folks. He spat out the window.

And then he heard it.

He heard it before he saw it. And he felt in his bones, knew beyond all doubt, that the siren signaled that his man was coming to him. His head suddenly felt light and giddy. And only when he picked up the BAR and watched the police car roar into the block and stop in front of the ambulance did his excitement leave him.

Captain Bull stepped out of the car. The brass buttons on his blue uniform pierced the gray twilight like rat's eyes. He, too, was dressed in flack jacket and helmet and carried a Thompson submachine gun at high port.

From his window he zeroed in on the gold captain's bars on the front of Bull's helmet and was about to squeeze off a round when a black newscaster, that station's roving black reporter in Harlem, stepped in front of Bull and began to interview him. He lowered his rifle and cursed under his breath. Time. I got plenty of time, he thought.

Bull, flanked by his sergeant, the newshawk, and his cameramen, walked to the ambulance. Bull stopped the attendants just as they were sliding Dap's body into the ambulance. Bull pulled back the sheet and looked at what was left of the man called Dapper Dude.

He had been watching the scene below so intently that

at first he had not heard the voices. Voices that were familiar to him.

"Do you know this man, Captain?"

"I've never seen him before in my life."

"Do you have any idea who killed him?"

"No."

"Why would anyone want to kill him, any idea?"

Then he turned around and saw that the scene below was being televised live and in color on the evening news. Ain't that a bitch, he thought. Good. Let the whole fuckin' world see it.

"The work of a madman, I'd say."

"Shit!" he said. "But you right; I'm mad as a bitch." He turned back to the window and saw Bull nod to the attendants, and they shoved Dap inside and slammed the door.

He saw that Bull and his sergeant were now joined by four cops. They pointed to the junkie. The junkie nodded and still pointed to the building near the corner. Bull led his men in that direction. In the gray twilight he caught Bull's white helmet in his sights. He led him, one, two, three, fired. He missed. He missed Bull's head by less than an inch. Bull dived under Dap's El D. His men scurried into the dark hallways and cellars. "Sonofabitch," he said. He switched the BAR to automatic and laid down a heavy field of fire at the El D. Nothing moved. Then he saw Bull rise on the street side of the El D and squeezed the trigger. Click. Click. Click. He moved to the table. He threw a clip into the BAR and another into his pants belt. When he returned to the window, he saw Bull and his men scurry into the apartment house directly across the street.

Well, that's that, he thought. It gonna go down different than I figured. Bull got to get him some high ground if he figure on takin' me. But he don't know I know that. Fool. He think I'm just some crazy nigger. Shit. I got right in my heart, a gun in my hand, and I'm the king of the world. Let's get the shit on.

He was sure the police knew exactly which window he had fired from. There would be no doubt in their minds; the last shots would frame it there forever. But he would not be in that window. He walked to the kitchen and was looking to the rooftops across the street when he heard Mae's voice.

"Yes, that's my apartment."

He turned around and saw Mae and the newshawk on

the television set in the living room. She was being interviewed behind the mobile unit downstairs. "Baby, whatcha doin' down there? Goddamn!"

"You're sure the shooting came from your apartment?" the newshawk asked.

"I told you once, yeah."

"You also said the gunman is your husband."

"Yeah, he my man. My husband and my man."

"Can you tell our audience why your husband . . . He has killed one man and is now engaged in a shoot-out with the police. Why?"

"He doin' what he's got to do."

"Er, er, I don't quite understand."

"He has to do what he's doin'. Nobody would understand."

"What kind of man is your husband? Had he been distraught, upset about something?"

Mae drew her thin black coat around her shoulders and clutched the manila envelope to her breast. The snow fell into her hair and crowned it with a strange majesty in the gray twilight, and she seemed to grow taller than her five feet, two inches, and he knew she would be all right. Nothing could touch her now. Her eyes were no longer red. She looked carefully, clearly, and directly into the newshawk's eyes and said, "He just a man. Just a man who had a son and lost him and didn't nobody care. He just a man, my man."

Mae looked lovely to him, a queen, and he loved her more than anything in this or any other world. He wished he had told her so more often. And tears came into his eyes; not tears of sadness or regret but of a terrible completeness of the order of things, their rightness in the universe. He saw the envelope in her hand and knew its contents: his G.I. insurance of ten thousand dollars that he had kept after his discharge; his paid-up life insurance from the Georgia Life Assurance and Burial Association that his mother had taken out shortly after he was born; the money he had withdrawn—$252.43—two days ago from the small bank account he had opened for Bobby to give him the little stake in life which he had never had; and the broken halfs of his Combat Infantry Badge. Why he put the medal in the envelope he was not quite sure. It had been in the cigar box in the bottom of his trunk with his papers, the blue background peeling off, leaving the rifle a stark white against the silver. And without thinking he picked it up and broke it easily in his large hand and dropped it into the envelope.

"Does your husband belong to any organization?" asked the newshawk.

"He don't belong to nobody but himself. . . ."

The first volley of shots, coming through the living-room window, hit the television set, splitting the image of Mae's head open, and the television was silent. The next volley hit the picture of the young Christ hanging above the television set and riveted it to the wall. "Ain't that a bitch," he said. "They done nailed J.C. to the wall with an overdose of America."

He crawled to the kitchen window and cautiously looked across to the rooftops. There were two of them, their funny little white helmets pinpricks against the gray sky. He stood to the side of the window and fixed them in his mind's eye. The rifleman was on his left, the tear-gas man on his right. He estimated the range and elevation—kept in mind that Bull and the other cops would try to break out from their hiding place—and whipped into the window, caught the rifleman about to squeeze off again, and blasted him. He knew the cop was dead and did not bother to watch him fall from the roof; instead, he laid down a sheet of fire in front of the door and into the hallway to keep Bull at bay until he was ready for him. He turned and caught the last cop in his sights just as the cop was about to fire his tear-gas gun. As he saw the cop's head explode, he smelled the acrid, pungent odor of tear gas in the living room.

He plunged into the living room, his eyes quickly tearing and put on his gas mask. While he was doing this, he did not, could not, see Bull and his four remaining men dart quickly across the street and into his building, their gas masks already on. But he heard them. He heard their outraged, stampeding feet as they raced up the stairs. And he knew they could not wait to get him. So he decided to make it easy for them; he unlocked the door to the apartment; then, threw a fresh clip into his rifle and calmly knelt behind the overstuffed chair and aimed at the door.

He was somewhat pleasantly surprised at Bull's methods; even though the door was cracked, he found it necessary to shoot the lock with his sub Thompson. You anxious, fool. Well, blast on, man, he thought, blast on in.

They rushed the apartment, firing at everything in sight, which was mostly smoke, and he caught them as they entered, and he fired steadily and evenly into their blue coats.

He rose from behind the overstuffed chair and fired into the four limp bodies without thought of mercy. Then he looked at them sprawled on the floor, their faces hidden behind green gas masks. Bull's helmet had been blown off, and he moved through the gray smoke among the still arms and legs and blown-away faces and saw that Bull had worn a wig. He pulled the mask from Bull's face and thought that he looked curiously like a fat old woman.

Then he heard the sirens and threw another clip into his Browning automatic rifle, and he waited as he had done many years ago in a land of unending mountains. Fuck 'em all. Fuck every goddamn one of 'em, he thought, and moved back to the window.

Dandy, or
Astride the Funky Finger of Lust

Ed Bullins

Ed Bullins is probably the leading black playwright in this country. He is co-founder of Black Arts West in San Francisco and a member of The Black Arts Alliance. Resident playwright at the New Lafayette Theatre in Harlem and editor of Black Theatre *Magazine, he has had a collection of his plays published and is the editor of an anthology of contemporary black plays,* Plays from the Black Theatre. *His first book of fiction,* The Hungered One, *was published in 1971.*

Dedicated to Malcom X . . .
who, too, wore a "zoot" suit.

"We're makin' a regular country boy outta you, Dandy Benson," Aunt Bessie said, wiping the flour from her hands.

Dandy laughed behind her back as she stopped to shove the biscuits in the oven and muttered "like hell" under his breath.

"What did you say?" she asked.

"Nothin'."

Dandy took his swatter and eased over in back of Marie Ann to smash the fly she was stalking.

"Git on away from here, Dandy Benson," she giggled. Her brown face burst into joy.

"This is man's work, Marie Ann," Dandy drawled.

She pulled at his wrist, and they began wrestling across the floor on the far side of the great kitchen from Aunt Bessie. Marie Ann's large muscular legs strained below her shorts as the two pushed and jerked. Dandy held her tight, on the sneak, to feel her young breasts.

"You kids, you kids break that up," Aunt Bessie yelled. "Break that up, you hear me, Dandy and Marie?"

They parted with Marie getting the last tap with her swatter on Dandy's rear.

"Dandy," Aunt Bessie said, "I want you to stay away from Marie," the middle-aged woman said for at least the hundredth time, Dandy thought. "You two are together too much, and if anything happens to that girl, Dandy Benson, I'm going to see that somebody goes to jail and that goes for you, too."

Dandy and Marie had heard Aunt Bessie's threats before; they had heard them as a regular part of their long summer days together; their being caught in childish play each day was almost routine, or the near miss of being discovered kissing or hugging, and then the following mock violence of the confrontation by the old lady they both loved. Even knowing that if they had been guilty, if Dandy were so fortunate as to be fully worthy of her suspicions, and the woman would have carried out her promises, they both knew that they would continue loving Aunt Bessie as nearly everyone did.

Aunt Bessie claimed love as her own, and in this manner she took the children of the poor and wretched and overworked into her warmth. She took those who would love her most.

Dandy looked out one of the windows surrounding the kitchen and wished that he had opportunity to test Aunt Bessie's threats.

Times were better now, he thought. There was so much more for him to like his second summer in Mary's Shore, Maryland. He liked the way the tan and brown of the sand and mud roads wound through the dried weed fields and meadows more this summer than his first lonely year, and he liked the animals: the dozen ducks, the eight pigs, the horse Jim, and the couple hundred chickens that Aunt Bess and Uncle Clyde kept on their sixteen-acre farm. He even kind of liked Uncle Clyde, a little bit at least, and surely the second summer's entire bunch better than the ones of his first vacation in Maryland. Even the year before that first one in Eastern Shore, spent in New Jersey with his near-white Aunt Martha, there wasn't the same dismal emptiness as the vacation of the first year with Aunt Bessie, even though there was no one in New Jersey with him but Aunt Martha and her maid, cook, and handyman who doubled at driving the shiny new black Buick and was called "the chauffeur."

The first summer with Aunt Bessie, the kids had been too young or either all from the same little town of Chester, Pennsylvania, except him, and Dandy couldn't stomach much of their attempting to convert the freedom of Aunt

Bess's farm into an extension of little Chester.

But this year there was Roy Howes, and there were Jack, Marie Ann, and Richard Bowen. And there was Ida.

Aunt Bessie boarded out kids for the state adoption, correction, and welfare agencies, and in the summer she and Uncle Clyde took in additional summer guests from the city. Dandy was from Philadelphia, that's why they had begun calling him Dandy, from his jitterbug clothes he arrived in and his cool impractical walk that was difficult to show on the soft dirt roads in his snake-skinned, pointy-toed shoes he had to abandon for loafers, but he still hadn't altogether dropped the strut because he *knew* the city had made him to be different from the other boys there in that farm land.

"Go out and empty the garbage, Dandy," Aunt Bessie said. "Uncle Clyde and Jack and the little boys will be home soon."

That was a job that Dandy did well. He enjoyed the pull the bucket gave his muscles when he lifted the tin container and carried the swishing mess outside and across the yard to the pig barrel. The two dogs, a young German shepherd named Pudgy, and a collie, Cisco, always followed him across the yard begging him to drop them a scrap or throw them crusts as he sometimes did.

A wooden cover covered the barrel, and Dandy had to slide it off with one hand while holding the bucket high so the dogs would not poke their snouts in and drag garbage around the yard and later get sick, having their stomach's contents heaved up, drawing flies. Whenever Aunt Bessie cleaned chickens, she especially warned Dandy, for one day Pudgy poked his head in the slop bucket quickly and pulled out a long chicken gut tied together with other chicken guts, and the shepherd and Cisco had dragged the garbage about the yard while several chickens who had slipped under their fence and constantly ran the yard chased after the scraps the dogs dropped and tore off. The hens pecked furiously away at the raw meat as if they didn't know they were devouring their brothers, and Aunt Bessie had gotten ill.

So with care Dandy lifted the bucket and sluiced the contents into the mixture. He stood and watched as the large pieces floated to the top and then were sucked under in the crawling stew while air bubbles burped and the mess stirred internally and gave off yeasty sounds and sourer smells. The dog's whines did not even muffle the popping of the pig's pudding.

Dandy stood just off the driveway, which half mooned around the house and cut the yard in two, pushing the workrooms, barn, and hen house into the background. The slop barrel hunkered beside an old wooden truck trailer that had been mounted on cinder blocks to the right of the house. Uncle Clyde used the trailer for a tool room and stored his pig and chicken feed in its cool wooden gloom.

The horse compound, stall, barn, and hen house with a shabby assortment of several other buildings formed a broken-toothed back wall to the yard. In front of the hen house grew a tree with a swing hanging from its lower branches. Dandy remembered the first summer when there were two little dark girls with the whitest of whites in their eyes to swing on the empty swing. He turned back and put the top back upon the barrel. In back of the barn and hen house and buildings was the manure pile, and down a small hill to ground spongy wet in the autumn rains was the pigpen with four large pigs in one half of the compound and four little porkers on the other side. Dandy would feed them after supper when it began to get dark and cool.

Behind the pigpens were woods for a quarter of a mile, and behind the trees were the church camp grounds; every year in August the Mary's Shore colored community gave an ole timey camp meetin'. Mary's Shore was in fact a town two miles away, two country miles, but where Aunt Bessie's farm sat was closer to the crossing of Mt. Holy. Three roads converged like blinded snakes; the road from Hamilton, the twisted and adventurous route from Bicksley, and the Biltmore dust highway. On one corner was a store with an ancient filling pump, an old-style one with gauges in the head and the liquid moving down the glass bulb like bubbling sand in an hourglass. On the other corner was Sister Ossie Mae Hewett's house and land. And at the apex of the triangle was the Mt. Holy Methodist church. Opposite Aunt Bessie's field, running a quarter mile toward the crossing, was the Mt. Holy cemetery. The small settlement of black farmers and laborers was more often called by themselves Mt. Holy than anything else.

"You sho drag feet, Dandy Wandy," Marie Ann said when he entered the kitchen. She tickled the back of his head with the fly swatter as he went past. Aunt Bessie was again bent over the oven. She was a large-boned, heavy-fleshed woman who eternally laughed and joked, showing her flashy store teeth. She was very proud of her teeth, almost as proud of them as she was of herself. Dandy thought that the way she managed things and worked the love and affection from people was like a pimp who psychs out his whores. She was a shrewd extrovert with a heart big enough to satisfy even herself. But Dandy knew her, knew she believed in nothing like he did, not even in the God she went in search of three times a week at the whitewashed church up the road, for she was what Dandy called a phony, though she was nice, one of his favorite people of all those he knew, so he liked her very much while not trusting her a bit.

"Why here they come," Aunt Bessie exclaimed in her booming voice. "Here come my boys."

An old Packard groaned around the driveway and halted. The front passenger door opened and a tall dark young man stepped out and turned away from the house and headed for the outhouse. From the rear doors skipped a brown laughing boy, and a thin dark one circled the car to join the other.

"Hey, hey, Fatso," the brown boy screamed in mirth as the dogs pranced and yapped about him.

"Ahhh, Roy, you better not tell," the darker one said. "Ahhh . . . Roy."

"Heee hee heee . . . Oooooo man," the brown boy laughed, and began running around the car with the dark one after him, the dogs completing the circle.

"Git on in the house and get ready fo' dinner," the man in the car said. He sat in his driver's place and shouted through the window.

The two boys came in the house, letting the screen door bang behind them.

"You little boys stop lettin' that screen door bang," Marie Ann shouted.

"Oh, shut up, girl," one of them said.

"Wait, wait . . . before you two little boys get ready for supper, I want you to walk up to Sister Ossie Mae Hewett's where Ida is workin'," Aunt Bessie said.

"Yes, Aunt Bessie," the dark boy said.

"Walk home with Ida, and Sister Ossie's goin' ta send back some tomatoes and peaches."

"Hee . . . hee . . ." Roy chortled.

"Didn't you hear Aunt Bess, boy," Marie Ann asked. "What's wrong with you little boys?"

"But Aunt Bess . . . hee hee," Roy tried to choke out, but his laugh bent him over near to the floor.

"Look at that silly boy," Aunt Bessie said, her face cracking into a smile for the joke that had to come.

"What's wrong with that boy?" Marie Ann wanted to know.

"Don't listen to him, Aunt Bessie," Richard said. "He's tryin' ta make fun ah me. Don't listen ta him, Aunt Bess."

"Aunt Bess, Fatso . . . he . . . he," Roy began, pointing at the thin boy. "He tried . . heee hee heeee.'"

"I don't want to hear about Richard Bowen," Aunt Bessie blustered when Roy stretched out on the floor and sobbed with mirth. "Get on up to Sister Ossie Mae's and get Ida."

The boys left finally, with Richard grabbing a slim stick from the woodshed in back of the trailer and crying "Oooo man" and chasing Roy around the drive and out in front of the house and up the road, with the old man's shouts from the car all the while warning that they better get about their little businesses.

Dandy was helping Marie Ann set the table when the tall youth came in and slammed the screen door.

"There's mah big son," Aunt Bess said, and shuddered when the door flew shut. "How did it go today son?"

"Awlright, Aunt Bessie," he said, deepening his voice on purpose to a musical baritone.

"How's my big bro' Bowen," Marie Ann said, pushing herself against the youth to make him lean sideways.

"What cha doin' dere, *Maurey*," the boy slipped into a playful drawl and began pushing her across the floor.

"Bo, stop pushen your little sister." Marie Ann giggled. She tried to tickle him as they jostled their way across the room.

"Dandy, come and pull this here girl offen me," Jack called.

"No Dandy don't you dare, Dandy," Marie screamed, laughing as she acted like she was about to be raped. "Help me, please help me, Dandy," she pleaded.

"I'm neutral," Dandy called out, watching their mock battle, seeing the sinews bulge in Marie Ann's legs and her solid behind below the narrow waist fight the material of the shorts.

"Dandy, you better help out one of them or ole Aunt Bessie's gonna jump in to even it up," the old woman teased, and began rolling up imaginary sleeves and wetting her thumbs on tongue as she threw up her dukes.

Dandy ran to the sink and pulled a damp towel from the rack and twirled it tight three times and ran across to the squirming couple and popped the towel on the seat of Marie Ann's shorts.

"Ohh . . . Dandy, you dirty dog," she whimpered.

And he popped her again, a loud and cracking whack.

"That's for the fly swatter, Marie," he said.

"Hey, what you kids doin' in dere?" the man in the car called in.

"See here, your Uncle Clyde is goin' to get you," Aunt Bess said, and moved over to the door, blocking the man's view.

"Jack Bowen, you go and clean up," she said.

The couple parted.

"Just don't worry so much about inside of here when you ain't in, Clyde," Aunt Bessie hollered. "Just don't stick your nose in so much," she said to the old man in the old Packard.

"I'll be stickin' mah foot somewhere if'en I don't git some peace around here," the man in the car said.

When Jack let Marie loose, Dandy spun around with the girl swinging at him. When they were inside the front room, he let her catch him, and she slapped at his grinning face until they began kissing. Aunt Bessie called her to finish setting the table.

Dandy didn't want to go back into the kitchen with his just having gotten kissed and then suddenly having to act like nothing had happened. He didn't know if he could be normal.

That time at Doris's he hadn't been normal, and he had really tried that time. No matter how he tried it always betrayed him. In fact, he knew it was *he* who betrayed himself.

He had met Doris at school. She was in his homeroom class, and Doris had been pretty hard to miss. She was the oldest of either girls or boys for having been put away in reform school for almost three years, and she was also the largest and loudest.

Doris was evil to his way of thinking . . . a type of evil that fascinated him. Not only did she curse like she wanted, she did everything else she wanted. She threatened the boys in class as well as the girls, but it was especially the boys who she had made fear her, and she didn't just bluff. Of course there was probable bluster in her statements to the boys that she could cut or pull their "things" off if they messed with her or got in her way, but most believed her, for she had been known to scratch girls up and hit the boys so hard on their arms and in the chest that they swore she hit like a man. Most fourteen-year-olds have not been struck by a man's full punch, but Doris's rep was secure.

Somehow she never bothered Dandy before they became friends. For all of Dandy's swagger, essentially, he was a quiet boy. After school he would go home and work on his motorbike, or hopelessly unable to find a defect, he and his friend Homer would take a ride or go by some girl's house. Homer lived next door to him, and they were the only two in their neighborhood that had motorbikes. Dandy had gotten his by begging his mother for two long weeks. Homer had gotten his six weeks later by taking an extra job after school. Some days Dandy didn't ride with Homer nor tamper with his bike's efficiency. He went around the corner to the Eighth Street gym in the basement of the police station. There he trained for the future. That's what he thought he would be some day, a fighter.

Columbia Avenue in North Philly in some of its neon stretches has a bar at every corner and one, two, or three in between. It is a street of pawn shops, trolley cars, pimps, markets, jazz, real-estate offices, hustlers, the hustled, lawyers, whores, junkies, blues, and more blues and bars and movies—the main artery of a ghetto, Dandy's neighborhood.

Up north, in the city, Dandy was mostly called Stevie. And the Saturday afternoon that Stevie Benson and Homer met Snoopy and his boys, the Avenue was jumpin', a drunk's delight and a cock-hound's carnival. Stevie and Homer had crossed Broad and passed the five-and-ten when they were stopped by the five boys who stepped from the alley next to the show.

"Hey, what's happenin', man?" the dark wiry leader said to Stevie.

"How's it goin', Homer?" one of the boys said to Stevie's friend.

"What the fuck is this supposed to be, man?" Homer asked. Homer was older than any of them, and the boys in front of him grinned and backed off. Stevie didn't know any of the gang.

"I said what's happenin'," the leader spoke again.

"Nothin', what's happen'n with you, man?" Stevie replied.

No one else spoke. Homer strolled to the curb and sat on the bumper of a car. The other boys faded aside, leaving the pair alone.

"How 'bout loanin' me a nickel, man?" the leader said.

"I ain't got it."

"Ain't cha goin'nin' da movie?"

"Yeah."

"Den wha'cha mean ya ain't got it? All I find I can have?" He reached toward Stevie's pocket.

Stevie stepped back into a fighting stance and shoved the boy's hand aside. From the edges of his eyes shapes moved.

"Don't worry 'bout yore back," Homer said. "This is just between you and him."

"What are ya supposed to be . . . bad, man?" the leader asked Stevie.

"Bad enough, man."

"I'll see ya 'round," he said, and he and his boys stepped back into the alley, glaring as they retreated.

There were three fights that afternoon in the movies. Two between rival gangs and one in the balcony between two gassed-head dudes over a girl who left with a third fellow. Homer told Stevie how well he had done with Snoopy, and they stayed out of hassles for the remainder of that day.

The rest of the weekend was spent with Homer instructing Stevie in what to look for and how to face it, for trouble was surely coming.

Monday morning was like many others. The dreary succession of junior high school classes passed with the same amount of perverse violence by the students and the exact amount of hate that big-city-slum schoolteachers can radiate. The erasers were thrown at Wild Leo in the third row by the hysterical, horn-rimmed redhead who taught something she said was social functioning; the zigging chalk whistled down the aisle at some pompadoured head in math class; the spitball that splattered upon the neck of the shell-shocked English teacher caused him to verbally fornicate with Jesus; the dragging of Pancho the Spic down to the principal's office for writing obscene suggestions to Rita the Jew; the accumulated deadening hate of packing fifty-one haters in a space where only thirty could possibly fit—Monday morning was like many others.

In this school Stevie had to hide always, had to hide his intelligence from teachers as well as students He had to hide his willingness to learn, his wanting to know and find out But now he knew how to hide his second year. In his first he was green and had found himself in fights each week; sometimes three or four in a gang would beat him up as he fought back wildly like a caged animal that didn't have instinct enough to run, even if the gate was opened. These fights usually ended when they hit him in the eyes, blinding him, and then pounding and kicking him to the ground as an added treat to the hundreds of schoolmates jeering the loser.

Force was what the crowd worshiped, Stevie learned. And for all the many good fights he had provided the mob, hardly anybody acknowledged him as a fighter. Losers are not often kept in mind as long as a year. And there had been no fight for Stevie for over a year since he had learned to hide so well.

After the lunch hour the kids formed lines to march back into classroom. Stevie waited in his line behind the numerous heads, not thinking of the long afternoon hours ahead, only sucking at the scraps of baloney caught between his teeth, from the king-sized hoagie he had eaten at the little lunch counter on Fifth Street.

"Hey, mahthafukker!" a voice at his side said loudly.

Stevie turned his head to see, as did the rest of the kids; it was Snoopy.

"I'll be waitin' fo' ya after school, ya little punk," Snoopy warned. "Don't try and git away."

A steady drone teased Stevie's ears the remainder of the afternoon. Guys and girls he didn't know stared at him and pointed and giggled. Some made pantomimed gestures —a boney fist smashing his mouth and the bugged-eyed expression of the punchdrunk, a mighty dig to the gut with a boloed right and the resulting doubling up and retching. The mood was intensifying for the afternoon's pagan dance.

Those who knew Stevie turned their heads or stayed far from him. Two friends from his neighborhood, his age, Brother and Timmy, looked knowingly and smiled and nodded among themselves, sharing this one more defeat of Stevie who they had known and seen defeated many other times. A few girls told him how sorry they were and for him to run out the side exit when the bell rang, or even before school ended. Who was Snoopy to create this total terror, he wondered. Stevie was out of his neighborhood, with no strong neighborhood friends to side with him, and had always been an outcast and foreigner during his school life because the schools closest him were so "bad" his mother threatened him with boarding school if he were ever compelled to go by the authorities. He constantly lied about his address. So, he had nobody there but himself. The Jewish boys he knew and the several Irish, Italian, and Polish guys wouldn't mix in a fight among Negroes even if one of them was a friend and the other a stranger with a gang to back him up. Fear of the gang was one more reason why he couldn't ask his few friends.

Toward the end of the last period Stevie raised his hand and asked to be excused from class. A tittering rustle rose about him as he got up and left the room. Inside the boys' toilet his stomach knotted as he sat on the john and tried to think of nothing and keep his legs from trembling, and after a while he straightened his clothes and in the mirror above the washbowl he feinted his left like Homer had shown him over the weekend and shadow-boxed a barrage of hooks and uppercuts into his imaginary opponent's surprised face. He then danced back, waiting for his dream adversary's vicious counterattack but stopped him cold with a low right hand thrown belt high as he charged in flailing, and Stevie finally creamed the shadow to the sidewalk with a left bolo to the kidneys. Before he left the cement room he pissed at the urinal, shaking the last drops into his palms and massaging the moist skin for luck.

"Little sucker, you gonna git your ass stomped *today*," Doris said, and he saw the joy of his return on his classmates' faces. "Fool, you should'a got away when ya had the chance," the big girl said when they lined up to leave school.

The fall sky was as gray as a morgue slab, and a pagan dance was held that day, a dance that marked the end and the beginning of something for Stevie Benson. The mob awaited the initiation, jostling and shoving to get better places. All the whites hurried home except for a few from over by the freight yards and from down the waterfront.

When Stevie came out his fire-tower exit, two boys bigger than he broke through the line and fell in step with him.

Doris ran up behind.

"Let me held your coat," she screamed above the gleeful mob.

Stevie pulled his jacket off and put it under his arm.

"Let me hold your coat, little sucker . . . you can't fight with a coat!"

He gave it to her. For blocks they walked, blocks of streets emptied except for Stevie, his two escorts, Doris, and the two hundred jostling figures. No one over eighteen stepped from a door, not a teacher or coach or administrator was seen seeking out his car or slinking to a bus stop that day until the dancers upon the concrete were blocks away, souls in time to the trotting and trucking of the savage song of the threshing floor.

Wild Leo screamed and whooped, pushing Pancho the Spic and grabbing leering Rita's hair. Black Delores, her face like a sooted Madonna with white rolling eyes, cried real tears, letting the streaks run over her lovely face like rain tracks upon coal. She stayed near but turned away and cried whenever Stevie glanced at her. Brother and Timmy, on the edges of the mob, smirked and stared straight at him when they got their chance.

The parade crossed Eighth Street, then Darien, and at last Ninth waited with a gravel vacant lot across the street from the train bridge. Snoopy squatted there sifting the grit through his fingers with at least ten street fighters around him.

"Dis is gonna be a fair fight, mahthafukker," Snoopy said when he rose and met the party. "I'm gonna kick yore ass until yore nose bleeds, punk." He took off his Eisenhower jacket and shrugged his shoulders to ripple his muscles. "You'll beg yore mamma to give you money ta bring ta me, ya understand!"

Stevie remained quiet. A burly boy with greasy green tam pulled down over his conked head acted as referee. Cheers and squeals rose among the crowd as the referee gave instructions, and pairs of anxious boys began body punching, the thuds and whacks beating out until the real fight began. Delores stood high on a stoop down the street, framed in the door, as alone as Stevie. Two bobby-socked girls picked up Snoopy's jacket and were on the verge of having a preliminary until the smaller backed down.

The referee pointed to Stevie: "When I say break, punk, you better scratch ass and git back like I tell you or you'll git yore little ass stomped today as well as whupped."

The two came to the center of the circle and began dancing like lightweights. Stevie was indeed an amateur lightweight but had only sparred with the boys in his neighborhood and the club fighters who used the police equipment on weekends. Snoopy's twenty-pound weight edge and his three-year advantage caused him to close fast with Stevie. Stevie won the first exchange by giving the clumsier boy two glancing jolts in the face with his left and right; Snoopy's swing swooshed above the little guy's head. They closed again immediately, and Stevie tied up his opponent

in a clinch and pumped quick shots to the kidneys and
gut like he had been taught. Surprised and ashamed at the
crowd's wild cheers for the underdog, Snoopy tried to butt
him, but Stevie had been waiting and dug his head into
the taller boy's chest, making him smash his nose. As they
broke, Stevie hit Snoopy again upon his bloodied nose. And
the referee stepped in.

"Here, man," he screamed, talking to Snoopy. "let me
take this mahthafukker." He had pulled his sweater off in
the late fall weather, and Snoopy stood between him and
Stevie as the mob surged out into the street.

"No, no, no, man," Snoopy pleaded. "I can take him.
I CAN TAKE THIS LITTLE PUNK ANYTIME I
WANT!"

The rest of the gang whispered among themselves, but
Snoopy wouldn't listen to them when they stepped into
the circle with the mob at their heels.

"C'mon, man," Snoopy said to Stevie, pushing his friends
back. "It's you and me now, little mahthafukker."

Stevie knew it was his fight and didn't think of anything
but winning. No more hiding, no more pulling punches and
not talking to the girls at school because he was out of
his neighborhood. No more copping out and eating shit.
No more, no more! They came for the dance, so now for
the floor show. I'm the best, he told himself; I'm the best,
and today we all find out.

The ring cleared, with even the referee pulled out, and
Stevie bobbed and weaved as he pressed in on the dark
boy, something he hadn't done before. He jabbed Snoopy
four times quickly around the arms and chest and landed
once in the throat. He danced, he danced so beautifully,
he knew, like to music, like to the sound of drums and
clashing cymbals. There was no other place in the universe
then for him but that dance floor with every fiber poised
and executing an ageless war dance passed down from his
father and his father's father before him and the black
fathers of his tribe before memory. He danced back, letting Snoopy's swing slip past and then feinted with his
left. Snoopy blinked and then stepped . . . the gang leader
woke up six minutes later with a busted mouth and nose,
one eye would be closed shut for two days, and his head
would ache for a time because of the mild concussion he
received when his skull cracked the curb. Stevie had stood
above him for a second after the feint and vicious combination of one, two, three, and more jabs pumped into
the big boy's face, and then the overhand right, and the

step behind the pivot and the hook that smashed into flesh and bone.

He waited for the fallen boy's counterattack.

"Here, mahthafukker," Doris screamed in the stunned second. "Run, mahthafukker, run . . . RUN!"

Stevie took his coat thrown at him and sped through the crowd behind him, speeding past smiling pearly-toothed Delores, running down the hill toward home. Running like he had never run in his life. All of Snoopy's boys seemed to be fifty steps behind, and behind them was the insane mob, crazy from the smash performance and lusting for added gore.

At the corner an old Hudson turned, and Stevie grabbed the door handle and leaped inside.

"What the hell?" the driver started, but the exhausted boy pointed back, and one look through the rear-view mirror gave the driver incentive to tramp on the gas.

After a week of negotiations between Homer and Snoopy and missing days at school with a couple running fights between Snoopy's boys and the ones Homer sent to escort Stevie back to his territory, the thing settled, and Brother and Timmy said: "You won!" and nodded their heads as they passed.

The following week Doris took Stevie to her house after school and ordered her little brother out. Then she showed Stevie how to really have sex, the way grown-ups did.

They met at her place every day after school for over a month. She told him about the other big guys she had at night, real men, she said, some even fathers and husbands that she had whenever she wanted. It seemed to Stevie that it was always she who wanted them from her way of telling it and who refused if they made demands upon her. She lived on the top floor of a tenement, and one day when Stevie was between her large dark thighs, his teeth nibbling at her earlobe the way she had showed him as they grunted and strained, they heard a loose step crack. He jumped up and ran to the window, and Doris pulled down her dress just as her girl friend pushed the door open and walked in.

"Don't ya know how to knock, bitch?" Doris growled.

"I've never had to before . . . was I interruptin' somethin'?" the girl asked. She was taller than Doris and almost as old. She was a grade ahead of both Stevie and Doris, and she and Doris ran around with a gang that called themselves The Controlerellas.

"How are you, Chuckie?" the girl asked Stevie. In this part of town he had a different nickname.

"Okay," he said over his shoulder.

He watched out the window. His fly had been buttoned just in time, but the front of his pants pushed out. He peered from the window as the girls talked, watching the trolley and cars go down Tenth Street, and the people on the streets that day, and looking south he saw the tall P.S.F.S. building rising from the gray dust of the slums, towering above them as if the structure's foundation were planted in the muck of the ghetto.

The street below looked small to Stevie and innocent, but he knew it was one of the main trails in the jungle. He liked being up high looking down at the people. He liked being there with Doris even though she bullied him in public; she was nice to him when they were alone, and best of all she said she liked the way he did it to her because he was young and strong and it took him a long time to finish.

"Give me a cigarette, Chuck," Doris's friend said.

He turned his head away from the window; she was smiling.

"Give me a cigarette, boy!"

He walked over to the couch and handed her a cigarette from his pack. She shrieked with laughter as she snatched it and leaned across Doris, choking and coughing. Stevie peeped down at his pants front.

He always betrayed himself, he knew. Always.

"Give me one, too." Doris said. She snatched the entire pack from his hands. "You don't need any, you silly little bastard."

Her friend laughed even louder.

Doris let him come to see her two more afternoons, but the times after that day of discovery when he asked to be let up her stairs, she told him no, though sometimes she would let him kiss her hurriedly in her vestibule. She stopped coming to school, and the kids gossiped that she had been thrown out because of being pregnant.

The week before she died Stevie and Homer were on Hutchinson Street, close to where Doris lived. They waited outside a girl's house who they were going to walk back to their neighborhood for a party. As they waited, Doris walked through the narrow streets with her tall, thin friend.

"Hey, lil' mahthafukker," she yelled to Stevie, "what'cha

doin' up this way?" She stopped, placing her hands on overblown hips, and stared at him through shiny eyes. "You know we don't allow little pricks up here."

She was loud and evil-sounding like the times at school when she threatened the boys, so Stevie knew she wasn't serious.

"Just hangin' out," he answered.

"What'cha been doin' lately?" she asked.

"Just eatin' fried chicken and fukkin' ev'va night, baby," he said, saying the line of the street song with a smile.

The girls flounced off in hobbling skirts and jeered at him to get out of "their" territory and swung their behinds in huge circles down the street, laughing, stumbling, and swearing.

"What'cha let that whore speak ta ya like that fo, man?" Homer had said. "You should'a punched that black bitch in da mouf."

Dandy had never told anyone about Doris. She had been his first, the first that mattered, for he had been playing sex games among the tenements since he was seven, but Doris had been the one who had made him feel for the first time that something which frightened and was vital to him. The only times before the quick afternoons with Doris on her couch was when he had had dreams he couldn't make out, but he awoke afterwards on his belly, wet and scared.

Since the first day with Doris he had sought out at least ten other girls. Slum girls who waited for any show of affection, especially from one their own age with a smooth brown face and who knew what to do. Dandy's challenge to Doris hadn't been entirely groundless even though sweet black Delores would only let him love her from across the aisle. He was out in the street every night. He knew Doris wanted to see him after the encounter on the side street, and her boisterous smile made him sweat some as he promised to go see her, for his feelings for the girl had grown suddenly proportional to his pants front, which moved out as he thought of her luscious warmth. He didn't make it to her place that week. The next, Doris died shortly after missing a fire net drawn under the window of her burning apartment.

Dandy stopped by to see her little brother some weeks later, and they both whispered of her and cried without thinking of being manly.

". . . And by the grace of God . . . Ahhh men," Uncle Clyde intoned.

"Pass the biscuits," Roy said.

"Just wait a minute, boy," Richard ordered, and acted cross and older than he was. "Shouldn't be so greedy!"

"Hush up, you two little boys," Ida James said. "All the way back from Sister Ossie Mae's you been at it."

"Yeah, keep quiet you little boy," Uncle Clyde said with a mouth filled with food.

"Here, Dandy," Ida said, and poured his lemonade for him.

"Why looky dere . . . old Dandy's makin' out like a madman," Jack Bowen slurred.

"Marie Ann, ya better look out or Ida will be takin' Dandy away from you," Roy said.

Marie shrugged and shoveled a spoonful of beans into her mouth. "Nobody's studden 'bout Dandy."

"Dandy, your city ways don't seem to be workin' any on Marie Ann," Aunt Bessie said. "What's wrong, boy?" She prodded Dandy, for she knew that he was working on her favorite, and he would have her if he got the chance.

"I don't know," Dandy answered. "I guess she thinks I'm a slicker."

"Hee hee heee . . ." Roy chortled. "Oooeee . . . hee heee . . ."

"Eat your supper, boy!"

"Well, that's what you is, boy," Jack drawled, and slipped tenses and syntax. "One of dem dere city slickers, and mah lil sister ain'ta gonna be fooled none any by y'all kind, *boy*." He made a private joke, though secretly he wanted his sister and Dandy to be more friendlier. Dandy would make a pretty fair brother-in-law, he thought, and he felt that any man who ever touched her would *have* to marry Marie Ann.

"Why are you so quiet, Sister Ida?" Uncle Clyde asked.

"Not much ta say, Unc' Clyde."

Ida was a stocky yellow girl who had been turned out by her mother after her father had taken her for over a period of two years and at last had succeeded in giving her his son. She was a ward of the state from being a minor and for having made herself available to any man in her town, forty miles south of Mary's Shore, who had the courage to talk to the fifteen-year-old for over five minutes. Many had the guts, and word finally got around to the authorities that a girl and baby were living in an abandoned shack close to town, and there were all sorts of carryings on. The powers couldn't charge Ida with anything more than vagrancy since she never asked for money from her numerous visitors, and not even vag stuck when it was found she was a teen-ager, though she seemed ten years older, or so it was assumed. Ida didn't talk much, and Dandy suspected that she was a bit dense since she was relieved that her baby had been taken from her. But she had enough sense to slip him a note his first day there that her heart was just about to actually burst from love of him.

She worked each day on a neighboring farm watching children or helping in the kitchen, for at least one member of each family in Mt. Holy had to go into town or farther to jobs in outlying districts. Some drove even to Dover and to Wilmington in Delaware.

Dandy knew his turn would come with Ida. Jack had told him how he would get her when he had the chance, not knowing that Dandy also schemed on her stubby flanks, for they both were sure that Ida James was as hot and ready as a ten-cent pistol.

"Dandy," Uncle Clyde asked. "When you comin' out with me or one of the boys on the job?"

"Any time, Uncle Clyde, how 'bout tomorrow?"

"Clyde, you know that boy don't want to work," Aunt Bessie said. She rubbed it in about Dandy being able to pay his board without working, for Dandy's mother had a civil-service job in the city, and the city slick Dandy was from Philly and had taken piano lessons and boxing lessons and singing and dancing lessons, and had a motorcycle (really only a motorbike). He was her current status symbol.

"No, he probably can't pull himself away from Marie Ann," Ida said, and peeped over her fork at the other girl across the table.

"I wish he could go somewheres," Marie Ann said, "I'm sure tired of lookin' at him."

The remainder of the table, except for Uncle Clyde, entered the conversation and bet about which of the girls would get Dandy, and the dinner ended with Aunt Bess promising that if anybody got Marie Ann they would go immediately to jail, whether or not they used "protection."

"NOW, BESSIE, YOU KNOW YOU SHOULDN'T BE TALKIN' LIKE DAT IN FRONT OF DESE HARE KIDS," Uncle Clyde hollered, nearly upsetting his greens.

"Well, all of them are big enough to take care of themselves, and none of mine ain't goin' 'round dumb for most of their lives, especially about somethin' that everybody has got ta do . . . or at least should try once, Clyde."

"Oh, hush up, woman."

"Well, I've told them already and even given them money to get 'em with," the old woman said. "All they have ta do is come and ask and I'll give them money to buy them. I ain't takin' the blame if somethin' happens. I'll tell the world it ain't Bessie's fault."

"You talk too much, Bessie."

It was a good dinner.

After dinner Dandy went to the trailer and poured hog feed into two large slop buckets and then carried them outside to the pig barrel. Setting them down, he lifted the large ladle and began filling the buckets a scoop at a time. The dogs had been tied for their evening feed, given by Roy coaxing and wheedling with puckered lips and many "Here boys" to the already leashed animals. As Dandy started on the second bucket, Marie Ann and Ida came out of the house, and they tugged at each other until one got the last tag, then Marie began trotting over toward the hen house where the outhouse stood.

"I'm goin' to get you when ya come back, Marie Ann," Ida called out.

"Ya know what you'll git, Ida," she said, turning around and making a fist and showing where on the light girl's face she would plant it. "And that goes double for your friend Dandy," she said before she entered the closetlike building.

Ida skipped over to the trailer and went inside. Dandy submerged the edge of the ladle in the thick broth and pulled it out with sucking sounds, pouring the mixture in the nearly filled last bucket. He heard the cracked corn rattling in the pan Ida used to feed the chickens.

"Come here, Dandy, I want ta show ya somethin'," she said from inside the trailer.

Dandy saw Roy cross the yard from the horse compound, and he stirred the pig's food until the boy was gone into the house.

"Dandy?"

Inside the trailer he found Ida in a dim corner and kissed her thick moist lips.

"I told Marie Ann that I loved you and she got mad."

"No, she didn't. You know that she likes Junior Kane."

"She did so get mad."

"She was teasin' you."

"No, she weren't, and she better not!"

"We better go," Dandy said after a while. "Someone will be out here looking for us."

"Okay. I have ta go ta choir rehearsal tonight, but I want ta talk ta ya when I git back."

Marie Ann was humming a hymn when Dandy passed the back of the outhouse with the heavy buckets.

The pigs were always ready to feed. No matter how Dandy filled their troughs to brimming, when he returned the next day, all had been swilled up and nothing remained but the stained, weathered boards of the troughs. When he turned the buckets up and splashed the food into the troughs, the pigs made oinking sounds that he had never gotten used to. He watched the fat beasts feeding, pushing each other aside, and remembered the story he had read of a man who had lain helpless in a pig pen and had been eaten alive.

On the way back to the house, climbing the stubbled trail beside the nearly grown summer corn, he saw three buzzards carried through the sky in the streams of invisible forces that he had been told were air currents. He found Jack Bowen waiting for him halfway up the rise.

"Well, howdy dowdy, Bowen?"

"Well, how yawhl doin', Mr. Benson?"

Jack was four years older than Dandy, but he allowed the younger boy to carry on rituals and treated him as an equal.

"How the girls treatin' ya, Bowen?" Dandy asked.

"Dey ain't treatin' one bit, partner, not a'tall."

Jack Bowen was more intelligent than Dandy; if he could break away from the farm and the series of mill-hand, packing-plant-helper jobs, he could be saved, Dandy knew but could not tell his friend. Jack lived as much for the future as for payday; he was forever participating in national contests that promised trips to Paris and mink coats and an occasional Cadillac. He purposely exaggerated his drawl, though he could speak better than Dandy could then; he could tell stories like nobody else and knew more about science, math, and those subjects' vocabularies. Dandy had never heard Jack's actual plans except once.

It was a day in early July that Jack took Dandy to the chicken plant to get on. Buddy Henderson drove them across the state line into Delaware where he and his girl worked. Buddy's girl, Betty Sue, was from Florida and chewed tobacco and wore men's pants because she had done so much field work she didn't "rightly take to dresses no mo'," and she couldn't read nor write much aside her name, Betty Sue. She had been living since spring in the shack village of itinerant workers behind the Hamilton Tomato packing plant until Buddy had gotten her to housekeep with hin..

The foreman hired everyone that day, for truckloads of birds waited to be slaughtered.

Dandy's job was to hang the chickens by their feet, pulling them from the crates as they flapped, squawked, and pecked, attaching the victims to metal clamps swinging under the conveyor. The belt ran, one clamp that had to be filled after another, and two farm boys worked beside Dandy and showed him how inadequate he was for hanging chickens at six bits an hour.

Sitting in a chair, ten feet down the line from Dandy, was an old fat man who cut the chickens' white throats. The man was black and wore a black rubber apron, the bib shielded his chest, the straps climbed up over his white-shirted shoulders and blended like dark bands with his neck. Dandy emptied crate after crate of white leghorns and sent them cackling down to the busy man with the blade. Sometimes a brown bird or a black with gray and white speckles found its way among the snowy ones and they added contrast, floating upended toward the chair, their red wattles dangling, then the brief last scream as one black hand reached out and anchored the head, and then the other hand moved, bringing red of a more alive hue streaming over their throats.

That lunch hour Dandy sat with Jack and Buddy Henderson and Betty Sue, eating homemade sandwiches of baloney and peanut butter.

"Hope ta gawd dese hare chickens hold out another two munts," Buddy remarked.

"I wouldn't care none if'in dey cut every last one's of da sonsabitches throats nex' hour," Jack said. "There ain't no future bein' a chicken plucker."

"Beats not eatin'," Buddy said. "What'cha do if dere were no job in'da chicken plant nor any in'da 'maters or any work a'tall?"

"Well, I don't know 'bout chauw, Buddy boy," Jack drawled, "but one ah dese hare days I'm hoppin' dat old Greyhound out on da road an' goin' up ta Philly an' git me ah job in 'da big post office up dere."

"Sheet, nigger," Betty Sue said. "When's de last time ya ev'va seen some nigger in a white shirt in da post office? Day get jest de job fo' all ya white-shirt niggers right here."

Jack didn't say anything for the rest of the lunch period, just munched his biscuit bread and peanut butter and looked mean. Everyone knew he would probably never go North to his post-office job.

Jack Bowen didn't seem like most brothers to Dandy. He didn't make threats nor get angry when Marie Ann first showed interest in him. Lots of times Jack would daydream aloud with Dandy. He would tell how he would one day visit Dandy in the city and maybe not go back to Mary's Shore. Secretly, Dandy knew Jack dreamed of visiting him and Marie Ann in their home in the wonderful city. But, nevertheless, they were real friends; they had mutual enemies.

"That goddamned Uncle Clyde is goin' ta git it one day," Jack said.

"What happened?"

"Wahl he just rides me, that's all. I was on the second floor of the mill today stackin' boxes like Mr. Harvey Wentley told me and Uncle Clyde came on up there and pulled me off the job."

"Yeah? That sounds bad."

"Sho nuf, hope ma gonna die but Harvey like ta pitched a bitch when he saw me traipsen my pretty black self down there on the mill floor amongst all them white gals."

"Yeah, I hear he don't like none of the young fellows ta be down dere near the girls, not even with himself dere."

"That's sho is right; Uncle Clyde is harmless; that's why he's foreman, but if he don't always stop fukkin' wit me . . . I'm goin' ta knock his ole rusty ass off."

They neared the rear of the outhouse and fell silent because they didn't know who might be inside.

After they passed, Jack said, "Junior Kane is comin' over, gonna go ov'va ta his place for some boozin' tonight."

"Yeah?"

"How 'bout goin'?"

"Why sho nuf, Mr. Bowen."

Junior Kane had a '34 Chevy and three half-sisters. The girls were young enough for Dandy and all attractive in their big-eyed, slow-talkin' country ways. Their reputations were of being fast girls for that part of the world.

Jack pulled out a pack of Chesterfields. He offered Dandy one, and they lit up. Dandy didn't like to smoke.

Before he began training, he smoked just enough to let his gang know that he did, and after he almost stopped completely. Since he had come down to Mt. Holy on his second vacation, he smoked whenever offered.

They walked into the kitchen, cigarettes in mouths. Uncle Clyde and Aunt Bessie were fussing.

"Now when I tell these little boys ta do somethin', Bessie, I meant it, ya hear?"

"These kids ain't for you to be always jumpin' on whenever you get ready, Clyde."

Marie Ann stood beside the sink with a dishtowel and gave approving looks to Aunt Bessie. Ida was over the sink with elbows in suds, softly singing a gospel song.

Jack and Dandy crept through the kitchen, crossed the front room, and climbed the second floor to their room. They passed Marie Ann and Ida's room first, then a spare room that was used when more guests arrived or during camp-meeting times when the house was jammed, and reached their large room at the end of the hall that ran the length of the house and had four large beds and a double-decker that Roy and Richard preferred to sleep in.

Jack stretched out on his bed, and Dandy sat on his, reaching for a Western magazine on the night stand between them.

"The Durango Kid sure gits into it, don't he?" Dandy commented.

Jack peered over his arms and said, "Sho do, I couldn't put that book there down until I had found out how the showdown would come off."

A tramping upon the stairs was heard.

"Stop it, Fatso," a cry came before the speeding tumble of tennis shoes.

"Hee heee heee . . ."

Roy and Richard burst around the corner at the stair's top, and Richard chased the giggling boy down the hallway into the bedroom.

Roy pulled himself into a corner between wall, bureau, and bed, and Richard, like a small scarecrow, thrashed at him with half-hearted pokes of his fists.

"Heee heee . . . Oooo, man," Roy called to his antagonist. "Fatso, stop!"

"Yeah, stop it, goddammit," Jack shouted.

"Oh, Bo," his brother protested. "Bo, he's always botherin' me."

"Heee . . . dat ain't right, Bowen," Roy said.

"SHUT UP, BOTH OF YOU! I DON'T WANT TA
HEAR ANYMORE OF IT!"

Richard stepped away from the hole where Roy
crouched and grumbled as he searched through a drawer.
Roy came out, hand over mouth, strangling on his laughs,
and finally hid his head under the double-decked bed, pretending to look for shoes.

"You guys goin' to choir meetin'?" Dandy asked the
younger boys.

"Yeah, Dandy," Richard said. "We goin', but I don't
know if'n we'll stay in the choir."

"Fatso's startin' a quartet," Roy spoke out.

"A quartet?" Jack said. "What makes ya think ya can
sing?"

"Well, it's like dis, Bo," one of them began. And they
spent the next half hour while changing their clothes to
describe the gospel quartet they were starting and how
when they were good enough their group, The Mt. Holy
Four, would go on nationwide tours, even to New York
City and Philly.

"Why don't you come on out and try to get on at the
mill tomorrow, Dandy?" Jack said after the boys had gone
downstairs.

"Oh, I'd like ta, Jack, but you remember the kiddin' I
got when I quit the chicken plant after three days."

"Awww, forgit that," Jack said. "Remember I quit two
days later."

"Yeah, but you work all the time, and I don't even have
ta unless I want ta have extra money."

"I know, but you're gittin' pretty tired 'round here all
day listenin' to Bessie . . . Say, are ya makin' much time
with mah little sister?" There was a guarded flash in his
eyes.

"Nawh, not much," Dandy said. "Aunt Bessie is around
all da time."

"Well, ya shouldn't mind comin' down ta da plant, then.
Thar's ah couple ah nice gals down there, and you can
always take Marie Ann ta the movies in Dover on Saturday nights."

"I'll ask Aunt Bessie."

A car chugged into the driveway; its wheezing engine
clanged in time to the barks and yips and prancing of the
newly unleashed dogs. The car's horn went AHHH
HUNNGGAA AHHH HUNNGGAAA AHHH HUNN-
GGAAA before the brittle pinging of the girls' giggles rose

above Aunt Bessie's voice bellowing welcomes to Junior Kane from the kitchen window.

Downstairs, Dandy stopped in the kitchen with Aunt Bess and Uncle Clyde as Jack strolled out to the car surrounded by the girls and two small boys on the old running boards.

"Howdy dere, Bowen," the driver yelled.

"Wahll if'n it ain't dat mule thief, Bro Kane."

The girls laughed more, their soft and syrupy drawls oozed over the heavy evening air as the sky glowed pink and violet and above trees to the east, twilight was promised by the gleam of a full moon on a pale blue-purple horizon.

"I'm goin' down ta the mill with Jack tomorrow, Aunt Bessie," Dandy said.

"Okay, son," the old woman answered.

"Wha ya say, Dandy?" the old man asked.

"I'm goin' ta try an' get on at da mill, Uncle Clyde."

"Shssucks . . . who you tryin' ta fool, boy? You don't wan' ta work."

"Ain't none of your business, Clyde," Aunt Bess said.

"Oh, dammit, Bessie! I don't care what he does, but he better know he's gon'na work when he's on mah crew. I don't play no favorites."

"We know you don't play favorites, Clyde," the woman said. "You'd work your mother to death if that white man wanted ya."

"NOW LISSEN HERE, BESSIE!"

Dandy went out the door and over to the car. Jack sat in the front next to the driver, and the remainder of the group stood by the windows.

"Howdy dere, Dandy," the driver said.

"Hi, Junior."

"What's goin' on with you, Dandy?"

"Wahll, I gues I'll be workin' with you guys startin' tomorrow."

Excitement rose, with everyone having something to add about Dandy's decision. Finally, Marie Ann went into the house, soon followed by Ida.

"Ain't you boys goin' ta choir rehearsal?" Dandy asked.

"Yeah, we goin' as soon as Ida gits ready. Shucks, she's been out hare makin' eyes at Junior Kane hare an' makin' us late."

Junior was a sun-darkened wiry boy in his late teens. He spoke with a coarse accent and laughed a lot.

"Stop dat fibbin'," Jack said. "You knows Marie Ann

has got Junior all staked out." Dandy saw Jack wink at him from behind Junior Kane's head. Junior broke into a great grin and showed tobacco-stained teeth.

"But, Bo!" one of the little boys protested.

"Shut up! Don't let me hear anything 'bout nobody flirtin' wit Marie Ann's boy friend."

"Here she comes."

Ida came out of the house wearing a red full-length coat. The hue heightened her bright skin and caused her teeth to flash within the scarlet-smeared mouth. She waved at Aunt Bessie through the kitchen-door window and turned toward the car and her admirers.

"See you, Junior," she said, and waved. "See you when I git home, Dandy and Bo." She hurried down the drive. "Come on, you little boys," she called while the two pups wagged their ends behind her heels.

"I'll race ya to Ida, Fatso."

"Oooo, man, we better catch her before she gets by the cemetery, or Aunt Bess will get on us."

And the boys were gone down the drive, laughing and squealing to the mingled barking of the dogs and the threatening yells of Ida.

Dandy opened the rear door and crawled in the back.

"Want a cigarette, Dandy?" Junior offered.

"Wow, a Raleigh!"

"Yeah, I save the coupons."

The radio played country music.

Rocks are mah cradle . . . da cole ground's mah bed da highway's mah home and I's might as well be dead . . .

Night came soon and the lights shone from the kitchen window and upstairs in Marie Ann's room. From under the seat Junior pulled four quarts of beer and opened each with a minimum of fizzing and handed Jack and Dandy one bottle.

"Ohhhee, Kane, you're really goin' ta do it tonight, boy," Jack said.

"Them sisters of mine have got some home brew ready, and we might as well git primed."

Thar I go . . . thare I go . . . thaaare I goo'oh . . . purty baby you's 's de soul that snaps mah control . . .

Marie Ann came out of the house wearing fresh short shorts and a white blouse outlining her young breasts.

"Ya ready ta go, Marie?" Junior asked as she got in the back of the car next to Dandy.

"Nawh, I didn't go ta choir meetin', and I better not go with yawhl."

"Why not, Marie? Jack will be dere." Junior handed her the last quart of beer, and she peered into the kitchen window to see if the old folks sat at the table. Aunt Bess and Uncle Clyde were in the front of the house; they sat in their bedroom off of the living room or watched television. Marie sipped at the beer. "Damn this is good." She leaned her elbows across the top of the front seat and placed her head between the half-turned heads of her brother and boy friend, Junior Kane.

"Sho gits dark quick around here," she said.

And night was outside, enclosing the blackened car as the pitter-patter of the returning dog's feet came from the road, and the cricket music and an occasional pig's oink and a drowsy duck quacked at the dark, while the white summer moon swung up into the black, star-pierced Southern heavens, and the stars that no city lights dimmed winked as if they, too, had secrets.

Wha ain't ya out'in da forest fighten dose grea' big ole grizzly bears?
I's a lady!
Dey got lady bears out dere'ah'ere.

"Dandy, you'll like it down the mill," Jack said.

"Ya sho will, boy," Junior Kane said. "Mr. Harvey Wentley's sho nice ta git along wit'."

"I'm sho glad yo goin', Dandy," Marie Ann teased. "Get real tired ah seein' yo face 'round here all the time."

Dandy's hand moved across the seat and caressed her bare legs; she flinched but took another sip of beer. Dandy had his bottle between his knees and drew on one of the cigarettes he took from Junior.

"Ya gonna buy me one of them great straw hats when ya git paid, Dandy?" Marie asked.

"One ah them Texas ones . . . shore will, Marie. I don't want ya ta git any blacker," he teased. "I'll git one with a string on it so ya can drop it back over ya neck and let ya hair fly."

"Ya never asked me fo ah ten-gallon straw hat, Marie Ann," Junior said.

And the music played.

*I found mah thrill on Blueberry Hill . . . on Blueberry
Hill . . . where I found you . . .*

"How's Ethel gittin' along?" Jack asked Junior.

"Oeewee, she's fit to be tied. Daisy and Helen came
down ta da mill, ya know, and got on. Now dere camp-
meetin' outfits' gonna be as purty as hers."

"Sho nuff?" Jack said.

"Hee heee . . ." Marie Ann simpered.

"Ah most like ta died, too, when I heard, Marie," Junior
said.

"Ahm jest glad I don' have ta work . . . got mah ole
big bro here," she said and caressed her brother's arm.

Dandy's fingers in the dark had crawled under the band
of her shorts and squeezed between the firm thighs and
around between the soft lips of the swelling labium. She
squirmed and hunched her boy friend and rested her head
upon her brother's shoulder.

"What y'all keep gigglin' fo, Marie Ann?" Junior Kane
asked.

"This is really some good beer," she said as she willed
herself to restrain the shudder that reached from her
center, and she opened her legs wide in the near-total
blackness and rested the rear end of her tight bottom on
the cushion and leaned fully forward with her knees bent
and her arms supporting herself.

"Give me a cigarette, Junior, pleez," she asked.

"I didn't know you did all this, gal," Junior kidded, and
giggled with her as he fished for his pack.

Marie Ann stretched farther over so that the light of
the match would not reach over the rim of the car seat,
and Dandy's moist moving finger flickered over her pursy
clitoris.

"Ummm . . ." she said, and hunched even farther forward.

"Wha you say, Marie?" Junior Kane asked.

"Just thinkin' . . ." she said.

Dandy took another long swallow of his beer, nearly
finishing the bottle. Jack tilted his up, and Junior got bold
enough to twist about and kiss Marie Ann full in the
mouth.

"Ummm . . ." she said between her lips, and Dandy's
finger worked like a lever. "Ohhh . . . that's so good," she
said as Junior pressed harder. Dandy wondered how the
two in front could not detect the heavy sweet funk odor.

"What'cha doin' ta mah baby sister," Jack Bowen kidded

in the dark. "Dandy, boy, you sittin' back dere and lettin'
Junior git away with the goods."

"Yeah, Junior's really makin' out," Dandy said.

"Shusss . . . ooeee . . . ummm . . ." Marie said, and
wriggled too much and lifted her girlish rear fully off the
back seat.

"Owww . . . Marie Ann," Junior Kane cried. "You know
how ta French kiss. Where did ya larn ta use yo tongue like
dat?"

"Okay, children," Jack spoke up, and put his hand on
Junior's shoulder. "That's enough for tonight."

Marie Ann sat back and gave a convulsive tremble as
she lowered herself fully upon Dandy's hand.

"Wha'cha shiverin' fo, Marie?" Junior asked as she
grabbed his hands and arm. "Bowen," he called out. "Dis
y'ere lil beer's got dis gal high as a Georgia pine."

And the radio never stopped.

*Mah pappa's a jockey an he teach me how ta ride . . .
Oh, yeah, mah pappa's a jockey an he teach me how ta ride
. . . He said git in'da middle son an' ya move from side to
side . . .*

"I have ta go," Marie said. She jerked across the seat
and stepped out. "Good night, Dandy."

"Good night, Marie Ann," Junior called.

"Night, Junior."

The screen door slapped shut, and the boys in the car
were quiet. A pig squealed from the pens, and the darkness
chirped with crickets.

*I's wan' ah bow legg'd w'man dat's all . . . I's want ah
bow legg'd woman dat's tall . . .*

"Sho was a good starter fo tonight," Junior said, and
lifted the last of his beer. "Here's the rest of Marie's,
Dandy, why don't ya finish it."

"Thanks, partner."

"Whall, let's be gittin' whare we ain't," Jack urged.

"Okay thar," Junior yelled, and turned on the ignition.

"Whall, that leaves me out, fellows," Dandy said, and
stepped into the yard. The dogs trotted up to him and
wagged their tails in the moonlight, their eyes glistened
yellow in the dark.

"Wha'cha say, Dandy?" Junior asked. "I thought ya was
comin' wit us."

"Can't. Startin' at the mill tomorrow, and the first day is always hell. It's almost eight now and I'll have ta get up at five-thirty."

"Shit," Jack said. "So do we."

"Yeah, but you're ust'ta it."

"Awww, c'mon, Dandy. I promised Helen I would bring ya back. She's fixin' up all fo ya," Junior said.

"Nawh . . . can't do it. I'll see her tomorrow at work and explain."

. . . wit' her big bow legs so wide apart . . .

The taillights of the '34 Chevy dipped up the road as the old car banged over potholes. Dandy entered the house and looked back through the screen at the two red lights jerking away.

"Good night, Uncle Clyde," Dandy said as he passed the old man sitting before the television screen, the set almost booming.

"I thought you were goin' with Jack and Junior," the old man said. "Your Aunt Bessie went ta sleep because she thought everybody was out."

"Nawh, have ta start work in the morning, so I better get some sleep."

"Whal, son . . . I didn't know ya had dat much sense."

The old woman slept, Dandy thought, because she didn't know anyone would be home but she and the old man. If she had known that Marie and him would be alone . . .

Dandy passed the girls' room; doorless, the entrance framed Marie lying face down upon the bed with her head toward the window.

Dandy went to his room and untied his shoes and let them drop loudly upon the floor. Then he undressed and changed into his pajamas. Later, with lights out, he tipped down the hallway and into the girls' room.

"Dandy, no!" Marie whispered when he turned her over on her back.

He put his finger to his lips and then tipped back to the door and clicked off the light. Moonlight spilled over the girl, her white blouse catching the light and showing dark valleys below her breasts.

"No, Dandy," she whispered, *"Aunt Bess will hear."*

"She's asleep!"

"Uncle Clyde!"

"You know he can't hear so good."

"No, Dandy, I can't," she murmured as he unbuttoned her shorts and pulled them with her panties down over her knees, down her brown moon-revealed thighs, down her long night-exposed legs to her tennis shoes.

She clamped her feet tight. Dandy tried to pry them apart, but she held them with all her strength, and he couldn't pull them apart unless he forced her with all his power.

The moonlight moved down over her brown body. Dandy moved up and kissed her lips as she rolled her head from side to side, and he kissed her shut eyes as she rolled her head, the muscles taut in her neck, and finally, after the pure white blouse was gone and the brassiere, he suckled her breasts in his starved mouth as her head shook no no no no no.

"No, Dandy, you gonna com' in me!"

"No, darling, I'll use protection," he said. "Don't you understand I love you. I'll take care of you. Trust me!"

"I'm sorry, Dandy. I can't. I just can't. I'm so sorry!"

Half an hour later, twin tear streaks running from Marie's eyes caught the moonlight and dripped into her matted hair and dampened the pillows and spread, and Dandy felt like adding to the deluge, for he had gotten no further in his conquest than inserting the same practiced finger and making the girl's dark nipples stand out like buttons. His finger worked, and his lips worked kissing away the tears and warming the tight eyelids and peppering the little nipple with pecks. His lips also pleaded in low prayer to the beautiful brown animal, and his eyes helped by the full moon fixed for moments on the curling pubic hair above his hand.

"Ahm sorry, Dandy; don't be mad at me . . . Will ya still git me the Texas hat?"

And the video still blared below.

Tonight we bring you the passionate saga of love and . . .

When Richard and Roy and Ida climbed the stairs to their bedrooms, Dandy had rolled Marie under the covers but had done little else.

"Good night," Aunt Bessie called up. "Is everybody home now?"

"Yes ma'am," Ida replied. "All cept'n Bo and Dandy."

"I'm goin' ta be da greatest lead tenor on da Eastern Shore," Roy promised.

"Awww, man, you ain't gonna be nothin'," Richard said as they passed the girls' doorway. "A chicken can crow better den you."

"Shut up, you little boys," Ida warned, and stepped into her room. "Don't be makin' a lot of fuss."

"Don't turn that light on, Ida," Marie Ann said.

The moon had been lost somewhere above the Mt. Holy church steeple when Jack Bowen crept up the stairs, slipped past his sister's and Ida's room, and sat on his bed.

"Damn . . ." he said. "Where's Dandy?"

"Heee . . . heee . . ."

"Wha ya say, Roy?" he asked.

"Yeah, Bo . . . heee heee . . ."

"Oooo, man, shut up," Richard warned.

"Well, I'll be damned," Jack said softly, and slipped under the covers.

Down the hall, the bed in the girls' room squeaked barely when a violent movement was made.

"Ohhh . . . ohhh . . . Dandy," Ida James whimpered. *"I love you."*

"Shusss . . ." he shushed her.

Marie Ann whimpered in her sleep, a captive in a bad dream, and beside her Dandy clutched the big yaller hot as a ten-cent-pistol gal to himself and worried about how he would tell Jack Bowen in the morning that he had never touched his baby sister.

Sonny's Not Blue

Sam Greenlee

*Sam Greenlee is a Chicago-born novelist. He has con-
tributed many short stories and articles to* Black World
(Negro Digest). *He is a member of Organization of
Black American Culture (OBAC) writers workshop.
He is author of the highly successful best-selling novel,*
The Spook Who Sat by the Door.

Sonny knew just what he was going to be when he grew
up. Sonny was going to be a basketball player. Red Beans
told him that basketball players made a lot of money when
they left college and played pro ball. Sonny was very surprised that somebody would pay you to do something like
play basketball. He was very happy to know that when he
grew up he could play basketball and make enough money
to take care of his mother and buy her things, too.

Sonny liked basketball better than anything: better than
the raisin bread from the health-food store on Sixty-third,
with strawberry jam on it, or homemade peach ice cream,
or cold watermelon in the summertime. Every day after
school he would play with the kids until the big boys
started playing basketball on the lot on Cottage Grove,
not far from the Afro-Arts Theater where Momma took
him sometimes to hear the music. He would stand near
one of the baskets and wave back at the big boys when
they noticed him. They called him their "mascot,"
and one time last summer they took him all the way to
DuSable High School to play basketball in the back of the
school with some big boys over there. DuSable was on
State Street all the way across Chicago. Sonny knew how
far it was because they walked over there from Thirty-
ninth and Cottage Grove Avenue, and he had never walked
so far in his life. Sonny didn't complain, and he kept up
with the big boys, but he was glad they took the bus back
to the block.

Three of the big boys who played on the block had been all-city, and three made honorable mention. Sonny didn't know what honorable mention meant, but he knew it was good—almost as good as all-city. Red Beans was the best: he could do everything, shoot, handle the ball, and jump very high and get it when it bounced off the backboard or the basket. Po Monty and Rooster were good, too, but not as good as Red Beans. Sonny was going to play just like Red Beans as soon as his hands got big enough to hold the basketball.

Last summer Sonny stood behind the backboard and ran after the ball when it went off the court when Red Beans practiced by himself after the other big boys went home. Sonny would go home and eat and come back, and Red Beans would still be practicing by himself. Red Beans would stay on the court until it was too dark for him to hit with his jump shot. Red Beans told Sonny that if he wanted to be good, Sonny would have to practice like that, too, and Sonny promised he would.

When school started, Sonny would watch the big boys every day and on the weekends, too, until basketball season started and the big boys practiced in the high school. Sonny knew the basketball coach at Phillips High School, so he got in free to see all the games there, and sometimes they would take him along when they went to play at Du-Sable and Forrestville and Dunbar, and one time he went all the way to Englewood High School with them, and Englewood was even farther away than DuSable. Sonny thought Englewood must be in California, and one time on the news on the television they talked about Inglewood in California, but Momma said it wasn't the same one, but Sonny wasn't so sure because Englewood High School was sure a long way, and he was glad they went on the bus instead of walking all the way.

Sonny would go home after the game between the big boys and let himself in with the key around his neck. Sonny was the only kid in his building with a key because his mother was the only one working and not on welfare in the building. Sonny was very proud he was big enough to have a key like some of the kids over in Ida B. Wells housing project. He would get the glass of Joe Louis milk out of the ice box and the raisin bread that came from the Fultonia health-food store on Sixty-third Street and eat it while looking at the television and wait until Momma came home to fix dinner. If Momma was going to be late, Sonny would eat with Rhoda, who lived down the hall.

All the kids loved Rhoda because she was so big and black and funny all the time. Rhoda was always smiling and laughing and hugging and pinching you, and she never had to go up side your head because all she had to do was change her big voice and all the kids did what she wanted. When you did something wrong, any of the mothers in the building would go up side your head, and the kids never got mad except when they really didn't do anything wrong, but you would even get mad at your own momma when that happened.

Momma always kept some kidney beans and lots of brown rice—she always said nothing white was good to eat and even bought brown sugar in the health-food store. Momma always kept beans and rice for when the welfare checks were late. All the women in the building would get their jaws tight when that happened, but the kids liked it because it meant a party. Momma would give Sonny some money, and he would run to the store to buy ham hocks and ground meat and maybe onions and things and then run back to the house. Momma would make red beans and rice for the grown folks, and Rhoda would make chili for the kids. Everybody stuck something away for when the welfare checks were late. Even Delfina, who was a wino, would put a bottle away, and she never touched it, even when she was uptight for a drink, because the bottle was only for when the welfare checks were late.

All the kids would be in Rhoda's and the grownups in Momma's, and a lot of them would be in Momma's and Rhoda's kitchen helping with the food and cussing the social workers and welfare and the white man, but as soon as they had a few drinks of wine or beer, or even sometimes somebody would put away a bottle of whiskey their boy friend didn't drink all of, they would get loud and happy, and it would be a party. Everybody had a lot of fun in the building.

Rhoda had more fun than anybody, and she was always laughing. Sometimes you could hear Rhoda laughing all the way out on the street, and she lived on the third floor in the back. Rhoda was on the welfare, too, but she usually had money because she did hair. She was always complaining that the women were costing her money because so many of them were wearing 'Fros nowadays, but nobody really believed Rhoda was really mad because she was the first one in the building to come out with a 'Fro. Only some of the older women still had their hair straightened, and the other women only bugged them once about that, and Rhoda really got mad and asked them who made them the Pope of soul. But everybody got real happy and had a party at Rhoda's whenever one of the women decided to stop straightening her hair, and they would all be down there to watch Rhoda wash it until it came out kinky and pretty. Rhoda didn't really lose all her money because they still came to have her wash and trim their 'Fros.

Rhoda used to have her own shop until her man ran off to California with one of Rhoda's young beauticians and all the money. Rhoda would fuss sometime about her no-good man, but she didn't really seem mad.

No men could live in the building because the women were all on the welfare, but there were always men around the place except when the social worker was expected, and the men were very careful ever since Bessie got kicked off the welfare when her boy friend forgot and left some of his clothes in the closet. When that happened, all the mothers had to go down and sit in the welfare office and feed Bessie until they got tired and put Bessie back on the welfare.

Momma's boy friend was around a lot, and Sonny had to mind him when he was there, but only Uncle Benny could punish Sonny when he had been real bad. Every Sunday morning Uncle Benny drove all the way from the West Side, and Momma would fix him what they called a real Mississippi breakfast: hot biscuits, fried chicken, scrambled eggs and grits and gravy, and then Momma would tell Uncle Benny if Sonny had been good or bad, and even when he had been bad, Uncle Benny would talk to him just like Sonny was grown and tell him why he had to be spanked. Like his Momma said, Sonny wasn't really a bad boy, but he had too much energy and imagination for his own good, and she told Uncle Benny they had to train that but never knock it out of Sonny.

Momma told Uncle Benny she didn't care how late he stayed out on Saturday or how much he drank, he better have his black self over there on Sunday because a boy needed a man to help him grow up, and everybody else in the building thought so, too, even the women who said they didn't like men much. Whenever Momma wanted to teach him something important, she always had a man do it.

Like the time Sonny wasn't doing anything in school, Momma talked to Red Beans, Po'Monty, and Tan Dan

the Ladies' Man, and they all came by the house. They
all sat around the kitchen table with Sonny just like he
was a big boy and ate Momma's peach cobbler. Red Beans
leaned over a little and looked right at Sonny like Sonny
was a big boy, too. Red Beans told Sonny that if Sonny
didn't do better in school, they wouldn't let him play
basketball in high school, and then he couldn't play in
college or ever play in the pros. Red Beans told Sonny
to remember about Uptight who used to be almost as
good as Red Beans, but he had flunked off the team, then
started shooting up until he had a habit so big they wouldn't
even let him push no more, and the summer before they
found Uptight in the alley dead from an O.D. Sonny had
to think about that for a few days because he knew
Momma had told Red Beans to talk to him, but he decided Momma and Red Beans were right and started
working in school, even if he didn't like the teacher because she was so stuck-up and hated the kids and was
always bugging them about the way they talked. The kids
thought the teacher was the one who talked funny because
everybody on the block talked like they did, and only the
teacher tried to talk like the people on the television. But
Sonny started doing better in school, and the teacher
seemed to like him even less. Sonny couldn't understand
that until Momma explained that anyone black who wanted
to be white was messed up in the mind, so Sonny went
along with it and didn't get his jaws tight about that
messed-up-in-the-mind teacher anymore. He knew the
teacher in the next grade was straight and everything
would be all right the next year. Uncle Benny told him
that getting a bad teacher for a year was like being in the
slam, and you just did your time and didn't let it bug you.

So Sonny watched the basketball games and waited for
his hands to get big enough and practiced his moves like
the big boys. He had a head fake like Red Beans and a
shoulder fake like Po' Monty, and he tried to get his foot-
work like Slick. Every day after he watched the big boys
play he would go home and watch the television if the
pros were playing. One time he asked Red Beans if Elgin
Baylor had ever seen Red Beans play, but Red Beans said
Sonny had it wrong and he was copying Elgin Baylor like
Sonny was copying him.

Sonny thought and thought about what he would buy
Momma when he signed his pro contract, and one day
when he was watching Lew Alcindor on the television he
knew what he would buy her. He would buy Momma a

Testimonial

Paula Hankins

Paula Hankins was born in Detroit twenty-three years ago. She has written plays for the Mausi Acting Company. Miss Hankins feels that Black literature only serves as a tool to educate the black masses in an effort to raise the level of consciousness and to motivate them to move toward political action.

News release

BLACK MILITANT ATTORNEY
KILLED IN FRONT OF BAR

Black militant attorney Joseph L. Anderson was killed today in front of the Pequin bar, on Detroit's east side. Anderson, considered one of the most brilliant black attorneys in this area of the country, publicly identified himself as a black revolutionary. Police say that the unidentified murderer has not been taken into custody. Anderson, who took part in several history-making court decisions, will be buried this Monday. Several thousand people from around the country are expected to attend.

"It's going to be like old home week at Joe's funeral. Everybody who considers himself a militant will be there. It's really going to be something."

"Shit, I sho don't want to be around no whiteys. Why do whitey have to be at his funeral, he was a black man. There shouldn't be no hunkies at his funeral."

"You know the pigs killed him. How come they haven't caught the man yet? If it had of been a pig killed, someone would have been arrested in ten minutes."

"Well he knew that he would die every time he opened his mouth to defend somebody. Revolution ain't no plaything, he knew that."

"You would have liked him if you had got a chance to meet him. You really would have liked him. Look, let me describe him to you. He was tall, thin, and black. That's all you need to know about his looks. After all, in the final analysis, looks become irrelevant, don't they. I never could see what all those women saw in him. I mean he had an ugly face. Well, anyway, you would have liked him because it's what's inside that counts. Still, if you would have seen a picture of him, you would have said to yourself, Who in the hell is this!?"

"Okay they shot him. They killed him, but understand this, brothers and sisters, his death will be avenged. We know who did it, and we are prepared to act upon it. We know why they did it, and it is important for all of you to understand why they did it. He was a revolutionary in the fullest sense of the word. What is a revolutionary? I'm asking you what is a revolutionary!?!!!? You mean to tell me that in a crowd of fifty thousand people not one of you can tell me what a revolutionary is? He was a lawyer, a father, a husband, a lover, a man, but above all he was a revolutionary. He believed that this system, this capitalist system we live under, was inhuman, corrupt, exploitive. He loved black people, he loved real people. He wanted to change this world so that everyone could be human. He died because of his beliefs. You'll have to excuse me if I'm not speaking as well as I usually do, but I'm upset, he was my friend. I'd like to seize upon this time not to engage in useless rhetoric but to educate those of you who are here today because he had a warm smile or because you thought he had a warm smile, or you thought he was a fiery speaker or because he was a good lawyer or because you thought he could screw good. I want you to know what the man was really all about. All of you should stop crying because crying ain't never changed shit. He wouldn't have cried for you, tears ain't no good. . . . He was a worker and that is what he was all about and for, workers. He knew that black workers built this country, were used by this country, and have been mistreated by this country. He also knew that black workers are the ones who are going to change this country. I don't think that there is anyone present today who doesn't agree that this country needs changing. Listen, he was a lawyer, but he knew how hard it was to hit those assembly lines in those automobile plants. He knew how it felt. How many of you know how it feels to have to stand on an assembly line for eight hours a day in a hot, dirty, and greasy factory? You have to raise your hand if you want to stop to use the bathroom. All the foreman is concerned about is that you meet production, meet production, meet production. Never mind how you feel about the weather. Never mind if your wife is sick in the hospital, you have to be there to meet production or bring an absence excuse. Never mind new books you've read, if you feel like reading when you get home you're so tired. Never mind anything, just meet production, forget the world, forget your feelings, forget your humanness, turn yourself into a robot and meet production. That's what industrial plants are all about, and Joe knew this. He knew this, and after he got his degree, he remembered us, we workers, and worked to dedicate his life for our liberation. What did he do? What was he all about? He was about taking calls twenty-four hours a day, getting this sister out of jail, that brother out of jail. What did he charge them, nothing. No money, he didn't ask them for money. He handled cases which no other black attorneys in the city would touch. And he won. He won case after case after case because he was good. He had to be good because he knew he had to be good for his people, for us. When he came out against the court system in this country, something no other black attorney in this country would do at the time, he knew he was putting his life on the line, but he did it for our liberation. You know, I can't stand to hear those tears. I can't stand it because they don't mean shit. All of you standing around here crying and for what. What are you going to do? You ain't going to do nothing, you ain't been doing nothing, and you come to this funeral like a bunch of hypocrites. It ain't about crying, it's about doing, doing. He did, he didn't just talk, he did. Ask yourself what are you going to do. Some of you brothers feel like you want to go out and kill up a bunch of whiteys. Well, let me tell you that there are some brothers who need to be killed. Because I'm willing to bet my life that it was a so-called brother hired by the C.I.A. who killed Joe. But the time now ain't for killing. The time now is for educating and organizing and educating and organizing and gaining power. And we will not be able to gain that power if all you people, yeah, all you

people, do is go to rallys and clap hands and come to
funerals and cry, then go home and turn on the idiot box
and talk about how funny Flip Wilson is. A revolutionary
devotes his life to the liberation of a people. Revolutions
are fought twenty-four hours a day, seven days a week,
three hundred and sixty-five days a year on some kind of
level. There is no such thing as a vacation or time off. It's
a lifetime thing. Joe knew this and he died for his beliefs.

"Joe was a man who was sensitive, warm, emotional,
and lonely. That's the way it goes with love. Nobody really
feels that anyone else can love as deeply as they do. That
is those individuals who have loved. That was the way Joe
felt. He thought that love was one of the most important
things in the world. He loved deeply and wanted to be
loved deeply. Only a few people knew of this desire he had
for love. He wanted the kind of love based on and understanding that human beings stink, spit, pee, shit, smile,
grin, have ambitions, have wants, fuck, have good days,
bad days, and make mistakes. People looked at him as if
he were a god and gods aren't supposed to have any of
those flaws. That's what's wrong with black people. They
elevate their leaders to the level of gods, then they destroy
them. That's what happen to Joe. People saw him as a god
and because it is the basic nature of men to hate gods,
they began to hate him. And because they began to hate
him, they began to do things against him, and because he
did not understand why, he became bitter. Few people saw
this, because although he began to dislike people, he still
did things for them, because he loved them. He knew that
gods are unloved, so he died unhappy, feeling unloved.

"There was one thing about him which few people knew,
he didn't like himself. He always felt that people liked him
for what he could do for them. He knew that he was intelligent and smart and he used that. But I think that deep
down inside, he felt that if he hadn't had a law degree, if
he hadn't saved so many brothers and sisters from going
to jail, then no one would have had anything to do with
him. Of course this wasn't true, those that loved him loved
him for what he was inside. If he had of been a junkie
instead of an attorney, he would have been the most popular junkie in the city. He'd of been a junkie god. A god in
the eyes of junkies. That's what it was, there was something different internally that made him different. He didn't
understand this, so he died alone, misunderstood, and, he
thought, really unloved. It's funny, when I was asked to

write something about him, the first thing I said to myself is that I'm going to write something to show people that he was a man. I've been in this movement so long, and I've watched so many of our leaders destroyed because we didn't realize that they were men, just men. Joe Anderson was a man, people, a man, a man. I thought about writing a political analysis of his death, but I couldn't because I knew that one of us had to deal with him as a man, a walking, living man.

"He was gentle, he was warm, that was his basic nature. When he found it necessary, he became harsh and vindictive. He was a revolutionary, he devoted his life to the development of a new world where everyone would be treated each according to his ability, each according to his need. He knew that he would never see that world. He knew that every time he spoke out against the injustices in this system, in this country as it really is, stripped of all its fancy clothing, he put his life in danger He revealed the racism, the injustice all at the expense of himself. He was a man, people. He was a man, people. He was a man, people, who loved his people, black people, and he used himself to help bring about their liberation.

"I've been sort of afraid to write all my feelings about him because to some people what I say might sound trite, romantic, and unreal. But because he is dead and because I loved him so much, and I know that I'll have to live without him, maybe if I let my feelings out, not keep them in, I'll feel better.

"Let's see, I loved him. Why? I loved him because he was warm, gentle, dedicated, and human. I loved his fuck-upness. He did have an ego problem; he began to see himself as being more important than he really was. I loved his harshness, and I loved him because he had a need for love. I loved him because he did love, and I loved him because he was a revolutionary. How did I love him? How much? Next to the revolution, he was the most important thing in my life. I put his wants and needs above my own. I loved to see him walk, smile, and I would walk down the street seeing his face. I loved everything about him, and I longed to have his baby. It's unfortunate but true that love ain't never and will never make a revolution. You know what I mean. Joe was a motherfucker. A revolutionary motherfucker. A black man made of steel iron. He was a bad motherfucker. He had a way with sisters, but he was a bad motherfucker. He never forgot those people on the street who because of certain objective conditions couldn't develop their potential as well as he did. He never forgot, never looked down on them. He never looked down because he realized that while he was scraping for tuition, some other black people were scraping for rent and food. And he realized that while he was scraping for rent and food, some other black people had just been laid off and evicted all in the same day. He never looked down on black folk because he understood the historical reasons for them being like they are. He was a motherfucker. While some of us was walking about bitching about this person or that person, he knew how to get them to do what he wanted them to do. He got me out of jail many a time, and I didn't give him one cent. Now I wish I could have given him something. He was a motherfucker, that man was almost a God. They should hang the motherfucker who killed him, if they ever catch him.

"He was born Joseph Lewis Anderson, the fifth of eleven children. His story, the story of his life, has been written about in a thousand different plays, novels, magazine articles, and newspapers. The poor black child with no parents, living, loving, and learning everything on his own. Poverty, drugs. He wanted to be a lawyer. When he was young, he wanted to be a politician. He had dreamed of maybe one day becoming the first black president of the United States of America. As he grew older and studied a little bit, and experienced life a little bit more, he realized the fallacy of his dream."

"I always wanted to see my own funeral. It's a desire I developed when I was young. I wondered what people would say about me, who would cry and who wouldn't. Contrary to what everyone thought, I did care about what other people thought about me. I didn't do anything that any other man with my conviction, dedication, and love wouldn't have done in my position.

"He died Joseph Lewis Anderson age thirty-five. Loved by many, hated by many, but he was a revolutionist. He realized that the country that he lived in was exploitive and oppressive and unjust. He realized that thousands of people starved everywhere in the world as a result of the oppression of the country he was born in. He loved, he hated, and he used the bathroom. He was considered a genius of God. He was a man. Those who knew him wished to be like him or loved by him. He was a worker, a philosopher, and a dreamer. The day of his funeral fifty thousand people attended, forty thousand people cried, twenty thousand vowed to be like him and carry on his work, ten thousand vowed to support those that carried on his work. After the funeral forty thousand people went home to dig Flip Wilson on the idiot box. Nine thousand nine hundred went home, packed a lunch to go to the city park because it was hot. One hundred people went on to carry on his work."

The Ray

Ron Milner

Ron Milner is a thirty-two-year-old Detroiter. He has received both the John Hay Whitney Fellowship and a Rockefeller Foundation Grant for his novel, Life of The Brothers Brown. *He is the author of the play* Who's Got His Own, *which opened at the American Place Theater. In 1967 it opened at the New Lafayette Theatre in Harlem. He has been published in* Best Short Stories by Negro Writers, *edited by Langston Hughes. His plays have also been published in* Black World. *Mr. Milner now lives and works in Detroit and New York.*

One slender stream of sunlight filled the slight hiatus between the closed drapes and plunged through the window down diagonally across the room. Bridging the small glass-doored bookcase beneath the window, which was an annex of the two larger bookcases that covered, excepting the window space, one full wall of the room. Passing over the moderate-sized, tasteful coffee table in front of the leather couch; not touching, on the table, the delicate wine glass or the bottle of sherry, nor the huge, black-leather-bound Bible with its red silk marker, the thick red edges of its pages.

The stream of sunlight touched none of this as it passed, but caused a reflective gleam on the silver badge pinned to the wallet lying open on the table alongside the closed Bible; a gleam which shone on the edge of a paper stamped SECURITY U.S. that peeped from the wallet's bill compartment. The stream did not touch that directly, merely caused a reflective gleam. For it dove as though magnetized, hypnotized *over the spread-eagle shoes, the rumpled argyle socks; over the brief flash of hair covered starkly pale-pink skin beneath the wrinkled pants; past the thick sweater which gave way to the leafs of the sportcoat flung immobilely out to the sides where the one hand appeared*

105

*so naked and virginal because the other hid behind the
dark heavy steel of the small revolver; past the untied bow
tie, the stiffly thrusted chin, the tight thin lips; not marking
the neat purple-edged hole at the left temple, nor the small
pool of drying blood that had escaped to the carpet and
now stopped running*—directly to the eyeglasses that had
been thrown just slightly to the right of the dead face by
the force of the low-caliber bullet.

The sunlight went, as an eager lover, straight to the eyeglasses; kissing them; blazing there in a frolicking glitter.
One ecstatic ray reflected off to the right, to the wall, to the
wooden edge of a glass-covered bulletin which hung there
proclaiming:

> DR. SAMUEL J. EVANSTON, FOR HIS
> OUTSTANDING WORK IN THE FIELD OF
> NUCLEAR RESEARCH, HAS BEEN AWARDED,
> ON THIS DAY, THE—.

The reflected ray danced ecstatically on the wooden
frame of the glass-covered bulletin, just above a large
sheet of note paper attached there by one tiny straight pin.
The ray danced from the frame onto the glass, glittering
playfully; then skipped toward the tiny straight pin and
jumped onto it, gleaming minutely. Sparkled there for an
instant, before leaping to the note paper and playing among
the large, neatly printed words:

> I SAW THE GREAT LIGHT BURN AWAY THE
>   DESERT
> AND I THOUGHT IT GOOD. THAT IT WOULD
>   FEED, AND WARM.
> THEN I SAW THE DESERT TURN TO GLASS,
>   AND HEARD
> BABES SCREAM IN TERROR! YET, STILL I
>   THOUGHT
> IT GOOD. THAT IT WOULD GIVE LIGHT AND
>   DO WORK. NOW I SEE THE DARKNESS!
> LO! WE HAVE DISCOVERED THE SECRET OF
>   FIRE,
> AND ARE BURNING AWAY THE FIELDS!
> O' OUR FATHER! WE KNOW WHAT WE DO!
> BUT CANNOT STOP OURSELVES!

The ecstatic ray played among the neatly printed words
until darkness came and devoured it.

A Good Season

John A. Williams

John A. Williams is the author of the following books:
The Man Who Cried I Am, Son of Darkness, Son of
Light, Sissie, *and* Night Song. *He has contributed stories and articles to all of the major magazines. He was
co-editor with Charles Harris of* Amistad.

I

It was almost midnight when Francisco entered the Riviera where he lived and worked. He had just returned from
Barcelona visiting his wife and three little daughters. It had
been his day off. It was his habit to return the same night
so he would be fresh the following morning for a day's
work behind the bar.

Francisco was surprised that the hotel front, that great
expanse of inslanted glass which sheathed the dining room,
bar, and lounge, was still lighted. He stepped through one
of the two still-unlocked glass doors and looked at the
women and Antonio.

The women were American—Francisco could tell that at
a glance. They sat at a front table, the only persons beside
Antonio, who was trying to take their order, in the dining
room. They were hotel guests, Francisco noted, too; he had
not passed a car on the track of the halfmoon driveway
which nestled against the hotel's low, concrete terrace, and
the women had only their purses with them.

He moved toward them, the thin, hard heels of his shoes
clicking like loose castanets on the terrazzo floor. At the
first click Antonio looked up and Francisco saw the smallest
expression of chagrin flash across his face and disappear in
a stiff smile. The women turned, too.

"Hello, Francisco," Antonio said in Spanish; he could
speak nothing else. "I cannot understand the *señoritas*. Will

107

you take their order?" To the women Antonio said as he nodded toward Francisco, *"Habla Inglés."*

Francisco bowed. He looked quickly at them; they were like most single women who traveled together, one attractive and the other, while not ugly, certainly not of romantic consequence. Francisco flipped out of his sweater as he walked to the bar. He replaced it with his white jacket with the gold and black epaulettes. He snapped on the black bow tie. With a pad and pencil in hand he walked back to the table. He smiled. "What will you like, misses?"

The attractive one gasped. "Beautiful English!"

"Yes," the unattractive one said. She looked curiously at Francisco.

"You're Spanish," the attractive one said.

Francisco smiled. "No, Hungarian."

"But you speak beautifully."

"Near the war's end," he said, "I am a prisoner in a British camp. I escape—run away—and come to Spain."

"You missed the revolution," the attractive one said archly. Then she looked at Antonio.

"Oh, no," Francisco said. "I go back to Budapest, and I am there for the revolution. After the trouble I come again to Spain." He moved the pencil above the pad. He smiled, and his green eyes slitted, his face seemed to flush. He jerked his head, and the rust brown hair flipped back into place.

"Can you make Old Fashioneds?" the attractive one asked. She had a soft, delicate face, black hair, and blue eyes. Had she been heavier and not quite so tall; had her face been more square, she might have been taken for a Catalana.

"Yes," Francisco said, writing. "Two?" He looked up.

The women looked at one another. The unattractive one said, "Why not? Two."

He finished taking the order, bowed, and returned to the bar to mix the drinks. "They want paella," he told Antonio. "Tell the cook." Antonio went to the kitchen and returned. He pulled up a barstool and sat down. He stared glumly at the glasses; this would be his last season. In the fall he would go into the army and he would be sent to Spanish Morocco. Antonio and Francisco spoke in Spanish.

"They are staying here?" Francisco asked as he worked.

"Yes," Antonio said. "The room at the far end. In front."

"How long will they be staying?"

Antonio shrugged. "They did not say."

"They *are* Americans?"

"Americanas," Antonio said. He stared at his fingernails.

Francisco gathered the drinks on a tray. He reached across the counter and patted Antonio on the cheek. "Already you are worried about which one you will get. When you speak a little English, you'll get the pretty ones."

"True, true," Antonio said with his dry little smile.

Francisco walked to the table. He bent from the waist and placed the drinks before the Americans. He stepped back holding the tray in front of him. He tilted his head to one side. "Please, you must taste it. Tell me how you like it."

Antonio did not understand the words, but he knew from Francisco's posture and the responses of the women what was taking place. Antonio smiled to himself and siphoned a glass of water.

"Wonderful!" the attractive one said.

"Pretty good," the other said.

"I'm happy you like it," Francisco said.

"We like," the unattractive one said. She looked thoughtfully at Francisco.

Francisco bowed away from the table and returned to the bar. Antonio had taken the thick brass locks and was crouching before the doors, twisting the keys to lock them. He stood with a grunt and motioned to Francisco to turn off the grounds lights. Blackness dropped quickly across the front. Then they stood, Francisco behind the bar, Antonio in front of it. They smoked and looked at the moon which was struggling up from behind the clouds which hovered down over the sea.

"It will be a good season," Francisco said.

"Yes," Antonio agreed.

"They have begun early. It is only the start of April."

"Yes, they are the smart ones, the *Americanas.*" Antonio ground out his cigarette. "Soon the place will be filled with foreigners."

Francisco nodded.

They exchanged cigarettes, Ganadors and Ideales. They smoked some more. Francisco asked, "How was business today?"

"Very bad. We have made only fifty pesetas each in tips."

"Well," Francisco said with a shrug, "it is fifty pesetas we didn't have before."

"Yes, that is true."

Francisco moved quickly in response to the lack of sound from the table. "They are finished," Antonio said without looking, but Francisco was halfway to the table. Before he could place the empty glasses on the bar, Antonio was beside the women, serving their paella.

"It's not in a pan," the unattractive one said.

"No," her friend said. She tapped the container with her knuckles. "It's the same sort of thing you use for baked beans. How odd; I thought they had to be made in pans."

Antonio retreated to the bar and sat in silence with Francisco until the women passed them, saying, "Goodnight."

When they were halfway up the stairs, Antonio asked in a soft voice, "What did they leave?"

"One peseta each," Francisco said.

"Phaaa," Antonio said.

"It does not matter. They will learn to leave more. Besides, Antonio, they both like you because you're handsome. It is a pity you do not know English."

"In matters of the heart, language is not important." Antonio took off his jacket and hung it carefully on a hook behind the bar.

"Besides," he said, "the look they have is familiar. Words mean little. They do not want too many words; just enough for the game."

Francisco smiled. He looked like a pale Oriental when he did. "Very good. You are right, my friend. You have learned much in only two seasons."

They started up the stairs to their rooms.

"I like *Americanas* best," Francisco said softly. "They are with love as if it were forbidden or rationed to them at home."

"That is true," Antonio said. "I remember the little one from the city of the angels two seasons ago when I began. Hoy!" Antonio shook his head and smiled pointedly at Francisco.

They were at the top of the stairs now. They paused and looked down the hall toward the room where the Americans were.

"Goodnight, Francisco."

"Goodnight, Antonio."

II

Toward the end of the third day, the Americans, Francisco noticed, were tired of their rented bicycles, their trips to the wine cellars in the pueblo, the hard-seated bus rides

to and from Barcelona, and walks along the still-empty
beaches. Americans, Francisco had observed, tired of things
more quickly than other foreigners. Miss Millet was the attractive one; Miss Judson was her friend. Miss Judson was
not really unattractive; there was something sometimes ugly
about her. She looked pasty and dark, like someone sick
from hunger. The other, Miss Millet, was pale and tall and
slender; she appeared weak and brittle like the women
Francisco had seen in the photographs in American magazines. The thing with Miss Judson was with her, too.

Their eating habits were neat and cautious. They drank
a little too much wine before, during, and after their meals.
The wines were strong. They had asked about the bullfights,
but Francisco had assured them that the best fights would
not be held until mid-summer when the bulls were best and
the matadors at the peak of condition.

During the *merienda* on that third day, Miss Judson
asked Francisco who had helped Antonio prepare the table.
"Do you and Antonio ever get time off?"

"We'd like you to show us where things are happening,"
Miss Millet explained. "Nobody, but nobody speaks English. Only you."

"Oh, misses," Francisco said. "We work every day from
early morning until there are no more people to serve in
the night."

"But," Miss Judson observed, stretching a thick leg from
beneath the table, "there isn't any business. Only us."

"Well, it is a little early, Anita," Miss Millet said.

"Yes." Francisco smiled appreciatively. "The season
has not really begun, but we must stay all day, for their
might be business."

Francisco laid the silver. The women watched in silence.
The dining room was a great rectangle. On the south wall
were modern paintings. Neat rows of white-topped tables
were set in lines. Outside the April sun rolled through
whorls of clouds above the neat pine groves just across the
road. Behind the groves were the *casas* and villas, hotels
and restaurants along the beach. The beach ran down from
Barcelona, dipping and jutting until it ran out against the
Monserrat Mountains, then continued southward past
Sitges. The highway—a wide, smooth asphalt band—ran
along the seacoast from Le Perthus on the French frontier
to Almeria all the way south before it curved sharply west
to Malaga.

"It is a very good spring day," Francisco said as he
straightened.

The women said nothing. Both held their chins in the palms of their hands. They stared at the road or at the sun. On the road, a giant truck—a Pegaso—its load hidden by canvas, thundered past a cyclist with his ragged little trailer filled with dried branches. A Seat going in the opposite direction, north, scuttled along like a frightened insect. Then the road was empty of traffic.

"Antonio speaks no English at all?" Miss Millet asked. She drew deeply on the cigarette she had just lighted. Her eyes danced, and Francisco smiled.

"No. He is very handsome, no?" He straightened a napkin. "You wish me to say something to him for you?"

"No, no," Miss Millet said. Francisco saw that she had exchanged glances with her friend. Miss Millet tapped her finger against the cigarette. The ash flew into the tray and crumpled.

Francisco retreated to his bar. He wiped glasses until Antonio joined him after serving the snack. "Let us close early tonight," Francisco said. "We will go with them to Bar Segoviana. It is small and dark there. They will like it. Besides, the wine is cheaper there than here."

"Good," Antonio said. "There will be another full moon. We will go by the beach."

"Camarero," they heard Miss Millet say. The two waiters exchanged smiles, Antonio went to them.

Francisco wiped his glasses and stared at the road until the cigarette man came on his motorcycle. He had four cartons of Chesterfields and a bottle of bourbon. Francisco carefully locked the items in the closet. He placed the key in his pocket. The boss would not be back from Genoa until the next week. It was nice when he was away. Not that he was a hard boss; he was just always there, in the way, his yellow sweater straining over his large stomach, his thin blue eyes darting this way and that, and always bowing. Francisco sighed and went to the table to tell the *Americanas* that if they wished, he and Antonio would take them to another restaurant that evening.

III

Miss Millet, who had confessed to Francisco that they (she and Miss Judson) had been wondering what they would drink that evening to get drunk, and Miss Judson had been eager to go.

"On one condition," Miss Millet said.

"What is that?" Francisco asked. He smiled; he hadn't quite understood about the getting drunk.

"That you call me Lorraine."

"Lor-ran?"

"Yes," Miss Millet said. Her name sounded wonderful when Europeans with their trilled Rs said it.

Now the four of them, Francisco and Antonio in front, the women behind, walked north on the beach. The low tide slid a white, foaming phosphorescent line against the beach, hissed itself flat in the sands, and trickled again to the sea. The beach was almost white in the cold white rays of the moon. The walk, the women agreed, seemed both unearthly and very lovely.

Two *carabineros,* their heads and shoulders covered with capes to check the stiff sea wind, loomed suddenly into the light. Behind them their tracks showed as ragged stitching in the fabric of bold white sand. The German guns on their backs and their peaked German caps made them appear grotesque moving as one unnamed, misshapen piece of machinery. They answered Francisco's and Antonio's greeting with a curt, "Hola," looking curiously at the women.

"What do they do?" Miss Judson asked when they had passed on.

"They guard against contraband coming in along the beaches," Francisco said. He had turned and walked backward a few steps as he answered. The women could see that his eyes were really on the soldiers. Involuntarily they turned and saw what Francisco saw; the *carabineros* had stopped and were looking toward them. Francisco spun around and resumed his pace with Antonio. The women followed and did not look back again.

After a while Anita Judson asked Lorraine Millet, "What do you think?" The question really meant, Lorraine, what is your idea of this affair we're going to have. Who gets whom?

Miss Millet said only, "What the hell," and they walked on in silence, each of them wondering what Francisco and Antonio were discussing in Spanish.

Antonio fell in beside Miss Judson and Francisco now walked beside Miss Millet. "It is not now far, Lor-ran," he said.

Beside them Antonio and Miss Judson talked in Miss Judson's poor Spanish. *"Me gusta mucho el mar,"* they heard her say.

"Bravo," Antonio answered, clapping his hands lightly. *"Habla Español muy bien."*

"No, no," Miss Judson said, but she laughed and Miss Millet could tell she was pleased, even if the entire business was artificial.

"Sí, sí," Antonio countered.

"It is here," Francisco said, guiding Miss Millet by the arm. They turned off the beach and passed through a breach in the seawall. The sand was very deep, and they all laughed softly as they struggled through it. Ahead of them they could see the lights from the window of the small restaurant; it sat in the center of a grove of young pines.

Behind them, a large wave—a shuddering, faceless, dark old man with flashing white hair—thrashed ashore, collapsed quietly, fizzed into the sand, then hissed back to the sea. The air was haunting, flat, and saline like the scent of freshly let blood.

The *carabineros* stepped out of the shadows. They were breathing heavily, and their breaths smelled of sausages and cognac. They spoke roughly to Francisco and Antonio.

"What do you wish?" Francisco asked in Spanish. "We have done nothing."

Antonio looked anxiously at his friend.

One of the soldiers, they couldn't tell which one, said, "You are the waiter who has no papers, are you not?"

"I have no papers, but the police know of this."

"You are on the beach late, foreigner."

"We have two *Americanas* who wish to visit the Bar Segoviana," Antonio said.

"Speak when you are spoken to, little one."

Francisco saw that the soldiers were looking at the women. "They are not business women," he said.

The *carabineros* chuckled. "We would like to speak with them."

"Yes," the other soldier said softly.

"They have done nothing," Francisco said.

"Another word, foreigner, and you will come to the jail on Via Layetana within the hour. You know this jail, no?"

"Yes, I was detained there when I came from Hungary. I was twice there."

"Did you like it?"

"No."

"We will speak with the *Americanas.*"

"We will wait here," Antonio said.

"No. You will go."

"They do not speak Spanish," Francisco said desperately.

He and Antonio had retreated a step as the soldiers stepped forward.

"Then you will tell them we wish to speak."

"What is it, Francisco?" Miss Millet asked. Miss Judson crowded close. Her eyes moved from the waiters to the soldiers to Miss Millet.

"The soldiers wish to speak to you," Francisco said in English. "They do not wish us to remain."

"But why?" Miss Judson asked.

"We haven't done anything," Miss Millet said. Her voice was suddenly shrill; a quality Francisco never associated with it. She clutched at Francisco's sleeve. "Stay with us."

"We cannot stay. We would be in great trouble. We must go."

Miss Judson stamped her foot in the sand and backed up, pulling Miss Millet by the elbow. "We're American citizens—"

"You can't do this," Miss Millet said.

Francisco and Antonio began to move away.

"Don't leave us," Miss Millet said. "We don't know how to get back."

"They know the way," Francisco said. He had stopped and turned; Antonio kept walking. "Don't run away from them," he said softly.

The *carabineros* adjusted their light machine guns on their backs and moved forward. "Say something," one snapped to Francisco, "to put them at their ease."

A little farther away now, Francisco stopped and turned. His face was very white in the moonlight. "Don't run from them," he said. He shrugged. "After all, what difference does it make?" He turned and vanished.

Miss Millet stared after him. She and Miss Judson were stepping backward carefully. The loose metal on the guns jingled as the soldiers stepped forward. "Is that how we look to them?" she said.

Miss Judson said nothing.

"Is that how we look to them?" Miss Millet repeated.

"Let's run. To hell with them," Miss Judson said. "At least let's not give up the right to choose."

"Which way?"

"Anyway except into the damned ocean."

"When I count three," Miss Millet said, and she was thinking of a Chaplin film where Chaplin was a boxer pantomiming each movement of his opponent. As the soldiers moved forward, they stepped backward.

"To hell with three," Miss Judson said. "Now!"

They ran holding hands. The *carabineros* chased them a few yards, then stopped. They muttered under their breaths. The women ran until they broke upon an asphalt road; there were lights ahead, and nearby they heard trucks on the main highway. When they were on it, walking toward the Riviera lights, they lighted cigarettes and walked a way in silence.

Finally Miss Millet said, "I don't know how I look, but I don't want to look like it anymore."

"Nor do I," Miss Judson said.

"Crazy," Miss Millet said.

"Yes."

They saw Antonio rushing to open the door for them. Francisco stood behind him; their faces were stolid.

"We are leaving in the morning, waiter," Miss Millet said to Francisco. "Please have our bill ready."

"Yes, misses," Francisco said with a bow.

"Bastards," Miss Judson said under her breath.

When the women were at the top of the stairs, Francisco said, "They ran."

"Yes," Antonio said. "We must not go again to Bar Segovania."

"No. It is good we found out about the new *carabineros*." Francisco slapped Antonio on the shoulder. "It will still be a good season, my friend."

"And why not," Antonio answered with his dry smile. "It is a lovely spring."

The Alternative

Imamu Amiri Baraka (LeRoi Jones)

Imamu Amiri Baraka (LeRoi Jones) was born in Newark, New Jersey, in 1934. He graduated from Howard at the age of 19. He is the acknowledged leader of the new Black arts movement. He has produced many volumes of poetry, books of plays, and a book on jazz. The books are: The System of Dante's Hell, Home, Tales, *etc. His plays are:* Slaveship, Dutchman, Toilet, The Slave, *and* A Recent Killing.

The leader sits straddling the bed, and the night, tho innocent, blinds him. (Who is our flesh. Our lover, marched here from where we sit now sweating and remembering. Old man. Old man, find me, who am I your only blood.)

Sits straddling the bed under a heavy velvet canopy. Homemade. The door opened for a breeze, which will not come through the other heavy velvet hung at the opening. (Each thread a face, or smell, rubbed against himself with yellow glasses and fear at their exposure. Death. Death. They (the younger students) run by screaming. Tho impromptu. Tho dead, themselves.

The leader, at his bed, stuck with 130 lbs. black meat sewed to failing bone. A head with big red eyes turning senselessly. Five toes on each foot. Each foot needing washing. And hands that dangle to the floor, tho the boy himself is thin small washed out, he needs huge bleak hands that drag the floor. And a head full of walls and flowers. Blinking lights. He is speaking.

"Yeh?" The walls are empty, heat at the ceiling. Tho one wall is painted with a lady. (Her name now. In large relief, a faked rag stuck between the chalk marks of her sex. Finley. Teddy's Doris. There sprawled where the wind fiddled with the drying cloth. Leon came in and laughed. Carl came in and hid his mouth, but he laughed. Teddy said, "Aw, Man."

117

"Come on, Hollywood. You can't beat that. Not with your years. Man, you're a schoolteacher 10 years after weeping for this old stinking bitch. And hit with a aspirin bottle (myth says)."

The leader, is sprawled, dying. His retinue walks into their comfortable cells. "I have duraw-ings," says Leon, whimpering now in the buses from Chicago. Dead in a bottle. Floats out of sight, until the Africans arrive with love and prestige. "Niggers." They say. "Niggers." Be happy your ancestors are recognized in this burg. Martyrs. Dead in an automat, because the boys had left. Lost in New York, frightened of the burned lady, they fled into those streets and sang their homage to the Radio City.

The leader sits watching the window. The dried orange glass etched with the fading wind. (How many there then? 13 Rue Madeleine. The Boys Club. They give, what he has given them. Names. And the black cloth hung on the door swings back and forth. One pork chop on the hot plate. And how many there. Here, now. Just the shadow, waving its arms. The eyes tearing or staring blindly at the dead street. These same who loved me all my life. These same I find my senses in. Their flesh a wagon of dust, a mind conceived from all minds. A country, of thought. Where I am, will go, have never left. A love, of love. And the silence the question posed each second. "Is this my mind, my feeling? Is this voice something heavy in the locked streets of the universe? Dead ends. Where their talk (these nouns) is bitter vegetable." That is, the suitable question rings against the walls. Higher learning. That is, the moon through the window clearly visible. The leader in seersucker, reading his books. An astronomer of sorts. "Will you look at that? I mean really, now, fellows. Cats!" (Which was Smitty from the City's entree. And him the smoothest of you American types. Said, "Cats. Cats. What's goin' on?" The debate.

The leader's job (he keeps it still, above the streets, summers of low smoke, early evening drunk and wobbling thru the world. He keeps it, baby. You dig?) was absolute. "I have the abstract position of watching these halls. Walking up the stairs giggling. Hurt under the cement steps, weeping . . . is my only task. Tho I play hockey with the broom & wine bottles. And am the sole martyr of this cause. A. B., Young Rick, T. P., Carl, Hambrick, Li'l' Cholley, Phil. O.K. All their knowledge "Flait! More! Way!" The leader's job . . . to make attention for the place. Sit along the sides of the water or lay quietly back under his own shooting vomit, happy to die in a new gray suit. Yes. "And what not."

How many here now? Danny (brilliant dirty curly Dan, the m.d.). Later, now, where you off to, my man. The tall skinny farmers, lucky to find sales and shiny white shoes. Now made it socially against the temples. This "hotspot" Darien drunk teacher blues . . . "and she tried to come on like she didn't even like to fuck. I mean, you know the kind. . . ." The hand extended, palm upward. I place my own in yours. That cross, of feeling. Willie, in his grinning grave, has it all. The place, of all souls, in their greasy significance. An armor, like the smells drifting slowly up Georgia. The bridge players change clothes, and descend. Carrying home the rolls.

Jimmy Lassiter, first looie. A vector. What is the angle made if a straight line is drawn from the chapel, across to Jimmy, and connected there, to me, and back up the hill again? The angle of progress. "I was talkin' to ol' Mordecai yesterday in a dream, and it's me sayin' 'dig baby, why don't you come off it?' You know."

The line, for Jimmy's sad and useless horn. And they tell me (via phone, letter, accidental meetings in the Village. "Oh he's in med school and married and lost to you, hombre." Ha. They don't dig completely where I'm at. I have him now, complete. Though it is a vicious sadness cripples my fingers. Those blue and empty afternoons I saw him walking at my side. Criminals in that world. Complete heroes of our time. (Add Allen to complete an early splinter group. Muslim heroes with flapping pants. Raincoats. Trolley car romances.)

And it's me making a portrait of them all. That was the leader's job. Alone with them. (Without them. Except beautiful faces shoved out the window, sunny days, I ran to meet my darkest girl. Ol' Doll. "Man, that bitch got a goddamn new car." And what not. And it's me sayin' to her, Baby, knock me a kiss.

Tonight the leader is faced with decision. Brown had found him drunk and weeping among the dirty clothes. Some guy with a crippled arm had reported to the farmers (a boppin' gang gone social. Sociologists, artistic arbiters of our times). This one an athlete of mouselike proportions. "You know," he said, his withered arm hung stupidly in the rayon suit, "That cat's nuts. He was sittin' up in that room last night with dark glasses on . . . with a yellow bulb . . . pretendin' to read some abstract shit." (Damn, even the color wrong. Where are you now, hippy, under this abstract shit. Not even defense. That you remain forever in that world. No light. Under my fingers. That you exist alone, as I make you. Your sin, a final ugliness to you. For the leopards, all thumbs jerked toward the sand.) "Man, we do not need cats like that in the frat." (Agreed.)

Tom comes in with two big bottles of wine. For the contest. An outing. "Hugh Herbert and W. C. Fields will now indian wrestle for ownership of this here country!" (Agreed.) The leader loses . . . but is still the leader because he said some words no one had heard of before. (That was after the loss.)

Yng Rick has fucked someone else. Let's listen. "Oh, man, you cats don't know what's happenin'." (You're too much, Rick. Much too much. Like Larry Darnell in them ol' italian schools. Much too much.) "Babes" he called them (a poor project across from the convents. Baxter Terrace. Home of the enemy. We stood them off. We Cavaliers. And then, even tho Johnny Boy was his hero. Another midget placed on the purple. Early leader, like myself. The fight of gigantic proportions to settle all those ancient property disputes would have been between us. Both weighing close to 125. But I avoided that like the plague, and managed three times to drive past him with good hooks without incident. Whew, I said to Love, Whew. And Rick, had gone away from them, to school. Like myself. And now, strangely, for the Gods are white our teachers said, he found himself with me. And all the gold and diamonds of the crown I wore he hated. Though, the new wine settled, and his social graces kept him far enough away to ease the hurt of serving a hated master. Hence "babes," and the constant reference to his wiggling flesh. Listen.

"Yeh. Me and Chris had these D.C. babes at their cribs." (Does a dance step with the suggestive flair.) "Oooooo, that was some good box."

Tom knew immediately where that bit was at. And he pulled Rick into virtual madness . . . lies at least. "Yeh, Rick. Yeh? You mean you got a little Jones, huh? Was it good?" (Tom pulls on Rick's sleeve like Laurel and Rick swings.)

"Man, Tom, you don't have to believe it, baby. It's in here now!" (points to his stomach.)

The leader stirs. "Hmm, that's a funny way to fuck." Rick will give a boxing demonstration in a second.

Dick Smith smiles, "Wow, Rick you're way," extending

his hand, palm upward. "And what not," Dick adds, for us to laugh. "O.K., you're bad." (At R's crooked jab.) "Huh, this cat always wants to bust somebody up, and what not. Hey, baby, you must be frustrated or something. How come you don't use up all that energy on your babes . . . and what not?"

The rest there, floating empty nouns. Under the sheets. The same death as the crippled fag. Lost with no defense. Except they sit now, for this portrait . . . in which they will be portrayed as losers. Only the leader wins. Tell him that.

Some guys playing cards. Some talking about culture, i.e., the leader had a new side. (Modesty denies. They sit around, in real light. The leader in his green glasses, fidgeting with his joint. Carl, in a brown fedora, trims his toes and nails. Spars with Rick. Smells his foot and smiles. Brady reads, in his silence, a crumpled black dispatch. Shorter's liver smells the hall and Leon slams the door, waiting for the single chop, the leader might have to share. The door opens, two farmers come in, sharp in orange suits. The hippies laugh, and hide their youthful lies. "Man, I was always hip. I mean, I knew about Brooks Brothers when I was 10." (So sad we never know the truth. About that world, until the bones dry in our heads. Young blond governors with their "dads" hip at the age of 2. That way. Which, now, I sit in judgment of. What I wanted those days with the covers of books turned toward the audience. The first nighters. Or dragging my two forwards to the Music Box to see Elliot Nugent. They would say, these dead men, laughing at us, "The natives are restless," stroking their gouty feet. Gimme culture, culture, culture, and Romeo and Juliet over the emerson.

How many there now? Make it 9. Phil's cracking the books. Jimmy Jones and Pud, two D.C. boys, famous and funny, study "zo" at the top of their voices. "Hemiptera," says Pud. "Homoptera," says Jimmy. "Weak as a bitch," says Phil, "Both your knowledges are flait."

More than 9. Mazique, Enty, operating now in silence. Right hands flashing down the cards. "Uhh!" In love with someone, and money from home. Both perfect, with curly hair. "Uhh! Shit, Enty, hearts is trumps."

"What? Ohh, shit!"

"Uhh!", their beautiful hands flashing under the single bulb.

Hambrick comes with liquor. (A box of fifths, purchased with the fantastic wealth of his father's six shrimp shops.)

"You cats caint have all this goddam booze. Brown and I got dates, that's why and we need some for the babes."

Brown has hot dogs for five. Franks, he says. "Damn, Cholley, you only get a half of frank . . . and you take the whole motherfucking thing."

"Aww, man, I'll pay you back." And the room, each inch, is packed with lives. Make it 12 . . . all heroes, or dead. Indian chiefs, the ones not waging their wars, like Clark, in the legal mist of Baltimore. A judge. Old Clark. You remember when we got drunk together and you fell down the stairs. Or that time you fell in the punch bowl puking, and let that sweet yellow ass get away? Boy, I'll never forget that, as long as I live. (Having died seconds later, he talks thru his rot.) Yeh, boy, you were always a card. (White man talk. A card. Who the hell says that, except that branch office with no culture. Piles of bullion, and casual violence. To the mind. Nights they kick you against the buildings. Communist homosexual nigger. "Aw man, I'm married and got two kids."

What could be happening? Some uproar. "FUCK YOU, YOU FUNNY-LOOKING SUNAFABITCH."

"Me? Funny-looking? Oh, wow. Will you listen to this little pointy head bastard calling *me* funny-looking. Hey, Everett. Hey Everett! Who's the funniest looking . . . me or Keyes?"

"Aww, both you cats need some work. Man, I'm trying to read."

"Read? What? You gettin' into them books, huh? Barnes is whippin' your ass, huh? I told you not to take Organic . . . as light as you are."

"Shit. I'm not even thinking about Barnes. Barnes can kiss my ass."

"Shit. You better start thinking about him, or you'll punch right out. They don't need lightweights down in the valley. Ask Ugly Wilson."

"Look, Tom, I wasn't bothering you."

"Bothering me? What's the matter with you ol' Jimmy. Commere boy, lemme rub your head."

"Man, you better get the hell outta here."

"What? . . . Why? What you gonna do? You can't fight, you little funny-looking buzzard."

"Hey, Tom, why you always bothering ol' Jimmy Wilson. He's a good man."

"Oh, oh, here's that little light ass Dan sticking up for Ugly again. Why you like him, huh? 'Cause he's the only cat uglier than you? Huh?"

"Tom's the worst looking cat on campus calling me ugly."

"Well, you are. Wait, lemme bring you this mirror so you can see yourself. Now, what you think. You can't think anything else."

"Aww, man, blow, will you?"

The pork chop is cooked and little charlie is trying to cut a piece off before the leader can stop him. "Ow, goddam."

"Well, who told you to try to steal it, jive ass."

"Hey, man, I gotta get somea that chop."

"Gimme some, Ray."

"Why don't you cats go buy something to eat. I didn't ask anybody for any of those hot dogs. So get away from my grease. Hungry ass spooks."

"Wait a minute, fella. I know you don't mean Young Rick."

"Go ask one of those D.C. babes for something to eat. I know they must have something you could sink your teeth into."

Pud and Jimmy Jones are wrestling under Phil's desk.

A. B. is playin' the dozen with Leon and Teddy. "Teddy are your momma's legs as crooked as yours?"

"This cat always wants to talk about people's mothers! Country bastard."

Tom is pinching Jimmy Wilson. Dan is laughing at them.

Enty and Mazique are playing bridge with the farmers. "Uhh! Beat that, jew boy!"

"What the fuck is trumps?"

The leader is defending his pork chop from Cholley, Rick, Brady, Brown, Hambrick, Carl, Dick Smith, (S from the City has gone out catting.

"Who is it?"

A muffled voice, under the uproar, "It's Mister Bush."

"Bush? Hey, Ray . . . Ray."

"Who is it?"

Plainer. "Mister Bush." (Each syllable pronounced and correct as a soft southern american can.) Innocent VIII in his bedroom shoes. Gregory at Canossa, raging softly in his dignity and power. "Mister Bush."

"Ohh, shit. Get that liquor somewhere. O.K., Mr. Bush, just a second. . . . Not there, asshole, in the drawer."

"Mr. McGhee, will you kindly open the door."

"Ohh, shit, the hot plate. I got it." The leader turns a wastepaper basket upside-down on top of the chop. Swings open the door. "Oh, Hello Mister Bush. How are you this evening?" About 15 boots sit smiling toward the door. Come in, Boniface. What news of Luther? In unison, now.

"Hi . . . Hello . . . How are you, Mister Bush?"

"Uh, huh." He stares around the room, grinding his eyes into their various hearts. An unhealthy atmosphere, this America. "Mr. McGhee, why is it if there's noise in this dormitory it always comes from this room?" Aww, he knows. He wrote me years later in the air force that he knew, even then.

"What are you running here, a boys' club?" (That's it.) He could narrow his eyes even in that affluence. Put his hands on his hips. Shove that stomach at you as proof he was an authority of the social grace . . . a western man, no matter the color of his skin. How To? He was saying, this is not the way. Don't act like that word. Don't fail us. We've waited for all you handsome boys too long. Erect a new world, of lies and stocking caps. Silence, and a reluctance of memory. Forget the slow grasses, and flame, flame in the valley. Feet bound, dumb eyes begging for darkness. The bodies moved with the secret movement of the air. Swinging. My beautiful grandmother kneels in the shadow weeping. Flame, flame in the valley. Where is it there is light? Where, this music rakes my talk?

"Why is it, Mr. McGhee, when there's some disturbance in this building, it always comes from here?" (Aww, you said that . . .)

"And what are all you other gentlemen doing in here? Good night, there must be twenty of you here! Really, gentlemen, don't any of you have anything to do?" He made to smile, Ha, I know some of you who'd better be in your rooms right now hitting those books . . . or you might not be with us next semester. Ha.

"O.K., who is that under that sheet?" (It was Enty, a student dormitory director, hiding under the sheets, flat on the leader's bed.) "You, sir, whoever you are, come out of there, hiding won't do you any good. Come out!" (We watched the sheet, and it quivered. Innocent raised his finger.) "Come out, sir!" (The sheet pushed slowly back. Enty's head appeared. And Bush more embarrassed than he.) "Mr. Enty! My assistant dormitory director, good night. A man of responsibility. Go-od night! Are there any more hiding in here, Mr. McGhee?"

"Not that I know of."

"All right, Mr. Enty, you come with me. And the rest

of you had better go to your rooms and try to make some better grades. Mr. McGhee, I'll talk to you tomorrow morning in my office."

The leader smiles, "Yes." (Jive ass.)

Bush turns to go, Enty following sadly. "My God, what's that terrible odor . . . something burning." (The leader's chop, and the wastepaper, under the basket, starting to smoke.) "Mr. McGhee, what's that smell?"

"Uhhh," (come-on, baby) "Oh, it's Strothers' kneepads on the radiator! (Yass) They're drying."

"Well, Jesus, I hope they dry soon. Whew! And don't forget, tomorrow morning, Mr. McGhee, and you other gentlemen had better retire, it's 2 in the morning!" The door slams. Charlie sits where Enty was. The bottles come out. The basket is turned right-side up. Chop and most of the papers smoking. The leader pours water onto the mess and sinks to his bed.

"Damn. Now I have to go hungry. Shit."

"That was pretty slick, ugly, the kneepads! Why don't you eat them they look pretty done."

The talk is to that. That elegance of performance. The rite of lust, or self-extinction. Preservation. Some leave, and a softer uproar descends. Jimmy Jones and Pud wrestle quietly on the bed. Phil quotes the *Post*'s sport section on Willie Mays. Hambrick and Brown go for franks. Charlie scrapes the "burn" off the chop and eats it alone. Tom, Dan, Ted and the leader drink and manufacture lives for each person they know. We know. Even you. Tom, the lawyer. Dan, the lawyer. Ted, the high-school teacher. All their proper ways. And the leader, without cause or place. Except talk, feeling, guilt. Again, only those areas of the world make sense. Talk. We are doing that now. Feeling: that, too. Guilt. That inch of wisdom, forever. Except he sits reading in green glasses. As, "No, no, the utmost share/Of my desire shall be/Only to kiss that air/That lately kissèd thee."

"Uhh! What's trumps, dammit!"

As, "Tell me not, Sweet, I am unkind,/That from the nunnery/Of thy chaste breast and quiet mind/To war and arms I fly."

"You talking about a lightweight mammy-tapper, boy, you really king."

Oh, Lucasta, find me here on the bed, with hard pecker and dirty feet. Oh, I suffer, in my green glasses, under the canopy of my loves. Oh, I am drunk and vomity in my room, with only Charley Ventura to understand my grace.

As, "Hardly are those words out when a vast image out of *Spiritus Mundi*/Troubles my sight: somewhere in sands of the desert/A shape with lion body and the head of a man/A gaze blank and pitiless as the sun,/Is moving its slow thighs, while all about it/Reel shadows of the indignant desert birds."

Primers for dogs who are learning to read. Tinkle of European teacups. All longing, speed, suffering. All adventure, sadness, stink, and wisdom. All feeling, silence, light. As, "Crush, O sea the cities with their catacomb-like corridors/And crush eternally the vile people,/The idiots, and the abstemious, and mow down, mow down/With a single stroke the bent backs of the shrunken harvest!"

"Damn, Charlie, We brought back a frank for everybody . . . now you want two. Wrong sunafabitch!"

"Verde que te quireo verde./Verde viento. Verdes ramas. /El barco sobre le mar/y el caballo en la montaña."

"Hey, man, I saw that ol' fagit Bobby Hutchens down in the lobby with a real D.C. queer. I mean a real way-type sissy."

"Huh, man he's just another *actor* . . . hooo."

"That cat still wearing them funny-lookin' pants?"

"Yeh, and orange glasses. Plus, the cat always needs a haircut, and what not."

"Hey, man you cats better cool it . . . you talkin' about Ray's main man. You dig?"

"Yeh. I see this cat easin' around corners with the cat all the time. I mean, talkin' some off the wall shit, too, baby."

"Yeh. Yeh. Why don't you cats go fuck yourselves or something hip like that, huh?"

"O.K., ugly Tom, you better quit inferring that shit about Ray. What you trying to say, ol' pointy head is funny or something?"

"Funny . . . how the sound of your voice . . . thri-ills me. Strange . . ." (the last à la King Cole.)

"Fuck you cats and your funny-looking families, too."

A wall. With light at the top, perhaps. No, there is light. Seen from both sides, a gesture of life. But always more than is given. An abstract infinitive. To love. To lie. To want. And that always . . . to want. Always, more than is given. The dead scramble up each side . . . words or drunkenness. Praise, to the flesh. Rousseau, Hobbes, and their betters. All move, from flesh to love. From love to flesh. At that point under the static light. It could be Shostakovich in Charleston, South Carolina. Or in the dull windows of Chicago, an unread volume of Joyce. Some black woman who will never hear the word *Negress* or remember your name. Or a thin preacher who thinks your name is Stephen. A wall. Oh, Lucasta.

"Man, you cats don't know anything about Hutchens. I don't see why you talk about the cat and don't know the first thing about him."

"Shit. If he ain't funny . . . Skippy's a punk."

"How come you don't say that to Skippy?"

"Our Own Boy, Skippy Weatherson. All-coon fullback for 12 years."

"You tell him that!"

"Man, don't try to change the subject. This cat's trying to keep us from talking about his boy, Hutchens."

"Yeh, mammy-rammer. What's happenin' McGhee, ol' man?"

"Hooo. Yeh. They call this cat Dick Brown. Hoooo!"

Rick moves to the offensive. The leader in his book, or laughs, "Aww, man, that cat ain't my boy. I just don't think you cats ought to talk about people you don't know anything about! Plus, that cat probably gets more ass than any of you silly-ass motherfuckers."

"Hee. That Ray sure can pronounce that word. I mean he don't say mutha' like most folks . . . he always pronounces the mother *and* the fucker, so proper. And it sure makes it sound nasty." (A texas millionaire talking.)

"Hutchens teachin' the cat how to talk . . . that's what's happening. Ha. In exchange for services rendered!"

"Wait, Tom. Is it you saying that Hutchens and my man here are into some funny shit?"

"No, man. It's you saying that. It was me just inferring, you dig?"

"Hey, why don't you cats just get drunk in silence, huh?"

"Hey, Bricks, what was Hutchens doin' downstairs with that cat?"

"Well, they were just coming in the dormitory, I guess. Hutchens was signing in that's all."

"Hey, you dig . . . I bet he's takin' that cat up to his crib."

"Yeh, I wonder what they into by now. Huh! Probably suckin' the shit out of each other."

"Aww, man, cool it, willya . . . Damn!"

"What's the matter, Ray, you don't dig love?"

"Hey, it's young Rick saying, that we oughta go up and dig what's happenin' up there?"

"Square motherfucker!"

"Votre mere!"

"Votre mere noir!"

"Boy, these cats in French One think they hip!"

"Yeh, let's go up and see what those cats are doing."

"Tecch, aww, shit. Damn, you some square cats, wow! Cats got nothing better to do than fuck with people. Damn!"

Wall. Even to move, impossible. I sit, now, forever where I am. No further. No farther. Father, who am I to hide myself? And brew a world of soft lies.

Again. *"Verde que te quiero verde."* Green. Read it again Il Duce. Make it build some light here . . . where there is only darkness. Tell them *"Verde, que te quiero verde."* I want you Green. Leader, the paratroopers will come for you at noon. A helicopter low over the monastery. To get you out.

But my country. My people. These dead souls, I call my people. Flesh of my flesh.

At noon, Il Duce. Make them all etceteras. Extras. The soft strings behind the final horns.

"Hey, Ray, you comin' with us?"

"Fuck you cats. I got other things to do."

"Damn, now the cat's trying to pretend he can read Spanish."

"Yeh . . . well let's go see what's happening cats."

"Cats, Cats, Cats . . . What's happenin'?"

"Hey, Smitty! We going upstairs to peep that ol' sissy Hutchens. He's got some big time D.C. faggot in there with him. You know, we figured it'd be better than 3-D."

"Yeh? That's pretty hip. You not coming, Ray?"

"No, man . . . I'm sure you cats can peep in a keyhole without me."

"Bobby's his main man, that's all."

"Yeh, mine and your daddy's."

Noise. Shouts, and Rick begs them to be softer. For the circus. Up the creaking stairs, except Carl and Leon who go to the freshman dorm to play ping-pong . . . and Ted who is behind in his math.

The 3rd floor of Park Hall, an old 19th-century philanthropy, gone to seed. The missionaries' words dead & hung useless in the air. "Be clean, thrifty, and responsible. Show the anti-Christs you're ready for freedom and God's true word." Peasants among the mulattos, and the postman's son squats in his glasses shivering at his crimes.

"Hey, which room is his?"

"Three Oh Five."

"Hey, Tom, how you know the cat's room so good? This cat must be sneaking, too."

"Huhh, yeh!"

"O.K. Rick, just keep walking."

"Here it is."

"Be cool, bastard. Shut up."

They stood and grinned. And punched each other. Two bulbs in the hall. A window at each end. One facing the reservoir, the other, the fine-arts building where Professor Gorsun sits angry at jazz. "Goddamnit, none of that nigger music in my new building. Culture. Goddamnit, ladies and gentlemen, line up and be baptized. This pose will take the hurt away. We are white and featureless under this roof. Praise God, from whom all blessings flow!"

"Bobby. Bobby, baby."

"Huh?"

"Don't go blank on me like that, baby. I was saying something."

"Oh, I'm sorry . . . I guess I'm just tired or something."

"I was saying, how can you live in a place like this. I mean, really, baby, this place is nowhere. Whew. It's like a jail or something eviler."

"Yes, I know."

"Well, why don't you leave it then. You're much too sensitive for a place like this. I don't see why you stay in this damn school. You know, you're really talented."

"Yeh, well, I figured I have to get a degree, you know. Teach or something, I suppose. There's not really much work around for spliv actors."

"Oh, Bobby, you ought to stop being so conscious of being colored. It really is not fashionable. Ummm. You know you have beautiful eyes."

"You want another drink, Lyle?"

"Ugg. Oh, that cheap bourbon. You know I have some beautiful wines at home. You should try drinking some good stuff for a change. Damn, Bob, why don't you just leave this dump and move into my place? There's certainly enough room. And we certainly get along. Ummm. Such beautiful eyes and hair, too."

"Hah. How much rent would I have to pay out there. I don't have penny the first!"

"Rent? No, no . . . you don't have to worry about that. I'll take care of all that. I've got one of those gooood jobs, honey. U.S. guvment."

"Oh? Where do you work?"

"The P.O. with the rest of the fellas. But it's enough for

what I want to do. And you wouldn't be an expense. Hmmp. Or would you? You know you have the kind of strong masculine hands I love. Like you could crush anything you wanted. Lucky I'm on your good side. Hmmp."

"Well, maybe at the end of this semester I could leave. If the offer still holds then."

"Still holds? Well why not? We'll still be friends then, I'm certain. Ummm. Say, why don't we shut off that light."

"Umm. Let me do it. There. . . . You know I loved you in Jimmy's play, but the rest of those people are really just kids. You were the only person who really understood what was going on. You have a strong maturity that comes through right away. How old are you, Bobby?"

"Nineteen."

"O baby . . . that's why your skin is so soft. Yes. Say, why wait until the end of the semester . . . that's two months away. I might be dead before that, you know. Umm."

The wind moves thru the leader's room, and he sits alone, under the drooping velvet, repeating words he does not understand. The yellow light burns. He turns it off. Smokes. Masturbates. Turns it on. *Verde, verde. Te quiero.* Smokes. And then to his other source. "Yma's brother," Tom said when he saw it. "Yma Sumac, Albert Camus. Man, nobody wants to go by their right names no more. And a cat told me that chick ain't really from Peru. She was born in Brooklyn, man, and her name's Camus, too. Amy Camus. This cat's name is probably Trebla Sumac, and he ain't French, he's from Brooklyn, too. Yeh. Ha!"

In the dark the words are anything. "If it is true that the only paradise is that which one has lost, I know what name to give that something tender and inhuman which dwells within me today."

"Oh, shit, fuck it. Fuck it." He slams the book against the wall, and empties Hambrick's bottle. "I mean, why?" Empties bottle. "Shiiit."

When he swings the door open, the hall above is screams. Screams. All their voices, even now right here. The yellow glasses falling on the stairs, and broken. In his bare feet. "Shiit. Dumb-ass cats!"

"Rick, Rick, what's the cat doing now?"

"Man, be cool. Ha, the cat's kissin' Hutchens on the face, man. Um-uh-mm. Yeh, baby. Damn, he's puttin' his hands all over the cat. Aww, rotten motherfuckers!"

"What's happening?"

"Bastards shut out the lights!"

"Damn."

"Gaw-uhd damn!"

"Hey, let's break open the door."

"Yeh, HEY, YOU CATS, WHAT'S HAPPENING IN THERE, HUH?"

"Yeh. Hee, hee. OPEN UP, FAGGOTS!"

"Wheee! HEY LET US IN, GIRLS!"

Ricky and Jimmy run against the door, the others screaming and jumping, doors opening all along the hall. They all come out, screaming as well. "LET US IN. HEY, WHAT'S HAPPENIN', BABY!" Rick and Jimmy run against the door, and the door is breaking.

"Who is it? What do you want?" Bobby turns the light on, and his friend, a balding queer of 40, is hugged against the sink.

"Who are they, Bobby? What do they want?"

"Bastards. Damn if I know. GET OUTTA HERE, AND MIND YOUR OWN DAMN BUSINESS, YOU CREEPS. Creeps. Damn. Put on your clothes, Lyle!"

"God, they're trying to break the door down, Bobby. What they want? Why are they screaming like that?"

"GET THE HELL AWAY FROM THIS DOOR, GOD-DAMNIT!"

"YEH, YEH. WE SAW WHAT YOU WAS DOIN', HUTCHENS. OPEN THE DOOR AND LET US GET IN ON IT."

"WHEEEEEE! HIT THE FUCKING DOOR, RICK! HIT IT!"

And at the top of the stairs the leader stops, the whole hall full of citizens. Doctors, judges, first negro directors of welfare chain, morticians, chemists, ad men, fighters for civil rights, all admirable, useful men. "BREAK THE FUCKIN' DOOR OPEN, RICK! YEH!"

A wall. Against it, from where you stand, the sea stretches smooth for miles out. Their voices distant thuds of meat against the sand. Murmurs of insects. Hideous singers against your pillow every night of your life. They are there now, screaming at you.

"Ray, Ray, comeon man help us break this faggot's door!"

"Yeh, Ray, comeon!"

"Man, you cats are fools. Evil stupid fools!"

"What? Man, will you listen to this cat."

"Listen, hell, let's get this door. One more smash and it's in. Comeon, Brady, let's break the fuckin' thing."

"Yeh, comeon you cats, don't stand there listenin' to that pointy head clown, he just don't want us to pop his ol' lady!"

"YEH, YEH. LET'S GET IN THERE. HIT IT HIT IT!"

"Goddamnit. Goddamnit, get the fuck out of here. Get outta here. Damnit Rick, you sunafabitch, get the hell outtahere. Leave the cat alone!"

"Man, don't push me like that, you lil' skinny ass, I'll bust your jaw for you."

"Yeh? Yeh? Yeh? Well you come on, you lyin' ass. This cat's always talking about all his 'babes' and all he's got to do is sneak around peeping in keyholes. You big lying asshole . . . all you know how to do is bullshit and jerk off!"

"Fuck you, Ray."

"Your ugly ass mama."

"Shiit. You wanna go 'round with me, baby?"

"Comeon. Comeon, big time cocksman, comeon!"

Rick hits the leader full in the face, and he falls backwards across the hall. The crowd follows screaming at this new feature.

"Aww, man, somebody stop this shit. Rick'll kill Ray!"

"Well, you stop it, man."

"O.K., O.K., cut it out. Cut it out, Rick. You win man. Leave the cat alone. Leave him alone."

"Bad Rick . . . Bad Rick, Bad ass Rick!"

"Well, man, you saw the cat fuckin' with me. He started the shit!"

"Yeh . . . tough cat!"

"Get up Ray."

And then the door does open and Bobby Hutchens stands in the half light in his shower shoes, a broom in his hands. The boys scream and turn their attention back to Love. Bald Lyle is in the closet. More noise. More lies. More prints in the sand, away, or toward some name. I am a poet. I am a rich famous butcher. I am the man who paints the gold balls on the tops of flagpoles. I am, no matter, more beautiful than anyone else. And I have come a long way to say this. Here. In the long hall, shadows across my hands. My face pushed hard against the floor. And the wood, old, and protestant. And their voices, all these other selves screaming for blood. For blood, or whatever it is fills their noble lives.

Strong Horse Tea*

Alice Walker

Alice Walker was born in Eatonton, Georgia, in 1944. She attended Spelman and Sarah Lawrence colleges, with a B.A. from Sarah Lawrence in 1966. Her book of poems, ONCE, was published by Harcourt Brace Jovanovich, Inc. in 1968. Her short stories have appeared in The Best Short Stories By Negro Writers, edited by Langston Hughes and published by Little, Brown in 1967, in The Denver Quarterly, Freedomways, The Negro Digest, and in many textbooks, paper texts and anthologies. Her essays have appeared in The Black Scholar, Moderator, and The American Scholar. Her novel, The Third Life of Grange Copeland, was published by Harcourt Brace Jovanovich, Inc. She is presently writer-in-residence at Tougaloo College, Tougaloo, Mississippi. She was recently awarded a fellowship (for her fiction) from The National Endowment for the Arts. She is married and has a daughter.

Rannie Toomer's little baby boy Snooks was dying from double pneumonia and whooping cough. She sat away from him gazing into a low fire, her long crusty bottom lip hanging. She was not married. Was not pretty. Was not anybody much. And he was all she had.

"Lawd, why don't that doctor come on here?" she moaned, tears sliding from her sticky eyes. She hadn't washed since Snooks took sick five days before, and a long row of whitish snail tracks laced her ashen face.

"What you ought to try is one of the old home remedies," Sarah urged. She was an old neighboring lady who wore magic leaves around her neck sewed up in possum skin next to a dried lizard's foot. She knew how magic came about and could do magic herself, people said.

* This story appeared in a slightly different version in *Negro Digest*, June 1968.

"We going to have us a doctor," Rannie Toomer said fiercely, walking over to shoo a fat winter fly from her child's forehead. "I don't believe in none of your swamp magic. The 'old home remedies' I took when I was a child come just short of killing me."

Snooks, under a pile of faded quilts, made a small oblong mound in the bed. His head was like a ball of black putty wedged between the thin covers and the dingy yellow pillow. His eyes were partly open as if he were peeping out of his hard wasted skull at the chilly room, and the forceful pulse of his breathing caused a faint rustling in the sheets near his mouth like the wind pushing damp papers in a shallow ditch.

"What time you reckon he'll git here?" asked Sarah, not expecting an answer. She sat with her knees wide apart under three long skirts and a voluminous Mother Hubbard heavy with stains. From time to time she reached down to sweep her damp skirts away from the live coals. It was almost spring, but the winter cold still clung to her bones, and she had to almost sit in the fireplace to get warm. Her deep, sharp eyes had aged a moist hesitant blue that gave her a quick dull stare like a hawk. She gazed coolly at Rannie Toomer and rapped the hearthstones with her stick.

"White mailman, white doctor," she chanted skeptically.

"They gotta come see 'bout this baby," Rannie Toomer said wistfully. "Who'd go and ignore a little sick baby like my Snooks?"

"Some folks we don't know well as we *thinks* we do might," the old lady replied. "What you want to give that boy of yours is one or two of the old home remedies, arrowsroot or sassyfrass and cloves, or a sugar tit soaked in cat's blood."

"We don't need none of your witch's remedies!" said Rannie Toomer. "We going to git some of them shots that makes people well. Cures 'em of all they ails, cleans 'em out and makes 'em strong, all at the same time." She grasped her baby by his shrouded toes and began to gently twist, trying to knead life into him the same way she kneaded limberness into flour dough. She spoke upward from his feet as if he were an altar.

"Doctor'll be here soon, baby. I done sent the mailman." She left him reluctantly to go and stand by the window. She pressed her face against the glass, her flat nose more flattened as she peered out at the rain.

She had gone up to the mailbox in the rain that morning, hoping she hadn't missed the mailman's car. She had sat down on an old milk can near the box and turned her drooping face in the direction the mailman's car would come. She had no umbrella, and her feet shivered inside thin, clear plastic shoes that let in water and mud.

"Howde, Rannie Mae," the red-faced mailman said pleasantly, as he always did, when she stood by his car waiting to ask him something. Usually she wanted to ask what certain circulars meant that showed pretty pictures of things she needed. Did the circulars mean that somebody was coming around later and give her hats and suitcases and shoes and sweaters and rubbing alcohol and a heater for the house and a fur bonnet for her baby? Or, why did he always give her the pictures if she couldn't have what was in them? Or, what did the words say? . . . Especially the big word written in red "S-A-L-E!"?

He would explain shortly to her that the only way she could get the goods pictured on the circulars was to buy them in town and that town stores did their advertising by sending out pictures of their goods. She would listen with her mouth hanging open until he finished. Then she would exclaim in a dull amazed way that *she* never had any money and he could ask anybody. *She* couldn't ever buy any of the things in the pictures—so why did the stores keep sending them to her?

He tried to explain to her that *everybody* got the circulars whether they had any money to buy with or not. That this was one of the laws of advertising, and he couldn't do anything about it. He was sure she never understood what he tried to teach her about advertising, for one day she asked him for any extra circulars he had, and when he asked her what she wanted them for—since she couldn't afford to buy any of the items advertised—she said she needed them to paper the inside of her house to keep out the wind.

Today he thought she looked more ignorant than usual as she stuck her dripping head inside his car. He recoiled from her breath and gave little attention to what she was saying about her sick baby as he mopped up the water she dripped on the plastic door handle of the car.

"Well, never *can* keep 'em dry; I mean, *warm* enough, in rainy weather like this here," he mumbled absently, stuffing a wad of circulars advertising hair dryers and cold creams into her hands. He wished she would stand back from his car so he could get going. But she clung to the side gabbing away about "Snooks" and "pneumonia" and "shots" and about how she wanted a *"real* doctor!"

To everything she said he nodded. "That right?" he injected sympathetically when she stopped for breath, and then he began to sneeze, for she was letting in wetness and damp, and he felt he was coming down with a cold. Black people as black as Rannie Toomer always made him uneasy, especially when they didn't smell good and when you could tell they didn't right away. Rannie Mae, leaning in over him out of the rain, smelled like a wet goat. Her dark dirty eyes clinging to his with such hungry desperation made him nervous.

"Well, ah, *mighty* sorry to hear 'bout the little fella," he said, groping for the window crank. "We'll see what we can do!" He gave her what he hoped was a big friendly smile. God! *He didn't want to hurt her feelings;* she did look so pitiful hanging there in the rain. Suddenly he had an idea.

"Whyn't you try some of old Aunt Sarah's home remedies?" he suggested brightly. He half believed along with everybody else in the county that the old blue-eyed black woman possessed magic. Magic that if it didn't work on whites probably would on blacks. But Rannie Toomer almost turned the car over shaking her head and body with an emphatic NO! She reached in a wet hand to grasp his shoulder.

"We wants us a doctor, a real doctor!" she screamed. She had begun to cry and drop her tears on him. "You git us a doctor from town!" she bellowed, shaking the solid shoulder that bulged under his new tweed coat.

"Like I say," he drawled patiently, although beginning to be furious with her, "we'll do what we can!" And he hurriedly rolled up the window and sped down the road, cringing from the thought that she had put her nasty black hands on him.

"Old home remedies! Old home remedies!" Rannie Toomer had cursed the words while she licked at the hot tears that ran down her face, the only warmth about her. She turned backwards to the trail that led to her house, trampling the wet circulars under her feet. Under the fence she went and was in a pasture surrounded by dozens of fat whitefolks' cows and an old gray horse and a mule. Cows and horses never seemed to have much trouble, she thought, as she hurried home.

Old Sarah dug steadily at the fire; the bones in her legs ached as if they were outside the flesh that enclosed them.

"White mailman, white doctor. White doctor, white mailman," she murmured from time to time, putting the poker down carefully and rubbing her shins.

"You young ones *will* turn to them," she said, "when it is *us* what got the power."

"The doctor's coming, Aunt Sarah. I know he is," Rannie Toomer said angrily.

It was less than an hour after she had talked to the mailman that she looked up expecting the doctor and saw old Sarah tramping through the grass on her walking stick. She couldn't pretend she wasn't home with the smoke from her fire climbing out the chimney, so she let her in, making her leave her bag of tricks on the porch.

Old woman old as that ought to forgit trying to cure other people with her nigger magic. Ought to use some of it on herself! she thought. She would not let Sarah lay a finger on Snooks and warned her if she tried anything she would knock her over the head with her own cane.

"He coming, all right," Rannie Toomer said again firmly, looking with prayerful eyes out through the rain.

"Let me tell you, child," the old woman said almost gently, sipping the coffee Rannie Toomer had given her. "*He ain't.*"

She had not been allowed near the boy on the bed, and that had made her angry at first, but now she looked with pity at the young woman who was so afraid her child would die. She felt rejected but at the same time sadly *glad* that the young always grow up hoping. It *did* take a long time to finally realize that you could only depend on those who would come.

"But I done told you," Rannie Toomer was saying in exasperation, "I asked the mailman to bring a doctor for my Snooks!"

Cold wind was shooting all around her from the cracks in the window framing; faded circulars blew inward from the walls.

"He done fetched the doctor," the old woman said, softly stroking her coffee cup. "What you reckon brung me over here in this here flood? It wasn't no desire to see no rainbows, I can tell you."

Rannie Toomer paled.

"*I*'s the doctor, child. That there mailman didn't git no further with that message of yours then the road in front of my house. Lucky he got good lungs—deef as I is I had myself a time trying to make out *what* he was yelling."

Rannie began to cry, moaning.

Suddenly the breathing from the bed seemed to drown out the noise of the downpour outside. The baby's pulse seemed to make the whole house shake.

"Here!" she cried, snatching the baby up and handing him to Sarah. "Make him well! Oh, my lawd, make him well!"

"Let's not upset the little fella unnecessarylike," Sarah said, placing the baby back on the bed. Gently she began to examine him, all the while moaning and humming a thin pagan tune that pushed against the sound of the wind and rain with its own melancholy power. She stripped him of his clothes, poked at his fiberless baby ribs, blew against his chest. Along his tiny flat back she ran her soft old fingers. The child hung on in deep rasping sleep, and his small glazed eyes neither opened fully nor fully closed.

Rannie Toomer swayed over the bed watching the old woman touching the baby. She mourned the time she had wasted waiting for a doctor. Her feeling of guilt was a stone.

"I'll do anything you say do, Aunt Sarah," she cried, mopping at her nose with her dress. "Anything you say, just, please God, make him git better."

Old Sarah dressed the baby again and sat down in front of the fire. She stayed deep in thought for several minutes. Rannie Toomer gazed first into her silent face and then at the baby whose breathing seemed to have eased since Sarah picked him up.

"Do something, quick!" she urged Sarah, beginning to believe in her powers completely. "Do something that'll make him rise up and call his mama!"

"The child's dying," said the old woman bluntly, staking out beforehand some limitation to her skill. "But," she went on, "there might be something still we might try . . ."

"What?" asked Rannie Toomer from her knees. She knelt before the old woman's chair, wringing her hands and crying. She fastened herself to Sarah's chair. How could she have thought anyone else could help her Snooks, she wondered brokenly, when you couldn't even depend on them to come! She had been crazy to trust anyone but the withered old magician before her.

"What can I *do*?" she urged fiercely, blinded by her new faith, driven by the labored breathing from the bed.

"It going to take a strong stomach," said Sarah slowly. "It going to take a mighty strong stomach, and most of you young peoples these days don't have 'em!"

"Snooks got a strong stomach," Rannie Toomer said, peering anxiously into the serious old face.

"It ain't him that's got to have the strong stomach," Sarah said, glancing at the sobbing girl at her feet. "*You* the one got to have the strong stomach . . . he won't know *what* it is he's drinking."

Rannie Toomer began to tremble way down deep in her stomach. It sure was weak, she thought. Trembling like that. But what could she mean her Snooks to drink? Not cat's blood! and not any of the other messes she'd heard Sarah specialized in that would make anybody's stomach turn. What did she mean?

"What is it?" she whispered, bringing her head close to Sarah's knee. Sarah leaned down and put her toothless mouth to her ear.

"The only thing that can save this child now is some good strong horse tea!" she said, keeping her eyes turned toward the bed. "The *only* thing. And if you wants him out of that bed you better make tracks to git some!"

Rannie Toomer took up her wet coat and stepped across the porch to the pasture. The rain fell against her face with the force of small hailstones. She started walking in the direction of the trees where she could see the bulky lightish shapes of cows. Her thin plastic shoes were sucked at by the mud, but she pushed herself forward in a relentless search for the lone gray mare.

All the animals shifted ground and rolled big dark eyes at Rannie Toomer. She made as little noise as she could and leaned herself against a tree to wait.

Thunder rose from the side of the sky like tires of a big truck rumbling over rough dirt road. Then it stood a split second in the middle of the sky before it exploded like a giant firecracker, then rolled away again like an empty keg. Lightning streaked across the sky, setting the air white and charged.

Rannie Toomer stood dripping under her tree hoping not to be struck. She kept her eyes carefully on the behind of the gray mare, who, after nearly an hour had passed, began nonchalantly to spread her muddy knees.

At that moment Rannie Toomer realized that she had brought nothing to catch the precious tea in. Lightning struck something not far off and caused a cracking and groaning in the woods that frightened the animals away from their shelter. Rannie Toomer slipped down in the mud trying to take off one of her plastic shoes, and the gray mare, trickling some, broke for a clump of cedars yards away.

Rannie Toomer was close enough to the mare to catch the tea if she could keep up with her while she ran. So, alternately holding her breath and gasping for air, she started after her. Mud from her fall clung to her elbows and streaked her frizzy hair. Slipping and sliding in the mud she raced after the big mare, holding out, as if for alms, her plastic shoe.

In the house Sarah sat, her shawls and sweaters tight around her, rubbing her knees and muttering under her breath. She heard the thunder, saw the lightning that lit up the dingy room, and turned her waiting face to the bed. Hobbling over on stiff legs, she could hear no sound; the frail breathing had stopped with the thunder, not to come again.

Across the mud-washed pasture Rannie Toomer stumbled, holding out her plastic shoe for the gray mare to fill In spurts and splashes mixed with rainwater she gathered her tea. In parting, the old mare snorted and threw up one big leg, knocking her back into the mud. She rose trembling and crying, holding the shoe, spilling none over the top but realizing a leak, a tiny crack, at her shoe's front. Quickly she stuck her mouth there over the crack, and, ankle deep in the slippery mud of the pasture, and freezing in her shabby wet coat, she ran home to give the good and warm strong horse tea to her baby Snooks.

A Love Song for Wing

Charles H. Fuller, Jr.

Charles H. Fuller, Jr., is a novelist and playwright living in Philadelphia. His work has appeared in Lib-erator and Black Dialogue. He is in the anthologies Blackfire and Black Arts. His play, The Rise, is in the Ed Bullins collection, Plays from The Black Thea-tre. His full-length play, The Perfect Party, has been produced off-Broadway.

At midafternoon on a Philadelphia Tuesday, Glory Ann, who had been named (her mother would tell her nostal-gically) after a one-time movie star (who had long since witnessed her decline in motion pictures and public mem-ory)—Glory Ann, a tall, thin, spindly-legged, twelve-year-old black girl, leaped from the steps of the Wanafowler Junior High School, where everyone when they were nasty called her "gass-ass," and laughing, screaming to the height of her voice, and unable to control her direction, collided head-on into Reuben Tate, the hippest fourteen-year-old in the ninth grade and found herself flat on her face. She was so embarrassed; she wanted to die. "What is wrong wif' you?" Reuben was on the ground when he said it. He was angry. There were streaks of it in his face as he brushed off his jacket and cursed.

"That's ole' gass-ass!" one of his friends shouted. "She ain't got good sense —do you, gass?"

"My name is Glory Ann—and I'm sorry!" was all she could say. She wanted to scream something else, but the situation was impossible. What pride she had before the leap had skidded into the street with her books. When she was standing, she and Reuben stared at one another, but he was quick to dismiss her with a cool "Dig yourself, girl. Next time you might git hurt," to which he added a *hip* turn, and *bopped* down Columbia Avenue in his double-breasted, wide-lapeled, high-vent jacket. That boy sure

141

could dress. "Later, gass!" his friend yelled. It was a put-down. Her two best friends were the first to let her know it.

"He sure put a thing on you, chile!" Rosalee sang.

"Oooo-weee!" shouted Willa Mae Johnson who always said, "oooo-weee! He ain' do nothin', though, did he," she observed. "Long as he ain' *break-bad* and do nothin', it don't even count. Talk is a check you can't cash!"

"He coulda' done you in," Rosalee enjoined. It was fuel to a raging fire in Glory Ann. "He's the *runner* of Tenth and Montgomery—Reuben is 'Little Blood,' girl! He holds all the *check* and is known for *juicin'* people just 'cause they smoke the wrong cigarettes! He just ain't wanna' hurt you, that's all—he gave you a break!"

She refused to respond to Rosalee's baiting. If all she wants to do is *signify*, I won't listen to her, she thought. The day, however, did look suddenly worse than it had from the screened windows of her last class. Why couldn't she have walked down? What had possessed her? She hadn't intended—or had she? Didn't she try to meet him several days ago? Wasn't the time she dropped her books in front of him deliberate? Certainly the day she tried to hit him with a spray of water from the fountain was. No, she finally admitted, the leap was no accident. She wanted to meet Reuben more than anything—but how? He was always surrounded by his friends, and she had no recollection of him ever talking to girls. Maybe he was afraid of girls. She laughed.

"I think he's scared of girls, myself!" She said it triumphantly.

"How come he useta go with Lois, then?" It was Rosalee, utterly destroying her sudden confidence. Glory Ann grumbled, turning off at Jefferson Street and glad to be rid of them.

"See you, gass!" Rosalee joked loudly.

"I'ma git you, girl!" Glory Ann responded angrily, raising a fist.

She slammed the door when she entered. It shook the glass. Almost immediately she heard her mother.

"What's wrong wif' you?" Her hands were on her hips. She sounded very much like Reuben.

Glory Ann stomped into the room and spit out, "Nothin'!"

"Then you betta go back an' close that damn door like you got good sense!"

"I got good sense," she shouted. "Y'all think I don't, but I ain't stupid! I ain't—!" The rest of it failed to come out.

Glory Ann was crying, the incident on the steps overflowing from her eyes, shaking her narrow frame, the memory of Reuben's look tormenting her.

"Hey! Glory Ann?"

"I-bumped-into-this-boy-named-Reuben—"

"Who?"

"Reuben! An-an-when-I-did—and-I-ain't-mean-it-everybody-called-me-stupid-and-gass-ass—"

"What?"

"Gass-ass!   And-I-said-that-ain't-my-name-and-I'm-sick-of-that-school-and-I-ain't-neva'-goin'-back!"

Her mother held her, running her hands down Glory Ann's arms. It felt good, as it had when she was little. Comforting—until her brother walked in, laughing at her tears.

"You git yourself outta here, boy!" Mother waved a dangerous fist at Henry.

"I ain't do nothin'!"

"OUT!" Henry left bewildered, moaning that he had not had his lunch and that, ". . . people 'roun' hea' is tryin to starve somebody out!" and he was immediately going to report his mother to the "cruelties."

"Do you like Reuben?"

"No!" she lied. "I can't stan' him, he walks 'roun' like he's a god or somethin'!" The thought had occurred to her that Reuben did occasionally act like a god—or someone with strange powers. No one ever touched him, and he wielded absolute authority over his friends without ever threatening them. She wondered if he was as *bad* as everyone said. He had to be, she convinced herself; if not, how could he be a runner? Yet she had never seen him fighting. In most instances Reuben would simply stare at whomever challenged his authority for a moment, turn sharply from them, and *bop* down the street without ever turning back. No one dared attack him from the rear.

"Why you so upset?"

"I ain't upset!" she dried her eyes. "Not ova' somebody like him!"

"Then, why don't you go up to him and tell—"

Glory Ann stopped listening. How dumb could her mother be? She must be insane! *Go* up to Reuben? Just *go* up to Little Blood? No wonder it was a generation-gap thing! Old people was crazy! You just don't *go* up to nobody like Reuben! He'd put you so far down you'd never get up. She pulled away from her mother and went upstairs. Nobody could be any more insane than that woman. Damn!

Through dinner and the evening, Glory Ann listened reluctantly to the advice of her "mentally disturbed" mother, telling herself no solution was possible because she had been born into a seriously ill family.

"I don't know who would like somebody ugly as you, anyway," said her brother for the fiftieth time before she went to bed. "You so ugly, you can turn out the lights in my room by just comin' to the door! You so ugly, you can make it night in midafternoon! You so . . ." He went on and on. She didn't answer him.

"Did you hear me, godzilla? You so ugly, you could strike a match . . ."

She was ugly—and not because Henry said so. How many boy friends had she? Rosalee was always telling her tales of this or that boy walking her home or meeting her at parties. Even "Oooo-weee," Willa Mae, was goin' with "Chop-Chop," the runner of Thirteenth and Poplar. The only boy who dared be seen with her was "Easy," and everyone in the world knew there was something wrong with him. As crazy as her mother was, Glory Ann had even heard her discussing the queerness in "Easy's" family.

"All those Robinsons act a little off," she had said. *"You know one of his sista's is out Byberry—and I think his fatha' comes home on weekend passes—simple as he acts!"*

She pulled the blanket over her face and cried. It wasn't Reuben. It was her—named after a movie star and looking like wolf-man. Sleep came swiftly to her twelve-year-old body, but her dreams were filled with Reuben. He stared quietly at her as she tried to climb a hill made of his friends.

"Mom, would you git mad if some boy walked me home?"

"If he was decent, I don't see why not."

On the way to school the thought bolstered her spirits. Not that anyone would walk her home. It seemed better, however, knowing *if* she were asked, her mother would permit it. In the hall, Rosalee leaned against a locker, breathing heavily into Ronald Jackson's face. He was the only boy everyone in school was certain would go on to college. Ronald Jackson was so smart the principal knew him by name! Glory Ann didn't like him. Aside from his I.Q. Ronald Jackson was a punk, set upon by everyone. He walked away when he saw her. She felt no sympathy for him.

"Hey there, Ronald Jack-ass," she laughed. Ronald disappeared up the stairs.

"Ronald just asked me to go to his party," Rosalee was smiling. "I told him if I got to go with a punk, I wanna be picked up in his fatha's Three-Twenty-Five Electra Buick, chile!"

"I can't stan' him!"

A group of boys ran down the hall, called her "gass-ass," and tried to pat her on the behind.

"Your motha'!" she yelled.

"You hear about the gang war?"

"No! Who's fightin'?"

"I heard," Rosalee began in her most secret voice, "that las' night Tenth and Montgomery *moved on* Twelf' and Thompson, and they comin' up hea' today to shoot Reuben and 'Dog-leg.'"

"Why they gonna' shoot Reuben?" She was suddenly frightened. Willa Mae ran up.

"Ooo-weee! You oughta see what Twelfth and Thompson got! Oooo-wee! Chop-Chop said they got a M-14 rifle!"

The news disturbed Glory Ann. Her excuse was hastily thought of, but with it she escaped her two friends. She had to find Reuben. She ran up the east staircase to the second floor. He wasn't in the hall. She took the flight to the third as if she had wings, but he wasn't there. Where was he? She couldn't believe he *punked out* and stayed away from school. Not Reuben. She went back down, again surveying the halls. Still no sign of him. On the ground level she went slowly to her locker and on to class as if bearing the weight of the world. It occurred to her, only after several pensive hours, that she wouldn't have known what to say if she had met him. The knowledge made her feel stupid. For the remainder of the day she moved quietly, trembling or crying on occasion whenever she thought of what might happen to him. By the time Twelfth and Thompson arrived she was near hysteria.

They came in their usual manner. A contingent moved up Tenth Street. Another group moved east on Columbia Avenue. The final force *bopped* up Eleventh Street to cut off any chance of escape. There were at least thirty of them, and they lined the sidewalk of Columbia Avenue like an army preparing to attack. "Durango," the *runner*, stood to the rear of his troops and when they were ready nodded to "Cornbread" the *warlord*, who moved to the center of the street screaming challenges to the school and Reuben.

It reminded Glory Ann of the movies. The students scrambled out of the way, in the same manner the storekeepers and drunks bolted in cowboy pictures The town would be silent as everyone waited for the gangs to ride in and shoot it out. But in her thoughts this was as it should be. Gangs fought. Today it was wrong somehow because Reuben might be the victim. Today someone she cared for might be hurt. Everything else she dismissed—the right or wrong was something adults talked about.

"Reuben Tate is a faggot!" Cornbread yelled.

"Blood is a pussy!" someone laughed. Glory Ann was shaking.

"Reuben is a punk!"

"He is not! He is not!" It was Glory Ann, screaming—running toward Cornbread crying. "He is not! He is not!" She charged into him swinging her books, her fists, closing her eyes and mind to what she was doing. Cornbread couldn't sidestep her, and her first blow struck him high in the face, blinding him momentarily. It was enough for him to miss Reuben and his gang *slide* easily around the corner. The second time Glory Ann swung, Cornbread danced back and threw a right solidly to her stomach. The girl twisted and went down on one knee screaming.

"*Ice* that bitch!" someone was shouting, but Cornbread had already turned from the groaning girl. He was facing Reuben, who walked slowly across the street toward him.

"Let's git it on!" Cornbread backed up, his fists in the air. Reuben said nothing. When he reached Glory Ann, he touched her on the shoulder.

"Git the hell off me," she yelled.

"Git up!"

She hadn't recognized the voice at first. Now she stared at his face, tears streaking down her cheeks, trying to smile.

"Let's make it, *Wing*," he said. She pulled herself up, and for one instant they took in each other's face. He had called her Wing. She almost told him that was not her name, but something stopped her. It was in his eyes. A simple command to take what he gave her. She straightened her dress and picked up her books. Reuben remained beside her. Today he was wearing his *boss* daishiki. Even in pain there was a sigh of admiration in her. When she was ready, he spun around and *bopped* her to his side of the street. With his own people, he gestured to a place for her, which she took proudly and obediently. He then faced Twelfth and Thompson.

"Y'all betta' make it! Ain't nobody gonna move on nobody today, yah dig? Nothin'!"

"Tomorra, Blood!" Durango stepped forward, his head and hands explaining in motion what his light voice could not convey. "Tomorra we gonna' *CAP* you, Blood! You!"

Reuben stared at them silently as they filed down Columbia Avenue.

They all left in the same direction. The last one to turn down Eleventh Street was "Racy," the runner of the Twelfth and Thompson "Juniors." He stopped, stood on the corner for a moment, put his hands inside his coat, and throwing it back, revealed his pistol. He pointed to it, then to Reuben, leaned back, and said, "jive mothafu . . . ," spun around quickly, and *bopped* down Eleventh Street, stopping occasionally with a mild challenge.

Tenth and Montgomery was silent. Reuben faced some of his people, and they moved off quickly, while the remainder gathered around him.

"This here is Wing," he said pointing to her.

"That's gass-ass!" someone said.

"It's Wing," Reuben re-enforced, and for all time it became Wing.

"Which way you goin', Wing?"

"Down thea'."

"You live 'round Twelf' and Thompson? She live 'roun' Twelf' and Thompson, Blood!"

"We goin' that way," he said. The others relented, and they crossed the street.

"Why you call me Wing?" She was gazing at him intently.

"You look like you flyin' when you run—plus wings is close to the eagle, you dig?" She shook her head, that she dug.

"You ain't hafta help me, I coulda' beat Cornbread!" Reuben smiled.

"How come they ain't do nothin' to you when you came out into the street?" The incident had been bothering her. Reuben had been alone. Twelfth and Thompson could have shot him, but no one had moved.

"I got a thing," he said. "It neutralizes people, you dig? All of us got it, but just the runners know how to use it. That's why I'm the runner."

She looked at him and smiled, wondering if she had it, and if she did, how it could be used. "All," he said. She didn't swell on it. Her mind was racing. What would Rosalee and Willa Mae say when they discovered Reuben had walked her home, given her a new name, and *in* Twelfth and Thompson territory? She could hear Willa Mae's "Oooo-wee" already. Rosalee would be speechless. In fact she was speechless. When they crossed Oxford Street Rosalee stood motionless on the corner following Glory Ann, Reuben, and the fifteen boys with her eyes. She started to wave but stole her hand back. Glory Ann nodded, smiled, and continued walking. When they reached her street, her mother was standing on the stoops. Upon seeing Glory Ann she began to race toward her, cursing at Reuben.

"Who you go wit'?" Reuben asked.

"Nobody right now," Wing replied. Reuben shook his head, then tilted it to the side and looked at her. She didn't hear her mother.

"Well—" she said it anxiously.

"Like, we'll rap, you know?" He pointed a quick finger and spun around *bopping* down the street, his boys comfortably behind him. Her mother was shouting. "YOU BETTA NOT LET ME GIT MY HANDS ON YOU— you little bastard! Don't you put your damn hands on her, you hea' me—if I catch your ass—" Glory Ann began to hear her.

"It wasn' him! It wasn' him! It was Cornbread, Momma! It wasn' Reuben!"

"Well—well, what you doin' wif' that boy? He ain't nothin' —I don't want you 'roun' him! Hear me?" She began to shake her Glory Ann. "Hea' me? Hea' me?"

"He stopped them!" Wing kept shouting until gradually the hysteria in her mother's voice and face dissipated and both began to cry. Through the tears Wing watched Reuben standing quietly on the corner before he disappeared. She vaguely heard, "Later, Wing!" and was pleased they had remembered. Her tears were filled with laughter. Inside she was new, more than twelve years could ever anticipate being—this little girl, Wing, sung inside and held her mother tightly. She had fought for her man, the way everyone said was necessary, and he had responded by protecting her, caring for her.

"I love him, Momma!"

Her mother didn't answer. They simply held one another in the middle of the street with everyone watching. Most of the black people felt like crying. The scene touched things inside them. This girl, this spindly-legged Glory Ann, almost twice the size of her mother—

BLAMMMMM!!   BLAMMMMM!!

"Oh God!" People were screaming, leaping off their steps.

"They shot him!"

"You see that? They shot that boy!" Everyone was running up the street.

"Git Racy! Racy did it!"

Racy ran terrified across the street. A car screeched.

"Ahhgghh!" The sound was loud. The glass shattered. Someone screamed. Racy tumbled twice before he hit the ground, the gun sliding across the pavement to the foot of a little boy.

"Gun! Gun! Gun, Mommy!"

"Don't you touch it, Michael!" She swept him up. There were sirens in the background. Crying. Wing running.

"It's Blood! Racy shot Blood in the back!"

"Oh Jesus! Jesus!"

Reuben was on his face. Blood on Blood on Reuben's dead. Wing running, screaming, crying, Wing howling, groaning, flying, Wing running, running, running to her dead man's side.

"Glory Ann!" Mother shouting. Wing bursting, twisting, shaking. Rosalee grabbed her and watched her vomit. Watched her life cave in. Watched Wing collapse beside her man. Her dead, dead Blood.

All night her mother held her, kissed her, calling endearing things, listening to Wing, listened to this twelve-year-old woman; heard her cry, heard this thin, spindly-legged child cry, until her throat was raw and belched out pain. All night with Wing, all night and every night until Wing's laughter returned, flowed into her face like black molasses, all night until Wing could whisper about it; until she could say she didn't need to be held; until, when she finally stood, her mother noticed more than the girl, noticed something else, and asked her Wing, her proud daughter, what it was and was told it was a *thing*.

"A thing," Wing said, "all of us have but few know how to use."

"Do you know how?"

"I know now, Momma. I know now."

The Convert

Lerone Bennett, Jr

*Lerone Bennett, Jr., was born in Clarksdale, Missis-
sippi, in 1928. Upon graduating from Morehouse
College, he joined the staff of the* Atlanta Daily
World, *first as a reporter and then as city editor. In
1960 he became the first senior editor of* Ebony
Magazine. *Among his books are* Before the May-
flower, The Negro Mood, What Manner of Man:
Biography of Martin Luther King, Jr., *and* Confrontation: Black and White. *Mr. Bennett is also a fellow
of the Black Academy of Arts and Letters.*

A man don't know what he'll do, a man don't know
what he is till he gets his back pressed up against a wall.
Now you take Aaron Lott: there ain't no other way to
explain the crazy thing he did. He was going along fine,
preaching the gospel, saving souls, and getting along with
the white folks; and then, all of a sudden, he felt wood
pressing against his back. The funny thing was that nobody knew he was hurting till he preached that Red Sea
sermon where he got mixed up and seemed to think Mississippi was Egypt. As chairman of the deacons' board, I
felt it was my duty to reason with him. I appreciated his
position and told him so, but I didn't think it was right
for him to push us all in a hole. The old fool—he just
laughed.

"Brother Booker," he said, "the Lord—He'll take care
of me."

I knew then that that man was heading for trouble.
And the very next thing he did confirmed it. The white
folks called the old fool downtown to bear witness that
the colored folks were happy. And you know what he
did: he got down there amongst all them big white folks
and he said: "Things ain't gonna change here overnight,
but they gonna change. It's inevitable. The Lord wants it."

Well sir, you could have bought them white folks for a penny. Aaron Lott, pastor of the Rock of Zion Baptist Church, a man white folks had said was wise and sound and sensible, had come close—too close—to saying that the Supreme Court was coming to Melina, Mississippi. The surprising thing was that the white folks didn't do nothing. There was a lot of mumbling and whispering, but nothing bad happened till the terrible morning when Aaron came a-knocking at the door of my funeral home. Now things had been tightening up—you could feel it in the air—and I didn't want no part of no crazy scheme, and I told him so right off. He walked on past me and sat down on the couch. He had on his preaching clothes, a shiny blue suit, a fresh starched white shirt, a black tie, and his Sunday black shoes. I remember thinking at the time that Aaron was too black to be wearing all them dark clothes. The thought tickled me, and I started to smile, but then I noticed something about him that didn't seem quite right. I ran my eyes over him closely. He was kinda middle-sized and he had a big clean-shaven head, a big nose, and thin lips. I stood there looking at him for a long time, but I couldn't figure out what it was till I looked at his eyes: they were burning bright, like light bulbs do just before they go out. And yet he looked contented, like his mind was resting somewheres else.

"I wanna talk with you, Booker," he said, glancing sideways at my wife. "If you don't mind, Sister Brown—"

Sarah got up and went into the living quarters. Aaron didn't say nothing for a long time; he just sat there looking out the window. Then he spoke so soft I had to strain my ears to hear.

"I'm leaving for the Baptist convention," he said. He pulled out his gold watch and looked at it. "Train leaves in 'bout two hours."

"I know *that*, Aaron."

"Yeah, but what I wanted to tell you was that I ain't going Jim Crow. I'm going first class, Booker, right through the white waiting room. That's the law."

A cold shiver ran through me.

"Aaron," I said, "don't you go talking crazy now."

The old fool laughed, a great big body-shaking laugh. He started talking 'bout God and Jesus and all that stuff. Now, I'm a God-fearing man myself, but I holds that God helps those who help themselves. I told him so.

"You can't mix God up with these white folks," I said.

"When you start to messing around with segregation, they'll burn you up and the Bible, too."

He looked at me like I was Satan.

"I sweated over this thing," he said. "I prayed. I got down on my knees, and I asked God not to give me this cup. But He said I was the one. I heard Him, Booker, right here (he tapped his chest) in my heart."

The old fool's been having visions, I thought. I sat down and tried to figure out a way to hold him, but he got up, without saying a word, and started for the door.

"Wait!" I shouted. "I'll get my coat."

"I don't need you," he said. "I just came by to tell you so you could tell the board in case something happened."

"You wait," I shouted, and ran out of the room to get my coat.

We got in his beat-up old Ford and went by the parsonage to get his suitcase. Rachel—that was his wife—and Jonah were sitting in the living room, wringing their hands. Aaron got his bag, shook Jonah's hand, and said, "Take care of your Mamma, boy." Jonah nodded. Aaron hugged Rachel and pecked at her cheek. Rachel broke down. She throwed her arms around his neck and carried on something awful. Aaron shoved her away.

"Don't go making no fuss over it, woman. I ain't gonna be gone forever. Can't a man go to a church meeting 'thout women screaming and crying."

He tried to make light of it, but you could see he was touched by the way his lips trembled. He held his hand out to me, but I wouldn't take it. I told him off good, told him it was a sin and a shame for a man of God to be carrying on like he was, worrying his wife and everything.

"I'm coming with you," I said. "Somebody's gotta see that you don't make a fool of yourself."

He shrugged, picked up his suitcase, and started for the door. Then he stopped and turned around and looked at his wife and his boy, and from the way he looked I knew that there was still a chance. He looked at the one and then at the other. For a moment there, I thought he was going to cry, but he turned, quick-like, and walked out of the door.

I ran after him and tried to talk some sense in his head. But he shook me off, turned the corner, and went on up Adams Street. I caught up with him, and we walked in silence, crossing the street in front of the First Baptist Church for whites, going on around the Confederate monu ment where, once, they hung a boy for fooling around with white women.

"Put it off, Aaron," I begged. "Sleep on it."

He didn't say nothing.

"What you need is a vacation. I'll get the board to approve, full pay and everything."

He smiled and shifted the suitcase over to his left hand. Big drops of sweat were running down his face and spotting up his shirt. His eyes were awful, all lit up and burning.

"Aaron, Aaron, can't you hear me?"

We passed the feed store, Bill Williams' grocery store, and the movie house.

"A man's gotta think about his family, Aaron. A man ain't free. Didn't you say that once, didn't you?"

He shaded his eyes with his hand and looked into the sun. He put the suitcase on the ground and checked his watch.

"Why don't you think about Jonah?" I asked. "Answer that. Why don't you think about your own son?"

"I am," he said. "That's exactly what I'm doing, thinking about Jonah. Matter of fact, he started *me* to thinking. I ain't never mentioned it before, but the boy's been worrying me. One day we was downtown here, and he asked me something that hurt. 'Daddy,' he said, 'how come you ain't a man?' I got mad, I did, and told him: 'I am a man.' He said that wasn't what he meant. 'I mean,' he said, 'how come you ain't a man where white folks concerned.' I couldn't answer him, Booker. I'll never forget it till the day I die. I couldn't answer my own son, and I been preaching forty years."

"He don't know nothing 'bout it," I said. "He's hotheaded, like my boy. He'll find out when he grows up."

"I hopes not," Aaron said, shaking his head. "I hopes not."

Some white folks passed, and we shut up till they were out of hearing. Aaron, who was acting real strange, looked up in the sky and moved his lips. He came back to himself after a little bit, and he said: "This thing of being a man, Booker, is a big thing. The Supreme Court can't make you a man. The NAACP can't do it. God Almighty can do a lot, but even He can't do it. Ain't nobody can do it but you."

He said that like he was preaching, and when he got through, he was all filled up with emotion, and he seemed kind of ashamed—he was a man who didn't like emotion outside the church. He looked at his watch, picked up his bag, and said, "Well, let's git it over with."

We turned into Elm, and the first thing I saw at the end of the street was the train station. It was an old red building, flat like a slab. A group of white men were fooling around in front of the door. I couldn't make them out from that distance, but I could tell they weren't the kind of white folks to be fooling around with.

We walked on, passing the dry goods store, the barber shop, and the new building that was going up. Across the street from that was the sheriff's office. I looked in the window and saw Bull Sampson sitting at his desk, his feet propped up on a chair, a fat brown cigar sticking out of his mouth. A ball about the size of a sweet potato started burning in my stomach.

"Please Aaron," I said. "Please. You can't get away with it. I know how you feel. Sometimes I feel the same way myself, but I wouldn't risk my neck to do nothing for these people. They won't appreciate it; they'll laugh at you."

We were almost to the station and I could make out the faces of the men sitting on the benches. One of them must have been telling a joke. He finished, and the group broke out laughing.

I whispered to Aaron: "I'm through with it. I wash my hands of the whole mess."

I don't know whether he heard me or not. He turned to the right without saying a word and went on in the front door. The string-beany man who told the joke was so shocked that his cigarette fell out of his mouth.

"Y'all see that," he said. "Why, I'll—"

"Shut up," another man said. "Go git Bull."

I kept walking, fast, turned at the corner, and ran around to the colored waiting room. When I got in there, I looked through the ticket window and saw Aaron standing in front of the clerk. Aaron stood there for a minute or more, but the clerk didn't see him. And that took some not seeing. In that room Aaron Lott stood out like a pig in a chicken coop.

There were, I'd say, about ten or fifteen people in there, but didn't none of them move. They just sat there with their eyes glued on Aaron's back. Aaron cleared his throat. The clerk didn't look up; he got real busy with some papers. Aaron cleared his throat again and opened his mouth to speak. The screen door of the waiting room opened and clattered shut.

It got real quiet in that room, hospital quiet. It got so quiet I could hear my own heart beating. Now Aaron knew who opened that door, but he didn't bat an eyelid. He turned around real slow and faced High Sheriff Sampson, the baddest man in South Mississippi.

Mr. Sampson stood there with his legs wide open, like the men you see on television. His beefy face was blood-red, and his gray eyes were rattlesnake hard. He was mad; no doubt about it. I had never seen him so mad.

"Preacher," he said, "you done gone crazy?" He was talking low-like and mean.

"Nosir," Aaron said. "Nosir, Mr. Sampson."

"What you think you doing?"

"Going to St. Louis, Mr. Sampson."

"You must done lost yo' mind, boy."

Mr. Sampson started walking toward Aaron with his hand on his gun. Twenty or thirty men pushed through the front door and fanned out over the room. Mr. Sampson stopped about two paces from Aaron and looked him up and down. That look had paralyzed hundreds of niggers; but it didn't faze Aaron none—he stood his ground.

"I'm gonna give you a chance, preacher. Git on over to the nigger side and git quick."

"I ain't bothering nobody, Mr. Sampson."

Somebody in the crowd yelled: "Don't reason wit' the nigger, Bull. Hit 'im."

Mr. Sampson walked up to Aaron and grabbed him in the collar and throwed him up against the ticket counter. He pulled out his gun.

"Did you hear me, deacon. I said, 'Git.' "

"I'm going to St. Louis, Mr. Sampson. That's cross state lines. The court done said—"

Aaron didn't have a chance. The blow came from no-where. Laying there on the floor with blood spurting from his mouth, Aaron looked up at Mr. Sampson, and he did another crazy thing: He grinned. Bull Sampson jumped up in the air and came down on Aaron with all his two hundred pounds. It made a crunchy sound. He jumped again, and the mob, maddened by the blood and heat, moved in to help him. They fell on Aaron like mad dogs. They beat him with chairs; they beat him with sticks; they beat him with guns.

Till this day, I don't know what come over me. The first thing I know I was running, and then I was standing in the middle of the white waiting room. Mr. Sampson was the first to see me. He backed off, cocked his pistol, and said: "Booker, boy, you come one mo´ step and I'll kill you. What's a matter with you niggers today? All y'all gone crazy?"

"Please don't kill him," I begged. "You ain't got no call to treat him like that."

"So you saw it all, did you? Well, then, Booker you musta saw the nigger preacher reach for my gun?"

"He didn't do that, Mr. Sampson," I said. "He didn't—"

Mr. Sampson put a big hairy hand on my tie and pulled me to him.

"Booker," he said sweetly. "You saw the nigger preacher reach for my gun, didn't you?"

I didn't open my mouth—I couldn't I was so scared—but I guess my eyes answered for me. Whatever Mr. Sampson saw there musta convinced him 'cause he throwed me on the floor beside Aaron.

"Git this nigger out of here," he said, "and be quick about it."

Dropping to my knees, I put my hand on Aaron's chest; I didn't feel nothing. I felt his wrist; I didn't feel nothing. I got up and looked at them white folks with tears in my eyes. I looked at the women sitting crying on the benches. I looked at the men. I looked at Mr. Sampson. I said, "He was a good man."

Mr. Sampson said, "Move the nigger."

A big sigh came out of me, and I wrung my hands.

Mr. Sampson said, "Move the nigger."

He grabbed my tie and twisted it, but I didn't feel nothing. My eyes were glued to his hands; there was blood under the fingernails, and the fingers—they looked like fat little red sausages. I screamed and Mr. Sampson flung me down on the floor.

He said, *"Move the nigger."*

I picked Aaron up and fixed his body over my shoulder and carried him outside. I sent for one of my boys, and we dressed him up and put him away real nice-like, and Rachel and the boy came and they cried and carried on, and yet somehow they seemed prouder of Aaron than ever before. And the colored folks—they seemed proud, too. Crazy people. Didn't they know? Couldn't they see? It hadn't done no good. In fact, things got worse. The Northern newspapers started kicking up a stink, and Mr. Rivers, the solicitor, announced they were going to hold a hearing. All of a sudden, Booker Taliaferro Brown became the biggest man in that town. My phone rang day and night: I got threats, I got promises, and I was offered bribes.

Everywhere I turned somebody was waiting to ask me: "Whatcha gonna do? Whatcha gonna say?" To tell the truth, I didn't know myself. One day I would decide one thing, and the next day I would decide another.

It was Mr. Rivers and Mr. Sampson who called my attention to that. They came to my office one day and called me a shifty, no-good nigger. They said they expected me to stand by "my statement" in the train station that I saw Aaron reach for the gun. I hadn't said no such thing, but Mr. Sampson said I said it, and he said he had witnesses who heard me say it. "And if you say anything else," he said, "I can't be responsible for your health. Now you know"—he put that bloody hand on my shoulder and he smiled his sweet death smile—"you *know* I wouldn't threaten you, but the boys"—he shook his head—"the boys are real worked up over this one."

It was long about then that I began to hate Aaron Lott. I'm ashamed to admit it now, but it's true: I hated him. He had lived his life; he had made his choice. Why should he live my life, too, and make me choose? It wasn't fair; it wasn't right; it wasn't Christian. What made me so mad was the fact that nothing I said would help Aaron. He was dead, and it wouldn't help one whit for me to say that he didn't reach for that gun. I tried to explain that to Rachel when she came to my office, moaning and crying, the night before the hearing.

"Listen to me, woman," I said. "Listen. Aaron was a good man. He lived a good life. He did a lot of good things, but he's *dead, dead, dead!* Nothing I say will bring him back. Bull Sampson's got ten niggers who are going to swear on a stack of Bibles that they saw Aaron reach for that gun. It won't do me or you or Aaron no good for me to swear otherwise."

What did I say that for? That woman liked to had a fit. She got down on her knees, and she begged me to go with Aaron.

"Go wit' him," she cried. "Booker. *Booker!* If you's a man, if you's a father, if you's a friend, go wit' Aaron."

That woman tore my heart up. I ain't never heard nobody beg like that.

"Tell the truth, Booker," she said. "That's all I'm asking. Tell the truth."

"Truth!" I said. "Hah! That's all you people talk about: truth. What do you know about truth? Truth is eating good and sleeping good. Truth is living, Rachel. Be loyal to the living."

Rachel backed off from me. You would have thought that I had cursed her or something. She didn't say nothing; she just stood there pressed against the door. She stood there saying nothing for so long that my nerves snapped.

"Say something," I shouted. "Say something—anything!"

She shook her head, slowly at first, and then her head started moving like it wasn't attached to her body. It went back and forth, back and forth, back and forth. I started toward her, but she jerked open the door and ran out into the night screaming.

That did it. I ran across the room to the filing cabinet, opened the bottom drawer, and took out a dusty bottle of Scotch. I started drinking, but the more I drank, the soberer I got. I guess I fell asleep 'cause I dreamed I buried Rachel and that everything went along fine until she jumped out of the casket and started screaming. I came awake with a start and knocked over the bottle. I reached for a rag and my hand stopped in mid-air.

"Of course," I said out loud and slammed my fist down on the Scotch-soaked papers.

I didn't see nothing.

Why didn't I think of it before?

I didn't see nothing.

Jumping up, I walked to and fro in the office. Would it work? I rehearsed it in my mind. All I could see was Aaron's back. I don't know whether he reached for the gun or not. All I know is that *for some reason* the men beat him to death.

Rehearsing the thing in my mind, I felt a great weight slip off my shoulders. I did a little jig in the middle of the floor and went upstairs to my bed, whistling. Sarah turned over and looked me up and down.

"What you happy about?"

"Can't a man be happy?" I asked.

She sniffed the air, said, "Oh," turned over, and mumbled something in her pillow. It came to me then for the first time that she was 'bout the only person in town who hadn't asked me what I was going to do. I thought about it for a little while, shrugged, and fell into bed with all my clothes on.

When I woke up the next morning, I had a terrible headache, and my tongue was a piece of sandpaper. For a long while I couldn't figure out what I was doing laying there with all my clothes on. Then it came to me: this was the big day. I put on my black silk suit, the one I wore for big funerals, and went downstairs to breakfast. I walked into the dining room without looking and bumped into Russell, the last person in the world I wanted to see. He was my only child, but he didn't act like it. He was always finding fault. He didn't like the way I talked to Negroes; he didn't like the way I talked to white folks. He didn't like this; he didn't like that. And to top it off, the young whippersnapper wanted to be an artist. Undertaking wasn't good enough for him. He wanted to paint pictures.

I sat down and grunted.

"Good morning, Papa." He said it like he meant it. He wants something, I thought, looking him over closely, noticing that his right eye was swollen.

"You been fighting again, boy?"

"Yes, Papa."

"You younguns. Education—that's what it is. Education! It's ruining you."

He didn't say nothing. He just sat there, looking down when I looked up and looking up when I looked down. This went on through the grits and the eggs and the second cup of coffee.

"Whatcha looking at?" I asked.

"Nothing, Papa."

"Whatcha thinking?"

"Nothing, Papa."

"You lying, boy. It's written all over your face."

He didn't say nothing.

I dismissed him with a wave of my hand, picked up the paper, and turned to the sports page.

"What are you going to do, Papa?"

The question caught me unawares. I know now that I was expecting it, that I wanted him to ask it; but he put it so bluntly that I was flabbergasted. I pretended I didn't understand.

"Do 'bout what, boy? Speak up!"

"About the trial, Papa."

I didn't say nothing for a long time. There wasn't much, in fact, I could say; so I got mad.

"Questions, questions, questions," I shouted. "That's all I get in this house—questions. You never have a civil word for your pa. I go out of here and work my tail off, and you keep yourself shut up in that room of yours looking at them fool books, and now soon as your old man gets his back against the wall, you join the pack. I expected better than that of you, boy. A son ought to back his pa."

That hurt him. He picked up the coffeepot and poured himself another cup of coffee, and his hand trembled. He took a sip and watched me over the rim.

"They say you are going to chicken out, Papa."

"Chicken out? What that mean?"

"They're betting you'll 'Tom.' "

I leaned back in the chair and took a sip of coffee.

"So they're betting, huh?" The idea appealed to me. "Crazy people—they'd bet on a funeral."

I saw pain on his face. He sighed and said: "I bet, too, Papa."

The cup fell out of my hand and broke, spilling black water over the tablecloth.

"You did what?"

"I bet you wouldn't 'Tom.' "

"You little fool." I fell out laughing, and then I stopped suddenly and looked at him closely. "How much you bet?"

"One hundred dollars."

I stood up.

"You're lying," I said. "Where'd you get that kind of money?"

"From Mamma."

"Sarah!" I shouted. "Sarah! You get in here. What kind of house you running, sneaking behind my back, giving this boy money to gamble with?"

Sarah leaned against the doorjamb. She was in her hot iron mood. There was no expression on her face. And her eyes were hard.

"I gave it to him, Booker," she said. "They called you an Uncle Tom. He got in a fight about it. He wanted to bet on you, Booker. *He* believes in you."

Suddenly I felt old and used up. I pulled a chair to me and sat down.

"Please," I said, waving my hand. "Please. Go away. Leave me alone. Please."

I sat there for maybe ten or fifteen minutes, thinking, praying. The phone rang. It was Mr. Withers, the president of the bank. I had put in for a loan, and it had been turned down, but Mr. Withers said there'd been a mistake. "New fellow, you know," he said, clucking his tongue. He said he knew that it was my lifelong dream to build a modern funeral home and to buy a Cadillac hearse. He said he sympathized with that dream, supported it, thought the town needed it, and thought I deserved it. "The loan will go through," he said. "Drop by and see me this morning after the hearing."

When I put that phone down, it was wet with sweat. I couldn't turn that new funeral home down, and Mr. Withers knew it. My father had raised me on that dream, and before he died, he made me swear on a Bible that I would make it good. And here it was on a platter, just for a word, a word that wouldn't hurt nobody.

I put on my hat and hurried to the courthouse. When they called my name, I walked in with my head held high. The courtroom was packed. The white folks had all the seats, and the colored folks were standing in the rear. Whoever arranged the seating had set aside the first two rows for white men. They were sitting almost on top of each other, looking mean and uncomfortable in their best white shirts.

I walked up to the bench and swore on the Bible and took a seat. Mr. Rivers gave me a little smile and waited for me to get myself set.

"State your name," he said.

"Booker Taliaferro Brown." I took a quick look at the first two rows and recognized at least ten of the men who killed Aaron.

"And your age?"

"Fifty-seven."

"You're an undertaker?"

"Yessir."

"You been living in this town all your life?"

"Yessir."

"You like it here, don't you, Booker?"

Was this a threat? I looked Mr. Rivers in the face for the first time. He smiled.

I told the truth. I said, "Yessir."

"Now, calling your attention to the day of May 17th, did anything unusual happen on that day?"

The question threw me. I shook my head. Then it dawned on me. He was talking about—

"Yessir," I said. "That's the day Aaron got—" Something in Mr. Rivers' face warned me, and I pulled up— "that's the day of the trouble at the train station."

Mr. Rivers smiled. He looked like a trainer who'd just put a monkey through a new trick. You could feel the confidence and the contempt oozing out of him. I looked at his prissy little mustache and his smiling lips, and I got mad. Lifting my head a little bit, I looked him full in the eyes; I held the eyes for a moment, and I tried to tell the man behind the eyes that I was a man like him and that he didn't have no right to be using me and laughing about it.

But he didn't get the message. The bastard—he chuckled softly, turned his back to me, and faced the audience.

"I believe you were with the preacher that day."

The water was getting deep. I scroonched down in my seat, closed the lids of my eyes, and looked dense.

"Yessir, Mr. Rivers," I drawled. "Ah was."

"Now, Booker—" he turned around— "I believe you tried to keep the nigger preacher from getting out of line."

I hesitated. It wasn't a fair question. Finally, I said: "Yessir."

"You begged him not to go in the white side?"

"Yessir."

"And when that failed, you went over to *your* side—the *colored* side—and looked through the window?"

"Yessir."

He put his hand in his coat pocket and studied my face.

"You saw *everything,* didn't you?"

"Just about." A muscle on the inside of my thigh started tingling.

Mr. Rivers shuffled some papers he had in his hand. He seemed to be thinking real hard. I pushed myself against the back of the chair. Mr. Rivers moved close, quick, and stabbed his finger into my chest.

"Booker, did you see the nigger preacher reach for Mr. Sampson's gun?"

He backed away, smiling. I looked away from him, and I felt my heart trying to tear out of my skin. I looked out over the courtroom. It was still; wasn't even a fly moving. I looked at the white folks in front and the colored folks in back, and I turned the question over in my mind. While I was doing that, waiting, taking my time, I noticed, out of the corner of my eye, that the smile on Mr. Rivers' face was dying away. Suddenly, I had a terrible itch to know what that smile would turn into.

I said, "Nosir."

Mr. Rivers stumbled backwards like he had been shot. Old Judge Sloan took off his glasses and pushed his head out over the bench. The whole courtroom seemed to be leaning in to me, and I saw Aaron's widow leaning back with her eyes closed, and it seemed to me at that distance that her lips were moving in prayer.

Mr. Rivers was the first to recover. He put his smile back on, and he acted like my answer was in the script.

"You mean," he said, "that you didn't see it. It happened so quickly that you missed it?"

I looked at the bait, and I ain't gonna lie: I was tempted. He knew as well as I did what I meant, but he was gambling on my weakness. I had thrown away my funeral home, my hearse, everything I owned, and he was standing there like a magician, pulling them out of a hat, one at a time, dangling them, saying: "Looka here, looka here, don't they look pretty?" I was on top of a house, and he was betting that if he gave me a ladder I would come down. He was wrong, but you can't fault him for trying. He hadn't never met no black man who would go all the way. I looked him in the eye and went the last mile.

"Aaron didn't reach for that gun," I said. "Them people, they just fell on——"

"Hold it," he shouted. "I want to remind you that there are laws in this state against perjury. You can go to jail for five years for what you just said. Now I know you've been conferring with those NAACP fellows, but I want to remind you of the statements you made to Sheriff Sampson and me. Judge——" he dismissed me with a wave of his hand—— "Judge, this *man*——" he caught himself and it was my turn to smile—— "this *boy* is lying. Ten niggers have testified that they saw the preacher reach for the gun. Twenty white people saw it. You've heard their testimony. I want to withdraw this witness, and I want to reserve the right to file perjury charges against him."

Judge Sloan nodded. He pushed his bottom lip over his top one.

"You can step down," he said. "I want to warn you that perjury is a very grave offense. You——"

"Judge, I didn't——"

"Nigger!" He banged his gavel. "Don't you interrupt me. Now git out of here."

Two guards pushed me outside and waved away the reporters. Billy Giles, Mr. Sampson's assistant, came out and told me Mr. Sampson wanted me out of town before sundown. "And he says you'd better get out before the Northern reporters leave. He won't be responsible for your safety after that."

I nodded and went on down the stairs and started out the door.

"Booker!"

Rachel and a whole line of Negroes were running down the stairs. I stepped outside and waited for them. Rachel ran up and throwed her arms around me. "It don't take but one, Booker," she said. "It don't take but one." Somebody else said: "They whitewashed it, they whitewashed it, but you spoiled it for 'em."

Russell came out then and stood over to the side while the others crowded around to shake my hands. Then the others sensed that he was waiting, and they made a little aisle. He walked up to me kind of slow-like and he said, "Thank you, sir." That was the first time in his whole seventeen years that that boy had said "sir" to me. I cleared my throat, and when I opened my eyes, Sarah was standing beside me. She didn't say nothing; she just put her hand in mine and stood there. It was long about then, I guess, when I realized that I wasn't seeing so good. They say I cried, but I don't believe a word of it. It was such a hot day and the sun was shining so bright that the sweat rolling down my face blinded me. I wiped the sweat out of my eyes, and some more people came up and said a lot of foolish things about me showing the white folks and following in Aaron's footsteps. I wasn't doing no such fool thing. Ol' Man Rivers just put the thing to me in a way it hadn't been put before—man to man. It was simple, really. Any man would have done it.

Not Your Singing, Dancing Spade

Julia Fields

Julia Fields was born in Alabama. She graduated from Knoxville College, studied toward the M.A. in English at the Bread Loaf School, and has studied for a summer at the University of Edinburgh. Miss Fields was writer-in-residence at Miles College in 1968 and at Hampton Institute in 1970. She is listed in Outstanding Young Women of America and in the Negro Almanac. Among her honors are also a Woodrow Wilson Fellowship and two grants from the National Endowment for the Arts and Humanities.

It was ridiculous to have an issue of such an insipidly written magazine in the apartment, he knew. Nevertheless, he picked it up again and began to read the article written about himself. The audacity of it, and the incredible and insane arrogance it suggested, made him feel helpless against the terrible tide of consciousness so established and so knowledgeable to him and to his people. His brains were sealed, signed for, and delivered like his body would have been in the previous century.

He focused his eyes and finished the article, his black hands and black eyes drooping wearily over the side of the plush gold sofa. Then he lay down upon it, keeping his shoes on. It was not very comforting at all.

The article stated clearly that his childhood dream had been to pursue and to possess a "blonde goddess," that he could never be happy without her. It made fun of a black entertainer he had dated. It said he paid her to give him his "freedom." There was no picture of her. But there was a listing and pictures of national and international ladies with fair hair to whom he had been linked romantically at one time or another.

There was a picture of him with his wife—his wife bright and grinning, and his teeth matching her fairness kilometer

167

for kilometer. His hair was falling into his eyes. It always
seemed to be falling into his eyes whenever he was playing
golf, or driving, or dancing, or singing. And he always had
to toss his head, give his neck a quick snappy jerk in order
to keep his tumbling hair neat. It always got into his eyes.
He bent over to light a cigarette. The hair fell into his eyes.
He used his free hand to brush it back, knowing that it
would tumble into his eyes again.

His wife entered the room. She was very, very white. He
had asked her to stay out of the sun. And the black maid
entered with a tray of beverages. The children liked the
maid, and his wife liked the maid. He hated her. She was
almost as black as himself, and her hair was short. He always felt like singing an old down-home blues whenever
he saw her . . . "I don't want no woman if her hair ain't no
longer'n mine; she ain't nothing but trouble and keep you
worried all the time." But no matter how much hatred he
showed toward her, the woman was always kind and
serene; yet, there was the very faintest hint of laughter and
incredible mockery in her eyes when she looked at him.
He knew the look. He himself had given it to others many
times. He remembered the party in Greenwich Village, the
interracial party with all the loud music and the loud dancing which belonged to a younger time than now.

There was a colored girl there, he was told, but all the
girls looked of the same race because there was not the
brightest lighting. Still he thought that he would know a
"Sapphire" if he saw one. The girl's white date had laughed
at him for saying this and slapped him on the back. He
had felt so clever, so able to take "it," so "free," so optimistic, so "in," and that was when he knew that he could
make it if he chose to make it in the big world of the
American dream. And this world, as he knew it, was not
white. It was a gray world with room in it for all the people.
He felt so "in" that he almost blessed Emma Lazarus.

A group of them were laughingly trying to sing a foolish
ditty with dirty words. They were all so happy and drunk.
And there was a girl whose hands kept going to her temple
and down behind her ears with long locks of hair which
she pushed over her shoulder. Then she would toss her hair,
or attempt to, but the long hair barely moved. The long
strands did not move freely. They seemed waxen, stuck
around her face like fetters. His hands went to his own
head in sudden derision and stuck in the Dixie Peach. The
girl swung her head again and caught his eyes. He looked

into her eyes as deeply as he could, and his bitterness spilled like a white sizzle across to her in mockery and despair and a tender, compassionate hatred.

The boy who had slapped him on the back moved toward the girl, caught her by the hand, and began to dance with her, his hips swaying brutally ungraceful in mock-Negro.

He went to the window. Dawn was moving up to the river and over the roofs. It was time for him to go. He knew that he would never go to another party with a Negro. No matter what color the Negro was—they were all embarrassing. He might go if he were the only one. Only if he were.

He knew that his wife somehow resulted from this promise which he had made to himself a long time ago at the Village party. He had come a long way. His name, his picture, his life, were on the lips and the life-sized posters of the world. Subway bums, whores, and dogs could lean against his photograph in most of the world's swinging cities. And he was very wealthy. He had his own entourage of jesters and the best hairdresser in the world—one who kept him well stocked with the best pomade.

The article in the magazine shouldn't have bothered him so much, he told himself. It wasn't the first time, nor would it be the last. He had to pay the price. They were requiring it of him, and he had to make it. He had to keep making it. It was too late to stop. Where would he go? There was no place elsewhere but down. Down to scorn. Back, slowly but certainly, to a world which had become alien, black, strange, and nameless. The wolves would chew him black.

Back to black indeed. Never. What did it matter? The whites had begun their assaults late; the blacks had berated him all his life. "Black bastard. Black bastard. Bad hair." "Boy, get a brush." And comparisons: "Almost Bunky's color." "No, not quite as black as Bunky." "Child, I couldn't see nuthin' but eyes and teeth." "I like him, sure, but my daddy would kill me if I married a man that black." "Child, I wouldn't want to mess up my children with that color." He was recalling the words of parents, relatives, and lovers. His yellow mother. His jet-black father who was his mother's footstool. His mother's freckles. Her rituals with Black and White ointment. Her "straight" nose. He hated his flat nose. All of his pictures were in profile. Except the one in the magazine. In that one, all of his black faults were on view. In that picture, the heat had turned the expensive pomade on his hair to plain and simple shining grease. Ah, chicken-eaters of the world unite. You have nothing to lose except your shame.

He began to dress, immaculately as always, for there was, his agent had said, a chance to make another million. Melanin and millions. Millions and melanin.

Numbly, he moved about the dressing room. Larger than his parents' living room had been.

Mutely, he dressed. Dejectedly, he faced himself in the mirror. Silently, the green gall of self-revulsion passed through his psyche and soul. Swiftly, he recalled the chance to make a million and the wife who would spend it on furs, jewels, fun, cosmetics, and servants. And the whole world would see what black bastards with millions and melanin could do. Yes, they would.

The agent's smooth voice, on the phone, reassured him about the million. There was nothing to reassure him about himself. Nothing. Nothing.

Down the stairs, voices were shrill suddenly. His little girl was sobbing. He heard the maid say, "Be quiet. You'll wake up your mama."

"But Cathy said my daddy's a nigger monkey."

"What do you care what Cathy says?"

"And Daddy puts gasoline in his hair to make it nice like her daddy's hair. Isn't Daddy's hair nice?"

"Of course it's nice. That little sickly Cathy with those strings hanging 'round her face. Don't pay her no attention. She's just jealous because your daddy's got the original beauty."

"The what?"

"The first, best beauty in the world. Black. Your daddy's a pretty man. That's why everybody likes him. Where've you seen Cathy's daddy's pictures? Not nearly's many places as your daddy. Your daddy is a beautiful man."

"Is he?"

"Yes. Of course he don't know how pretty he is. Anyhow, it's easy to be pale. Like milk. It ain't got nothing in it. Like vanilla ice cream. See? Now take any other flavor. Take chocolate. Milk with cocoa. You love chocolate malt, don't you?"

"Yes."

"Take strawberry. Any ice cream. It's nothing as just plain milk. What goes in makes it beautiful. It can be decorated, but by itself, it lacks a lot. Your daddy was born decorated. Born a pretty king. Born beautiful. Don't believe Cathy. She's dumb."

"Born beautiful. Daddy was born beautiful. That silly

Cathy. She's a dumb one. My daddy is pretty. I always thought so."

"Yes, I always thought so, too."

Numbly, he stood there. He had to listen. The annihilated searching, seeking to be. Terror. Who had first given assumption and such supreme arrogance to the captives? He knew she had read the article which had denied her existence. A black female. The race and sex which, according to them, could never move him to love, to cherish, to desire. *Caldonia, Caldonia, what makes your big head so hard?*

He remembered his boyhood. And all the lyrics which laughed at and lamented black womanhood. Blackness. Black manhood. Black childhood. Black.

They had made the world for him, had set all the traps. He had been born to it. The horror of blackness. They had outdone themselves. They had outdone him. And it was not meant that he should ever be saved. He must believe. And they could assume postures and lies. And they could believe in his self-hatred. And they could rest comfortably believing that he believed and continue their believing.

They were so arrogant, so stupefied by history and circumstances that they could accept any incredible thing they said about him. Terror. Who was the bondsman? Who was the freed man? He knew.

Life began to flow again. His blood sang vital and red. Freedom. Power, even. Yes I *am* beautiful. Born black. Born with no lack. Decorated. Born decorated.

At the foot of the stairs, he could hear the maid again, angrily muttering. With dancer's feet, he moved nearer. Nearer to hear, nearer to self, to recovery.

"Lies, lies, lies. Sometimes we have to lie to make it. Even to live. We got to lie to ourselves, to our friends, and to our enemies. To those we love and to those we hates. If they so smart they ain't got to b'leve us."

He saw her throw the movie magazine clear down his long, sumptuous living room. And he heard his little daughter laughing as she went to get the magazine.

"Here. Put it in the trash can."

"But it's got Daddy's picture. Daddy's picture's in it."

"Your daddy's picture's everywhere. Besides, that's not a good picture of him. Some fool took it. Here." The child obeyed.

"Arrogant, uppity folks'll believe anything. Let 'em pay. And pay. White bastards."

"What? What?" The child questioned.

"Nothing. Go on to the playroom until I call you for lunch. I got to vacuum up this room."

Then he was there standing in the beautiful, luxurious room facing the black woman with the short hair.

"Humph," he heard her say as she turned to push a low, red, incredulously plush and ridiculously expensive chair aside for her vacuuming.

"Here, let me be of service," he said.

"Never mind."

"Let me!" he said again, and gently pushed her aside.

"Humph," she said again. But he got a glimpse of her face, which had years of anger and defiance and hope written in chicken-scratch wrinkles and crows' feet. And there was the mockery he always saw there. And yet, a kindness, a laughter which was very sweet and strong And the barest hint of tears in the eyes, tears like monuments to despair.

When he replaced the chairs and kissed his wife and child, he said his good-bye to the black woman and sang a snatch of his latest recording as he walked to the elevator. He felt light—weightless and yet strong and pretty. "I feel pretty," he thought. Well, not that kind of pretty, he mocked himself. But it was surprising that he sang, for he had promised himself that he was only an entertainer, that he wasn't your singing, dancing spade, that he, a professional only, wouldn't be caught dead, drunk, or straitlaced singing off the stage or away from the T.V. cameras, or dancing like some ham-hocking gig-a-boo.

Nevertheless, his chauffeur smiled happily when he cut a step from his latest musical sensation as he entered the limousine with the sacrilegious words, "I feel pretty," floating, cake-walking from his lips.

A Happening in Barbados

Louise M. Meriwether

*Louise M. Meriwether is a graduate of the University
of California in Los Angeles. She is currently writing
a series of Black historical sketches for the kindergarten set. The Freedom Ship of Robert Smalls, to be
published by Prentice-Hall, relates to hijacking of a
Confederate gunboat by eight slaves during the Civil
War. Following will be a capsule of the life of Dr.
Daniel Hale Williams, who performed the world's
first successful heart surgery in 1893. She is a member of the Harlem Writers Guild. Short stories and
articles have appeared in the Antioch Review,
Ebony, Essence, Black World, Frontier, etc. She is
the author of the best-selling novel, Daddy Was a
Number Runner.*

The best way to pick up a Barbadian man, I hoped, was
to walk alone down the beach with my tall, brown frame
squeezed into a skin-tight bathing suit. Since my hotel was
near the beach and Dorothy and Alison, my two traveling
companions, had gone shopping, I managed this quite well.
I had not taken more than a few steps on the glittering,
white sand before two black men were on either side of me
vying for attention.

I chose the tall, slim-hipped one over the squat, muscle-
bound man who was also grinning at me. But apparently
they were friends because Edwin had no sooner settled me
under his umbrella than the squat one showed up with a
beach chair and two other boys in tow.

Edwin made the introductions. His temporary rival was
Gregory, and the other two were Alphonse and Dimitri.

Gregory was ugly. He had thick, rubbery lips, a scarcity
of teeth, and a broad nose splattered like a pyramid across
his face. He was all massive shoulders and bulging biceps.
No doubt he had a certain animal magnetism, but person-

173

ally I preferred a lean man like Edwin, who was well built but slender, his whole body fitting together like a symphony. Alphonse and Dimitri were clean-cut and pleasant looking

They were all too young—twenty to twenty-five at the most—and Gregory seemed the oldest. I inwardly mourned their youth and settled down to make the most of my catch.

The crystal blue sky rivaled the royal blue of the Caribbean for beauty, and our black bodies on the white sand added to the munificence of colors. We ran into the sea like squealing children when the sudden raindrops came, then shivered on the sand under a makeshift tent of umbrellas and damp towels waiting for the sun to reappear while nourishing ourselves with straight Barbados rum.

As with most of the West Indians I had already met on my whirlwind tour of Trinidad and Jamaica who welcomed American Negroes with open arms, my new friends loved their island home, but work was scarce and they yearned to go to America. They were hungry for news of how Negroes were faring in the States.

Edwin's arm rested casually on my knee in a proprietary manner, and I smiled at him. His thin, serious face was smooth, too young for a razor, and when he smiled back, he looked even younger. He told me he was a waiter at the Hilton, saving his money to make it to the States. I had already learned not to be snobbish with the island's help. Yesterday's waiter may be tomorrow's prime minister.

Dimitri, very black with an infectious grin, was also a waiter, and lanky Alphonse was a tile setter.

Gregory's occupation was apparently women, for that's all he talked about. He was able to launch this subject when a bony, white woman—more peeling red than white, really—looking like a gaunt cadaver in a loose-fitting bathing suit, came out of the sea and walked up to us. She smiled archly at Gregory.

"Are you going to take me to the Pigeon Club tonight, Sugar?"

"No, mon," he said pleasantly, with a toothless grin. "I'm taking a younger pigeon."

The woman turned a deeper red, if that were possible, and, mumbling something incoherent, walked away.

"That one is always after me to take her some place," Gregory said. "She's rich, and she pays the bills but, mon, I don't want an old hag nobody else wants. I like to take my women away from white men and watch them squirm."

"Come down, mon," Dimitri said, grinning. "She look like she's starving for what you got to spare."

We all laughed. The boys exchanged stories about their experiences with predatory white women who came to the islands looking for some black action. But, one and all, they declared they liked dark-skinned meat the best, and I felt like a black queen of the Nile when Gregory winked at me and said "The blacker the berry, mon, the sweeter the juice."

They had all been pursued and had chased some white tail, too, no doubt, but while the others took it all in good humor, it soon became apparent that Gregory's exploits were exercises in vengeance.

Gregory was saying "I told that bastard, 'You in my country now, mon, and I'll kick your ass all the way back to Texas The girl agreed to dance with me, and she don't need your permission.' That white man's face turned purple, but he sat back down, and I danced with his girl. Mon, they hate to see me rubbing bellies with their women 'cause they know once she rub bellies with me she wanna rub something else, too."

He laughed, and we all joined in. Serves the white men right, I thought. Let's see how they liked licking *that* end of the stick for a change.

"Mon, you gonna get killed yet," Edwin said, moving closer to me on the towel we shared. "You're crazy. You don't care whose woman you mess with. But it's not gonna be a white man who kills you but some bad Bajian."

Gregory led in the laughter, then held us spellbound for the next hour with intimate details of his affair with Glenda, a young white girl spending the summer with her father on their yacht Whatever he had, Glenda wanted it desperately, or so Gregory told it.

Yeah, I thought to myself, like LSD, a black lover is the thing this year I had seen the white girls in the Village and at off-Broadway theatres clutching their black men tightly while I, manless, looked on with bitterness. I often vowed I would find me an ofay in self-defense, but I could never bring myself to condone the wholesale rape of my slave ancestors by letting a white man touch me.

We finished the rum, and the three boys stood up to leave, making arrangements to get together later with us and my two girl friends and go clubbing.

Edwin and I were left alone. He stretched out his smoothly muscled leg and touched my toes with his. I smiled at him and let our thighs come together. Why did he have to be so damned young? Then our lips met, his warm and demanding, and I thought, what the hell, maybe I will.

I was thirty-nine—goodbye, sweet bird of youth—an ungay divorcee, up tight and drinking too much, trying to disown the years which had brought only loneliness and pain. I had clawed my way up from the slums of Harlem via night school and was now a law clerk on Wall Street. But the fight upward had taken its toll. My husband, who couldn't claw as well as I, got lost somewhere in that concrete jungle. The last I saw of him he was peering under every skirt around, searching for his lost manhood.

I had always felt contempt for women who found their kicks by robbing the cradle. Now here I was on a Barbados beach with an amorous child young enough to be my son. Two sayings flitted unbidden across my mind "Judge not that ye be not judged," and "The thing which I feared is come upon me." I thought, ain't it the goddamned truth?

Edwin kissed me again, pressing the length of his body against mine.

"I've got to go," I gasped. "My friends have probably returned and are looking for me. About ten, tonight?"

He nodded. I smiled at him and ran all the way to my hotel.

At exactly ten o'clock the telephone in our room announced we had company downstairs.

"Hot damn," Alison said, putting on her eyebrows in front of the mirror "We're not going to be stood up."

"Island men," I said loftily, "are dependable, not like the bums you're used to in America "

Alison, freckled and willowy, had been married three times and was looking for her fourth. Her motto was, if at first you don't succeed, find another mother. She was a real estate broker in Los Angeles, and we had been childhood friends in Harlem.

"What I can't stand," Dorothy said from the bathroom, "are those creeps who come to *your* apartment, drink up *your* liquor, then dirty up *your* sheets. You don't even get a lousy dinner out of the deal "

She came out of the bathroom in her slip. Petite and delicate with a pixie grin, at thirty-five Dorothy looked more like one of the high school girls she taught than their teacher. She had never been married. Years ago, while she was holding onto her virginity with a miser's grip, her fiancé had messed up and knocked up one of her friends.

Since then, all of Dorothy's affairs had been with married men, displaying perhaps a subconscious vendetta against all wives.

By ten-twenty we were downstairs and I was introducing the girls to our four escorts who eyed us with unconcealed admiration. We were looking good in our Saks Fifth Avenue finery. They were looking good, too, in soft shirts and loose slacks, all except Gregory, whose bulging muscles confined in clothing made him seem more gargantuan.

We took a cab and a few minutes later were squeezing behind a table in a small, smoky room called the Pigeon Club. A Trinidad steel band was blasting out the walls, and the tiny dance area was jammed with wiggling bottoms and shuffling feet. The white tourists, trying to do the hip-shaking calypso, were having a ball and looking awkward.

I got up to dance with Edwin. He had a natural grace and was easy to follow. Our bodies found the rhythm and became one with it while our eyes locked in silent, ancient combat, his pleading, mine teasing.

We returned to our seats and to tall glasses of rum and cola tonic. The party had begun.

I danced every dance with Edwin, his clasp becoming gradually tighter until my face was smothered in his shoulder, my arms locked around his neck. He was adorable. Very good for my ego. The other boys took turns dancing with my friends, but soon preferences were set—Alison with Alphonse and Dorothy with Dimitri. With good humor Gregory ordered another round and didn't seem to mind being odd man out, but he wasn't alone for long.

During the floor show featuring the inevitable limbo dancers, a pretty white girl, about twenty-two, with straight, red hair hanging down to her shoulder, appeared at Gregory's elbow. From his wink at me and self-satisfied grin, I knew this was Glenda from the yacht.

"Hello," she said to Gregory. "Can I join you, or do you have a date?"

Well, I thought, that's the direct approach.

"What are you doing here?" Gregory asked.

"Looking for you."

Gregory slid over on the bench next to the wall, and Glenda sat down as he introduced her to the rest of us. Somehow her presence spoiled my mood. We had been happy being black, and I resented this intrusion from the white world. But Glenda was happy. She had found the man she set out to find and a swinging party to boot. She beamed a dazzling smile around the table.

Alphonse led Alison onto the dance floor, and Edwin and I followed. The steel band was playing a wild calypso, and I could feel my hair rising with the heat as I joined in the wildness.

When we returned to the table, Glenda applauded us, then turned to Gregory. "Why don't you teach me to dance like that?"

He answered with his toothless grin and a leer, implying he had better things to teach her.

White women were always snatching our men, I thought, and now they want to dance like us.

I turned my attention back to Edwin and met his full stare.

"I want you," he said, his tone as solemn as if he were in church.

I teased him with a smile, refusing to commit myself. He had a lusty, healthy appetite, which was natural, I supposed, for a twenty-one-year-old lad. Lord, but why did he have to be *that* young? I stood up to go to the ladies' room.

"Wait for me," Glenda cried, trailing behind me.

The single toilet stall was occupied, and Glenda leaned against the wall waiting for it while I flipped open my compact and powdered my grimy face.

"You married?" she asked.

"Divorced."

"When I get married, I want to stay hooked forever."

"That's the way I planned it, too," I said drily.

"What I mean," she rushed on, "is that I've gotta find a cat who wants to groove only with me."

Oh Lord, I thought, don't try to sound like us, too. Use your own sterile language.

"I really dug this guy I was engaged to," Glenda continued, "but he couldn't function without a harem. I could have stood that maybe, but when he didn't mind if I made it with some other guy, too, I knew I didn't want that kind of life."

I looked at her in the mirror as I applied my lipstick. She had been hurt, and badly. Shook right down to her naked soul. So she was dropping down a social notch, according to her scale of values, and trying to repair her damaged ego with a black brother.

"You gonna make it with Edwin?" she asked, as if we were college chums comparing dates.

"I'm not a one-night stand." My tone was frigid. That's another thing I can't stand about white people. Too familiar, just because we're colored.

"I dig Gregory," she said, pushing her hair out of her eyes. "He's kind of rough, but who wouldn't be, the kind of life he's led."

"And what kind of life is that?" I asked.

"Didn't you know? His mother was a whore in an exclusive brothel for white men only. That was before, when the British owned the island."

"I take it you like rough men?" I asked.

"There's usually something gentle and lost underneath," she replied.

A white woman came out of the toilet, and Glenda went in. Jesus, I thought. Gregory, gentle? The woman walked to the basin, flung some water in the general direction of her hands, and left.

"Poor Daddy is having a fit," Glenda volunteered from the john, "but there's not much he can do about it. He's afraid I'll leave him again, and he gets lonely without me, so he just tags along and tries to keep me out of trouble."

"And pays the bills?"

She answered with a laugh. "Why not? He's loaded."

Why not, I thought with bitterness. You white women have always managed to have your cake and eat it, too. The toilet flushed with a roar like Niagara Falls. I opened the door and went back to our table. Let Glenda find her way back alone.

Edwin pulled my chair out and brushed his lips across the nape of my neck as I sat down. He still had not danced with anyone else, and his apparent desire was flattering. For a moment I considered it. That's what I really needed, wasn't it? To walk down the moonlit beach wrapped in his arms, making it to some pad to be made? It would be a delightful story to tell at bridge sessions. But I shook my head at him, and this time my smile was more sad than teasing.

Glenda came back and crawled over Gregory's legs to the seat beside him. The bastard. He made no pretense of being a gentleman. Suddenly, I didn't know which of them I disliked the most. Gregory winked at me. I don't know where he got the impression I was his conspirator, but I got up to dance with him.

"That Glenda," he grinned, "she's the one I was on the boat with last night. I banged her plenty, in the room right

next to her father. We could hear him coughing to let us
know he was awake, but he didn't come in."

He laughed like a naughty schoolboy, and I joined in.
He was a nerveless bastard all right, and it served Glenda
right that we were laughing at her. Who asked her to crash
our party, anyway? That's when I got the idea to take
Gregory away from her.

"You gonna bang her again tonight?" I asked, a new
teasing quality in my voice. "Or are you gonna find something better to do?" To help him get the message I rubbed
bellies with him.

He couldn't believe this sudden turn of events. I could
almost see him thinking. With one stroke he could slap
Glenda down a peg and repay Edwin for beating out his
time with me on the beach that morning.

"You wanna come with me?" he asked, making sure of
his quarry.

"What you got to offer?" I peered at him through half-
closed lids.

"Big Bamboo," he sang, the title of a popular calypso.
We both laughed.

I felt a heady excitement of impending danger as Gregory pulled me back to the table.

The men paid the bill, and suddenly we were all standing
outside the club in the bright moonlight. Gregory deliberately uncurled Glenda's arm from his and took a step
toward me. Looking at Edwin and nodding in my direction,
he said: "She's coming with me. Any objections?"

Edwin inhaled a mouthful of smoke. His face was in-
scrutable. "You want to go with him?" he asked me quietly.

I avoided his eyes and nodded. "Yes."

He flipped the cigarette with contempt at my feet and
lit another one. "Help yourself to the garbage," he said,
and leaned back against the building, one leg braced behind
him. The others suddenly stilled their chatter, sensing
trouble.

I was holding Gregory's arm now, and I felt his muscles
tense. "No," I said, as he moved toward Edwin. "You've
got what you want. Forget it."

Glenda was ungracious in defeat. "What about me?" she
screamed. She stared from one black face to another, her
glance lingering on Edwin. But he wasn't about to come
to her aid and take Gregory's leavings.

"You can go home in a cab," Gregory said, pushing her
ahead of him and pulling me behind him to a taxi waiting
at the curb.

Glenda broke from his grasp. "You bastard. Who in the hell do you think you are, King Solomon? You can't dump me like this." She raised her hands as if to strike Gregory on the chest, but he caught them before they landed.

"Careful, white girl," he said. His voice was low but ominous. She froze.

"But why," she whimpered, all hurt child now. "You liked me last night. I know you did. Why are you treating me like this?"

"I didn't bring you here," his voice was pleasant again, "so don't be trailing me all over town. When I want you, I'll come to that damn boat and get you. Now get in that cab before I throw you in. I'll see you tomorrow night. Maybe."

"You go to hell." She eluded him and turned on me, asking with incredible innocence: "What did I ever do to you?" Then she was running past us toward the beach, her sobs drifting back to haunt me like a forlorn melody.

What had she ever done to me? And what had I just done? In order to degrade her for the crime of being white I had sunk to the gutter. Suddenly Glenda was just another woman, vulnerable and lonely, like me.

We were sick, sick, sick. All fucked up. I had thought only Gregory was hung up in his love-hate, black-white syndrome, decades of suppressed hatred having sickened his soul. But I was tainted, too. I had forgotten my own misery long enough to inflict it on another woman who was only trying to ease her loneliness by making it with a soul brother. Was I jealous because she was able to function as a woman where I couldn't, because she realized that a man is a man, color be damned, while I was crucified on my anti-white-man cross? What if she were going black trying to repent for some ancient Nordic sin? How else could she atone except with the gift of herself? And if some black brother wanted to help a chick off her lily-white pedestal, he was entitled to that freedom, and it was none of my damned business anyway.

"Let's go, baby," Gregory said, tucking my arm under his.

The black bastard. I didn't even like the ugly ape. I backed away from him. "Leave me alone," I screamed. "Goddammit, just leave me alone!"

For a moment we were all frozen into an absurd fresco —Alison, Dorothy, and the two boys looking at me in shocked disbelief, Edwin hiding behind a nonchalant smoke screen, Gregory off balance and confused, reaching out toward me.

I moved first, toward Edwin, but I had slammed that door behind me. He laughed, a mirthless sound in the stillness. He knew. I had forsaken him, but at least not for Gregory.

Then I was running down the beach looking for Glenda, hot tears of shame burning my face. How could I have been such a bitch? But the white beach, shimmering in the moonlight, was empty. And once again, I was alone.

Early Autumn

Langston Hughes

*Langston Hughes was born in Joplin, Missouri, in
1902. In 1925 he received his first poetry award in a
contest conducted by* Opportunity *magazine. He is
the best-known and the most versatile writer produced by the Harlem Literary Renaissance. His literary career extends over a period of more than forty
years. Among his books are* The Weary Blues, Not
Without Laughter, The Big Sea, *and the books about
the urban folk-hero, Jesse B. Simple. Langston
Hughes died in May 1967.*

When Bill was very young, they had been in love. Many
nights they had spent walking, talking together. Then
something not very important had come between them,
and they didn't speak. Impulsively, she had married a man
she thought she loved. Bill went away, bitter about women.

Yesterday, walking across Washington Square, she saw
him for the first time in years.

"Bill Walker," she said.

He stopped. At first he did not recognize her, to him she
looked so old.

"Mary! Where did you come from?"

Unconsciously, she lifted her face as though wanting a
kiss, but he held out his hand. She took it.

"I live in New York now," she said.

"Oh"—smiling politely. Then a little frown came quickly
between his eyes.

"Always wondered what happened to you, Bill."

"I'm a lawyer. Nice firm, way downtown."

"Married yet?"

"Sure. Two kids."

"Oh," she said.

A great many people went past them through the park.

People they didn't know. It was late afternoon. Nearly sunset. Cold.

"And your husband?" he asked her.

"We have three children. I work in the bursar's office at Columbia."

"You're looking very . . ." (he wanted to say *old*) ". . . well," he said.

She understood. Under the trees in Washington Square, she found herself desperately reaching back into the past. She had been older than he then in Ohio. Now she was not young at all. Bill was still young.

"We live on Central Park West," she said. "Come and see us sometime."

"Sure," he replied. "You and your husband must have dinner with my family some night. Any night. Lucille and I'd love to have you."

The leaves fell slowly from the trees in the Square. Fell without wind. Autumn dusk. She felt a little sick.

"We'd love it," she answered.

"You ought to see my kids." He grinned.

Suddenly the lights came on up the whole length of Fifth Avenue, chains of misty brilliance in the blue air.

"There's my bus," she said.

He held out his hand, "Good-by."

"When . . ." she wanted to say, but the bus was ready to pull off. The lights on the avenue blurred, twinkled, blurred. And she was afraid to open her mouth as she entered the bus. Afraid it would be impossible to utter a word.

Suddenly she shrieked very loudly, "Good-by!" But the bus door had closed.

The bus started. People came between them outside, people crossing the street, people they didn't know. Space and people. She lost sight of Bill. Then she remembered she had forgotten to give him her address—or to ask him for his—or tell him that her youngest boy was named Bill, too.

Just Like A Tree

Ernest Gaines

*Ernest J. Gaines was born on a Louisiana plantation
in 1933 and spent much of his childhood working in
the fields. At fifteen he moved to California, where he
completed his education and graduated from San
Francisco State College in 1957. The following year
he won a Wallace Stegner Creative Writing Fellowship at Stanford University. In 1959 he received the
Joseph Henry Jackson Literary Award; and his first
novel,* Catherine Carmier, *was published in 1964. His
second novel,* Of Love and Dust, *was published in
1967 by The Dial Press, Inc. He had a book of short
stories,* Bloodline, *published in 1969. His latest novel
is* The Autobiography of Miss Jane Pittman.

> *I shall not;*
> *I shall not be moved.*
> *I shall not;*
> *I shall not be moved.*
> *Just like a tree that's*
> *planted 'side the water.*
> *Oh, I shall not be moved.*
>
> *I made my home in glory;*
> *I shall not be moved.*
> *Made my home in glory;*
> *I shall not be moved.*
> *Just like a tree that's*
> *planted 'side the water.*
> *Oh, I shall not be moved.*

(from an old Negro spiritual)

Chuckkie

Pa hit him on the back and he jeck in them chains like he pulling, but ever'body in the wagon know he ain't, and Pa hit him on the back again. He jeck again like he pulling, but even Big Red know he ain't doing a thing.

"That's why I'm go'n get a horse," Pa say. "He'll kill that other mule. Get up there, Mr. Bascom."

"Oh, let him alone," Gran'mon say. "How would you like it if you was pulling a wagon in all that mud?"

Pa don't answer Gran'mon; he just hit Mr. Bascom on the back again.

"That's right, kill him," Gran'mon say. "See where you get mo' money to buy another one."

"Get up there, Mr. Bascom," Pa say.

"You hear me talking to you, Emile?" Gran'mon say. "You want me hit you with something?"

"Ma, he ain't pulling," Pa say.

"Leave him alone," Gran'mon say.

Pa shake the lines little bit, but Mr. Bascom don't even feel it, and you can see he letting Big Red do all the pulling again. Pa say something kind o' low to hisself, and I can't make out what it is.

I low' my head little bit, 'cause that wind and fine rain was hitting me in the face, and I can feel Mama pressing close to me to keep me warm. She sitting on one side o' me and Pa sitting on the other side o' me, and Gran'mon in the back o' me in her setting chair. Pa didn't want bring the setting chair, telling Gran'mon there was two boards in that wagon already and she could sit on one of 'em all by herself if she wanted to, but Gran'mon say she was taking her setting chair with her if Pa liked it or not. She say she didn't ride in no wagon on nobody board, and if Pa liked it or not, that setting chair was going.

"Let her take her setting chair," Mama say. "What's wrong with taking her setting chair."

"Ehhh, Lord," Pa say, and picked up the setting chair and took it out to the wagon. "I guess I'll have to bring it back in the house, too, when we come back from there."

Gran'mon went and clambed in the wagon and moved her setting chair back little bit and sat down and folded her arms, waiting for us to get in, too. I got in and knelt down 'side her, but Mama told me to come up there and sit on the board 'side her and Pa so I could stay warm.

Soon 's I sat down, Pa hit Mr. Bascom on the back, saying what a trifling thing Mr. Bascom was, and soon 's he got some mo' money he was getting rid o' Mr. Bascom and getting him a horse.

I raise my head to look see how far we is.

"That's it, yonder," I say.

"Stop pointing," Mama say, "and keep your hand in your pocket."

"Where?" Gran'mon say, back there in her setting chair.

" 'Cross the ditch, yonder," I say.

"Can't see a thing for this rain," Gran'mon say.

"Can't hardly see it," I say. "But you can see the light little bit. That chinaball tree standing in the way."

"Poor soul," Gran'mon say. "Poor soul."

I know Gran'mon was go'n say "poor soul, poor soul," 'cause she had been saying "poor soul, poor soul" ever since she heard Aunt Fe was go'n leave from back there.

Emile

Darn cane crop to finish getting in and only a mule and a half to do it. If I had my way I'd take that shotgun and a load o' buckshots and—but what's the use.

"Get up, Mr. Bascom—please," I say to that little dried-up, long-eared, tobacco-color thing. "Please, come up. Do your share for God sake—if you don't mind. I know it's hard pulling in all that mud, but if you don't do your share, then Big Red'll have to do his and yours, too. So, please, if it ain't asking you too much to—"

"Oh, Emile, shut up," Leola say.

"I can't hit him," I say, "or Mama back there'll hit me. So I have to talk to him. Please, Mr. Bascom, if you don't mind it. For my sake. No, not for mine; for God sake. No, not even for His'n; for Big Red sake. A fellow mule just like yourself is. Please, come up."

"Now, you hear that boy blaspheming God right in front o' me there," Mama say. "Ehhh, Lord—just keep it up. All this bad weather there like this whole world coming apart—a clap o' thunder come there and knock the fool out you. Just keep it up."

Maybe she right, and I stop. I look at Mr. Bascom there doing nothing, and I just give up. That mule know long 's Mama's alive he go'n do just what he want to do. He know when Papa was dying he told Mama to look after him, and he know no matter what he do, no matter what he don't do, Mama ain't go'n never let me do him anything. Sometimes I even feel Mama care mo' for Mr. Bascom 'an she care for me her own son.

We come up to the gate, and I pull back on the lines.

"Whoa up, Big Red," I say. "You don't have to stop, Mr. Bascom. You never started."

I can feel Mama looking at me back there in that setting chair, but she don't say nothing.

"Here," I say to Chuckkie.

He take the lines, and I jump down on the ground to open the old beat-up gate. I see Etienne's horse in the yard, and I see Chris new red tractor 'side the house, shining in the rain. When Mama die, I say to myself, Mr. Bascom, you going. Ever'body getting tractors and horses, and I'm still stuck with you. You going, brother.

"Can you make it through?" I ask Chuckkie. "That gate ain't too wide."

"I can do it," he say.

"Be sure to make Mr. Bascom pull," I say.

"Emile, you better get back up here and drive 'em through," Leola say. "Chuckkie might break up that wagon."

"No, let him stay down there and give orders," Mama say, back there in that setting chair.

"He can do it," I say. "Come on, Chuckkie boy."

"Come up, here, mule," Chuckkie say.

And soon 's he say that, Big Red make a lunge for the yard, and Mr. Bascom don't even move, and 'fore I can bat my eyes I hear *pow-wow; sagg-sagg; pow-wow.* But above all that noise, Leola up there screaming her head off. And Mama—not a word; just sitting in that chair, looking at me with her arms still folded.

"Pull Big Red," I say. "Pull Big Red, Chuckkie."

Poor little Chuckkie up there pulling so hard till one of his little arms straight out in back; and Big Red throwing his shoulders and ever'thing else in it, and Mr. Bascom just walking there just 's loose and free, like he's suppose to be there just for his good looks. I move out the way just in time to let the wagon go by me, pulling half o' the fence in the yard behind it. I glance up again, and there's Leola still hollering and trying to jump out, but Mama not saying a word—just sitting there in that setting chair with her arms still folded.

"Whoa," I hear little Chuckkie saying. "Whoa up, now."

Somebody open the door, and a bunch o' people come out on the gallery.

"What the world—?" Etienne say. "Thought the whole place was coming to pieces there."

"Chuckkie had a little trouble coming in the yard," I say.

"Goodness," Etienne say. "Anybody hurt?"

Mama just sit there about ten seconds, then she say something to herself and start clambing out the wagon.

"Let me help you there, Aunt Lou," Etienne say, coming down the steps.

"I can make it," Mama say. When she get on the ground she look up at Chuckkie. "Hand me my chair there, boy."

Poor little Chuckkie, up there with the lines in one hand, get the chair and hold it to the side, and Etienne catch it just 'fore it hit the ground. Mama start looking at me again, and it look like for at least a' hour she stand there looking at nobody but me. Then she say, "Ehhh, Lord," like that again, and go inside with Leola and the rest o' the people.

I look back at half o' the fence laying there in the yard, and I jump back on the wagon and guide the mules to the side o' the house. After unhitching 'em and tying 'em to the wheels, I look at Chris pretty red tractor again, and me and Chuckkie go inside: I make sure he kick all that mud off his shoes 'fore he go in the house.

Leola

Sitting over there by that fireplace, trying to look joyful when ever'body there know she ain't. But she trying, you know; smiling and bowing when people say something to her. How can she be joyful, I ask you; how can she be? Poor thing, she been here all her life—or the most of it, let's say. 'Fore they moved in this house, they lived in one back in the woods 'bout a mile from here. But for the past twenty-five or thirty years, she been right in this one house. I know ever since I been big enough to know people I been seeing her right here.

Aunt Fe, Aunt Fe, Aunt Fe, Aunt Fe; the name's been 'mongst us just like us own family name. Just like the name o' God. Like the name of town—the city. Aunt Fe, Aunt Fe, Aunt Fe, Aunt Fe.

Poor old thing; how many times I done come here and

washed clothes for her when she couldn't do it herself. How many times I done hoed in that garden, ironed her clothes, wrung a chicken neck for her. You count the days in the year and you'll be pretty close. And I didn't mind it a bit. No, I didn't mind it a bit. She there trying to pay me. Proud—Lord, talking 'bout pride. "Here." "No, Aunt Fe; no." "Here, here; you got a child there, you can use it." "No, Aunt Fe. No. No. What would Mama think if she knowed I took money from you? Aunt Fe, Mama would never forgive me. No. I love doing these thing for you. I just wish I could do more."

And there, now, trying to make 'tend she don't mind leaving. Ehhh, Lord.

I hear a bunch o' rattling round in the kitchen, and I go back there. I see Louise stirring this big pot o' eggnog.

"Louise," I say.

"Leola," she say.

We look at each other, and she stir the eggnog again. She know what I'm go'n say next, and she can't even look in my face.

"Louise, I wish there was some other way."

"There's no other way," she say.

"Louise, moving her from here's like moving a tree you been used to in your front yard all your life."

"What else can I do?"

"Oh, Louise, Louise."

"Nothing else but that."

"Louise, what people go'n do without her here?"

She stir the eggnog and don't answer.

"Louise, us'll take her in with us."

"You all no kin to Auntie. She go with me."

"And us'll never see her again."

She stir the eggnog. Her husband come back in the kitchen and kiss her on the back o' the neck and then look at me and grin. Right from the start I can see I ain't go'n like that nigger.

"Almost ready, honey?" he say.

"Almost."

He go to the safe and get one o' them bottles of whiskey he got in there and come back to the stove.

"No," Louise say. "Everybody don't like whiskey in it. Add the whiskey after you've poured it up."

"Okay, hon."

He kiss her on the back o' the neck again. Still don't like that nigger. Something 'bout him ain't right.

"You one o' the family?" he say.

"Same as one," I say. "And you?"

He don't like the way I say it, and I don't care if he like it or not. He look at me there a second, and then he kiss her on the ear.

"Un-unnn," she say, stirring the pot.

"I love your ear, baby," he say.

"Go in the front room and talk with the people," she say.

He kiss her on the other ear. A nigger do all that front o' public got something to hide. He leave the kitchen. I look at Louise.

"Ain't nothing else I can do," she say.

"You sure, Louise? You positive?"

"I'm positive," she say.

The front door open, and Emile and Chuckkie come in. A minute later Washington and Adrieu come in, too. Adrieu come back in the kitchen, and I can see she been crying. Aunt Fe is her godmother, you know.

"How you feel, Adrieu?"

"That weather out there," she say.

"Y'all walked?"

"Yes."

"Us here in the wagon. Y'all can go back with us."

"Y'all the one tore the fence down?" she ask.

"Yes, I guess só. That brother-in-law o' yours in there letting Chuckkie drive that wagon."

"Well, I don't guess it'll matter too much. Nobody go'n be here, anyhow."

And she start crying again. I take her in my arms and pat her on the shoulder, and I look at Louise stirring the eggnog.

"What I'm go'n do and my nan-nane gone? I love her so much."

"Ever'body love her."

"Since my mama died, she been like my mama."

"Shhh," I say. "Don't let her hear you. Make her grieve. You don't want her grieving, now, do you?"

She sniffs there 'gainst my dress few times.

"Oh, Lord," she say. "Lord, have mercy."

"Shhh," I say. "Shhh. That's what life's 'bout."

"That ain't what life's 'bout," she say. "It ain't fair. This been her home all her life. These the people she know. She don't know them people she going to. It ain't fair."

"Shhh, Adrieu," I say. "Now, you saying things that ain't your business."

She cry there some mo'.

"Oh, Lord, Lord," she say.

Louise turn from the stove.

"About ready now," she say, going to the middle door. "James, tell everybody to come back and get some."

James

Let me go on back here and show these country niggers how to have a good time. All they know is talk, talk, talk. Talk so much they make me buggy round here. Damn this weather—wind, rain. Must be a million cracks in this old house.

I go to that old beat-up safe in that corner and get that fifth of Mr. Harper (in the South now; got to say Mister), give the seal one swipe, the stopper one jerk, and head back to that old wood stove. (Man, like, these cats are primitive —goodness. You know what I mean? I mean like wood stoves. Don't mention TV, man, these cats here never heard of that.) I start to dump Mr. Harper in the pot and Baby catches my hand again and say not all of them like it. You ever heard of anything like that? I mean a stud's going to drink eggnog, and he's not going to put whiskey in it. I mean he's going to drink it straight. I mean, you ever heard anything like that? Well, I wasn't pressing none of them on Mr. Harper. I mean, me and Mr. Harper get along too well together for me to go around there pressing.

I hold my cup there and let Baby put a few drops of this egg stuff in it; then I jerk my cup back and let Mr. Harper run a while. Couple of these cats come over (some of them aren't so lame) and set their cups, and I let Mr. Harper run for them. Then this cat says he's got 'nough. I let Mr. Harper run for this other stud, and pretty soon he says, "Hold it. Good." Country cat, you know. "Hold it. Good." Real country cat. So I raise the cup to see what Mr. Harper's doing. He's just right. I raise the cup again. Just right, Mr. Harper; just right.

I go to the door with Mr. Harper under my arm and the cup in my hand, and I look into the front room where they all are. I mean, there's about ninety-nine of them in there. Old ones, young ones, little ones, big ones, yellow ones, black ones, brown ones—you name them, brother, and they were there. And what for? Brother, I'll tell you what for.

Just because me and Baby are taking this old chick out of
these sticks. Well, I'll tell you where I'd be at this moment
if I was one of them. With that weather out there like it is,
I'd be under about five blankets with some little warm
belly pressing against mine. Brother, you can bet your hat
I wouldn't be here. Man, listen to that thing out there. You
can hear that rain beating on that old house like grains of
rice; and that wind coming through them cracks like it
does in those old Charlie Chaplin movies. Man, like you
know—like *whooo-ee; whooo-ee.* Man, you talking about
some weird cats.

I can feel Mr. Harper starting to massage my wig, and I
bat my eyes twice and look at the old girl over there. She's
still sitting in that funny-looking little old rocking chair and
not saying a word to anybody. Just sitting there looking
into the fireplace at them two pieces of wood that aren't
giving out enough heat to warm a baby, let alone ninety-
nine grown people. I mean, you know, like that sleet's falling out there like all get-up-and-go, and them two pieces
of wood are lying there just as dead as the rest of these
way-out cats.

One of the old cats—I don't know which one he is—
Mose, Sam, or something like that—leans over and pokes
in the fire a minute; then a little blaze shoots up, and he
raises up, too, looking as satisfied as if he'd just sent a rocket
into orbit. I mean, these cats are like that. They do these
little bitty things, and they feel like they've really done
something. Well, back in these sticks, I guess there just
isn't nothing big to do.

I feel Mr. Harper touching my skull now—and I notice
this little chick passing by me with these two cups of eggnog. She goes over to the fireplace and gives one to each of
these old chicks. The one sitting in that setting chair she
brought with her from God knows where, and the other
cup to the old chick that Baby and I are going to haul from
here sometime tomorrow morning. Wait, man, I mean like,
you ever heard of anybody going to somebody else's house
with a chair? I mean, wouldn't you call that an insult at
the basest point? I mean, now, like tell me what you think
of that? I mean—dig—here I am at my pad, and in you
come with your own stool. I mean, now, like man, you
know. I mean that's an insult at the basest point. I mean,
you know . . . you know, like way out. . . .

Mr. Harper, what you trying to do, boy?—I mean, *sir.*

(Got to watch myself, I'm in the South. Got to keep watching myself.)

This stud touches me on the shoulder and raise his cup and say, "How 'bout a taste?" I know what the stud's talking about, so I let Mr. Harper run for him. But soon 's I let a drop get in, the stud say, " 'Nough." I mean I let about two drops get in, and already the stud's got enough. Man, I mean, like you know. I mean these studs are 'way out. I mean like 'way back there.

This stud takes a swig of his eggnog and say, "Ahhh." I mean this real down-home way of saying "Ahhhh." I mean, man, like these studs—I notice this little chick passing by me again, and this time she's crying. I mean weeping, you know. And just because this old ninety-nine-year-old chick's packing up and leaving. I mean, you ever heard of anything like that? I mean, here she is pretty as the day is long and crying because Baby and I are hauling this old chick away. Well, I'd like to make her cry. And I can assure you, brother, it wouldn't be from leaving her.

I turn and look at Baby over there by the stove, pouring eggnog in all these cups. I mean, there're about twenty of these cats lined up there. And I bet you not half of them will take Mr. Harper along. Some way-out cats, man. Some way-out cats.

I go up to Baby and kiss her on the back of the neck and give her a little pat where she likes for me to pat her when we're in the bed. She say, "Uh-uh," but I know she likes it, anyhow.

Ben O

I back under the bed and touch the slop jar, and I pull back my leg and back somewhere else, and then I get me a good sight on it. I spin my aggie couple times and sight again and then I shoot. I hit it right square in the middle and it go flying over the fireplace. I crawl over there to get it and I see 'em all over there drinking they eggnog, and they didn't even offer me and Chuckkie none. I find my marble on the bricks, and I go back and tell Chuckkie they over there drinking eggnog.

"You want some?" I say.

"I want shoot marble," Chuckkie say. "Yo' shot. Shoot up."

"I want some eggnog," I say.

"Shoot up, Ben O," he say. "I'm getting cold staying in one place so long. You feel that draft?"

"Coming from that crack under that bed," I say.

"Where?" Chuckkie say, looking for the crack.

"Over by that bedpost over there," I say.

"This sure's a beat-up old house," Chuckkie say.

"I want me some eggnog," I say.

"Well, you ain't getting none," Gran'mon say, from the fireplace. "It ain't good for you."

"I can drink eggnog," I say. "How come it ain't good for me? It ain't nothing but eggs and milk. I eat chicken, don't I? I eat beef, don't I?"

Gran'mon don't say nothing.

"I want me some eggnog," I say.

Gran'mon still don't say no more. Nobody else don't say nothing, neither.

"I want me some eggnog," I say.

"You go'n get a eggnog," Gran'mon say. "Just keep that noise up."

"I want me some eggnog," I say; "and I 'tend to get me some eggnog tonight."

Next thing I know, Gran'mon done picked up a chip out o' that corner and done sailed it back there where me and Chuckkie is. I duck just in time, and the chip catch old Chuckkie side the head.

"Hey, who that hitting me?" Chuckkie say.

"Move, and you won't get hit," Gran'mon say.

I laugh at old Chuckkie over there holding his head, and next thing I know here's Chuckkie done haul back there and hit me in my side. I jump up from there and give him two just to show him how it feel, and he jump up and hit me again. Then we grab each other and start tussling on the floor.

"You, Ben O," I hear Gran'mon saying. "You, Ben O, cut that out. Y'all cut that out."

But we don't stop 'cause neither one o' us want be first. Then I feel somebody pulling us apart.

"What I ought to do is whip both o' you," Mrs. Leola say. "Is that what y'all want?"

"No'm," I say.

"Then shake hand."

Me and Chuckkie shake hand.

"Kiss," Mrs. Leola say.

"No, ma'am," I say. "I ain't kissing no boy. I ain't that crazy."

"Kiss him, Chuckkie," she say.

Old Chuckkie kiss me on the jaw.

"Now, kiss him, Ben O."

"I ain't kissing no Chuckkie," I say. "No'm. Uh-uh. You kiss girls."

And the next thing I know, Mama done tipped up back o' me and done whop me on the leg with Daddy belt.

"Kiss Chuckkie," she say.

Chuckkie turn his jaw to me, and I kiss him. I almost wipe my mouth. I even feel like spitting.

"Now, come back here and get you some eggnog," Mama say.

"That's right, spoil 'em," Gran'mon say. "Next thing you know, they be drinking from bottles."

"Little eggnog won't hurt 'em, Mama," Mama say.

"That's right, never listen," Gran'mon say. "It's you go'n suffer for it. I be dead and gone, me."

Aunt Clo

Be just like wrapping a chain 'round a tree and jecking and jecking, and then shifting the chain little bit and jecking and jecking some in that direction, and then shifting it some mo' and jecking and jecking in that direction. Jecking and jecking till you get it loose, and then pulling with all your might. Still it might not be loose enough and you have to back the tractor up some and fix the chain 'round the tree again and start jecking all over. Jeck, jeck, jeck. Then you hear the roots crying, and then you keep on jecking, and then it give, and you jeck some mo', and then it falls. And not till then that you see what you done done. Not till then you see the big hole in the ground and piece of the taproot still way down in it—a piece you won't never get out no matter if you dig till doomsday. Yes, you got the tree—least got it down on the ground, but did you get the taproot? No. No, sir, you didn't get the taproot. You stand there and look down in this hole at it, and you grab yo' axe and jump down in it and start chopping at the taproot, but do you get the taproot? No. You don't get the taproot, sir. You never get the taproot. But, sir, I tell you what you do get. You get a big hole in the ground, sir; and you get another big hole in the air where the lovely branches been all these years. Yes, sir, that's what you get.

The holes, sir, the holes. Two holes, sir, you can't never fill no matter how hard you try.

So you wrap yo' chain 'round yo' tree again, sir, and you start dragging it. But the dragging ain't so easy, sir, 'cause she's a heavy old tree—been there a long time, you know—heavy. And you make yo' tractor strain, sir, and the elements work 'gainst you, too, sir, 'cause the elements, they on her side, too, 'cause she part o' the elements, and the elements, they part o' her. So the elements, they do they little share to discourage you—yes, sir, they does. But you will not let the elements stop you. No, sir, you show the elements that they just elements, and man is stronger than elements, and you jeck and jeck on the chain, and soon she start to moving with you, sir, but if you look over yo' shoulder one second you see her leaving a trail—a trail, sir, that can be seen from miles and miles away. You see her trying to hook her little fine branches in different little cracks, in between pickets, 'round hills o' grass, 'round anything they might brush 'gainst. But you is a determined man, sir, and you jeck and you jeck, and she keep on grabbing and trying to hold, but you stronger, sir—course you the strongest—and you finally get her out on the pave road. But what you don't notice, sir, is just 'fore she get on the pave road she leave couple her little branches to remind the people that it ain't her that want leave, but you, sir, that think she ought to. So you just drag her and drag her, sir, and the folks that live in the houses 'side the pave road, they come out on they gallery and look at her go by, and then they go back in they house and sit by the fire and forget her. So you just go on, sir, and you just go and you go—and for how many days? I don't know. I don't have the least idea. The North to me, sir, is like the elements. It mystify me. But never mind, you finally get there, and then you try to find a place to set her. You look in this corner, and you look in that corner, but no corner is good. She kind o' stand in the way no matter where you set her. So finally, sir, you say, "I just stand her up here a little while and see, and if it don't work out, if she keep getting in the way, I guess we'll just have to take her to the dump."

Chris

Just like him, though, standing up there telling them lies when everybody else feeling sad. I don't know what you do without people like him. And yet, you see him there, he sad just like the rest. But he just got to be funny. Crying on the inside, but still got to be funny.

He didn't steal it, though; didn't steal it a bit. His grandpa was just like him. Mat? Mat Jefferson? Just like that. Mat could make you die laughing. 'Member once at a wake. Who was dead? Yes—Robert Lewis. Robert Lewis laying up in his coffin dead as a door nail. Everybody sad and droopy. Mat look at that and start his lying. Soon, half o' the place laughing. Funniest wake I ever went to, and yet—

Just like now. Look at 'em. Look at 'em laughing. Ten minutes ago you would 'a' thought you was at a funeral. But look at 'em now. Look at her there in that little old chair. How long she had it? Fifty years—a hundred? It ain't a chair no mo', it's little bit o' her. Just like her arm, just like her leg.

You know, I couldn't believe it. I couldn't. Emile passed the house there the other day, right after the bombing, and I was in my yard digging a water drain to let the water run out in the ditch. Emile, he stopped the wagon there 'fore the door. Little Chuckkie, he in there with him with that little rain cap buckled up over his head. I go out to the gate, and I say, "Emile, it's the truth?"

"The truth," he say. And just like that he say it. "The truth."

I look at him there, and he looking up the road to keep from looking back at me. You know, they been pretty close to Aunt Fe ever since they was children coming up. His own mon, Aunt Lou, and Aunt Fe, they been like sisters, there, together.

Me and him, we talk there little while 'bout the cane cutting, then he say he got to get on to the back. He shake the lines and drive on.

Inside me, my heart feel like it done swole up ten times the size it ought to be. Water come in my eyes, and I got to 'mit I cried right there. Yes sir, I cried right there by that front gate.

Louise come in the room and whisper something to Leola, and they go back in the kitchen. I can hear 'em moving things 'round back there, still getting things together they go'n be taking along. If they offer me anything, I'd like that big iron pot out there in the back yard. Good for boiling water when you killing hog, you know.

You can feel the sadness in the room again. Louise brought it in when she come in and whispered to Leola. Only, she didn't take it out when her and Leola left. Every pan they move, every pot they unhook keep telling you she leaving, she leaving.

Etienne turn over one o' them logs to make the fire pick up some, and I see that boy, Lionel, spreading out his hands over the fire. Watch out, I think to myself, here come another lie. People, he just getting started.

Anne-Marie Duvall

"You're not going?"

"I'm not going," he says, turning over the log with the poker. "And if you were in your right mind, you wouldn't go, either."

"You just don't understand, do you?"

"Oh, I understand. She cooked for your daddy. She nursed you when your mama died."

"And I'm trying to pay her back with a seventy-nine-cents scarf. Is that too much?"

He is silent, leaning against the mantel, looking down at the fire. The fire throws strange shadows across the big, old room. Father looks down at me from against the wall. His eyes do not say go nor stay. But I know what he would do.

"Please go with me, Edward."

"You're wasting your breath."

I look at him a long time, then I get the small package from the coffee table.

"You're still going?"

"I am going."

"Don't call for me if you get bogged down anywhere back there."

I look at him and go out to the garage. The sky is black. The clouds are moving fast and low. A fine drizzle is falling, and the wind coming from the swamps blows in my face. I cannot recall a worse night in all my life.

I hurry into the car and drive out of the yard. The house stands big and black in back of me. Am I angry with Edward? No, I'm not angry with Edward. He's right. I should not go out into this kind of weather. But what he does not understand is I must. Father definitely would have gone if he were alive. Grandfather definitely would have gone, also. And, therefore, I must. Why? I cannot answer why. Only, I must go.

As soon as I turn down that old muddy road, I begin to

pray. Don't let me go into that ditch, I pray. Don't let me go into that ditch. Please, don't let me go into that ditch.

The lights play on the big old trees along the road. Here and there the lights hit a sagging picket fence. But I know I haven't even started yet. She lives far back into the fields. Why? God, why does she have to live so far back? Why couldn't she have lived closer to the front? But the answer to that is as hard for me as is the answer to everything else. It was ordained before I—before father—was born—that she should live back there. So why should I try to understand it now?

The car slides toward the ditch, and I stop it dead and turn the wheel, and then come back into the road again. Thanks, Father. I know you're with me. Because it was you who said that I must look after her, didn't you? No, you did not say it directly, Father. You said it only with a glance. As grandfather must have said it to you, and as his father must have said it to him.

But now that she's gone, Father, now what? I know. I know. Aunt Lou, Aunt Clo, and the rest.

The lights shine on the dead, wet grass along the road. There's an old pecan tree, looking dead and all alone. I wish I was a little nigger gal so I could pick pecans and eat them under the big old dead tree.

The car hits a rut but bounces right out of it. I am frightened for a moment, but then I feel better. The windshield wipers are working well, slapping the water away as fast as it hits the glass. If I make the next half mile all right, the rest of the way will be good. It's not much over a mile now.

That was too bad about that bombing—killing that woman and her two children. That poor woman; poor children. What is the answer? What will happen? What do they want? Do they know what they want? Do they really know what they want? Are they positively sure? Have they any idea? Money to buy a car, is that it? If that is all, I pity them. Oh, how I pity them.

Not much farther. Just around that bend and—there's a water hole. Now what?

I stop the car and just stare out at the water a minute; then I get out to see how deep it is. The cold wind shoots through my body like needles. Lightning comes from toward the swamps and lights up the place. For a split second the night is as bright as day. The next second it is blacker than it has ever been.

I look at the water, and I can see that it's too deep for

the car to pass through. I must turn back, or I must walk the rest of the way. I stand there a while wondering what to do. Is it worth it all? Can't I simply send the gift by someone tomorrow morning? But will there be someone tomorrow morning? Suppose she leaves without getting it, then what? What then? Father would never forgive me. Neither would grandfather or great-grandfather, either. No, they wouldn't.

The lightning flashes again, and I look across the field, and I can see the tree in the yard a quarter of a mile away. I have but one choice: I must walk. I get the package out of the car and stuff it in my coat and start out.

I don't make any progress at first, but then I become a little warmer, and I find I like walking. The lightning flashes just in time to show up a puddle of water, and I go around it. But there's no light to show up the second puddle, and I fall flat on my face. For a moment I'm completely blind, then I get slowly to my feet and check the package. It's dry, not harmed. I wash the mud off my raincoat, wash my hands, and I start out again.

The house appears in front of me, and as I come into the yard, I can hear the people laughing and talking. Sometimes I think niggers can laugh and joke even if they see somebody beaten to death. I go up on the porch and knock, and an old one opens the door for me. I swear, when he sees me, he looks as if he's seen a ghost. His mouth drops open, his eyes bulge—I swear.

I go into the old crowded and smelly room, and every one of them looks at me the same way the first one did. All the joking and laughing has ceased. You would think I was the devil in person.

"Done, Lord," I hear her saying over by the fireplace. They move to the side and I can see her sitting in that little rocking chair I bet you she's had since the beginning of time. "Done, Master," she says. "Child, what you doing in weather like this? Y'all move; let her get to that fire. Y'all move. Move, now. Let her warm herself."

They start scattering everywhere.

"I'm not cold, Aunt Fe," I say. "I just brought you something—something small—because you're leaving us. I'm going right back."

"Done, Master," she says. Fussing over me just like she's done all her life. "Done, Master. Child, you ain't got no business in a place like this. Get close to this fire. Get here. Done, Master."

I move closer, and the fire does feel warm and good.

"Done, Lord," she says.

I take out the package and pass it to her. The other niggers gather around with all kinds of smiles on their faces. Just think of it—a white lady coming through all of this for one old darky. It is all right for them to come from all over the plantation, from all over the area, in all kinds of weather: this is to be expected of them. But a white lady, a white lady. They must think we white people don't have their kind of feelings.

She unwraps the package, her bony little fingers working slowly and deliberately. When she sees the scarf—the seventy-nine-cents scarf—she brings it to her mouth and kisses it.

"Y'all look," she says. "Y'all look. Ain't it the prettiest little scarf y'all ever did see? Y'all look."

They move around her and look at the scarf. Some of them touch it.

"I go'n put it on right now," she says. "I go'n put it on right now, my lady."

She unfolds it and ties it 'round her head and looks up at everybody and smiles.

"Thank you, my lady," she says. "Thank you, ma'am, from the bottom of my heart."

"Oh, Aunt Fe," I say, kneeling down beside her. "Oh, Aunt Fe."

But I think about the other niggers there looking down at me, and I get up. But I look into that wrinkled old face again, and I must go back down again. And I lay my head in that bony old lap, and I cry and I cry—I don't know how long. And I feel those old fingers, like death itself, passing over my hair and my neck. I don't know how long I kneel there crying, and when I stop, I get out of there as fast as I can.

Etienne

The boy come in, and soon, right off, they get quiet, blaming the boy. If people could look little farther than the tip of they nose— No, they blame the boy. Not that they ain't behind the boy, what he doing, but they blame him for what she must do. What they don't know is that the boy didn't start it, and the people that bombed the house didn't start it, neither. It started a million years ago. It started when one man envied another man for having a

penny mo' 'an he had, and then the man married a woman
to help him work the field so he could get much 's the other
man, but when the other man saw the man had married a
woman to get much 's him, he, himself, he married a
woman, too, so he could still have mo'. Then they start
having children—not from love; but so the children could
help 'em work so they could have mo'. But even with the
children one man still had a penny mo' 'an the other, so
the other man went and bought him a ox, and the other
man did the same—to keep ahead of the other man. And
soon the other man had bought him a slave to work the ox
so he could get ahead of the other man. But the other man
went out and bought him two slaves so he could stay ahead
of the other man, and the other man went out and bought
him three slaves. And soon they had a thousand slaves
apiece, but they still wasn't satisfied. And one day the
slaves all rose and kill the masters, but the masters (knowing slaves was men just like they was, and kind o' expected
they might do this) organized theyself a good police force,
and the police force, they come out and killed the two
thousand slaves.

So it's not this boy you see standing here 'fore you
'cause it happened a million years ago. And this boy here's
just doing something the slaves done a million years ago.
Just that this boy here ain't doing it they way. 'Stead of
raising arms 'gainst the masters, he bow his head.

No, I say; don't blame the boy 'cause she must go. 'Cause
when she's dead, and that won't be long after they get her
up there, this boy's work will still be going on. She's not
the only one that's go'n die from this boy's work. Many
mo' of 'em go'n die 'fore it's over with. The whole place—
everything. A big wind is rising, and when a big wind rise,
the sea stirs, and the drop o' water you see laying on top
the sea this day won't be there tomorrow. 'Cause that's
what wind do, and that's what life is. She ain't nothing but
one little drop o' water laying on top the sea, and what
this boy's doing is called the wind . . . and she must be
moved. No, don't blame the boy. Go out and blame the
wind. No, don't blame him 'cause tomorrow, what he's
doing today, somebody go'n say he ain't done a thing.
'Cause tomorrow will be his time to be turned over just
like it's hers today. And after that, be somebody else time
to turn over. And it keep going like that till it ain't nothing
left to turn—and nobody left to turn it.

"Sure, they bombed the house," he say, "because they
want us to stop. But if we stopped today, then what good

would we have done? What good? Those who have already died for the cause would have just died in vain."

"Maybe if they had bombed your house, you wouldn't be so set on keeping this up."

"If they had killed my mother and my brothers and sisters, I'd press just that much harder. I can see you all point. I can see it very well. But I can't agree with you. You blame me for their being bombed. You blame me for Aunt Fe's leaving. They died for you and for your children. And I love Aunt Fe as much as anybody in here does. Nobody in here loves her more than I do. Not one of you." He looks at her. "Don't you believe me, Aunt Fe?"

She nods—that little white scarf still tied 'round her head.

"How many times have I eaten in your kitchen, Aunt Fe? A thousand times? How many times have I eaten tea cakes and drank milk on the back steps, Aunt Fe? A thousand times? How many times have I sat at this same fireplace with you, just the two of us, Aunt Fe? Another thousand times—two thousand times? How many times have I chopped wood for you, chopped grass for you, ran to the store for you? Five thousand times? How many times have we walked to church together, Aunt Fe? Gone fishing at the river together—how many times? I've spent as much time in this house as I've spent in my own. I know every crack in the wall. I know every corner. With my eyes shut, I can go anywhere in here without bumping into anything. How many of you can do that? Not many of you." He looks at her. "Aunt Fe?"

She looks at him.

"Do you think I love you, Aunt Fe?"

She nods.

"I love you, Aunt Fe, much as I do my own parents. I'm going to miss you much as I'd miss my own mother if she were to leave me now. I'm going to miss you, Aunt Fe, but I'm not going to stop what I've started. You told me a story once, Aunt Fe, about my great-grandpa. Remember? Remember how he died?"

She looks in the fire and nods.

"Remember how they lynched him—chopped him into pieces?"

She nods.

"Just the two of us were sitting here beside the fire when you told me that. I was so angry I felt like killing. But it was you who told me get killing out of my mind. It was you who told me I would only bring harm to myself and sadness to the others if I killed. Do you remember that, Aunt Fe?"

She nods, still looking in the fire.

"You were right. We cannot raise our arms. Because it would mean death for ourselves, as well as for the others. But we will do something else—and that's what we will do." He looks at the people standing 'round him. "And if they were to bomb my own mother's house tomorrow, I would still go on."

"I'm not saying for you not to go on," Louise says. "That's up to you. I'm just taking Auntie from here before hers is the next house they bomb."

The boy look at Louise, and then at Aunt Fe. He go up to the chair where she sitting.

"Good-bye, Aunt Fe," he say, picking up her hand. The hand done shriveled up to almost nothing. Look like nothing but loose skin's covering the bones. "I'll miss you," he say.

"Good-bye, Emmanuel," she say. She look at him a long time. "God be with you."

He stand there holding the hand a while longer, then he nods his head and leaves the house. The people stir 'round little bit, but nobody say anything.

Aunt Lou

They tell her good-bye, and half of 'em leave the house crying, or want cry, but she just sit there 'side the fireplace like she don't mind going at all. When Leola ask me if I'm ready to go, I tell her I'm staying right there till Fe leave that house. I tell her I ain't moving one step till she go out that door. I been knowing her for the past fifty some years now, and I ain't 'bout to leave her on her last night here.

That boy, Chuckkie, want stay with me, but I make him go. He follow his mon and paw out the house, and soon I hear that wagon turning 'round. I hear Emile saying something to Mr. Bascom even 'fore that wagon get out the yard. I tell myself, well, Mr. Bascom, you sure go'n catch it, and me not there to take up for you—and I get up from my chair and go to the door.

"Emile?" I call.

"Whoa," he say.

"You leave that mule 'lone, you hear me?"

"I ain't done Mr. Bascom a thing, Mama," he say.

"Well, you just mind you don't," I say. "I'll sure find out."

"Yes'm," he say. "Come up here, Mr. Bascom."

"Now, you hear that boy. Emile?" I say.

"I'm sorry, Mama," he say. "I didn't mean no harm."

They go out in the road, and I go back to the fireplace and sit down again. Louise stir 'round in the kitchen a few minutes, then she come in the front where we at. Everybody else gone. That husband o' hers, there, got drunk long 'fore midnight, and Emile and them had to put him to bed in the other room.

She come there and stand by the fire.

"I'm dead on my feet," she say.

"Why don't you go to bed," I say. "I'm go'n be here."

"You all won't need anything?"

"They got wood in that corner?"

"Plenty."

"Then we won't need a thing."

She stand there and warm, and then she say good night and go 'round the other side.

"Well, Fe?" I say.

"I ain't leaving here tomorrow, Lou," she say.

" 'Course you is," I say. "Up there ain't that bad."

She shake her head. "No, I ain't going nowhere."

I look at her over in her chair, but I don't say nothing. The fire pops in the fireplace, and I look at the fire again. It's a good little fire—not too big, not too little. Just 'nough there to keep the place warm.

"You want sing, Lou?" she say, after a while. "I feel like singing my 'termination song."

"Sure," I say.

She start singing in that little light voice she got there, and I join with her. We sing two choruses, and then she stop.

"My 'termination for Heaven," she say. "Now—now—"

"What's the matter, Fe?" I say.

"Nothing," she say. "I want get in my bed. My gown hanging over there."

I get the gown for her and bring it back to the fireplace. She get out of her dress slowly, like she don't even have 'nough strength to do it. I help her on with her gown, and she kneel down there 'side the bed and say her prayers. I sit in my chair and look at the fire again.

She pray there a long time—half out loud, half to herself. I look at her kneeling down there, little like a little old girl. I see her making some kind o' jecking motion there, but I feel she crying 'cause this her last night here and 'cause she got to go and leave ever'thing behind. I look at the fire.

She pray there ever so long, and then she start to get up. But she can't make it by herself. I go to help her, and when I put my hand on her shoulder, she say, "Lou? Lou?"

I say, "What's the matter, Fe?"

"Lou?" she say. "Lou?"

I feel her shaking in my hand with all her might. Shaking, shaking, shaking—like a person with the chill. Then I hear her take a long breath, longest I ever heard anybody take before. Then she ease back on the bed—calm, calm, calm.

"Sleep on, Fe," I tell her. "When you get up there, tell 'em all I ain't far behind."

Not We Many

Clarence L. Cooper, Jr.

Clarence L. Cooper, Jr., is the author of the highly successful novels Weed, Dark Messenger, The Scene, *and* The Farm. *His collection of short stories,* Black!, *was published by Regency Books. His short stories have appeared in* Esquire, Playboy, *and* Rogue.

I told the Captain of the Fruit, Brother Harvey, that I just didn't give a damn. Those were my words, and I could hear the gasps from the ordered black lines of my brother Muslims.

Brother Harvey had been quizzing me on my listlessness, my uncertainty of direction, not only in the ranks of fleshed blue suits and sun-red ties and forefront eyes but in quite evident inner-mind.

It was youth, and impatience, he said, and lack of faith in our Leader's way, and inbred Devil's ignorance, he added; those were my ailments.

And that's when I said I didn't give a damn.

And that's not all I said.

I said, You're lambs, too, just like that dead nigger in the street who *hasn't* heard the message of the Prophet and prefers the white man's boot, and loves his pork chops—but that's not all I said:

"If I'm to die or live for Islam, then let it be *now*. Not waiting for some goddamn eastern cloud to show up on the horizon. If Armageddon's to come, then let *us* bring it to pass—here, now!"

Then I shouted, in a way that made his shocked black face wince, raising my fist as though it held a slashing sword of vengeance.

"*Allahu Akbar!* In the name of God!"

I was immediately expelled for ninety days and denied all contact with the Temple.

There was rain on the roof, and I was poor. Plus my mother was sick; and the white man at the grocery store on 80th wouldn't increase my salary.

Man, I loathed this shittness of living!

I loathed Brother Harvey, Brother Minister, who called all shots in the Temple's policy subject to He Most Knowing, and I hated Craig, my friend from boyhood, who'd introduced me to Islam months before and was more shocked than anyone else at my obscene explosiveness—who could not, damn him, understand my pain and need and demand for expression of the gall that boiled, seeking access from my throat.

I even hated my dying mother who'd brought me into this hell, who now whiningly sought surcease and vindication through her dying.

"David . . . ?"

It was her; and the plaintiveness of her voice—the not-understanding faint timber of it—made me feel ashamed of the things I'd been thinking.

I listened to it, sitting by the window in my small room, watching the haze of evening blackened with rain and cloaklike above the crap-pile crowns of the dirty city five stories below our tenement tower—and felt a kind of inside gnawing, kneading, mouth.

"David . . . son?"

I couldn't understand what was happening to me. At twenty-five, I didn't feel *too young*, too withheld from a *knowing* of myself and what I wanted:

That was just the trouble—I wanted more than merely the vision of early-autumn gold and silver intermixed in the rain and dust-lifted, mote-laden halo of my city's filthy crests—I wanted the gold and silver alone, without the dirt of people's making and pain.

And more—much more than I could know at that moment—I wanted peace and an awareness of something other than hate, something that would spring with sweet freshness to my morning's tongue—something I couldn't understand just then.

Slowly, I rose and went into the apartment's remaining room, my mother's, the dining, living, and everything-else place, made secondary by her presence.

"Yeah, Ma?" I said, standing over her.

"It's you I want, David," she said slowly.

"I ain't got time for talkin, Ma."

"Don't put me back, David—I'm your mother . . ."

"I know who you are . . ."

"Then sit," she commanded.

And I sat.

"We have things to talk about, my son," she said in a voice stronger than I had heard in many years.

I waited, trying to close my heart.

"We're not close, David—we haven't been close since your father died ten years ago."

"I don't remember him."

"Yes . . . I know."

I had not seen her face, and now when I looked purposely, I found it in shadow.

"Want me to turn on a light?" I asked.

"No, please . . . there's another sort of light we need, you and I."

And now I waited again, anticipating in wonder yet knowing all the while what was about to come, dreading the words I'd never heard spoken.

I'd lied deliberately about my father—I remembered him only too well—his strength, the fount from which I'd drawn my height, the clear bright goodness that was invulnerable to everything but the tuberculosis bacilli.

But now I waited, lying. To her, to myself, to my inner yearning yet unknown.

"David, I know your feeling . . ."

"Do you?"

"Please, let me finish."

"Go on."

"It's because . . ." She paused and shifted a little on the bed so that her face revealed itself in the listless light, starkly. "It's because having a white mother is not an easy thing—"

"I gotta go, Ma." I stood up, watching the pain erode slowly over the sharp angles, the soft breast-bows, of her features. "I'll be late for work."

"David—"

"I only gotta work a few hours—"

"Please . . ."

But I cruelly ignored the word, snatching up my jacket from the couch where I'd thrown it angrily arriving home from the Fruit meeting.

"David," she said softly, that second before I could fully close the door behind me, ". . . your father and I loved each other."

And I had to hurry before the flood burst entirely and I rushed back to her arms and comfort . . .

Like the night my father died.

Here's my world—Niggerville—my sore, my shame, since the first time I realized it as a thing of fact and not some Cracker's cartoon strip:

Greasy Bones 'N' Cracklin's, the Shine epicure's constancy of eternal chopping jaws; the lighted neoned otherworlds, where whiskey-whining woes found expression in B.B.'s blues and *Blinky's* hues of black and low-trash white; those slinking Johns, consorting with sly-eyed, fearful laughs, futilely measuring their acceptance here, dickering with some black Horror's whore for that slice of ecstasy that was not life unto themselves, *was* oblivion to the whore and what she represented to her environment—like screwing death, I thought disgustedly.

My world, man:

Yes, dopeys and drugmen and dapper mocking Dans—the fuzz and pussy and pussy-collared: the *Jesus, please* exhorters on cornerfronts, in candy stores converted; the hurried, harried, hungry, for whom despair and life composed a litany—a dirge—preceding, yes, overlasting, their damned-faced passing.

Mine.

And me. I'm them.

So see as I have seen, have been, am now, will remain:

When I walk streets, I see with different nigger's eyes . . . The pool-packed, pulsing poolroom is no longer fraternity house where clicking balls in undulating unbroken colored continuity caused by reefer's exciting illusion and inconstancy is now a mortuary replete with stupidly staring, insipid-eyed corpses—with nowhere else to be but here and being dead this way.

Lazarus, the Prophet called us.

Hi, Laz, old buddy, I say to myself in passing—all you Lazs in *Abraham's Pool Emporium* . . .

His bosom.

Niggerville, Hooverhill, Stupidstill.

That was it—*still,* rather than anything else, forever, like all-ways, always this way, unchanging, without the usual boredom of such things, *like* things (though not another world is *like* this one of mine), undifferently different, daily.

I walked and felt the cooling nighttime stink against my cheeks and saw myself reflected sadly in the garish glass façades. There was no other world in which I could escape my fate, no ash or sackcloth to redeem my father's guilt, his father's past, that past-time savage's acquiescence to slavery's sloppy mouth, her whorish kiss . . .

Seventy-fourth Street.

Oh, my people's city within the black bloated white whale's belly! Unmasticated, swallowed whole in dirty, acid bilish unfelt torment—

I see here an Avenue of lavish lights, of luscious, lazy abstraction—of irresponsible life—and I goddamn its refusal of me, of my question, of my quest for identification—

"Because you could *tell* me," I say, in a way that makes a passing man turn as though he really could.

—and denying me, in its complacent comfort, that pit-small piece of peace which is my heritage's right.

I despise and loathe you, each and every nigger, now, before, to come, who make me prisoner and shameful recipient of a deeper unrealized repulsion.

Only your deaths—and mine—would make me accept the way things are!

"Listen, Dave, would you tell me straight? It's just a thing that crossed my mind, and you and me are pretty tight around the store—just a question to prove my point 'bout progress, and brotherhood and such."

I looked deep in Arnie's light blue eyes and saw the lecher gleam. Another question about sex—and me.

"You ever had a white woman, Dave?"

It was the same, the question that was not asked by them for knowing's sake—more for self-substantiation. It was one that always rankled me, nothing like the "how big's yours?" or "can ya really strike bottom with a colored girl?" kind: this query demanded self-incrimination, and it left no fifth-amendment exit.

I looked at him, his face, the palishness that was a glow to *know*. His covering skin was the same as my mother's, but the difference here was a distention of abstraction that dissolved into complete racelessness. I mean . . .

I felt the burn of it—I *hated* him. And her, too, my Ma. But still, they didn't seem to be the same, her and Arnie: she, in her hiding, bedridden twilight of prolonged dying, and he—he the cousin of my boss, my co-mate superior in the supermarket's well-stocked stockroom of floresced people-needs.

He—this—here—was what I seemed to *know* in her but couldn't ever see in fact. It was frustrating, and I was helpless. Futility,

That drove my fingers into hard-rock black fists.

That made me rise—actually *rise*—as though to sunder Murder's virgin cherry.

"You know what I mean, Dave? Huh?"

Again I looked at him, examining his flushed, pink throat: his talk of women's asses, tits, pussy, hungry, consuming mouths—had drawn hot blood to his reddish skull and caused a shiny wetness at the corners of his mouth.

I raised a carton to chest level and placed it on another just the same.

"No," I said, avoiding him, unsure of myself as I'd never been before.

"What?"

"You heard me."

He wiped the moisture and stockroom dustiness on his apron front and sat on two ass-high cartons of Campbell's soup.

"Aw, Dave, come off it . . . I know you City College boys—"

"I only went for a couple semesters . . ."

"But that's enough! You musta met *some* hot young blonde—they've got a reputation over there."

"They didn't earn it because of me—I went to CC to get an education—" I was angry now, and I turned on a pivot that warmed my calves and thighs, clear to my chest and pounding heart. "—not a piece of tail that all it knows how to *be* is tail—that means no more to me than *your* ass!"

"Now listen . . ." he said, rising.

"No, *you* listen—" And I saw him back away a little, shocked by the thing in my eyes.

"My religion tells me you're scum," I said in a low, steady, unmistakable voice.

"What are you talkin about, Dave?"

"That you're filthy. From your sex habits and psychosis to your useless effort to return head-first to the womb through some brother-faggot's rump—"

"Hey—" he said in an almost scream, as though I'd struck him.

"Now!" I said, impressed with our aloneness, the inspiration of death in my hands. "It's gotta come now—not when Fard decides its ready—*our* time is ready!" My head was buzzing with a surging new strength.

"What's the *matter* with you, Dave?" Arnie said, aghast. He moved behind the boxes, trembling in a manner that gave the gutty stone at the pit of me an urgent implosion.

We both knew it, what was to come, in a way that was more than fear, or orgasm—or death: even more than the thing itself. I found myself crouched, somehow overly huge and anticipatory, like a jungle animal that had surprised its natural prey breaking thirst, and now there was no shelter or escape for it, as though there had *never* been, as though God had never meant there to be a haven from its natural death.

"Dave," Arnie whimpered, "for chrissakes, pull yourself together!"

As I had sensed natural death, so now did I sense an innate, almost historical, fear. A congenital thing, just as Brother Harvey and the Leader had apprised us of in the teachings. Before me was the face of a *criminal*—a murderer and rapist—who had been caught in the act and now dreaded the final, absolute consequences of his acts . . . Revelation's Beast of the Bottomless Pit who would cry to Heaven on the day of exposure, seeking mercy where there is none—the serpent of the original garden: Baal, Satan.

The Devil.

"Dave," he said, trembling uncontrollably, "the way you're lookin . . . you're *scarin* me! Dave, I never did *nothin* to you—why do you wanna do this?"

Involuntarily, my mind and body were released from the strange—yes, *selfish*—tension, and it was as if my eyes had been opened after a week's slumber. And what I saw, through the dying storm of my lust, was not a devil at all but merely a prefab human—certainly a prototype of the Master of the World—a cardboard Tarzan whose hard-ons came vicariously . . . who, for some indefinable reason not completely explained to my satisfaction in the teachings, bore an insuperable weight of guilt, of envy, of masochistic love-hate, in the person of a contradictory personage—the black man.

Why I stopped to grapple with, to rationalize, my *hatred* (but was it *mine*? I wondered; wasn't it shared by others?) I didn't know.

My anger was unceasing—indeed, it had increased, soared, in an illimitable abundance, not upward but Heavenward, eastward, toward Mecca, receiver of my five-times-a-day genuflections—and the God of another age whose evil black mind had predestined my torment presently with His creation—*glad* creation—of a plague-race, and the current-day Allah, W. D. Fard Muhammad, whose patience in the divine city was my pain.

And I cursed aloud, and the quivering, pre-ordained Adam before me quivered anew, mewlingly, so sickeningly humbled by his own unknown fear that I felt like retching.

I turned away in guilty disgust.

This was not the kind of thing that I, if God's seed I was, could make war on.

Yakub, the God of Genesis, had been successful in his command, *"Come, let us make Man in our own image . . ."*

For an *image* was all he succeeded in creating.

The boss regarded me as though I was mad—and I guess I was, maniacally—when I told him to shove his job and collected the pay I had coming. I didn't see his face—it had idiotically grown too pale to realize, diaphanous—nor hear his words of not-understanding: nor even, really, feel myself as a person—more as a dissociated entity that was *eyes*, watching me go through a series of motions at the checkout counter, glaring low-browed in a way to cause the watcher to feel that *me* was staring inwardly at some inward horror, or had, finally, terrifyingly, come aware of a rot that had existed there unnoticed all along, too long, and that putrescence was steadily, intransigently, occupying the *all* of *me*.

I watched me come slowly out of the market, shoving the few bills to the coarse pocket bottom, separating the few coins from the crinkling mass so that they came between the first joint of each finger, tediously.

He glanced over the long, black, brighted, nighttime street pointlessly, for he knew now there was nowhère to go from here. Above, the sky had grown black as his thalamic pit; the wings of his heart fluttered accusingly. Yes—and *his* soul was tightening about his entire being like a garrote.

His eyes, darting ahead of his brain, recognized the next, people-cluttered block as the one nestling the Muslim restaurant, Shabazz, and he knew many Brothers would be there now, indulging a good-night's repast. The urge to enter was almost overpowering as he passed, but he knew their voices would lower if he did, their eyes would not see him, their minds would deny his outcast abstraction.

Inside this heart sped with longing as he came staring by were the brightly lit, sterile cleanliness of Brotherhood, and Brothers' close-cropped heads, neatly nodding to sup, the smell of onion-sopped beef expertly cooked by Sister Dahlil, Brother Harvey's fat, jolly ebony-skinned wife, which brought saliva bitter and yearning to his tongue—and he quickened the passage of his feet a bit in going by the luscious place of belonging.

Behind him, he heard footsteps discreetly chasing his,

and turned to see Brother Forest, tall as a Watusi, and his sister, Famat, who was but an inch or two shorter, led in a mild, soldierly trot by Brother Carl.

"Brother David . . ." he called.

But he already waited, weirdly empty, as they came abreast.

"As salaam aliekum," Brother Carl said, and so did the others.

"Wa 'liekum salaam," he answered.

Brother Carl was somehow abashed, rather ashamed, it seemed; and the others—their eyes watched him with expectancy—and for the first time he knew Famat's intense white smile, the way it was embossed by large, generous lips; the way her nose flared, like a doe that has been frightened suddenly—the way that her smooth skin was, now, not black and monotonous as he believed all black skins to be, but lustrous, myriadly brilliant and kaleidoscopic with the variance of night lights, and abruptly it was one of the most beautifully pigmented tissues he'd ever seen.

"We saw you pass by Shabazz, Brother," his friend told him, now so different from the embarrassed, facially reticent young man he'd spoken with after the Fruit meeting, earlier.

"You shouldn't have left your meals," he told Carl quietly, supernaturally aware of himself *above* himself, hovering, it seemed, like some message of black importance.

Concerned. Yes, their faces watching him, the looks in their eyes, were concerned.

"Is anything wrong? Brothers? Sister?"

Famat tensed visibly at his reference, and boldly set precedence by answering before any of the males, invoking quick, obvious displeasure from her brother.

"Brother David . . . we wondered—at least, we . . . *I* . . . heard about what happened tonight. I'm sorry."

"Of course we are," Brother Forest said, putting emphasis on "we."

"We weren't eating," Brother Carl told him. "We were just talking when you came by. Brother Forest intends to record a little of the Teachings . . ."

"We wondered if you would like to come by," Brother Forest said politely. "We don't feel, because of your suspension, you should be denied Allah's most abundant food—we don't feel any Black Brother should be ostracized, in this respect."

"That's kind of you," he told them.

Famat's face brightened. "Then you *will* come along?"

"I'm sorry . . ."

"Please, David," Carl said kindly. "It'll take your mind off things."

"My mind isn't troubled, Brother, thank you."

He saw Carl's face flush, an accent of lemon on thin, sensitive, Asiatic features, and felt ashamed of the pain he'd caused his only friend.

Now his eyes shifted to Famat once more, and there was something about the way she watched him, not that prim generality of surveillance used by the modest Pearls of Islam but a frank, open gaze, white and clear, which accentuated her full, unpainted character of face; and the trunk of her, he saw self-consciously, with a tiny tickle of physicality, was full to bursting with youth under the plain dress emulated by all Sisters of the Pearl: breasts high, full and proper over the wide, receptive pelvis, carried on thick thighs and slim smooth legs he had come to recognize as those belonging to the pedigree of black female blood—the mark of an honored tribe.

And he wondered what had kept his eyes from seeing her before. In this peculiar, pleasing way.

"I was on my way home," he began, watching the way her lids raised at the sound of his voice.

"Oh, please, Brother David—Allah would be pleased if you came along," she said.

From above, from a plane, an eyrie perspective, that seemed to sway his heart irrepressibly in a way he'd never felt before, he saw, and felt, his mouth form the words.

"If . . . I won't bother anyone," he agreed.

"You won't," Famat said, showing a wide, comforting smile.

They struck a pace, and Carl fell in beside him.

"I stopped by your place not long ago," he said quietly. "Your mother told me you'd gone to the market."

"I quit tonight." But he offered no further explanation, and Carl did not press. He turned to Brother Forest and Famat, who followed behind, and directed their attention to an eastern star.

"Mine," he announced, like a song. "Brother Dawud cast my horoscope, and that's my direction, he said. The star of faith."

Brother Forest nodded with dark inscrutability. "You have as much of that as anyone I know, Brother Carl."

"Thank you, Brother."

They walked in silence up to 112th Street, then over a block past the teeming nightshade tenements, where black men and women and running, playing children lived in unlikely prosperous vivacity, enthusiastic, perhaps for tomorrow, perhaps the next day, in love with life's living and each personal moment, contained in the fallacy of God's benevolence, in a kind of drug-like deprivation that induced a false, comforting elation in an immediacy that was really death. And more.

Was really the World in miniature, was frightening, truly, if one stopped to look at it. And he *had*—suddenly had.

Carl noticed the slight change in step. "I'm glad we saw you tonight, Brother . . . I didn't have a chance to speak with you as fully—after the Fruit gathering—as I would have liked . . ."

"Yes. I'm sorry now. What I said," he told Carl in a funny, different voice he'd never heard his mouth make before.

"No, Bro—David." He watched Carl's profile and, when he could see them, the small, radiant eyes that seemed to emanate a feeling of sincerity, of brotherly dedication to the cult of—brotherhood.

And he smiled with the thought, not with discovery but with a heavy weight of judgment. For he had known all along that there was something each man endeavored to achieve—something, he didn't know what, that even *he* desired over and above the very fact of life.

In simply knowing this, he knew what it was Carl wanted —and he despised Carl for it. But if Carl wanted it . . .

Didn't Brother Harvey? Brother Forest and all the other Brothers?

Even the Leader himself?

Were it not for his detachment, he could have answered the most important questions. But it didn't seem to mean so much now, not now that he was aware of Carl, and his hunger, and the hunger about them as they walked, and the black above, with Carl's star dimly insinuated, and his own heart thumping wildly as he made himself aware of Famat's full, blossomed presence behind and how much he would like to touch her flowered skin, to know its warmth with his own.

Perhaps . . .

"This is my place, Brothers," Forest said, pointing to a stoop just ahead where several black people sat drinking beer, two women and a man, who was cursing one of the women unangrily but steadily and did not pause as they came up and entered.

"Sometimes the dead Brother is disgusting," Brother Forest commented in the dark, unlit gloominess of the hallway.

Like his own apartment building, Brother Forest's was a musical of despair; the stairway looped rather than ascended to the third floor, around hedges of battered-faced doors and limp iron railings, where the darkness grew more penetrable as they went higher, shafted by beams of the night-sky's varied illumination from the dull skylight above the fifth floor.

"The darkest part of the temple," Brother Forest noted grimly, referring to a Masonic ritual.

At one of the rear doors on the third floor, he stopped and inserted a key. The room was neat and plumpily furnished. In one corner was a television set, with a black plaster bust of a long-dead Egyptian queen atop. On one wall was an almost full-sized eastern tapestry of a desert scene—two camel drovers trading with what appeared to be a rich merchant whose eyes on their wares were greedy and lascivious rather than brotherly—very beautifully and expertly done.

All the couches were purposely fat, cushioned in the opulent eastern harem fashion, and he felt misplaced, the softness sucking at his rump as he sat, and much out of place.

A tall, dark-skinned, smiling woman came through the kitchen doorway, bowing slightly. "As salaam aliekum."

"Wa 'liekum salaam," they replied.

"I heard you come in," she said in a gently deep voice. "I have some coffee ready."

"That's fine, Mother," Famat said. "I'll help you with it."

They both bowed almost imperceptibly in united grace as they left for the kitchen.

"Your sister is a fine-looking woman, Brother Forest," he heard himself say involuntarily. "And your mother is quite handsome."

He noticed vaguely Carl's glance in his direction, that seemed to make his skin prickle, and he turned his eyes toward the door the women had entered. Over the archway was the blood-red Muslim flag, the sun, the crescent of the moon, the tranquility of the stars. Freedom, Justice, and Equality.

Brother Forest went into an adjoining room and returned with a portable tape recorder and a sheaf of papers in a manila folder.

"I'll have to review a bit, Brother Carl; Brother Dawud and I did quite a lot of recording earlier today." He set it down next to an overlarge easy chair, unlatched the top, and plugged the cord into one of the wall outlets.

"Here's the coffee," Famat said, entering again with a tray. "I hope you like it black—there's no cream."

He watched her as she smiled at him, handing over a cup and saucer tentatively. "Brother David . . .?"

"Thank you," he said, and watched the salience of her long dark legs as she took a seat facing him. And he could not take his eyes from her face, knowing all the while she was aware of his attention.

"There it is," Brother Forest said, with a final tape adjustment. He consulted the typewritten pages in the folder. "Where shall we begin, Brother Carl? Brother David?"

"Well," said Carl, "the European evolutionary stage—the Devil's development there. I don't think we've done it yet." He sipped hugely of his coffee.

Brother Forest objected with an upraised finger and polite smile. "I have the tapes by Brother Charles X, which were done last fall."

"They're kind of shabby now, Brother," Famat addressed her blood. "Why don't we begin with The Creation? We're all familiar with it, and maybe you Brothers can contribute taped portions without the benefit of the Leader's notes."

Whenever she spoke, he noticed, a certain quiet prevailed afterward, accentuating the tone, the resonance, of her rather deep voice, giving the words an impact of forwardness and presumption he was sure she did not intend to convey.

"Why not let Brother David begin?" she added, and it might as well have been the sharp explosion of a pistol.

Carl looked at him quickly. "Yes, David, why don't you start it off for me?"

And he felt himself saying, against his will, "I don't know how it'll turn out . . . but I wouldn't mind trying."

Brother Forest stood up from his seat. "Sit here, Brother. I'll adjust the machine as you speak."

He saw himself rise, take the place, take the microphone along with Brother Forest's brotherly smile, and, with one last glance at the calm-faced Famat and a signal from Brother Forest, he was surprised to hear himself begin:

"As salaam aliekum. By the benevolence of Allah, the One God, the following is an interpretation of The Creation, as revealed to our Leader by Allah the All Merciful, in the voice of Brother David X, devotee of Muhammad's Temple of Islam, eastern district."

Brother Forest snapped the off-button. "Now, Brother

David, that was a fine introduction. Take your time; there's thirty minutes of tape."

He cleared his throat, not nervous as he'd expected himself to be and, peculiarly, not even aware what his first words would be. He took a deep drink of the bitter Arabic coffee.

They waited expectantly. Brother Forest started the machine again.

"About eight thousand years ago, in the Holy City of Mecca," he began, "there occurred the birth of a man whose name, Allah tells us, was Yakub—the God of his time. Yakub's birth had been foretold through the prophets in the twenty-two million-year-old dynasty of the black man.

"Now. When Yakub was born it was, therefore, no secret. The people, as well as the Sidi and the twenty-four prophets, knew of his coming and what his coming would mean to the world and countless generations to follow.

"Yakub, in fact, told his uncle, at the age of eight, that he would create a race more powerful than any the world of Godmen had yet seen . . . and his statement was not taken lightly. For even his destiny had been foretold, also— even so the evil it would bring . . ."

His voice now took a branch of discourse they were not familiar with, indelibly stamped in the twisting spool, and he felt the strange warmth in the eyes as they watched him.

"However, no action was taken to prevent the coming of this scourge predicted to last six thousand years, neither by previous Gods, who could have easily misdirected the genetic stream, or the God of Yakub's day, who could have blunted the seed, telepathically, in his mother's womb . . ."

Unconsciously, he stopped. The statement was unpremeditated but far from subtle. It was a rebuke, a criticism, plain and simple, an irritating granule of thought that had grated his whole conscience since the day he'd embraced Islam, the unasked why that could not, as Brother Minister and Brother Harvey claimed, be "explained mathematically, as could all things in Islam," for no mathematical solution seemed sufficient enough an *excuse,* a *vindication,* of the Godheads who were supposedly aware of the havoc this new devil race would disseminate on ensuing generations.

No.

Mathematically, he was forced to see, it was imperfect— and ridiculous to consider it any other way.

Six thousand years of hell as balanced against *what*? Tomorrow, which was an abstract one could not compute along with yesterday's facts and today's reality—was, therefore, the imponderable fraction, the key denominator in a final solution?

No, he told himself impassively.

No.

"Go on, Brother," Brother Forest said softly, watching him. They all watched him, like stuffed drovers anticipating a wealth's barter he could not yet fully honor.

Brother Forest waited with finger on key, having deigned the full, raging, thunderous catharsis of enlightening silence they'd just heard.

He raised the microphone close to his lips again and licked them.

Click.

"Yakub came to be," he heard himself say, "the first God of evil, Baal, the first black Devil ever to exist in Heaven-Mecca. He was a genius of dissension, sedition, subterfuge, coming at a time when a certain portion of the world's population was socially satisfied while a smaller percentage was not. It was to these malcontents he appealed when arranging his master plan. They followed him unquestioningly into the whirlpools of political unrest he fomented, never doubting his assertion of their own *special* divinity under his leadership, and even, when Yakub was no longer tolerable to those of ruling authority, followed him into exile —a small island off the coast of North Africa.

"As a result of Yakub's concentrated attacks and other ingenious methods contrived to create turmoil, the civilization of the Original God suffered schisms of belief; new faiths arose; Godman isolated himself in groups on other portions of the globe and went into wild tangents of religiosity . . . the clashes were enough to draw attention away from the insidious God Yakub and the Frankensteinian scheme he set toward consummation.

"Yakub—or, as the Bible calls him: Luther, the Archangel—you see, was followed by fifty-nine thousand, nine hundred ninety-nine believers, whom he was to employ in this Gargantuan plan. And it took four hundred and sixty-odd years."

Brother Forest snapped the recorder off. "Brother David, I think you ought to say a word or two about the pre-Yakub world."

"It's pertinent," Carl agreed. "Anyone hearing this for the first time, David—say, one of the dead Brothers— couldn't help being a little confused."

Famat smiled at him. "You're doing beautifully, Brother David."

Click.

"A footnote should be added here," his voice rang solidly inside his head. "Before the coming of Yakub, for thousands—yes, for millions of years—Original man had existed upon the Earth in complete sensual serenity. He was the *mind* of the universe, the God of Perfection, capable of self-reproduction, the like of which is observed today in certain amoebic life forms; it was much later, after realization of his intellectual supremacy, that he decided to form the female entity separate of himself. No one knows, save Allah in His greatness, how Original man evolved. But no one doubts the facts of his unique dominion for countless centuries. From the life force of his mere being he had caused the existence of the Earth, moon, and surrounding planets through a calculated explosion of our nova. Even the crinkly hair of certain black people is directly attributed to one of these Original men—a casual whim of his.

"This was a period of total oneness, a time in which man communicated with his brother through the medium of telepathy; when he traveled by the light-like instantaneousness of teleportation; when one thought, one discovery, was simultaneously flashed to the corporate mind.

"One may ask why man didn't continue this indescribably perfect state—and that one has every right to have his question answered."

But here Brother Forest stopped the machine and looked at him a long time before speaking. "I don't think we should stray too far off the point, Brother David."

"I don't intend to."

Brother Forest nodded in a way that did not necessarily indicate concession. "Let us continue, then."

He licked his lips and felt his voice lower to a throbbing, strengthful octave of emotion.

"It was because," he went on, "that Original man was *not* as perfect as he led himself to believe . . ."

Click.

Brother Forest now stood from his kneeling position by the machine. There was almost a vibratory emanation of quiet confusion in his rigid stance, unwavering eyes, and dark-set black face. "I think we'd better erase that part, Brother David."

"Wait," he heard Famat's soft voice say. "I don't think Brother David completed his thought."

"What he's saying is not doctrine," her brother said with

what was now an unmistakable chill in his voice. He looked to Carl for—not *support*—confirmation.

And Carl said, not looking at his friend,

"Yes, sir. We're listening to personal interpretation."

"But I thought that's what we agreed on from the beginning," she protested, "a rendition of *personal* perspectives." She shifted her bulk, the fineness of her living electric beauty, to him where he sat waiting with the microphone. "How else are we expected to gain the *essence* of the Leader's truth other than by interpretive individuality? No one truth is the same in the eyes of all the people, Brother, because each man's conception is colored by his *own values* and experiences. But this doesn't change the truth from being *truth*—nothing, no one, could do that. No matter how you dress it, no matter how many lying drugs are injected to make it stand at a false attention—not even artificially changing its sex or origin."

She paused now, and seemed about to go on for a moment. Then she smiled at him under the glowering cascade of her brother's distemper.

"Please go on, Brother David," she said softly.

He cleared his throat, not feeling nervous at all—actually anxious to go on, embraced by the necessity of expression and the pulse of a foreign passion.

After a brief hesitation, Brother Forest stooped to start the machine again.

"Somewhere, during his various metamorphic stages, Original man lost his originality," he said unflinchingly. "After countless years of duplication of his perfection and him*self*, the first God became more *man* than God, for through his own formulation, his basic cognizance of the unavoidability of—the primary prerequisite of all creation —the cycle of three hundred and sixty degrees, man-God *inversed* himself, taking on more manlike attributes at the sake of aggravating the God-core—originality—thereby fusing the flesh and that which was omnipotent into an unholy alliance. In other words, there were too many Gods for God's own good—too many omnipresent pretenders for the throne of omniscience.

"Mathematically, then, there was little these unfused God-intellects could do, in the eons falling on the coming of Yakub, to keep from degenerating into mere men.

"And so concerned they were with the inward contemplation of the wonders in the evolution of their slowly vanishing Godseeds, the growing inaction of the God*seat*—the brain—that there was damned little they cared to do about it."

"That's about all," Brother Forest said harshly, cutting off the machine with a loud snapping noise that rang around the void of All-things and yanked the past, the present, into the *here* . . . and *me* into *myself*.

"But I'm not finished," I said, looking at him in his eyes until our four eyes were glued, and I could feel the fear as he hovered menacingly above me, from both of us.

"You are as far as I'm concerned," he said rather loudly.

"Brother—" Famat started. "Forest . . . Brother David is our guest—we *won't* show him any discourtesy."

"It's Brother David who's shown the discourtesy," he said lividly. "He's shown it to the Holy Koran, our Honorable Leader, and Allah Himself in that order—any one of which is excuse enough to take his blaspheming head!"

"Forest!" Famat said.

Carl stood to go over to him. "Brother . . . peace, Brother, *please*. It's only that Brother David's interpretation of known truth isn't as exact as it *could* be—he needs further study . . ."

"He needs total expulsion from the Temple," Brother Forest said venomously, and I knew he hated me—but the hatred was because of another thing, because of his sister, whose plain prim dress I had raised over her hips as soon as I knew that the wrongness I was experiencing was the dress itself, the doctrine, the *peace be with you* in hell, as though there could *ever* be the sudden, good, human-again feeling. . . . Someone, some voice, some*thing*, was laughing at us, at all of us, at me, because of some vague, shadowy, goddamn lie we'd been conned to believe in.

I could see the sides of Brother Forest's cheeks bunching in sharp muscles, rocky, black huge mountain definitions, as he looked down on me. "This young man is dangerous to himself, to us, and to the cause of the lost-found black nation here in the hell of North America. I heard him earlier tonight, with his filthy devil's mouth, heaping abuse on Brother Harvey in the midst of a Fruit discussion, and if it hadn't been for you, Brother Carl, I'd never have allowed him in my home."

"Brother—" Carl started.

I now stood myself. "That's all right, Carl. Brother Forest, I want you to know something—"

"I don't want your apologies . . ."

"I wasn't about to give them."

"Then you can get out of here."

"Forest!" Famat said.

Her mother came through the kitchen door and stood watching us quietly.

"Now I've got something to say," Famat's voice rose surprisingly, and I could see now a glimmering coat of anger in her smooth features that somehow gave me a feeling of extreme excitement. "And I'm going to say it whether you like it or not. You Brothers all seem to feel that we Sisters have no right to think. Well, that's wrong. That we have no voice—that we're merely receptacles for your holy seed and the teats for its nourishment. Well, you're wrong again!" she said feelingly. "We *do* think, and we *are* more than homemakers and brood cows—"

"Famat," Brother Forest said tensely. "I command you to shut your mouth."

"And I refuse to!" she said defiantly. "And from now on I'm going to refuse *all* commands I think are unjust. Don't you provoke me, Brother," she warned, "because I'll go further than Brother David and question the tenet called Freedom, Justice, and Equality under Islam. I thank Allah for the capacity to make my own judgments and to seek my own answers." Her ire caused her to appear lost for words for a moment.

Then she glanced at me, a soft thing, feline and heartful. "If you're going to expel Brother David from the Fruit, then you'd better expel *me* from the Pearl."

"Famat!" her mother said, shocked.

"That's the way it must be," Famat went on strongly. "Because I have questions, too, and I'll never stop asking for the answers until I have them—to *my* satisfaction. Even though we were raised in Islam, Forest—please. Even though our father raised us in Islam, he never established— no, decreed—our positions as his children—"

"*I* am Allah's spear of judgment," her brother said proudly. "I offer my life to the war, and victory, of Armaggedon."

"Yes, you," Famat answered dimly. "You're a warrior of Allah—you know your place. But what about me? What about me, Mother?" she said, looking up. "Us? Why is it we've got to take the back seat? Is my only duty to Islam to teach day after endless day fourth-grade classes in the Temple classroom—when what I want to do is use my mind—contribute what I *know* is a good intellect—to a common cause, a common good? Is it only to birth strong black babies whose only purpose will be to give up their lives in some stinking war whose cause—whose back-

ground—whose beginning—is too profound for them to
understand? So that all they've got to feed their warfire is a
bunch of slogans and thrilling semantics? No! I refuse.
Again I refuse! Because I don't know—and I've *got* to know
before I follow *any* command. Allah says that I am his
separate self. That under the law I am equal, free, and
subject to every justice rendered my male counterpart. I
choose, as Brother David apparently does, to *demand* confirmation of my heritage, and as long as I don't get it, I'm
going to question the dogma of men—because God, not
man, is the only infallibility." She stared unafraidly at her
brother. "I hereby assume my better judgment to be the
final decider, and from it *only* will I follow orders—because, of all things I know to be God-given and *mine* only,
this is most obvious."

Brother Forest, without a doubt, regarded me as sole
cause of his sister's impassioned rebellion, and I began to
hope fervently that I *was*.

The chill had increased in Brother Forest's eyes. "You've
said quite enough, Famat. I'm sure you don't want Brother
David's departure to become any more complicated."

I went to the door, nodded slightly, "As salaam aliekum,"
and left.

I noticed that no one, with the exception of Famat,
wished me peace in going.

> ". . . We wore silk robes and slippers of gold;
> We were the finest people, I'm told;
> Now we're the poorest of the poor . . .
> Nobody wants us at his door.
>   "So, my friends, it is easy to tell
>   White man's heaven is a black man's hell."

The loudspeaker outside a record shop on Eighth Avenue
defiantly blared the deeply emotional voice and haunting
melody. I paused for a moment and listened, moved against
my will as the rhythmic strains flooded the lull of the
late nighttime, existed in sweet deprecation:

> ". . . With his white woman and firewater,
> Tricks and lies he stole America . . .
> The Original owner of this nation
> Is cooped up on a reservation.
>   "So, my friends, it is easy to tell
>   White man's heaven is a black man's hell."

I walked slowly toward home, strangely calm and introspective in a way that seemed in accord with the night and all its things. As though, a moment before, I hadn't been locked in self-conflict, hadn't engaged and warred within myself to strict and gruesome culmination. *Had* been the victor.

Now the taste of it—this first victory, the only one I'd ever won—overcame me, and I tasted it hot and sweet-bitter, like the wonderful soothing taste of Famat's good black coffee.

I crossed over to the mall where an empty bench faced the traffic and sat down, feeling washed and free—possessed of an alien knowledge that had come under my control through a cultivation I had not been aware of.

I listened intently for a while to the message from the loudspeaker, listened to it trace a history of slavery in chilling, graphic detail right up to the present day, which saw the status of the slave unchanged—in fact, more deeply ingrained through a process of indoctrination that deadened the collective senses and hardened the arteries of mass response.

I wondered at myself, compared my new audacity of self-awareness to that of a molecular chain, framed much like the scheme of stars overhead pointing the way to the arid answers of space.

I now had my path indicated, unspecified, but happy, and I wondered about it all, intoxicated, like the first time I had tasted liquor hidden discreetly by my father from my mother's attention: frightened yet exhilarated, sickened yet cured, warmed and cooled simultaneously, both inside and out, in gut and epidermis.

Brother Forest had said I was dangerous. And he'd been right. I was. But more than anything else, the Nation included, to myself—to my sudden sanity. And the thought of this suddenly made me quite afraid. Suppose I should lose it?

I got up and strode slowly into the street and traffic, narrowly missed by roaring convertibles loaded with carousing, drunk-eyed teenagers, chased without pretense by grinning juggernaut trucks.

Slightly out of breath, I made the other side, standing now in front of the record shop, Muslim, I saw now, by the fact of the young black woman sitting behind the counter with her hair covered, in the traditional Pearl manner, with a colorful silk bandanna.

"The greatest crime is his
Who kills new dust of the womb,
Sterile father of Death and the Tomb;
The snake of the Garden and Tree,
  "Despiser of Man's trunk and Earth;
  But in Love we find truth and rebirth."

The words were strange to me. I stopped and listened closely.

*"We find ourselves a part of plots
So desperately made,
But love is not easily swayed;
Our task is a one to be praised,
Allah has directed our ways,
To roads that the future has paved.
  "Come flee with me to new land,
  Where evil disdains our way and kind.
"Someday, my darling, we will gift our
Kinsmen with passion's harvest:
New men who'll rule the world and stars—
Our sons, the Children of the Outside."*

Something about the song caused me to linger to its finale. Unlike *White Man's Heaven Is A Black Man's Hell*, it spoke of love, and woman, and an end to all iniquity through adoration and physical delight.

"That's called *Outsiders*," someone behind me said, and I turned with a thrill of recognition to look in Famat's smiling eyes. "It's very beautiful, isn't it?"

"Yes," I said.

"The author is unknown."

"Perhaps he isn't."

She lowered her eyes, but not in a way that was shy—was, oddly, a gesture meant only for me. "Would you like me to tell you the story of *Outsiders*?"

"I'd like that more than anything else."

"Let's walk," she said, taking my arm.

I hesitated. "My mother is alone. I should've *been* back to see about her. I was on my way home when I met you at Shabazz."

"I'll walk with you," she said.

"It's late. Too late for you to be out, Sister."

"I'm not afraid, David," she told me with a confident smile. "This neighborhood, these people, are mine; they know me. They wouldn't hurt me in any way."

I looked at the dress parade of slouching winos and whores as we passed, the peanut hawkers and profane children, the neat pimps in ambiguous Cadillacs, the other twisted sores of Harlem's blackened face, and said, "These people belong to someone else—not you, Famat. The leader's right—they're zombies, the walking dead—slaves of the Devil."

"What did you mean?" she said suddenly.

"About what?"

"About the song—about its author possibly being known?"

"I'll have to wait, to hear the story you're going to tell me; I've heard them all and know their creators. They're just so many story roots, even in Islam."

"This isn't Islam, David . . ."

"Then what is it?"

She lowered her eyes again as I glanced in her direction. "It's a love tale. It's simply about two people."

I waited—because it wasn't embarrassment she felt, but a tenuity that abruptly trilled through us both.

In silence we walked, in silent agreement, in solitude of self, if that is expressionable; this was an outlying venue that did not at all portend an eventual disaster but was much like a fairy forest full with need of *having*: the need to be *had* by another individual, that should be a coupling of two differences into one fact.

As we neared the place I lived in, I felt a new fear pull accusingly at my knowledge of the present.

"Carl has spoken of your mother," I heard her say dimly. "I hope my neglect in introducing you to my mother formally won't stop you from making me known to yours, as your friend."

"She might not be yours," I said frankly.

"Why shouldn't she be?"

"Why was the white man created?"

"That's such a difficult question, David. That's why we're here together, tonight. Maybe that was the reason—to bring us here together."

She turned her eyes as I met them.

"It's a question that Islam . . . attempts to answer," she went on softly. "But the explanation has always puzzled me and seemed—*sadistic*. I guess you've felt the same way."

"I've felt . . . confused," I confessed.

Now her eyes brightened, impish flashes, and I grew warm in their glow. "Have you ever felt—not quite right, David? I mean . . ."

"What *do* you mean?"

"Well, as though—" She struggled for the evasive words, clutched them resolutely: "As though you were where you belonged but didn't really belong there at all."

I smiled, "I've never known how to express the feeling— till now."

My street arrived, like a dirty laugh, a carousel of crude buildings and denuded life sucking at long-emptied bowels of contrived surcease advertised as *newly redeckorated or money, love, happiness peace Madam Nosall Basement front Lucky Spirits;* gallons of uncapped noisome garbage that belonged now—had belonged for more than three days —to the City of New York, and had multiplied, as though by some celestial command, until it reeked in worship, in a way that was sacrificial, the gush of its own fierce, filthy immortality.

"This is where I live," I said quietly—but no longer ashamed in the way I had been at one time—which had only been a few hours before.

I sat on the stoop, and she placed herself closely beside me, so that I could feel the heat of her and the unfamiliar thing it seemed to stir in the pit of my belly. "Now," I said, "tell me about the *Outsiders*."

"Well," she said, in a voice I could imagine as one she used in her classroom with the Godseed of the Fruit and Pearl, "the *Outsiders* are two people aware of the Devil's evil and his attempt to annihilate them. But rather than fight him, they find it easier to escape his reservations and make the outer world their home: *We two, we few, we Nomads, must love desperately, use love's disguise,* they tell themselves."

"I noticed you sang that, and it was beautiful." I touched her long, relaxed fingers. "I feel there's another stanza following that. Please sing it."

After a moment's hesitation, she purred softly, *"Thus when our bodies meet in fusion comprising a total one-ship, we know our home: the heart of destiny—existing on the Outside . . ."*

And then, for a long time, when there was no sound in the street, or the world, we stared at each other.

Silently, I took her hand again and held it firmly in the mouth of my palm. "Sing, Famat, sing . . ."

And her cooing words enveloped me:

"It's true, my darling, you're the finest
Treasure I've owned;
No precious stone breaches your tone:

Contrasting black skin, whitest soul.
My ending life isn't hard when
Love's the best place to go,
And I've been. . . .
I've won, I've failed, but you know:
They don't get along, Man's laws and mine.
So when you pray for me, remember our
Good feasts and love mem'ries *as* me;
No man or God may touch what is to be:
"Our hearts are on the Outside."

Now the stars grouped in, and the night, and all things
indeed became a solitude of our one existence.

"Do you understand?" she asked me.

"How can one understand something he's never known?"

"David . . . you didn't ask me why I followed you tonight. Why I've come this far."

It wasn't the question so much as the realization that I
knew the answer, not even really that her speech was not a
question at all—more like an accusation that drew me into
a frightening, unplumbed vortex.

And I said, "I didn't intend to be the reason—"

"But you *are,* David, whether you want to be or not,"
she told me. "You can't—if you have the slightest belief in
Islam—help believing in destiny, in fate, in predestination,
David," she said firmly, and I could feel her breath warm
and Famat-fragrant against my cheek. "We both felt it tonight. I could tell it, oh, so long ago, when I first saw your
face and the pain on it, in the Temple—that first Sunday
you came, do you remember? When you came to the rear
after Brother Minister spoke, to accept your letter of entrance into the Temple: I was passing them out . . . Oh,
David, I knew you then, and you *looked* at me for such a
time, for such a time that seemed so long a time . . . *And I
was warmed through with you—*"

She stopped abruptly.

"Please . . ." I said.

"You probably think I'm mad . . ."

"But I *don't,* Famat."

"I don't know what's wrong with me," she said vaguely,
turning her head away. "I'm just acting like a fool . . ."

"Listen, Famat, how can I tell you how *I* feel?" I said
desperately. "Because what you say *is* true . . ." But now my
words would not come, and I sat with her in silence, waiting for the flood of our emotions to pass. And they *would*

not; they grew huger, monolithic, and sweet. Her hand was warm and moist in mine.

"David," she said at length, "do you think—do you think I've been shameless? I mean—I don't want you to *think* I'm not without shame because I feel it about so *many* things—about the way my mind refutes so much of the leader's testaments—which *must* be good, for Allah has seen fit to reveal them to us—that confuse me. In my prayers, I beg for forgiveness, but Allah doesn't see fit to give me comfort from this torment . . . David, my Brother," she said passionately, turning her face close to mine, "my *self* —*tell* me!"

"There *is* peace, Famat . . ."

"But where? Is it really on the outside? Are *we* the Outsiders?"

I felt a strange and sobering fear. "Why should we be? All we need to do is keep our mouths shut. Keep our minds shut, opening them only to what *should* be absorbed by them. Stop thinking." Then I suddenly saw the fateless futility of that fear. "Walk to the beat of that certain drummer, remain just one of a billion faceless faces. Stay harmless, and lambs—the way we were born to be!"

"Stop it!" she said harshly.

So I stopped, but merely stopping did not restore the ungentled plane of balance.

"How can—we—compromise, David?" she said finally.

"Ourselves?" I asked. "That wouldn't be the end."

"No, but it might make a beginning."

I smiled. And she smiled, too.

"It's the first time I've seen you look so beautiful," she said.

Now I blushed.

I stood. "Would you like to meet . . . my mother?"

"I couldn't think of anything I'd enjoy more," she said, rising in a single fluid motion.

But now I paused, anticipating, imagining her reaction to the place I called my home—the woman who was my mother.

Now, she did *not* know, and the magnetism I felt between us was not false, nor did it stem from some cataract of illusion; it was a bond, the caul, in fact, of a newborn entity that superceded our very existence, thrust from a womb of non-identification. But there *was* a specter of identity between us, and I wondered at her response once she set eyes on it.

It was a very difficult moment for me. I was on the

threshold of discovering Famat, as a woman who had come to represent something unutterably valuable among all the things I had, up to now, considered tinsel and gilt, the tender of desiccated demigods. Yes, and discovering *myself* as a man—not merely the inflation of the genitals: yet more, the inflation of the heart to painfully gigantic and pleasant proportions I'd never before experienced.

I was afraid of losing her, and yet, more afraid of losing myself.

"David . . . ?" I heard her voice probe at my indecision.

Without another word I took her hand and led her into the fetid building, she bringing along a warmth beside me that, curiously, was chilling to my flesh.

When we entered, I could see that my mother had found the strength to rise and turn on the lights. There was a residual scent of cooking, leftover spoils that mixed sourly with the ever-present smell of my mother's strange sickness.

Now she reposed in bed, limp and tiredly pale, eyes shining fitfully as we entered, and I felt the guilt of my neglect pounce unmercifully on my mental shoulders, heavily bending its back. I remembered belatedly that I had the unsavory task of telling her that I'd quit my job.

"David." I heard her say. "I was becoming worried . . ."

Behind me I felt Famat come to an abrupt halt, and I was almost frozen, as I said, without turning,

"Famat, this is my mother, Mrs. Kane."

"Oh, *hello*," Ma said, trying feebly to rise, to preen herself, to become other than the semi-invalid she was.

I felt Famat brush past me and, strangely, watched her bend over the bed to take my mother's half-raised hand. And Famat was smiling down—*smiling*.

"Mrs. Kane," she said in that soft voice, "I'm very happy to meet you."

My mother's face seemed electrified with an unusual surge of new life. "*Famat*, did you say? Oh, you dear girl! David, get Famat a chair and put it here by the bed. Oh, you dear girl," she said in a totally happy way that was strange for my ears to hear. "Are you a friend of David's? But that's silly—of *course* you are! My dear, you don't know how happy I am that you came by. David doesn't bring many friends by. Carl, of course—but *you*: child, you're the first girl David's ever brought home to me!"

I went and found the chair. Then I made coffee while they talked of inconsequential things, women things, and I sat on the couch and watched them as Ma bubbled on and the night crept slyly to ravish morning, and the thing between them developed until I hungrily realized they were two women I desired intensely and was not, because the laws of other men said I could not be, allowed to have, and I strained at the chains until I felt the snapping of a link, a vitally important one, that bound the biceps of my brain, till the free formation of my *own* new laws expanded their vast, clumsy arms to embrace the two differences of those living, human souls to the point of oneness, and there was no longer distinction, nor distillation, nor detraction.

"Famat, I've kept you *so* long," Ma said at last. "Please go home, child, and rest. But promise me you'll come back."

"Any time you want," Famat smiled. "I'll stop later this evening if you don't mind."

I saw Ma shoot me a hesitant glance. "I'd be very happy if you did, Famat . . . I don't get many visitors."

"Well, you've got a regular from now on, Mrs. Kane—before it's over, you'll have a stomach full of me."

My mother's smile was vivid and fond. "Have no fear about that. I've got a year of conversation for anyone who'll listen."

I couldn't help feeling relieved as I led Famat out and down the stairs.

Outside the day had come with an early ferocity that soundly slapped the cheeks of the dirty sidewalks.

We walked silently up to Eighth, where the motorized sweepers and street-washers had already begun their early-morning dirty work.

Finally, as we walked, and the marvel of the new day, with an ambivalently clean fresh smell of the city, surrounded us, I couldn't help saying what I knew Carl had thought all along but would not reveal to others because of our friendship:

"Now, it's plain what my sin is . . ."

Famat's face was surprisingly radiant as she looked at me. "There *is* no sin, David."

My laugh was dull and tarnished by what I considered an irreconcilable fact of origin. "Having just come from the den of the Devil, you can say that?"

I felt the pressure of her arm as it passed through mine.

"It is not the Devil within that matters, my David," she said softly, "but the one without."

Two weeks later I had found my way. With Famat's help, studying with her in my room after she'd left the Temple in the evening, I came to grasp an ology that was an inter-mixture of Ax, orthodox Islam, and theory.

Sometimes Famat would stare inexpressibly at me for long periods, which usually ended with, "You need so desperately to *believe,* David."

I took the Ax Muslim mathematical equations and reviewed them:

One:—The Beginning.

Two:—A nation: man and woman.

Three:—The light of the world: the sun, moon, and stars.

Four:—The square by which all things are equal, i.e., $4 \times 9 = 36$, which points to 9 as the beginning of One.

Five:—The number of Allah, Who is just to the obedient.

Six:—The Dragon's number—the number of a man who was six hundred years in the making, has six thousand years to rule, at which time his cycle of life will be complete—and he will die forever from the face of the Earth.

Seven:—Is complete in itself, causing the first to come last and the last to come first.

Eight:—Yakub's number, signifying the maker and the made.

Nine:—Is exact and the beginning of One.

This was an advocated formula, panacea for all the black man's ills. But study as I might, I could not adjust its semantics to any practical use.

"It's not applicable," I told Famat, after a few interminable sessions.

"Maybe we're trying too hard, David."

"It's not that," I protested. "There *is* truth in its numerical sense, but there's fallacy in the semantic denominator. All right, let's look at One, the Beginning. I've searched the teachings, the Koran, the Bible, and they all only *allude* to it."

She nodded. "That makes it an unknown factor."

"And possibly the key," I agreed. "I'm sure death will reveal the answer, but death takes us right back to One and Nine. Two and Three are incontestable truths. Now, look what happens when we come to Four, the oddball, which subtly inveigles Nine into its scope of reasoning."

Famat concentrated, her brow creased beautifully. "This could be the root."

"But how?" I said, showing her my list of contentions. "Where was the Beginning, in One, Two, or Four? Not only do these suggest origin, but so do Seven and Nine. Why?"

"Go on to Two," she smiled. "That's the one I like best —and I didn't make a pun on purpose."

"What can I say about Two that we don't already know?" I said softly.

I saw her begin a speech, but she paused and started again. "What do you think of Three?"

"The sun, moon, and stars? The flag used by *all* Muslim followers the world over. But it's something to be considered of unusual importance. Whether it's of mythical or original significance will involve further study, Famat, and I'd like you to dig up all you can about the subject."

"Four?"

"Isn't *Two* just as practical? It's easier to arrive at 36 two times eighteen than 4 times nine. I wonder . . .'"

"What about Five?"

"We've been taught to look on the One God as an entity rather than a divisible quantum—unless—and I say this hypothetically—Five represents the five senses possessed by man: the pillars of the human temple. But we know that man may be in charge of *more* than five senses, so it's difficult to proceed on the God-man theory when we know Allah is the All-knowing, All-bountiful, All-giving. Let's go on."

"Six, the Dragon's number, the number of a man," she said.

"This is *knowledge*, Famat. I've seen provocative references in the Koran. And there's something to it; what, I don't know. A profounder intellect than mine'll have to point out the nuances and cement the seams of my logic."

"What about the Caucasian's proclivity for burying his dead six feet underground," she said, "his sailing measurement of sounding, using six fathoms of depth as the gradient?"

I agreed with a nod. "There're numerous others, the six thousand-year reign, et cetera. There's no doubt his racial history is scanty, at best, past six thousand years. But there's also the fact that the black rulers of Egypt had Caucasian slaves in abundance, and this goes back more than eight thousand years. I can't find any mathematical consistency here—"

" 'Six hundred years to make, six thousand to rule . . .' "

"Exactly. But I'm not so concerned about this fallacy as I am about the stress it puts on the imagination of the un-initiated. It's like giving a dog the bone first and the meat later."

"Seven," Famat went on with a relentless little pleasure. I shrugged, and then she said sharply, "Eight."

"The year Eight Thousand, right?"

"I'm asking you, David. It's *you* who must answer these questions so that I'll know and be able," she said, looking away self-consciously, "to teach my children."

"We're told Eight Thousand was the year of Yakub's coming—"

"More than eight thousand years ago."

"Okay. We *know* this is the year Fifteen thousand and forty-five, which should have put the final creation of Yakub's mutant around the year Nine Thousand and a little more, since Yakub's *exact* birthday was Eight Thousand Four Hundred. This I'll accept at face value until investigation changes my mind."

"But you don't like it."

"I didn't say that. It's not a question of my liking or disliking this wealth of submitted evidence but whether or not I *accept* into my personal values items which are, thus far, poorly substantiated."

She pouted at me. "What about Nine?"

"It's *unexact* since its root is 3, not 2 or 4. *Unless*—" I became excited with the thought. "Unless One and Three are indicative to some chemical composite in relation to Five, Seven, and Nine."

"I don't follow you, David . . ."

"Look, Famat, what makes *active* life? I mean, atomically?"

She studied for a moment. "Well, there's the proton, neutron, and electron . . ."

"The sun—energy, alias proton," I said. "The moon—the feminine gender, the neuter, the receiver of life's seed; and the stars, that unknown binding quotient of all life, the thing that intersperses man's void and connects each living tissue. Famat—!"

"I understand, David," she said intensely. "Two, in conjunction with Five—no, with Three—that gives us *Five*—man and woman, the nation: *Allah.*"

"Seven," I rushed on, unable to contain myself, "gives us—procreation, male and female births out of the nation, making the first come last and the last come first!"

"And Nine—" She suddenly clasped me about the neck and rained sweet, new kisses on my glowing face.

"Oh, David," she said as I took her in my arms. "We've discovered *God* . . . ."

I got a job near the close of the summer which was sufficient to pay the rent and feed my mother and myself. It was a semi-white collar position as ledger-filer in a Negro insurance company where I came into first-hand contact with the unscrupulous exploitation employed by one brother against another—and a huge black brother who was my superior, and who (it was my misfortune to reveal it unthinkingly one day) knew I followed the Muslim faith. His name was Charles Benson.

"Y'all teach hate over there, doncha?" he asked me early one morning in the filing storeroom.

"What?"

"Y'all Mooslums," he said impatiently. "Don't y'all teach each other to hate the white man?"

"I don't know what you mean," I answered vaguely, going about my work, not wanting to get involved in an argument.

"Well?" said Charles Benson.

"Well what?"

His pancake face, black and pious, crinkled a little comically. "Well, *do* ya or *doncha* teach hate, you Mooslums?"

"No, we don't," I said, wondering at a way to tell him I no longer attended the Temple, by my *own* choice, now that my suspension period was up. "We teach merely that those things which go against our survival are the ones to be shunned—not hated."

"Like the white man?" Charles Benson said craftily, reminding me of Arnie, but in a more malicious, more insidious way.

"If he threatens our survival, yes."

Charles Benson laughed and sat next to the filing cabinet where I worked. "Boy, you sure is dumb—all you niggers!"

"Okay," I said, promising myself not to get angry, "suppose you tell me why."

"Because," he said, stabbing a pink and black finger into his palm, "the white man give us everything we got, that's why. If it hadn't been for him, where'd we be today?"

"You tell me."

"In Africa, that's where!" he said violently. "Agitatin' ain't gonna get you nothin', don't you know that? Look at it the way it is: See how far we've got since slavery days?

The black man ain't never advanced so much, so far, at one time. And integration's on the way."

"And what does that mean?"

"It means freedom!" Charles Benson said indignantly.

"But don't you already *have* that?" I asked him in the strictest seriousness. "The Fourteenth Amendment guaranteed—"

"You *know* what I mean . . . freedom to eat in the same place the white man does, go to school where he goes, swim where he swims—not be discriminated against."

"But look—integration doesn't change your color: You're still *black*. How can anyone imagine that a law can, overnight, convert a man who wasn't a man yesterday into a man today?"

Charles Benson bristled. "Are you sayin' I *ain't* a man?"

"No—but the white man *is*, by the very insinuation of his integrating laws." Now I warmed. "There may be some sad things said about Islam in the U.S., but the thing you can't deny is the fact that its followers stand on their own two feet and don't need a bunch of laughing-up-the-sleeve laws to tell 'em they're free and *equal*—not through white men's laws, but God's!"

Charles Benson laughed in a way that infuriated me momentarily. "I hear that talk all the time up on 125th Street, but it ain't knockin' down no walls the white man don't *want* down."

I was a little amazed. "In one breath you say the white is the black's last hope, and in the next you admit he is a suppressor who allows racial walls to fall at *his* discretion."

"Well, it's *his* country, ain't it? You Mooslums talk about how *inferior* he is—but I want to thank ya, he *ain't* no punk. It took a *man* to raise this, the most powerful country in the world. How can the black man, with nuthin', stand up against the maker of the A-bomb and H-bomb?"

"Who said anything about standing up against him?" I said. "The Black Muslims of America ask for *separation*."

Charles Benson shook his head mockingly. "And what's that gonna getcha?"

"*Freedom*," I said harshly. "That thing which you seem to think integration will bring you."

"All right, suppose you do get separation like you want— two or three states just for the black man to live in: how ya gonna get along without the white man's goods. his machines, his factories, his food?"

"We'll *make* them ourselves."

"Don't make me laugh!"—and he did so derisively.

"You'll never get a bunch of niggers to cooperate in some-thin' like that. I know from my own experience, from workin' right here in this place." He squinted up at me.

"The way it is, with the nigger, he's used to followin' the white man's orders, and he'll be lost without the bossman to tell 'im what to do."

I was about to speak, but saw he was going to continue.

"I don't care *what* you say, man, you or none of them people on 125th—a black nation here in America won't ever work."

"Why?" I said.

"Why? *Why?*" His eyes got big. "Because *the black man stopped bein' a black man a long time ago—in this country.*"

Now I had to stop working—the little I was doing—and take a seat facing him. At the moment, he and I were the only ones in the filing room, and the opening of the outer office door would signal a new entry with the hum and clatter of office machines.

"What do you mean?" I asked Charles Benson carefully.

"Just what I said," he told me adamantly.

"No, explain yourself. You said this country's black man is no longer black. If I've got the right understanding, you mean he's become a *white* man."

"That's *just* what I mean! That's where you Mooslums goin' wrong, can'tcha see? The nigger's been chuggin' up-hill for more'n a hundred years after equality through—through *association.* Hell," he said, stabbing his palm again, "look at magazines like *Ebony,* where they got niggers in ads doin' the same things whites do in the identical ads in *Life,* or *Look.* This just goes to show ya . . ."

"What?" I insisted.

"That y'all is *wrong,*" he went on fervently. "You think after all this strugglin' and strivin' to be like the white man, you could get more'n a handful of people to throw 'way that hard work? Boy, shit!" he said disgustedly, "you'd bet-ter take another look at it for the way it *is.* Even your Mooslums, dedicated the way they say they is—give 'um one week away from the subways, hollerin' Harlem, and the easy-pay plans on 125th, and they'll be *scramblin'* to get back."

"But, why?"

"Because they got a germ in 'um," he told me sagely. "You got it, I got it, everybody and everything with a drop of nigger blood in him's got it. It's a thing that won't allow no *separation, brotheration,* or *concentration* The same old self-sickness we fed on right out of our mothers' tits—and even before that, the bossman made sure we knew how to use this sick germ 'gainst ourselves, first and forever. And that's why I know not eatin' pork, smokin' cigarettes, or prayin' to Mecca ain't gonna make a damn bit of difference."

Now I shifted, and when I looked in Charles Benson's wide, stark white eyes, I knew he wasn't the fool I took him to be.

After a while, I asked the question he was waiting on.

His eyes twinkled. "Don't you know, boy? It's that thing you first denied knowin' anything about: hate."

Famat met me after work and, as I anticipated, sensed the current of new thought running rampant in my mind.

"What is it, David?" she said as we threaded our way through the evening crowd on 125th.

"Nothing serious. A man just gave me food for—seeing, I guess you'd say. . . ."

"Tell me about it."

I smiled. "I will, but not now, honey. We'll take a walk later, okay?"

She smiled and took my arm without another word.

When we arrived home, I was surprised to see my mother up and arranging a cold salad on three plates. "Hi, there," she said brightly. "I didn't expect you two so early."

"We took the tram," Famat said with a resonant but deep-soft laugh—and again I was surprised, for I never suspected their relationship would touch on secret-joke elements that concerned my mother's adolescence in England. As a child I had been fascinated by her endless tales of a strange, pale, proud, powerful people and cities that were composed of heathers and moors and vales and sheep, and an unfeminine person called a Queen, who was loved by everyone she ruled and ruled by a church called England.

Too soon—and impatiently after my father died—I'd come to look on her stories more as fairy tales than fact. But now I couldn't help envying Famat, knowing she had entered a phase of my mother's life that I had spurned—and it was an emotion that quickly grew to an almost physical sensation of pain as I watched them talk animatedly over the meal. And I could appreciate fully now the solitude and loneliness this white woman who was my mother must have suffered in the years following my father's death, how it had been intensified through the uncommunicativeness of her *only* link with humanity—her son. . . .

Because she could never be accepted fully by the black brethren of her husband, and because she had shorn all ties to have him, she was never again acceptable to the peers of her natural origin!

Each minute, studied cruelty I had exercised against her came back to me vividly. I'd always felt like a freak—but not because my skin color or tone was different to show the oddity, which they were not—but primarily:

Primarily because she *was* my mother and white and you could look at me and not be able to tell a damn bit of difference. I tried once to explain this to Carl, but I'd never been able to make him see what I meant, he never failing to reply maddeningly: "One drop of God's blood makes you whole, Brother."

That wasn't it at all: I wasn't solely my father's child . . . I was my mother's, too, there was no getting away from it. But yet I *wasn't* at all, can I make myself understood? With my coloring belying my maternal heritage on one side and certain Gaelic features casting aspersions on the identity of my sire, there was really *no racial classification reserved for me.*

Yet my environmental acclimation was Negroid, my thoughts, my motivation and militant impetus—even the basic mistrust of my mother.

It's hard to explain here . . . for it went—and goes—much farther than what I've put down here: to tell of the *black* feeling one black experiences at all times; the tenacity and choke of racial somnambulism because of that same innate blackness; the panorama viewed by *black* eyes that may not consciously regard but cannot help psychosomatically registering, which shows plainly the *difference,* the injustice, the pain, physical and psychic, the lust writ on the faces and hands of the pale executioner, whether in the midst of a lynch mob or white citizens' public orgy, or firm stroke of a slum landlord as the tip of his pen nips the roof from the heads of a rent-delinquent family, that makes *being* black, a Negro, Nigra, Spade, nigger—any of a dozen colorful synonyms—nothing less than a crime.

Shit, I said to myself, watching Famat and Mrs. Kane carry on as though there were no such things as racial propriety or pride, I would rather be a tree or rock or a clear white drop of cloud moisture with a moment's life than be an American so-called Negro, who can be compared to a pig who'd suddenly found himself within the Holy City of Mecca.

I ate silently, relishing the self-loathing Charles Benson had warned was inescapably incident to all like myself.

It was getting dark when Famat and I walked down to Riverside Drive, and the park. From the battlement hedging the green growth below—while around us young couples with new, stumbling, first-stepping children and aged Jewish haves, and ancient have-nots, hot-blooded, running, yelling children attacking flat-skulled water fountains near the staircase to the lower level, swarmed interminably—we watched the shimmering Hudson in the dying blue-gold of the sun's depressed half-moon (cool orange now over Jersey and pleasant to look at directly), and saw the lights from the other side's city flicker on in fear of insurgent night.

She took my hand in hers, and I turned at the gesture to look levelly into her big, becalmed eyes and see a moment's peace there.

"What are we going to do, David?" she said quietly.

"I don't know," I admitted.

"I . . . saw you, when we were eating. You were thinking so deeply."

I didn't answer.

"David," she said, and the tone, the tightening, of her voice made me turn to her. "There's something I've got to tell you . . ."

"Yes?" I said, noting that the tempo of my heart had accelerated.

"Forest . . . is going to—he and some others of the Fruit, including Carl—recommend that you be expelled permanently from the Temple."

"Oh . . ."

"Did you understand me, David?" she said anxiously.

"Yes . . ." Then I took her arm and guided her to the lower level, coming close, down the flagstone paths to the guard rail fronting the river and time-and-water-rotted wharfs of another era. I found a bench, and we sat in silence, watching, feeling, smelling night approach.

"It doesn't matter, Famat," I said after a long while. "I've come to realize that the real Temple is the soul—what you feel inside, the thing that overrides the laws and orders of other men." I shook my head. "They can't take anything away from me."

Strangely, as had more frequently been the case with us lately, I could feel she had more to say.

"What *is* it, Famat, please . . .?"

When she turned to me, it all came in a rush. "Forest has been following me—I told him I've been coming over regularly and don't intend to stop, how much I love your mother—" She stopped, and when she did, I took her in my arms and cast her body into the mould of myself, made her mouth mine, made it yield its passion's fruit until mine was full of its sweetness and need.

And the coming night became a cloak to time our love, where we found it on the featherbed of grass and protecting overhang of rock formation God had made a million years before to serve this moment.

"You're mine, Famat," I said over her at last, "my flesh, my woman. Any man who tries to take you from me will risk—and lose—his life."

The next week, early in the evening, I took a kitchen ladder—borrowed from a neighbor on my floor—and went down on 125th, right across from the Hotel Teresa.

It was Saturday and brisk along Seventh. Sidewalk hawkers, junkies with hot suits, trousers, dresses, winos, and whores had plunged into the evening's river, struggling, some successfully, against the tide.

I hadn't told Famat what I'd planned, and now, as I watched the steaming, surging, people-flood, I felt the first tinge of doubt.

Allah is with me, I told myself resolutely, and crossed to the vacant corner facing west and downtown and set up the ladder. I climbed to the wide flat top and looked about me. Two white-faced patrolmen on the east side of the street watched me disinterestedly; they were used to the racial harangues of nationalist and Ax Islamic speakers and probably considered me no more dangerous than the rest.

"Watcha gonna do up there, man?"

I looked down and saw a crooked, bent little old black man staring up at me.

"You gettin' ready to preach?" He carried a worn black shopping bag, the top of which exposed the limp fluffy heads of tired lettuce.

"No," I told him, smiling down, "I'm going to speak if I can get anyone to listen."

The old man cackled a pleasant laugh. "Well, boy, you'll get plenty people to listen—all you gotta do is start talkin'." He raised his toothless chin in a listening position.

I rubbed my sweating hands together and stretched my arms outward, Christlike. "Brothers . . . Sisters . . . give me your attention!"

"Yews got it," laughed the old man. "Start talkin', boy."

A few passersby had stopped—two teenage girls licking flavored ice chips in paper cones, a soldier in summer khakis and an old woman carrying a bag who might have been the old man's wife or twin sister.

"I want you to know," I began nervously, "that I come to you this evening on a mission of the gravest importance . . ."

"Mebbe, mebbe not," said the old man. "You let *us* 'cide how important it is."

"You bringin' God's word?" the bag-carrying old woman inquired snappily. " 'Cause if you ain't, I kin get right on home to what *is* important."

I cleared my throat. "The word I bring *is* God's," I said strongly, "Whose real name is Allah . . ."

"I knew it," said the old woman, turning stoutly to walk away with her bag. "Any man callin' God by two names *couldn't* know what he talkin' 'bout!"

Her exodus caused a snicker to ripple through my slowly growing audience.

"Go wan, boy, I'm witcha," the old man laughed. "Some calls a spade a tool, an' others say it's a man, but that don't change neither one of 'em from bein' what they *is*."

This statement encouraged me, and I looked out at the spray of new black faces with a growing confidence.

"Brothers and Sisters," I said, "it's only fair for me to tell you that I *am* of the faith called Islam." I saw the torso of the crowd begin to shift and sway. "Wait! I know what you've heard of the Black Muslim movement, and I know what you've heard *from* it. But what I want to tell you about Islam is another thing—maybe it's crazy, maybe it's unreasonable—but it's mine: one man's belief in the reality of his own existence—and I want you to listen, if you will."

Somehow, through some affinity peculiar to crowds, they collectively assented to stay, and I was assailed by a new problem: what to say next.

"Well, go wan, boy," prompted my accomplice—or Nemesis—the old man. "Tell us whatcha been thinkin' 'bout."

"I just want to dispel some common notions, first of all," I went on bravely, "that most people connect with Islam. It doesn't teach hate; it doesn't teach intolerance; it doesn't teach revolt. But it does teach love, acceptance, and compatibility; cleanliness, both physical and mental, and union, through brotherly recognition."

"You talk good, boy," the old man said, "but the words

is so big they bust a dumb man's brain. Just tell us in plain words whatchu learned from all this teachin'."

I glanced sharply at the old man, for he had touched a chord that had been eluding me, a sensitive and slightly painful one—yet all the while I knew it was the very thing that had brought me here, as though before some *en-masse* receiver of my confessional.

For this was guilt, wasn't it? This need to reveal my aching total and sums of indigenous skepticism?

"Go wan, boy, time's a-gittin'! We all be dead and gone 'fore you get through."

"Maybe he's got nothing to say at all," said a new but familiar voice, and I looked over the heads of the crowd to recognize the expressionless face of Brother Forest. Carl and another grim-faced Brother from the Temple were flanking him.

The crowd was waiting. For a fiery instant Brother Forest and I threw our eyes together.

Then I began to speak.

"I came into Islam many months ago. I came because, like so many of you Brothers and Sisters here today, I needed belief to tide me over the swells of the white man's unfailing suppression—or his constant attempts at suppressing—my basic sense of individuality and the need to be free.

"Now, that may not say much, the way I've put it, and there may be a tighter way for me to make plain what I want to say . . ."

"What *do* you want to say?" Brother Forest's voice rose threateningly over my last words.

"That, when I say I wanted to be free," I went on strongly, "I didn't necessarily mean *physical* freedom. I've always been told that Lincoln *gave* me that—not God but Lincoln. What I want to make plain is, I knew I *was* in a special sort of slavery that required no shackles or chains, or any other physical restrainer—but detained its prisoners through subtler, more ingenious, methods. Methods that involved the book called the Bible—which invoked fear of The Great One and adherence to commands better suited to gods than men; indoctrination, utilizing this same book, which proposed that those without, those meek and poor, and *black,* should suffer the slings and arrows of outrageous hell without rancor or despair or hate in anticipation of the Promised Land where all the atrocities ever committed against them would be righted in the greatest war-crime trial ever held, and the enemies of man would burn in the everlasting hellfire of The Great One's judgment."

"Amen, boy, now you sayin' the Word!"

"All right," I said, voice trembling a little. "So this was the way it had to be. The Book said so. And who was I to suggest that it wasn't quite justice enough, from *my* way of looking at it? . . . That's what I want you to remember—that this is just *my* way of looking at it . . . Or that there wouldn't be much of eternity left after this trial of trials, since *billions* of defendants, from time immemorial, had to stand before the bar of the Almighty. Or, for many of those defendants, their crimes were determined by the Almighty Himself in the eons before they were born. Or, in *my* opinion, it should be the Almighty *Himself* standing in the judgment of men since He had started the whole unholy mess in the first place."

The crowd swayed again, a huge black serpent now, with angry growlings in the dark pit of its bowels.

"Let me remind you," I went on, "that these are *my* feelings—not anything that's taught in Islam. Not any belief held by any man I know . . . I am the only man I know who suggests God is a war criminal." I looked around me, not afraid—in fact, elated—but tentative. "May I go on?"

"Speak yer piece, brother," a woman's voice hollered up at me.

I tried to find Brother Forest's face in the black, rippling pond, and when I did it was indistinct, but it seemed to have grown in size and appeared now like a huge black balloon hovering masklike, the face of a witch doctor, over the unpeaceful attention of my audience.

"So I came into Islam," I said.

"Why?" was Brother Forest's angry voice.

"To board the transport to a *new* outlook toward the Supreme," I shouted back. "One that exposed *my* roots as those among the countless which are inextricably linked to the One God, Allah. But—"

"*But* what?" cried Brother Forest.

"But I found *duplication* amid the truth!" I answered. "I found man had inserted his ego here in the same manner white man had inserted his in Christianity. I found Allah the same knowing criminal, the same omnipotent originator of this present Earthly hell, the same Promiser of Peace through Armageddon's final bloodshed—the same great Big Daddy overseeing each beginning and end with the relish of his divinity: but, unwittingly, He had given me the formula to the composite structure of *all* things,

"*And I saw Him.* No longer could He hide behind the sacred cloak of Godhood because it had been rent by the lightning blast of His own indiscretion—I saw Him and knew Him, and *see Him* now."

I pointed my finger at the black belly of the crowd. "Take your genitals in hand, you Great Deceiver, for they are the crown of Him Who was, Who is, Who *will* be—to the end of eternity!"

The moon had come down. Thunder rolled across the muted sky. From the east, a chiding shatter of angry rain had risen to briefly drench me where I stood, the ladder folded and held under my arm.

I stood trembling from some inner violence.

Looking toward the chastening east, the sharp rain daggers, cold and accurate, stabbing my vision I could see vaguely the blinking neons of theaters and bars and novelty chains, and people and dogs (one stopping to crap happily in a well-trained gutter manner) and slickered cops smoking on duty—and westward, the heavens were lit sickly by some upper ozone, twinkling in dying: and it halved the skyscrapered trillion-bricked dwellings, like the wand of the Devil had passed over its brow, as it had touched the crown of Sodom.

And I stood trembling. The night grew blacker. My audience had left—Brother Forest and the others quickly, after I'd finished. And I had answered the questions of tired, wrinkled black women and men smelling of charm water and galloping death, assuring them I had no "church" and did not want their alms or blessings, or a good "figure," and had felt good when they thanked me for speaking even though they didn't understand half of what I'd said.

I stood trembling in the rain, resigned in the cleansing eastern reprimand. I'd said too much to gain so little, for what I'd earned was baptismal and simply each man's right. I'd carried my public confirmation to dangerous lengths, and I began to sense the—to anticipate the—consequences of my actions. It wasn't myself I was worried about, but Famat . . .

I began to walk in the downpour. Famat would be coming by now. Surely she would. She *must*.

At 123rd Street, a little man, a midget, a black little gnome-faced creature, came up and plucked at my sleeve.

"As salaam aliekum, Brother," he greeted me in a crackly voice.

"Wa aliekum salaam," I replied.

He double-timed to keep up with my pace. "You Ammaddiayia Muslim, Brother?"

"No," I said, hurrying on.

"But you's a Muslim, right?"

"I follow certain tenets of the Muslim faith, Islam," I said.

"Well, I heard you talkin', that's all. See," he said in the sharp voice, snapping at my sleeve again, "I'm *bein'* a Muslim myself."

The rain became stronger, and I ducked into an open doorway for shelter, the midget on my heels.

"Man, it's really rainin', ain't it?"

"It'll let up in a minute," I predicted.

"Now, listen," said the midget, "I heard you speakin', like I say, and I'm just learnin' Islam. I want you to help me, Brother, 'cause I got a problem."

"Well, I'll help all I can, Brother," I said, looking down in his wide, almost catlike eyes, full with something that bespoke shock—or pain. "What is it?"

"Jazak-Allah, Brother," he thanked me. "What I wanna know is this: In Islam, I is supreme with God, 'cause I is black, like the Original man, havin' seven layers of skin, seven-an-a-half ounces of brains, and comin' into my own in the seventh-thousandth year. Is that right?"

"I have been taught that, Brother, yes."

"Jazak-Allah. Now, look here: if I is God, like you say, how is I gonna keep from over*lookin'* myself on Judgment Day?"

When I looked down, he was looking up at me and bursting, a fat black toy panda, with his own hilarious, cackling laughter.

"David!"

It was Carl who grabbed my arm as I came around my corner. The rain obscured my mind's picture of him, and it was only the stark angry yellow skin that stood out ominously.

"I'm in a hurry, Brother Carl—"

"So am I, David. Listen to me—you're no longer my Brother! And Famat has been promised to me—leave her alone!"

"Let me go, Carl . . ."

"You've blasphemed, David! I should have known that Devil mother of yours—"

"If you don't release me, Carl," I said tightly, "I'll forget that peace *has* existed between us. I wouldn't want that to happen."

I felt his hand drop from my arm. "You'll pay for this treachery, David . . ." I saw his head turn toward the tenement I lived in, and I was suddenly overcome by an unknown menace.

I squinted through the rain at Carl, feeling my fists clench and bulge the muscles of my forearms. "What are you talking about?"

"Allah demands the heads of all Devils, therefore—"

I reached out blindly, and before I realized it, his face was level with mine, and I could feel his breath of fear. "David . . . you're choking me!"

"Where is Brother Forest?" I almost screamed at him.

"I don't know!"

I squeezed until there was no resistance, and the flesh of his throat was escaping the prison of my maddened fingers.

"Wait," he gasped. "*Wait,* David!"

The vise of my fingers relaxed, and I could hear the babbling of his terrified voice. The red-hot insanity found exit in the wild dash I made toward the apartment. Twice I stumbled over the garbage cans lining the walk, rising, filthy and reeking with the slush of discarded human waste, to plummet on, not daring to imagine the scene I might find in the apartment.

Almost out of breath, I stumbled up the staircase and onto the floor that was mine.

The door moved inward at a single twist of the knob, and I froze inwardly.

It was not caution that made me enter slowly—not even fear. It was more than that—not death, no, not the condemned finally meeting the instrument of his execution—not even that exquisite moment . . .

How can I explain the way my insides had *flown?* Had deserted me laughingly?

Death was here, surely.

I first saw—*first*—my mother. On the cot. Eyes closed. Mouth partly opened, pale, thin lips. Faded hair cascaded nobly about the sheet-whiteness of her face. Worry wrinkles relaxed, muscles sagged. Like a ghost, even now, not tomorrow's but yesterday's remembered wraith.

Then in the shadows cast off the lamp's periphery, I saw

Brother Forest, abnormally tall, cloaked, it seemed, like a master messenger of fate.

And I knew she was dead—perhaps not now, not yet, but dying, and dead, because of what he suggested, and was.

"Your mother was kind enough to permit me to enter," he said, at length.

"What have you done?" I said slowly.

"Nothing, *Brother* David," he said, advancing out of the shadows and into the light of the room. "I haven't touched her." He looked down at her, almost amusedly. "Of course, I *wouldn't*, you know. I stopped by simply to inquire after Famat—she seemed quite glad to meet Famat's brother. We had an interesting chat . . ."

"About what?" I said, feeling that thing rise within me that Charles Benson had spoken of.

He shrugged. "You. Famat. Your mother. Her background. Her *history*—her racial history—"

I took a step toward him.

"Peace, Brother," he said, smiling.

"Never again," I said.

"Be rational, Brother David. After all, she was highly enlightened—and excited—to find that you had studied the facts of her origin." He smiled again, and I felt a chill come over me, numbing my brain. "Such things as, well, finding out how Yakub arrived at his final creation through a series of birth elimination experiments from the guinea-pig following of 59,999. How he murdered each black baby, driving pins through their heads and lying to the mothers about the fates of the newborn, until his doctors delivered the first all-white children . . . Oh, she was very glad to find out your studies were so broad—"

He was suddenly sitting on the floor, and my fist was aching, the fingers locked.

"David . . ." It was her voice, and I rushed over to the bed.

"Ma . . ."

She opened her eyes briefly, then she saw me, and I watched her mouth tremble into a frightened smile.

"Please don't hate me too much, my son," she said in a voice I could barely hear. "I just didn't know . . . I didn't know God made mistakes, too . . ."

"Ma . . ." I said. *"Mother!"*

When I looked around, when I raised my head from her

breast, there was darkness in the lamp glow, Forest was gone . . .

And she was dead.

I stood and looked at her, this wax-white, doll-like dead thing, eyes closed to the world—the womb of my coming. No more.

Lost. Strength in the loss that shored my ignorance and claim to manhood . . . child tears, like those of my first moment's birth, and a man's voice to sob them out.

I turned and left, closing the door of that other world.

I met Famat coming up the staircase. I did not have to tell her. I saw the shimmering loss in her eyes for a moment only, and then she said, "I have left my household and the people of my birth. I come to you with my arms open and the dowery of my heart. I come to weld my life with yours, my David. Forever."

I took her, and we went into the hell of the night, walking, and she once asked, not really caring, "Where?"

And I answered, with a dream of tomorrow and the knowledge of our good marriage in the eyes of Allah:

"The Outside . . ."

See What Tomorrow Brings

James W. Thompson

James W. Thompson has been published in various periodicals and anthologies in America and Europe: Transatlantic Review, Présence Africaine, Negro Digest, Umbra, Negro History Bulletin, America Sings, Sixes And Sevens, I am the New Negro, Beyond the Blues, *and* We Speak As Liberators. First Fire, *his latest volume of poetry, was published by Paul Breman Ltd., London.*

Laughter exploding in an extremely hollow room, that's how this day has been. Its echoes will linger to haunt Muhdear, for days to come. I could tell, immediately, when I came home that she had worried herself sick. She flew from the kitchen like a startled sparrow, her hands perched nervously upon her hips—all set to raise the roof!

"Not going through this worry tomorrow," she commanded. "Soon . . . school is out, you bring your butt home—just the way you leave here— in that station wagon. You hear me?" She frowned. Before I could open my mouth, she smiled. The little wrinkles about her eyes curved like tooled icing on a chocolate cake. "Wasn't too bad, was it Honey. And tomorrow will be easier. First of anything's always the worst to take. You get used to it." Turning toward my father and sister, who were sitting in the living room, she sighed: "Guess we can eat now." Muhdear went back to the kitchen to re-heat the supper that had turned cold.

"Humphf," Ella Mae said, "you really showed out today —worrying everybody. Like I always say, you don't think about nobody but yourself." It's my sister's habit to accuse others of the crimes she's most guilty of committing. "You knew just as well we'd be worried." I can't imagine Ella worrying about anything, most of all me. "When those deputies come here and said you was nowhere to be found,

Muhdear almost died. She sent daddy to hunt you up. The whole neighborhood was up in arms." I knew that there wasn't any way for me to explain my reason for having come home late and unescorted, at least not to Ella. My father, to my surprise, remained stony and silent. During supper he stared at me with granite eyes.

Muhdear had prepared my favorite meal: pork chops, smothered in onions, with fried corn and mashed potatoes. "Honey-boy," Muhdear winked at me, "guess what! I made new curtains for your room." She tapped her plate, intermittently, with her fork. "Know what," she said, "think maybe we can get that studio bed you been just raving to have." Muhdear looked at me, then she looked at my plate. I wasn't hungry. I tried to eat. Ella kept interrupting with questions. "Well, what's it gonna be like tomorrow," she wanted to know. I wouldn't dignify that question with an answer. There are so many tomorrows, and today had just been one of them.

When I discovered the sun, I had been dressed for over an hour. It inched across the sky, a flaming snail on a bleached rock. The sound of Muhdear fussing over her extra-special breakfast drifted from the kitchen along with the scent of cinnamon and strong coffee. It was a wonderful breakfast. (Muhdear makes the best cinnamon pancakes in the world, and these had banana bits in them.) It was an important morning. I was one of four Negroes entering Central High. I was the only one whose parents weren't professionals. I didn't feel half as anxious as the rest of the family. The neighbors had discussed it with the relish of vultures pecking over a delicate dish. You would have thought that I was going to visit the Queen. As I sat looking out of the window, for a moment I wished that I had had their enthusiasm. I didn't feel at all shook; if anything, I felt numb. All I could think of was the time I sat on the front porch with Daddy (The yard lay damp with dew, and the sweetness of evening burst in wisteria and rose, jasmin and mint, mixed with the stinging scent of Dad's cigar and kerosene from the porch lamp—where moths dizzied themselves and the light. Daddy insists on using this lamp), talking about his job and my future. He looked at me. A deep sigh ended in a smile. He spoke softly, "Honey, sometimes . . . I look upon apples as they hang in trees and wish to have their ripe indifference. One day . . . *you'll* know the feeling."

Muhdear was standing on the porch with me when the two deputies came. She had been reminding me of how I should act. She repeated the same words over, and over, and over. I had ceased listening long ago. "Com'on, boyah," one of the deputies shouted. "Jesse," my mother called, "it's time!" My father stepped onto the porch. He stood, his thumbs tucked in his overalls, his fingers rolled in huge fists. His face, a tight, dark mask, was enlivened only by the brown eyes that darted from the deputies to our front walk (the walk that he had made with bright reddish-brown bricks). The way his head was cocked, the way he held his body, cheered and frightened me. Muhdear monkeyed with my collar again. And for what must have been the twentieth time, she smoothed my tie. "There'll be a pack out there," Muhdear began, "don't let them get your goat, honey. They're more afraid of you than you are of them." Her eyes squinted toward the guards and widened into mine. They hovered over me. Daddy pinched the back of my neck and thumped the back of my head with his fingers. Muhdear dried cool hands on her apron. She does this at the strangest times . . .

When news came that Archie, the rebel hereabouts, had been chased and shot by the Rensalar Boys, she rushed over to his house. I was right on her tail. The other neighbors were leaving when we got there. Muhdear still had on her apron. Mrs. Matthews and Muhdear sat in the front room. I lingered in the hall. She tried to console Mrs. Matthews, who was trying hard not to cry.

"Louise, they kilt my baby."

"Now, Lucille, don't talk about it any more."

"I gotta talk about it—I gotta make myself believe it. I knowed Archie were always on for devilment, only this time . . . You know, I tole him time and time again, 'Archie.' (Her voice cracked. She paused, and her hands armored her head; she looked across the room at Archie's picture on the mantelpiece, anchored in a sea of lace.) 'Archie,' I'd say, 'if you so hot on gettin' back at the world, you'll just have to rise above it.' You knowed Archie . . . never paid a mind to me. I think, maybe, he kinda thought I was crazy. Oh, I know . . . some things I tole him sounded strange. Louise . . . it was *all* I knew." (The whole time she spoke, Muhdear dried cool hands in the folds of her apron.)

"Well, Lucille, if you just gotta talk about it . . ."

"You know them Rens'lar Boys. Archie worked for their father, sometime, at the gas station. They shot him! They were drunk . . . Wanted some fun . . . Seems they tole Archie they wanted a live coon to hunt, and he were it. They went and got their guns and hounds, play-acting, you

know. It seems that when Archie conceived their seriousness, he started to run. Why he didn't just com'on home I'll
never know. Instead, he lit out behind the gas station into
those woods. They chased him . . . shot him down . . ."
(She stopped. For a long while she seemed not to breathe.
She rocked back and forth on that old red leather chair, her
arms clasped across her stomach so tight I could see the
veins in her arms from where I stood in the hall.)

"IN THE BACK . . . shot him . . . MY BABY. (She took a
deep breath.)

"And they CUT him."

"Henry, you can go on the porch now."

Muhdear said this without looking in my direction. I
knew better than to object, so I went out and sat under
the window. I heard Mrs. Matthews ending, "They had no
call to do that . . . no call." Then she cried bitterly, and I
went back in to see what I could do. Muhdear hadn't
moved. She wasn't even crying. In the folds of her apron,
she dried cool hands, just as she had done this morning.

When we neared the school, the sun that I'd found so
beautiful was crashing over the entrance of Central High.
It fell in fake golden specks at the foot of the steaming
crowd, casting acute shadows through the calm green trees.
They hung like hothouse specimens adopted by a bleak
season. (It seems that I read that somewhere.) School. The
thought hit me. The chilled air bit the whites of those
glaring eyes surrounding the station wagon. Every face that
I looked into, as the car crawled, glistened. The din: "Two,
four, six, eight, we don't wanna in-urr-grate," split the
morning. Arms flailed the air with homemade signs. Bodies
hunched. Jaws were thrust dangerously forward, cutting
grotesque lines: carving one massive and miserably tortured crowdface. I sat in the back of the station wagon, my
back pressed against the hot leather seat. A tomato splashed
against the window on my left. I didn't flinch. I felt suddenly tired and tense. I looked out at them, and I could
have killed them all and never have felt a thing.

The men, lurching about, were wearing washable work
clothes. I spotted an occasional white shirt. And the women,
the ones that I could see, wore cotton housedresses and
light coats. They looked as though many lusty infants had
suckled at their breasts far too long. The fat ones sagged
like old sows. I wanted to laugh. They looked useless and
extremely weary. Yet there they were, as my father says,
their infernal female spirits stirring. They had come to

nourish a dying tradition. It was from them that the men had gathered their will, succored their violence which is the bottom of their fear, and strangely, it was for the women that the men now raged in a barbaric marriage, to the accompaniment of flashbulbs.

The car stopped. The pack writhed and screamed in a wild revival beat. "Two, four, six, eight, we don' wanna in-urr-grate." Little children were sewn in cardboards. NIGGERS NEVER. GOD SAVE US FROM NIGGERS. NO BLACKS IN OUR SCHOOLS. I didn't know whether I should feel angry or proud. Dad had said, way back during the summer after we'd made up following weeks of silence, that when this day came, I should feel proud. "The beautiful story that will become history," he'd said, "is all about you, honey, and you must hold to your dignity and not be daunted." I held. Their children stood, in their huge signs, blank and bewildered. I saw a few burrow between knees in fright when the voice of the rout rose threateningly. They were pummeled, squized, held high, knocked and shaken. I was locked behind glass and steel, waiting for their parents to calm down. Their pathetic little bodies reacted to the changing pressures with wails and tears. They were not soothed. The attention of their mothers and fathers was focused on me. The deputy had maneuvered the car so that it stood directly in front of the entrance, ringed on both sides by the Army and the State Police. When the door opened for me, the frenzy increased. The white-topped helmets of the troopers bobbed, sparkling in the sunlight, a striking contrast to the damp disheveled heads they fought to restrain. I wondered if their ears were ringing like mine. They were closer to the den.

Locked between the shoulders of the deputies, I began climbing the steps. I knew that in the minds of those two who were protecting me there was also the feeling that I was an invader. They had not made their feelings secret—I had been told during the drive. The patience of my fathers who had defied the singular death of time, who had traversed from chattel to changling was now concrete in me; I was the black challenger mounting forbidden stairs; and all of the forces of their depressed and fantastic heritage were fermenting within me. It has yet to erupt! I felt as though I moved in a vacuum, my objective receding, my movement motionless. It was all Jules Verne. The shrill screams of the pack behind me set my stomach on fire. My throat felt parched. I think that I swallowed constantly. "Say, yeh black bastard, we don' wancha here," fell on my ears—gnawed at the back of my brain. It seemed as though the sun cracked over me, a huge egg, depositing a hot yoke. I wished for a big mirror to turn upon the crowd, then a machine gun. And I wondered, what was it, other than stupidity, that was supposed to be so damned superior about these people. They're barbaric, I told myself. For some reason I stopped on the steps for a moment. One of the guards caught me by the arm. "Com'on now, Nigra," he drawled, "we gotta git you inside." I looked over the face of the building. The American flag fell over the heavily carved masonry of the peaked entrance. I smiled. Vines crept up the dark brick walls, mint-green on brown. The Army stood, legs spread, guns bayoneted held at their sides. I wanted suddenly to shout "TENCHUT." They were silent and unblinking. "Here, blackie," someone yelled. "Two, four, six, eight, we don' wanna in-urr-grate," the crowd chanted. I don't know what possessed me, but I spun around. Flash bulbs, popping, blinded me momentarily. My two heavy-set guards, puffing and sweating, and swearing, too, grabbed my arms. They drug me up the two remaining steps. I looked back once more before entering the building. A white man, very tall and very red, screamed to me. "That's right, black-boy, show'em what you're made of." I think that he would have said more, but he was swallowed by men with clubs, flying. I could not see him any longer. I wonder who he was?

Inside, I was greeted by six students. Four boys and two girls. They had come to wish me luck. Each class today was trying. I'm a senior, and the other three are juniors, so we don't have classes together. And we have a different lunch hour. A redhead tripped me in my history class. And now that I know who he is I have decided to fix him. I don't know what I'm going to do. I don't intend to let him get away without paying. Maybe they should not have chosen me for this; Daddy is not a professional, and he has taught me several different ways to skin a cat, and that redhead doesn't know it yet, but he's got a skinning coming. It will have to be quiet and very indirect, and something that he will not forget.

I knew that among the students I was very visible, and I knew, too, that no one really wanted to see me. Before the last bell I made for the side exit hoping to avoid the deputies. The black and white station wagon was there in front of the door. I was relieved when I saw that it was empty. I was on the sidewalk in seconds. The street looked as though it had been abandoned after a parade. Bits of string, cardboards, and cigarette butts littered the sidewalk. Dark pools of water stood in the gutter, morning's souvenirs, left by the fire hose that had been used to disperse the crowd. I walked along quickly, looking back, hoping that no one would spot me. When I reached my hideaway in the grove at the edge of town, I sat down. I was trembling, so I threw stones in the stream with all of my might. I heard my heart pounding, and I was shocked by the stinging taste of tears. I jumped up, and in an effort to relieve the tremors, I started singing. The road that leads to the grove looked wide and endless beneath the fading arc of trees. I bet my voice must have echoed into the mountain of the evening as I walked singing just as loud as I could, "Hurry down sunshine . . . See what tomorrow brings." And the sun died, bleeding across the sky.

A Coupla Scalped Indians

Ralph Ellison

Ralph Ellison was born in Oklahoma in 1914 and studied at Tuskegee Institute. In 1936 he met Richard Wright in the WPA and thereafter began to write. Since 1939 his work has appeared in national magazines and anthologies. His first novel, Invisible Man, *published in 1952, received the National Book Award and the Russwurm Award. From 1955 to 1957 he was a fellow of the American Academy in Rome. He has served as Visiting Professor of Writing at Rutgers University. Much of his work has been collected in* Shadow and Act.

They had a small, loud-playing band, and as we moved through the trees, I could hear the notes of the horns bursting like bright metallic bubbles against the sky. It was a faraway and sparklike sound, shooting through the late-afternoon quiet of the hill; very clear now and definitely music, band music. I was relieved. I had been hearing it for several minutes as we moved through the woods, but the pain down there had made all my senses so deceptively sharp that I had decided that the sound was simply a musical ringing in my ears. But now I was doubly sure, for Buster stopped and looked at me, squinching up his eyes with his head cocked to one side. He was wearing a blue cloth headband with a turkey feather stuck over his ear, and I could see it flutter in the breeze.

"You hear what I hear, man?" he said.

"I *been* hearing it," I said.

"Damn! We better haul it outta these woods so we can see something. Why didn't you say something to a man?"

We moved again, hurrying along. Until suddenly we were out of the woods, standing at a point of the hill where the path dropped down to the town, our eyes searching. It was close to sundown, and below me I could see the red clay of the path cutting through the woods and moving past a white, lightning-blasted tree to join the river road, and the narrow road shifting past Aunt Mackie's old shack and on, beyond the road and the shack, I could see the dull, mysterious movement of the river. The horns were blasting brighter now, though still far away, sounding like somebody flipping bright handfuls of new small change against the sky. I listened and followed the river swiftly with my eyes as it wound through the trees and on past the buildings and houses of the town—until there, there at the farther edge of the town, past the tall smokestack and the great silver sphere of the gas storage tower, floated the tent, spread white and cloudlike with its bright ropes of fluttering flags.

That's when we started running. It was a dogtrotting Indian run, because we were both wearing packs and were tired from the tests we had been taking in the woods and in Indian Lake. But now the bright blare of the horns made us forget our tiredness and pain, and we bounded down the path like young goats in the twilight; our army-surplus mess kits and canteens rattling against us.

"We late, man," Buster said. "I told you we was gon' fool around and be late. But naw, you had to cook that damn sage hen with mud on him just like it says in the book. We coulda barbecued a damn elephant while we was waiting for a tough sucker like that to get done. . . ."

His voice grumbled on like a trombone with a big, fat, pot-shaped mute stuck in it, and I ran on without answering. We had tried to take the cooking test by using a sage hen instead of a chicken because Buster said Indians didn't eat chicken. So we'd taken time to flush a sage hen and kill him with a slingshot. Besides, he was the one who insisted that we try the running endurance test, the swimming test, *and* the cooking test all in one day. Sure it had taken time. I knew it would take time; especially with our having no Scout Master. We didn't even have a troop, only the Boy Scout's Handbook that Buster had found, and—as we'd figured—our hardest problem had been working out the tests for ourselves. He had no right to argue anyway, since he'd beaten me in all the tests—although I'd passed them, too. And he was the one who insisted that we start taking them today even though we were both still sore and wearing our bandages, and I was still carrying some of the catgut stitches around in me. I had wanted to wait a few days until I was healed, but Mister Know-it-all Buster challenged me by saying that a real stud Indian could take the

tests even right after the doctor had just finished sewing on
him. So, since we were more interested in being *Indian*
scouts than simply *boy* scouts, here I was running toward
the spring carnival instead of being already there. I wondered how Buster knew so much about what an Indian
would do, anyway. We certainly hadn't read anything about
what the doctor had done to us. He'd probably made it up,
and I had let him urge me into going to the woods even
though I had to slip out of the house. The doctor had told
Miss Janey (she's the lady who takes care of me) to keep
me quiet for a few days, and she dead-aimed to do it. You
would've thought from the way she carried on that she was
the one who had the operation—only that's one kind of
operation no woman ever gets to brag about.

Anyway, Buster and me had been in the woods, and now
we were plunging down the hill through the fast-falling
dark to the carnival. I had begun to throb, and the bandage
was chafing, but as we rounded a curve, I could see the
tent and the flares and the gathering crowd. There was a
breeze coming up the hill against us now, and I could almost smell that cotton candy, the hamburgers, and the
kerosene smell of the flares. We stopped to rest, and Buster
stood very straight and pointed down below, making a big
sweep with his arm like an Indian chief in the movies when
he's up on a hill telling his braves and the Great Spirit that
he's getting ready to attack a wagon train.

"Heap big . . . teepee . . . down yonder," he said in
Indian talk. "Smoke signal say . . . Blackfeet . . . make . . .
heap much . . . stink, buck-dancing in tennis shoes!"

"Ugh," I said, bowing my suddenly war-bonneted head,
"ugh!"

Buster swept his arm from east to west, his face impas-
sive, "Smoke medicine say . . . heap . . . *Big* stink! Hot toe
jam!" He struck his palm with his fist, and I looked at his
puffed-out cheeks and giggled.

"Smoke medicine say you tell heap big lie," I said. "Let's
get on down there."

We ran past some trees, Buster's canteen jangling.
Around us it was quiet except for the roosting birds.

"Man," I said, "you making as much noise as a team of
mules in full harness. Don't no Indian scout make all that
racket when he runs."

"No scout-um now," he said. "Me go make heap much
pow-wow at stinkydog carnival!"

"Yeah, but you'll get yourself scalped, making all that
noise in the woods," I said. "Those other Indians don't give

a damn 'bout no carnival—what does a carnival mean to them? They'll scalp the hell outta you!"

"Scalp?" he said, talking Colored now, "Hell, man—that damn doctor scalped me last week. Damn near took my whole head off!"

I almost fell with laughing. "Have mercy, Lord," I laughed, "we're just a coupla poor scalped Indians!"

We laughed. Buster stumbled about, grabbing a tree for support. The doctor had said that it would make us men, and Buster had said, hell, he was a man already—what he wanted was to be an Indian. We hadn't thought about it making us scalped ones.

"You right, man," Buster said. "Since he done scalped so much of my head away, I must be crazy as a fool. That's why I'm in such a hurry to get down yonder with the other crazy folks. I want to be right in the middle of 'em when they really start raising hell."

"Oh, you'll be there, Chief Baldhead," I said.

He looked at me blankly. "What you think ole Doc done with our scalps?"

"Made him a tripe stew, man."

"You nuts," Buster said, "he probably used 'em for fish bait."

"He did, I'm going to sue him for one trillion, zillion dollars, cash," I said.

"Maybe he gave 'em to ole Aunt Mackie, man. I bet with them she could work up some out*rageous* spells!"

"Man," I said, suddenly shivering, "don't talk about that old woman, she's evil."

"Hell, everybody's so scared of her. I just wish she'd mess with me or my daddy, I'd fix her."

I said nothing—I was afraid. For though I had seen the old woman about town all my life, she remained to me like the moon, mysterious in her very familiarity; and in the sound of her name there was terror:

Ho, Aunt Mackie, talker-with-spirits, prophetess-of-disaster, odd-dweller-alone in a riverside shack surrounded by sunflowers, morning-glories, and strange magical weeds (Yao, as Buster during our Indian phase, would have put it, Yao!); Old Aunt Mackie, wizen-faced walker-with-a-stick, shrill-voiced ranter in the night, round-eyed malicious one, given to dramatic trances and fiery flights of rage; Aunt Mackie, preacher of wild sermons on the busy streets of the town, hot-voiced chaser of children, snuff-dipper, visionary; wearer of greasy headrags, wrinkled gingham aprons, and old men's shoes; Aunt Mackie, nobody's sister but still

Aunt Mackie to us all (Ho, yao!); *teller of fortunes, con-cocter of powerful, body-rending spells* (Yao, Yao!); *Aunt Mackie, the remote one though always seen about us; night-consulted adviser to farmers on crops and cattle* (Yao!); *herb-healer, root-doctor, and town-confounding oracle to wildcat drillers seeking oil in the earth*—(Yaaaah-Ho!). It was all there in her name and before her name I shivered. Once uttered, for me the palaver was finished; I resigned it to Buster, the tough one.

Even some of the grown folks, both black and white, were afraid of Aunt Mackie, and all the kids except Buster. Buster lived on the outskirts of the town and was as unimpressed by Aunt Mackie as by the truant officer and others whom the rest of us regarded with awe. And because I was his buddy I was ashamed of my fear.

Usually I had extra courage when I was with him. Like the time two years before when we had gone into the woods with only our slingshots, a piece of fatback, and a skillet and had lived three days on the rabbits we killed and the wild berries we picked and the ears of corn we raided from farmers' fields. We slept each rolled in his quilt, and in the night Buster had told bright stories of the world we'd find when we were grown up and gone from hometown and family. I had no family, only Miss Janey, who took me after my mother died (I didn't know my father), so that getting away always appealed to me, and the coming time of which Buster liked to talk loomed in the darkness around me rich with pastel promise. And although we heard a bear go lumbering through the woods nearby and the eerie howling of a coyote in the dark, yes, and had been swept by the soft swift flight of an owl, Buster was unafraid, and I had grown brave in the grace of his courage.

But to me Aunt Mackie was a threat of a different order, and I paid her the respect of fear.

"Listen to those horns," Buster said. And now the sound came through the trees like colored marbles glinting in the summer sun.

We ran again. And now, keeping pace with Buster, I felt good; for I meant to be there, too, at the carnival; right in the middle of all that confusion and sweating and laughing and all the strange sights to see.

"Listen to 'em now, man," Buster said. "Those fools is starting to shout amazing grace on those horns. Let's step on the gas!"

The scene danced below us as we ran. Suddenly there was a towering Ferris wheel revolving slowly out of the dark, its red and blue lights glowing like drops of dew dazzling a big spider web when you see it in the early morning. And we heard the beckoning blare of the band now shot through with the small, insistent, buckshot voices of the barkers.

"Listen to that trombone, man," I said.

"Sounds like he's playing the dozens with the whole wide world."

"What's he saying, Buster?"

"He's saying. 'Ya'll's mamas don't wear 'em. Is strictly without 'em. Don't know nothing 'bout 'em. . . .' "

"Don't know about what, man?"

"Draw's, fool; he's talking 'bout draw's!"

"How you know, man?"

"I hear him talking, don't I?"

"Sure, but you been scalped, remember? You crazy. How he know about those peoples' mamas?" I said.

"Says he saw 'em with his great big ole eye."

"Damn! He must be a Peeping Tom. How about those other horns?"

"Now that there tuba's saying:

"They don't play 'em, I know they don't.
They don't play 'em, I know they won't.
They just don't play no nasty dirty twelves. . . ."

"Man, you *are* a scalped-headed fool. How about that trumpet?"

"Him? That fool's a soldier, he's really signifying. Saying,

"So ya'll don't play 'em, hey?
So ya'll *won't* play 'em, hey?
Well pat your feet and clap your hands,
'Cause I'm going to play 'em to the promised land. . . ."

"Man, the white folks know what that fool is signifying on that horn, they'd run him clear on out the world. Trumpet's got a real *nasty* mouth."

"Why you call him a soldier, man?" I said.

" 'Cause he's slipping 'em in the twelves and choosing 'em, all at the same time. Talking 'bout they mamas and offering to fight 'em. Now he ain't like that ole clarinet; clarinet so sweet-talking he just *eases* you in the dozens."

"Say, Buster," I said, seriously now. "You know, we gotta stop cussing and playing the dozens if we're going to be boy scouts. Those white boys don't play that mess."

"You doggone right they don't," he said, the turkey feather vibrating above his ear. "Those guys can't take it, man. Besides, who wants to be just like them? Me, *I'm* gon' be a scout and play the twelves, too! You have to, with some of these old jokers we know. You don't know what to say when they start easing you, you never have no peace. You have to outtalk 'em, outrun 'em, or outfight 'em and I don't aim to be running and fighting all the time. N'mind those white boys."

We moved on through the growing dark. Already I could see a few stars, and suddenly there was the moon. It emerged bladelike from behind a thin veil of cloud, just as I heard a new sound and looked about me with quick uneasiness. Off to our left I heard a dog, a big one. I slowed, seeing the outlines of a picket fence and the odd-shaped shadows that lurked in Aunt Mackie's yard.

"What's the matter, man?" Buster said.

"Listen," I said. "That's Aunt Mackie's dog. Last year I was passing here and he sneaked up and bit me through the fence when I wasn't even thinking about him. . . ."

"Hush, man," Buster whispered, "I hear the sonofabitch back in there now. You leave him to me."

We moved by inches now, hearing the dog barking in the dark. Then we were going past and he was throwing his heavy body against the fence, straining at his chain. We hesitated, Buster's hand on my arm. I undid my heavy canteen belt and held it, suddenly light in my fingers. In my right I gripped the hatchet which I'd brought along.

"We'd better go back and take the other path," I whispered.

"Just stand still, man," Buster said.

The dog hit the fence again, barking hoarsely; and in the interval following the echoing crash I could hear the distant music of the band.

"Come on," I said, "let's go 'round."

"Hell, no! We're going straight! I ain't letting no damn dog scare me, Aunt Mackie or no Aunt Mackie. Come on!"

Trembling, I moved with him toward the roaring dog, then felt him stop again, and I could hear him removing his pack and taking out something wrapped in paper.

"Here," he said, "you take my stuff and come on."

I took his gear and went behind him, hearing his voice suddenly hot with fear and anger saying, "Here, you 'gator-mouthed egg-sucker, see how you like this sage hen," just as I tripped over the straps of his pack and went down. Then I was crawling frantically, trying to untangle myself and hearing the dog growling as he crunched something in his jaws. "Eat it, you buzzard," Buster was saying. "See if you tough as he is," as I tried to stand, stumbling and sending an old cooking range crashing in the dark. Part of the fence was gone, and in my panic I had crawled into the yard. Now I could hear the dog bark threateningly and leap the length of his chain toward me, then back to the sage hen; toward me, a swift leaping form snatched backwards by the heavy chain, turning to mouth savagely on the mangled bird. Moving away I floundered over the stove and pieces of crating, against giant sunflower stalks, trying to get back to Buster when I saw the lighted window and realized that I had crawled to the very shack itself. That's when I pressed against the weathered-satin side of the shack and came erect. And there, framed by the window in the lamp-lit room, I saw the woman.

A brown naked woman, whose black hair hung beneath her shoulders. I could see the long graceful curve of her back as she moved in some sort of slow dance, bending forward and back; her arms and body moving as though gathering in something which I couldn't see but which she drew to her with pleasure; a young, girlish body with slender, well-rounded hips. _But who?_ flashed through my mind as I heard Buster's _Hey, man; where'd you go? You done run out on me?_ from back in the dark. And I willed to move, to hurry away—but in that instant she chose to pick up a glass from a wobbly old round white table and to drink, turning slowly as she stood with backward-tilted head, slowly turning in the lamplight and drinking slowly as she turned, slowly; until I could see the full-faced glowing of her feminine form.

And I was frozen there, watching the uneven movement of her breasts beneath the glistening course of the liquid, spilling down her body in twin streams drawn by the easy tiding of her breathing. Then the glass came down and my knees flowed beneath me like water. The air seemed to explode soundlessly. I shook my head, but she, the image, would not go away, and I wanted suddenly to laugh wildly and to scream. For above the smooth shoulders of the girlish form I saw the wrinkled face of old Aunt Mackie.

Now I had never seen a naked woman before, only very little girls or once or twice a skinny one my own age who looked like a boy with the boy part missing. And even though I'd seen a few calendar drawings, they were not alive like this, nor images of someone you'd thought familiar through having seen them passing through the streets of the town; nor like this inconsistent, with wrinkled face mismatched with glowing form. So that mixed with my fear of punishment for peeping there was added the terror of her mystery. And yet I could not move away. I was fascinated, hearing the growling dog and feeling a warm pain grow beneath my bandage—along with the newly risen terror that this deceptive old woman could cause me to feel this way, that she could be so young beneath her old baggy clothes.

She was dancing again now, still unaware of my eyes, the lamplight playing on her body as she swayed and enfolded the air or invisible ghosts or whatever it was within her arms. Each time she moved, her hair, which was black as night now that it was no longer hidden beneath a greasy headrag, swung heavily about her shoulders. And as she moved to the side I could see the gentle tossing of her breasts beneath her upraised arms. *It just can't be,* I thought, *it just can't* and moved closer, determined to see and to know. But I had forgotten the hatchet in my hand until it struck the side of the house and I saw her turn quickly toward the window, her face evil as she swayed. I was rigid as stone, hearing the growling dog mangling the bird and knowing that I should run even as she moved toward the window, her shadow flying before her, her hair now wild as snakes writhing on a dead tree during a springtime flood. Then I could hear Buster's hoarse-voiced, *Hey, man! where in hell are you?* even as she pointed at me and screamed, sending me moving backwards and I was aware of the sickle-bladed moon flying like a lightning flash as I fell, still gripping my hatchet, and struck my head in the dark.

When I started out of it someone was holding me and I lay in light and looked up to see her face above me. Then it all flooded swiftly back, and I was aware again of the contrast between smooth body and wrinkled face and experienced a sudden warm yet painful thrill. She held me close. Her breath came to me, sweetly alcoholic as she mumbled something about, "Little devil, lips that touch wine shall never touch mine! That's what I told him, understand me? Never," she said loudly. "You understand?"

"Yes, ma'm. . . ."

"Never, never, NEVER!"

"No, ma'm," I said, seeing her study me with narrowed eyes.

"You young, but you young'uns understand, devilish as you is. What you doing messing 'round in my yard?"

"I got lost," I said. "I was coming from taking some boy scout tests and I was trying to get by your dog."

"So that's what I heard," she said. "He bite you?"

"No, ma'm."

"Course not, he don't bite on the new moon. No, I think you come in my yard to spy on me."

"No, ma'm, I didn't," I said. "I just happened to see the light when I was stumbling around trying to find my way."

"You got a pretty big hatchet there," she said, looking down at my hand. "What you plan to do with it?"

"It's a kind of boy scout axe," I said. "I used it to come through the woods. . . ."

She looked at me dubiously. "So," she said, "you're a heavy hatchet man, and you stopped to peep. Well, what I want to know is, is you a drinking man? Have your lips ever touched wine?"

"Wine? No, ma'm."

"So you ain't a drinking man, but do you belong to church?"

"Yes, ma'm."

"And have you been saved and ain't no backslider?"

"Yessum."

"Well," she said, pursing her lips, "I guess you can kiss me."

"MA'M?"

"That's what I said. You passed all the tests, and you was peeping in my window. . . ."

She was holding me there on a cot, her arms around me as though I were a three-year-old, smiling like a girl. I could see her fine white teeth and the long hairs on her chin, and it was like a bad dream. "You peeped," she said, "now you got to do the rest. I said kiss me, or I'll fix you. . . ."

I saw her face come close and felt her warm breath and closed my eyes, trying to force myself. *It's just like kissing some sweaty woman at church,* I told myself, *some friend of Miss Janey's.* But it didn't help, and I could feel her drawing me, and I found her lips with mine. It was dry and firm and winey and I could hear her sigh. "Again," she said, and once more my lips found hers. And suddenly she drew me to her and I could feel her breasts soft against me as once more she sighed.

"That was a nice boy," she said, her voice kind, and I opened my eyes. "That's enough now, you're both too young and too old, but you're brave. A regular lil' chocolate hero."

And now she moved, and I realized for the first time that my hand had found its way to her breast. I moved it guiltily, my face flaming as she stood.

"You're a good brave boy," she said, looking at me from deep in her eyes, "but you forget what happened here to-night."

I sat up as she stood looking down upon me with a mysterious smile. And I could see her body up close now, in the dim yellow light; see the surprising silkiness of black hair mixed here and there with gray, and suddenly I was crying and hating myself for the compelling need. I looked at my hatchet lying on the floor now and wondered how she'd gotten me into the shack as the tears blurred my eyes.

"What's the matter, boy?" she said. And I had no words to answer.

"What's the matter, I say!"

"I'm hurting in my operation," I said desperately, knowing that my tears were too complicated to put into any words I knew.

"Operation? Where?"

I looked away.

"Where you hurting, boy?" she demanded.

I looked into her eyes and they seemed to flood through me, until reluctantly I pointed toward my pain.

"Open it, so's I can see," she said. "You know I'm a healer, don't you?"

I bowed my head, still hesitating.

"Well open it, then. How'm I going to see with all those clothes on you?"

My face burned like fire now and the pain seemed to ease as a dampness grew beneath the bandage. But she would not be denied and I undid myself and saw a red stain on the gauze. I lay there ashamed to raise my eyes.

"Hmmmmmmm," she said, "a fishing worm with a head-ache!" And I couldn't believe my ears. Then she was look-ing into my eyes and grinning.

"Pruned," she cackled in her high, old woman's voice, "pruned. Boy, you have been pruned. I'm a doctor but no tree surgeon— No, lay still a second."

She paused, and I saw her hand come forward, three clawlike fingers taking me gently as she examined the band-age.

And I was both ashamed and angry, and now I stared at her out of a quick resentment and a defiant pride. *I'm a man*, I said within myself. *Just the same I am a man!* But I could only stare at her face briefly as she looked at me with a gleam in her eyes. Then my eyes fell and I forced myself to look boldly at her now, very brown in the lamplight, with all the complicated apparatus within the globular curvatures of flesh and vessel exposed to my eyes. I was filled then with a deeper sense of the mystery of it, too, for now it was as though the nakedness was nothing more than another veil; much like the old baggy dresses she always wore. Then across the curvature of her stomach I saw a long, puckered, crescent-shaped scar.

"How old are you, boy?" she said, her eyes suddenly round.

"Eleven," I said. And it was as though I had fired a shot.

"Eleven! Git out of here," she screamed, stumbling backwards, her eyes wide upon me as she felt for the glass on the table to drink. Then she snatched an old gray robe from a chair, fumbling for the tie cord which wasn't there. I moved, my eyes upon her as I knelt for my hatchet and felt the pain come sharp. Then I straightened, trying to arrange my knickers.

"You go now, you little rascal," she said. "Hurry and git out of here. And if I ever hear of you saying anything about me I'll fix your daddy and your mammy, too. I'll fix 'em, you hear?"

"Yes, ma'm," I said, feeling that I had suddenly lost the courage of my manhood, now that my bandage was hidden and her secret body gone behind her old gray robe. But how could she fix my father when I didn't have one? Or my mother, when she was dead?

I moved, backing out of the door into the dark. Then she slammed the door, and I saw the light grow intense in the window, and there was her face looking out at me, and I could not tell if she frowned or smiled, but in the glow of the lamp the wrinkles were not there. I stumbled over the packs now and gathered them up, leaving.

This time the dog raised up, huge in the dark, his green eyes glowing as he gave me a low disinterested growl. *Buster really must have fixed you, I thought. But where'd he go?* Then I was past the fence into the road.

I wanted to run but was afraid of starting the pain again, and as I moved, I kept seeing her as she'd appeared with her back turned toward me, the sweet undrunken movements that she made. It had been like someone dancing by herself and yet like praying without kneeling down. Then she had turned, exposing her familiar face. I moved faster now, and suddenly all my senses seemed to sing alive. I heard a night bird's song, the lucid call of a quail arose. And from off to my right in the river there came the leap of a moon-mad fish and I could see the spray arch up and away. There was wisteria in the air and the scent of moonflowers. And now moving through the dark I recalled the warm, intriguing smell of her body and suddenly, with the shout of the carnival coming to me again, the whole thing became thin and dreamlike. The images flowed in my mind, became shadowy, no part was left to fit another. But still there was my pain, and here was I, running through the dark toward the small, loud-playing band. It was real, I knew, and I stopped in the path and looked back, seeing the black outlines of the shack and the thin moon above. Behind the shack the hill arose with the shadowy woods and I knew the lake was still hidden there, reflecting the moon. All was real.

And for a moment I felt much older, as though I had lived swiftly long years into the future and had been as swiftly pushed back again. I tried to remember how it had been when I kissed her, but on my lips my tongue found only the faintest trace of wine. But for that it was gone, and I thought forever, except the memory of the scraggly hairs on her chin. Then I was again aware of the imperious calling of the horns and moved again toward the carnival. Where was that other scalped Indian, where had Buster gone?

Come Out the Wilderness

James Baldwin

James Baldwin *was born in New York in 1924. His
first novel,* Go Tell It On the Mountain *(1952), was
acclaimed by the literary world. His stories and essays have since appeared in* Harper's, Esquire, Atlan-
tic Monthly, The Reporter, *etc. Among his other
books are* Notes of a Native Son, Giovanni's Room,
Nobody Knows My Name, Another Country, Going
to Meet the Man, *and* Tell Me How Long the Train's
Been Gone. *He now lives and writes in Europe.*

Paul did not yet feel her eyes on him. She watched him.
He went to the window, peering out between the slats in
the Venetian blinds. She could tell from his profile that
it did not look like a pleasant day. In profile, all of the
contradictions that so confounded her seemed to be revealed. He had a boy's long, rather thin neck, but it supported a head that seemed even more massive than it
actually was because of its plantation of thickly curling
black hair, hair that was always a little too long or else,
cruelly, much too short. His forehead was broad and
high, but this austerity was contradicted by a short, blunt,
almost ludicrously upturned nose. And he had a large
mouth and very heavy, sensual lips, which suggested a
certain wry cruelty when turned down but looked like the
mask of comedy when he laughed. His body was really
excessively black with hair, which proved, she said, since
Negroes were generally less hairy than whites, which race,
in fact, had moved farthest from the ape. Other people
did not see his beauty, which always mildly astonished her
—it was like thinking that the sun was ordinary. He was
sloppy about the way he stood and sat, that was true, and
so his shoulders were already beginning to be round. And
he was a poor man's son, a city boy, and so his body could
not really remind anyone of a Michelangelo statue as she

277

—"fantastically," he said—claimed; it did not have that luxury or that power. It was economically tense and hard and testified only to the agility of the poor, who are always dancing one step ahead of the devil.

He stepped away from the window, looking worried. Ruth closed her eyes. When she opened them, he was disappearing away from her down the short, black hall that led to the bathroom. She wondered what time he had come in last night; she wondered if he had a hang-over; she heard the water running. She thought that he had probably not been home long. She was very sensitive to his comings and goings and had often found herself abruptly upright and wide awake a moment after he, restless at two-thirty in the morning, had closed the door behind him. Then there was no more sleep for her. She lay there on a bed that inexorably became a bed of ashes and hot coals, while her imagination dwelt on every conceivable disaster, from his having forsaken her for another woman to his having somehow ended up in the morgue. And as the night faded from black to gray to daylight, the telephone began to seem another presence in the house, sitting not far from her like a great, malevolent black cat that might, at any moment, with one shrill cry, scatter her life like dismembered limbs all over this tiny room. There were places she could have called, but she would have died first. After all—he had only needed to point it out once, he would never have occasion to point it out again—they were not married. Often she had pulled herself out of bed, her loins cold and all her body trembling, and gotten dressed and had coffee and gone to work without seeing him. But he would call her in the office later in the day. She would have had several stiff drinks at lunch and so could be very offhand over the phone, pretending that she had only supposed him to have gotten up a little earlier than herself that morning. But the moment she put the receiver down she hated him. She made herself sick with fantasies of how she would be revenged. Then she hated herself; thinking into what an iron maiden of love and hatred he had placed her, she hated him even more. She could not help feeling that he treated her this way because of her color, because she was a colored girl. Then her past and her present threatened to engulf her. She knew she was being unfair; she could not help it; she thought of psychiatry; she saw herself transformed, at peace with the world, herself, her color, with the male of indeterminate color she would have found. Always, this journey 'round her skull ended with tears, resolutions, prayers, with Paul's face, which then had the power to reconcile her even to the lowest circle of hell.

After work, on the way home, she stopped for another drink, or two or three; bought Sen-Sen to muffle the odor; wore the most casually glowing of smiles as he casually kissed her when she came through the door.

She knew that he was going to leave her. It was in his walk, his talk, his eyes. He wanted to go. He had already moved back, crouching to leap. And she had no rival. He was not going to another woman. He simply wanted to go. It would happen today, tomorrow, three weeks from today; it was over, she could do nothing about it; neither could she save herself by jumping first. She had no place to go, she only wanted him. She had tried hard to want other men, and she was still young, only twenty-six, and there was no real lack of opportunity. But all she knew about other men was that they were not Paul.

Through the gloom of the hallway he came back into the room and, moving to the edge of the bed, lit a cigarette. She smiled up at him.

"Good morning," she said. "Would you light one for me, too?"

He looked down at her with a sleepy and slightly shame-faced grin. Without a word he offered her his freshly lit cigarette, lit another, and then got into bed, shivering slightly.

"Good morning," he said then. "Did you sleep well?"

"Very well," she said lightly. "Did you? I didn't hear you come in."

"Ah, I was very quiet," he said teasingly, curling his great body toward her and putting his head on her breast. "I didn't want to wake you up. I was afraid you'd hit me with something."

She laughed. "What time *did* you come in?"

"Oh"—he raised his head, dragging on his cigarette, and half-frowned, half-smiled—"about an hour or so ago."

"What did you do? Find a new after-hours joint?"

"No. I ran into Cosmo. We went over to his place to look at a couple new paintings he's done. He had a bottle, we sat around."

She knew Cosmo and distrusted him. He was about forty, and he had had two wives; he did not think women were worth much. She was sure that Cosmo had been giving Paul advice as to how to be rid of her; she could imagine, or believed she could, how he had spoken about

her, and she felt her skin tighten. At the same moment
she became aware of the warmth of Paul's body.

"What did you talk about?" she asked.

"Oh. Painting. His paintings, my paintings, all God's
chillun's paintings."

During the day, while she was at work, Paul painted in
the back room of this cramped and criminally expensive
Village apartment where the light was bad and where
there was not really room enough for him to step back
and look at his canvas. Most of his paintings were stored
with a friend. Still, there were enough, standing against the
wall, piled on top of the closet and on the table, for a
sizable one-man show. "If they were any good," said Paul,
who worked very hard. She knew this despite the fact that
he said so rather too often. She knew, by his face, his
distance, his quality, frequently, of seeming to be like a
spring, unutterably dangerous to touch. And by the ex-
haustion, different in kind from any other, with which he
sometimes stretched out in bed.

She thought—of course—that his paintings were very
good, but he did not take her judgment seriously. "You're
sweet, funnyface," he sometimes said, "but, you know,
you aren't really very bright." She was scarcely at all
mollified by his adding, "Thank heaven. I hate bright
women."

She remembered, now, how stupid she had felt about
music all the time she had lived with Arthur, a man of
her own color who had played a clarinet. She was still
finding out today, so many years after their breakup, how
much she had learned from him—not only about music,
unluckily. If I stay on this merry-go-round, she thought,
I'm going to become very accomplished, just the sort of
girl no man will ever marry.

She moved closer to Paul, the fingers of one hand playing with his hair. He lay still. It was very silent.

"Ruth," he said finally, "I've been thinking . . ."

At once she was all attention. She drew on her cigarette,
her fingers still drifting through his hair, as though she
were playing with water.

"Yes?" she prompted.

She had always wondered, when the moment came, if
she would make things easy for him or difficult. She still
did not know. He leaned up on one elbow, looking down
at her. She met his eyes, hoping that her own eyes reflected nothing but calm curiosity. He continued to stare
at her and put one hand on her short, dark hair. Then,

"You're a nice girl," he said irrelevantly, and leaned down and kissed her.

With a kiss! she thought.

"My father wouldn't think so," she said, "if he could see me now. What is it you've been thinking?"

He still said nothing but only looked down at her, an expression in his eyes that she could not read.

"I've been thinking," he said, "that it's about time I got started on that portrait of you. I ought to get started right away."

She felt, very sharply, that his nerve had failed him. But she felt, too, that his decision now to do a portrait of her was a means of moving far enough away from her to be able to tell her the truth. Also, he had always said that he could do something wonderful with her on canvas —it would be foolish to let the opportunity pass. Cosmo had probably told him this. She had always been flattered by his desire to paint her, but now she hoped that he would suddenly go blind.

"Anytime," she said, and could not resist, "Am I to be part of a gallery?"

"Yeah. I'll probably be able to sell you for a thousand bucks," he said, and kissed her again.

"That's not a very nice thing to say," she murmured.

"You're a funny girl. What's not nice about a thousand dollars?" He leaned over her to put out his cigarette in the ash tray near the bed; then took hers and put it out, too. He fell back against her and put his hand on her breast.

She said tentatively: "Well, I suppose if you do it often enough, I could stop working."

His arms tightened, but she did not feel that this was due entirely to desire; it might be said that he was striving now to distract her. "If I do *what* enough?" he grinned.

"Now, now," she smiled, "you just said that I was a nice girl."

"You're one of the nicest girls I ever met," said Paul soberly. "Really you are. I often wonder . . ."

"You often wonder what?"

"What's going to become of you."

She felt like a river trying to run two ways at once: she felt herself shrinking from him, yet she flowed toward him, too; she knew he felt it. "But as long as you're with me," she said, and she could not help herself, she felt she was about to cry; she held his face between her hands, pressing yet closer against him. "As long as you're with me." His face was white, his eyes glowed; there was a war in him, too. Everything that divided them charged, for an instant, the tiny space between them. Then the veils of habit and desire covered both their eyes.

"Life is very long," said Paul at last. He kissed her. They both sighed. And slowly she surrendered, opening up before him like the dark continent, made mad and delirious and blind by the entry of a mortal as bright as the morning, as white as milk.

When she left the house, he was sleeping. Because she was late for work and because it was raining, she dropped into a cab and was whirled out of the streets of the Village —which still suggested, at least, some faint memory of the individual life—into the grim publicities of midtown Manhattan. Blocks and squares and exclamation marks, stone and steel and glass as far as the eye could see; everything towering, lifting itself against, though by no means into, heaven. The people, so surrounded by heights that they had lost any sense of what heights were, rather resembled, nevertheless, these gray rigidities and also resembled, in their frantic motion, people fleeing a burning town. Ruth, who was not so many years removed from trees and earth, had felt in the beginning that she would never be able to live on an island so eccentric; she had, for example, before she arrived, dreamed of herself as walking by the river. But apart from the difficulties of realizing this ambition, which were not inconsiderable, it turned out that a lone girl walking by the river was simply asking to be victimized by both the disturbers and the defenders of the public peace. She retreated into the interior, and this dream was abandoned—along with others. For her as for most of Manhattan, trees and water ceased to be realities; the nervous, trusting landscape of the city began to be the landscape of her mind. And soon her mind, like life on the island, seemed to be incapable of flexibility, of moving outward, could only shriek upward into meaningless abstractions or drop downward into cruelty and confusion.

She worked for a life insurance company that had only recently become sufficiently progressive to hire Negroes. This meant that she worked in an atmosphere so positively electric with interracial good will that no one ever dreamed of telling the truth about anything. It would have seemed, and it quite possibly would have been, a spiteful act. The only other Negro there was male, a Mr. Davis, who was very highly placed. He was an expert, it appeared, in some way about Negroes and life insurance, from which Ruth had ungenerously concluded that he was the company's expert on how to cheat more Negroes out of more money and not only remain within the law but also be honored with a plaque for good race relations. She often —but not always—took dictation from him. The other girls, manifesting a rough, girl-scoutish camaraderie that made the question of their sincerity archaic, found him "marvelous" and wondered if he had a wife. Ruth found herself unable to pursue these strangely overheated and yet eerily impersonal speculations with anything like the indicated vehemence. Since it was extremely unlikely that any of these girls would ever even go dancing with Mr. Davis, it was impossible to believe that they had any ambition to share his couch, matrimonial or otherwise, and yet, lacking this ambition, it was impossible to account for their avidity. But they were all incredibly innocent and made her ashamed of her body. At the same time it demanded, during their maddening coffee breaks, a great deal of will power not to take Paul's photograph out of her wallet and wave it before them, saying, *"You'll never lay a finger on Mr. Davis. But look what I took from you!"* Her face at such moments allowed them to conclude that she was planning to ensnare Mr. Davis herself. It was perhaps this assumption, despite her phone calls from Paul, that allowed them to discuss Mr. Davis so freely before her, and they also felt, in an incoherent way, that these discussions were proof of their democracy. She did not find Mr. Davis "marvelous," though she thought him good looking enough in a square, stocky, gleaming, black-boyish sort of way.

Near her office, visible from her window and having the air of contraband in Caesar's market place, was a small gray chapel. An ugly neon cross jutted out above the heads of passers-by, proclaiming "Jesus Saves." Today, as the lunch hour approached and she began, as always, to fidget, debating whether she should telephone Paul or wait for Paul to telephone her, she found herself staring in some irritation at this cross, thinking about her childhood. The telephone rang and rang, but never for her; she began to feel the need of a drink. She thought of Paul sleeping while she typed and became outraged, then thought of his painting and became maternal; thought of his arms and paused to light a cigarette, throwing the most pitying of glances toward the girl who shared her office, who still had a crush on Frank Sinatra. Nevertheless, the sublimatory tube still burning, the smoke tickling her nostrils and the typewriter bell clanging at brief intervals like signals flashing by on a railroad track, she relapsed into bitterness, confusion, fury: for she was trapped. Paul was a trap. She wanted a man of her own, and she wanted children, and all she could see for herself today was a lifetime of typing while Paul slept or a lifetime of typing with no Paul. And she began rather to envy the stocky girl with the crush on Frank Sinatra since she would settle one day, obviously, for a great deal less, and probably turn out children as Detroit turned out cars and never sigh for an instant for what she had missed, having indeed never, and especially with a lifetime of moviegoing behind her, missed anything.

"Jesus Saves." She began to think of the days of her innocence. These days had been spent in the South, where her mother and father and older brother remained. She had an older sister, married and with several children, in Oakland, and a baby sister who had become a small-time night club singer in New Orleans. There were relatives of her father's living in Harlem, and she was sure that they wrote to him often complaining that she never visited them. They, like her father, were earnest churchgoers, though, unlike her father, their religion was strongly mixed with an opportunistic respectability and with ambitions to better society and their own place in it, which her father would have scorned. Their ambitions vitiated in them what her father called the "true" religion, and what remained of this religion, which was principally vindictiveness, prevented them from understanding anything whatever about those concrete Northern realities that made them at once so obsequious and so venomous.

Her innocence. It was many years ago. She remembered their house, so poor and plain, standing by itself, apart from other houses, as nude and fragile on the stony ground as an upturned cardboard box. And it was nearly as dark inside as it might have been beneath a box, it leaked when the rain fell, froze when the wind blew, could scarcely be entered in July. They tried to coax sustenance out of a soil that had long ago gone out of the business. As time went on, they grew to depend less and less on the soil and more on the oyster boats, and on the wages and leftovers brought home by their mother, and then herself, from the white kitchens in town. And her mother still struggled in these white kitchens, humming sweet hymns, tiny, mild-eyed, and bent, her father still labored on the oyster boats; after a lifetime of labor, should they drop dead tomorrow, there would not be a penny for their burial clothes. Her brother, still unmarried, nearing thirty now, loitered through the town with his dangerous reputation, drinking and living off the women he murdered with his love-making. He made her parents fearful, but they reiterated in each letter that they had placed him, and all of their children, in the hands of God. Ruth opened each letter in guilt and fear, expecting each time to be confronted with the catastrophe that had at last overtaken her kin; anticipating, too, with a selfish annoyance that added to her guilt, the enforced and necessary journey back to her home in mourning; the survivors gathered together to do brief honor to the dead, whose death was certainly, in part, attributable to the indifference of the living. She often wrote her brother asking him to come North, and asked her sister in Oakland to second her in this plea. But she knew that he would not come North —because of her. She had shamed him and embittered him, she was one of the reasons he drank.

Her mother's song, which she, doubtless, still hummed each evening as she walked the old streets homeward, began with the question, *How did you feel when you come out the wilderness?*

And she remembered her mother, half-humming, half-singing, with a steady, tense beat that would have made any blues singer sit up and listen (though she thought it best not to say this to her mother):

Come out the wilderness,
Come out the wilderness.
How did you feel when you
  come out the wilderness,
Leaning on the Lord?

And the answers were many: *Oh, my soul felt happy!* or, *I shouted hallelujah!* or, *I do thank God!*

Ruth finished her cigarette, looking out over the stone-cold, hideous New York streets, and thought with a strange new pain of her mother. Her mother had once been no older than she, Ruth, was today, she had probably been pretty, she had also wept and trembled and cried beneath the rude thrusting that was her master and her life, and children had knocked in her womb and split her as they came crying out. Out, and into the wilderness: she had placed them in the hands of God. She had known nothing but labor and sorrow, she had had to confront, every day of her life, the everlasting, nagging, infinitesimal details, it had clearly all come to nothing, how could she be singing still?

"Jesus Saves." She put out her cigarette, and a sense of loss and disaster wavered through her like a mist. She wished, in that moment, from the bottom of her heart, that she had never left home. She wished that she had never met Paul. She wished that she had never been touched by his whiteness. She should have found a great, slow, black man, full of laughter and sighs and grace, a man at whose center there burned a steady, smokeless fire. She should have surrendered to him and been a woman, and had his children, and found, through being irreplaceable, despite whatever shadows life might cast, peace that would enable her to endure.

She had left home practically by accident: it had been partly due to her brother. He had grown too accustomed to thinking of her as his prized, adored little sister to recognize the changes that were occurring within her. This had had something to do with the fact that his own sexual coming of age had disturbed his peace with her —he would, in good faith, have denied this, which did not make it less true. When she was seventeen, her brother had surprised her alone in a barn with a boy. Nothing had taken place between herself and this boy, though there was no saying what might not have happened if her brother had not come in. She, guilty though she was in everything but the act, could scarcely believe and had not, until today, ever quite forgiven his immediate leap to the obvious conclusion. She began screaming before he hit her, her father had had to come running to pull her brother off the boy. And she had shouted their innocence in a steadily blackening despair, for the boy was too badly beaten to be able to speak, and it was clear that no one believed her. She bawled at last: "Goddamit, I wish I had, I wish I had. I might as well of done it!" Her father slapped her. Her brother gave her a look and said: "You dirty . . . you dirty . . . you black and dirty—" Then her mother had had to step between her father and her brother. She turned and ran and sat down for a long time in the darkness on a hillside, by herself, shivering. And she felt dirty, she felt that nothing would ever make her clean.

After this she and her brother scarcely spoke. He had wounded her so deeply she could not face his eyes. Her father dragged her to church to make her cry repentance, but she was as stubborn as her father, she told him she had nothing to repent. And she avoided them all, which was exactly the most dangerous thing that could have happened, for when she met the musician, Arthur, who was more than twenty years older than she, she ran away to New York with him. She lived with him for more than four years. She did not love him all that time. She simply did not know how to escape his domination. He had never made the big-time himself, and he therefore wanted her to become a singer; and perhaps she had ceased to love him when it became clear that she had no talent whatever. He was very disappointed, but he was also very proud, and he made her go to school to study shorthand and typing, and made her self-conscious about her accent and her grammar, and took great delight in dressing her. Through him, she got over feeling that she was black and unattractive, and as soon as this happened, she was able to leave him. In fleeing Harlem and her relatives there, she drifted downtown to the Village where, eventually, she found employment as a waitress in one of those restaurants with candles on the tables. Here, after a year or so and several increasingly disastrous and desperate liaisons, she met Paul.

The telephone rang several desks away from her and, at the same instant she was informed that Mr. Davis wanted her in his office. She was sure that it was Paul telephoning, but she picked up her pad and walked into Mr. Davis's cubbyhole. Someone picked up the receiver cutting off the bell, and she closed the door of Mr. Davis's office behind her.

"Good morning," she said.

"Good morning," he answered. He looked out of his window. "Though, between you and me, I've seen better mornings. This morning ain't half trying."

They both laughed, self-consciously amused and relieved by his "ain't."

She sat down, her pencil poised, looking at him questioningly.

"How do you like your job?" he asked her.

She had not expected his question, which she immediately distrusted and resented, suspecting him, on no evidence whatever, of acting now as a company spy.

"It's quite pleasant," she said in a guarded, ladylike tone, and stared hypnotically at him as though she believed that he was about to do her mischief by magical means and she had to resist his spell.

"Are you intending to be a career girl?"

He was giving her more attention this morning than he ever had before, with the result that she found herself reciprocating. A tentative friendliness wavered in the air between them. She smiled. "I guess I ought to say that it depends on my luck."

He laughed—perhaps rather too uproariously, though, more probably, she had merely grown unaccustomed to his kind of laughter. Her brother bobbed briefly to the surface of her mind.

"Well," he said, "does your luck seem likely to take you out of this office anytime in the near future?"

"No," she said, "it certainly doesn't look that way," and they laughed again. But she wondered if he would be laughing if he knew about Paul.

"If you don't mind my saying so, then," he said, *"I'm* lucky." He quickly riffled some papers on his desk, putting on a business air as rakishly as she had seen him put on his hat. "There's going to be some changes made around here—I reckon you have heard that." He grinned. Then, briskly: "I'm going to be needing a secretary. Would you like it? You get a raise"—he coughed—"in salary, of course."

"Why, I'd love it," she heard herself saying before she had had time for the bitter reflection that this professional advance probably represented the absolute extent of her luck. And she was ashamed of the thought, which she could not repress, that Paul would probably hang on a little longer if he knew she was making more money.

She resolved not to tell him and wondered how many hours this resolution would last.

Mr. Davis looked at her with an intentness almost personal. There was a strained, brief silence. "Good," he said at last. "There are a few details to be worked out, like getting me more office space"—they both smiled—"but you'll be hearing directly in a few days. I only wanted to sound you out first." He rose and held out his hand. "I hope you're going to like working with me," he said. "I think I'm going to like working with you."

She rose and shook his hand, bewildered to find that something in his simplicity had touched her very deeply. "I'm sure I will," she said gravely. "And thank you very much." She reached backward for the doorknob.

"Miss Bowman," he said sharply—and paused. "Well, if I were you, I wouldn't mention it yet to"—he waved his hand uncomfortably—"the girls out there." Now he really did look rather boyish. "It looks better if it comes from the front office."

"I understand," she said quickly.

"Also, I didn't ask for you out of any—racial—considerations," he said. "You just seemed the most *sensible* girl available."

"I understand," she repeated; they were both trying not to smile. "And thank you again." She closed the door of his office behind her.

"A man called you," said the stocky girl. "He said he'd call back."

"Thank you," Ruth said. She could see that the girl wanted to talk, so she busily studied some papers on her desk and retired behind the noise of her typewriter.

The stocky girl had gone out to lunch, and Ruth was reluctantly deciding that she might as well go, too, when Paul called again.

"Hello. How's it going up there?"

"Dull. How are things down there? Are you out of bed already?"

"What do you mean, already?" He sounded slightly nettled and was trying not to sound that way, the almost certain signal that a storm was coming. "It's nearly one o'clock. I got work to do, too, you know."

"Yes. I know." But neither could she quite keep the sardonic edge out of her voice.

There was a silence.

"You coming straight home from work?"

"Yes. Will you be there?"

"Yeah. I got to go uptown with Cosmo this afternoon, talk to some gallery guy. Cosmo thinks he might like my stuff."

"Oh"—thinking *Damn Cosmo!*—"that's wonderful, Paul. I hope something comes of it."

Nothing whatever would come of it. The gallery owner would be evasive—*if* he existed, if they ever got to his gallery—and then Paul and Cosmo would get drunk. She would hear, while she ached to be free, to be anywhere else, *with* anyone else, from Paul, all about how stupid art dealers were, how incestuous the art world had become, how impossible it was to *do* anything—his eyes, meanwhile, focusing with a drunken intensity, his eyes at once arrogant and defensive.

Well. Most of what he said was true, and she knew it, it was not his fault.

Not his fault. "Yeah. I sure hope so. I thought I'd take up some of my water colors, some small sketches—you know, all the most *obvious* things I've got."

This policy did not, empirically, seem to be as foolproof as everyone believed, but she did not know how to put her uncertain objections into words. "That sounds good. What time have you got to be there?"

"Around three. I'm meeting Cosmo now for lunch."

"Oh"—lightly—"why don't you two, just this once, order your lunch before you order your cocktails?"

He laughed, too, and was clearly no more amused than she. "Well, Cosmo'll be buying, he'll have to, so I guess I'll leave it up to him to order."

Touché. Her hand, holding the receiver, shook. "Well, I hope you two make it to the gallery without falling flat on your faces."

"Don't worry." Then, in a rush, she recognized the tone before she understood the words, it was his you-can't-say-I-haven't-been-honest-with-you tone: "Cosmo says the gallery owner's got a daughter."

I hope to God she marries you, she thought. I hope she marries you and takes you off to Istanbul forever where I will never have to hear of you again, so I can get a breath of air, so I can get out from under.

They both laughed, a laugh conspiratorial and sophisticated, like the whispered, whisky laughter of a couple in a night club. "Oh?" she said. "Is she pretty?"

"She's probably a pig. She's had two husbands already, both artists."

She laughed again. "Where has she buried the bodies?"

"Well"—really amused this time but also rather grim—"one of them ended up in the booby hatch and the other turned into a fairy and was last seen dancing with some soldiers in Majorca."

Now they laughed together, and the wires between them hummed, almost, with the stormless friendship they both hoped to feel for each other someday. "A powerful pig. Maybe you *better* have a few drinks."

"You see what I mean? But Cosmo says she's not such a fool about painting."

"She doesn't seem to have much luck with painters. Maybe you'll break the jinx."

"Maybe. Wish me luck. It sure would be nice to unload some of my stuff on somebody."

You're doing just fine, she thought. "Will you call me later?"

"Yeah. Around three-thirty, four o'clock, as soon as I get away from there."

"Right. Be good."

"You, too. Good-by."

"Good-by."

She put down the receiver, still amused and still trembling. After all, he had called her. But he would probably not have called her if he were not actually nourishing the hope that the gallery owner's daughter might find him interesting; in that case he would have to tell Ruth about her, and it was better to have the way prepared. Paul was always preparing the way for one unlikely exploit or flight or another, it was the reason he told Ruth "everything." To tell everything is a very effective means of keeping secrets. Secrets hidden at the heart of midnight are simply waiting to be dragged to the light, as, on some unlucky high noon, they always are. But secrets shrouded in the glare of candor are bound to defeat even the most determined and agile inspector, for the light is always changing and proves that the eye cannot be trusted. So Ruth knew about Paul nearly all there was to know, knew him better than anyone else on earth ever had or probably ever would, only—she did not know him well enough to stop him from being Paul.

While she was waiting for the elevator, she realized, with mild astonishment, that she was actually hoping that the gallery owner's daughter would take Paul away. This hope resembled the desperation of someone suffering from a toothache who, in order to bring the toothache to an end, was almost willing to jump out of a window. But she found herself wondering if love really ought to be like a toothache. Love ought—she stepped out of the elevator, really wondering for a moment which way to turn—to be a means of being released from guilt and terror. But Paul's touch would never release her. He had power over her not because she was free but because she was guilty. To enforce his power over her he had only to keep her guilt awake. This did not demand malice on his part, it scarcely demanded perception—it only demanded that he have, as, in fact, he overwhelmingly did have, an instinct for his own convenience. His touch, which should have raised her, lifted her roughly only to throw her down hard; whenever he touched her, she became blacker and dirtier than ever; the loneliest place under heaven was in Paul's arms.

And yet—she went into his arms with such eagerness and such hope. She had once thought herself happy. Was this because she had been proud that he was white? But—it was she who was insisting on these colors. Her blackness was not Paul's fault. Neither was her guilt. She was punishing herself for something, a crime she could not remember. *You dirty . . . you black and dirty . . .*

She bumped into someone as she passed the cigar stand in the lobby and, looking up to murmur, "Excuse me," recognized Mr. Davis. He was stuffing cigars into his breast pocket—though the gesture was rather like that of a small boy stuffing his pockets with cookies, she was immediately certain that they were among the most expensive cigars that could be bought. She wondered what he spent on his clothes —it looked like a great deal. From the crown of rakishly tilted, deafeningly conservative hat to the tips of his astutely dulled shoes, he glowed with a very nearly vindictive sharpness. There were no flies on Mr. Davis. He would always be the best-dressed man in *any*body's lobby.

He was just about the last person she wanted to see. But perhaps his lunch hour was over and he was coming in.

"Miss Bowman!" He gave her a delighted grin. "Are you just going to lunch?"

He made her want to laugh. There was something so incongruous about finding that grin behind all that manner and under all those clothes.

"Yes," she said. "I guess you've had your lunch?"

"*No,* I ain't had no lunch," he said. "I'm hungry just like you." He paused. "I be delighted to have your company, Miss Bowman."

Very courtly, she thought, amused, and the smile is extremely wicked. Then she realized that she was pleased that a man was *being* courtly with her, even if only for an instant in a crowded lobby, and at the same instant made the discovery that what was so widely referred to as a "wicked" smile was really only the smile, scarcely ever to be encountered anymore, of a man who was not afraid of women.

She thought it safe to demur. "Please don't think you have to be polite."

"I'm never polite about food," he told her. "Almost drove my mamma crazy." He took her arm. "I know a right nice place nearby." His stride and his accent made her think of home. She also realized that he, like many Negroes of his uneasily rising generation, kept in touch, so to speak, with himself by deliberately affecting, whenever possible, the illiterate speech of his youth. "We going to get on real well, you'll see. Time you get through being *my* secretary, you likely to end up with Alcoholics Anonymous."

The place "nearby" turned out to be a short taxi ride

away, but it was, as he had said, "right nice." She doubted that Mr. Davis could possibly eat there every day, though it was clear that he was a man who liked to spend money.

She ordered a dry Martini and he a bourbon on the rocks. He professed himself astonished that she knew what a dry Martini was. "I thought you was a country girl."

"I *am* a country girl," she said.

"No, no," he said, "no more. You a country girl who came to the city, and that's the dangerous kind. Don't know if it's safe, having you for my secretary."

Underneath all this chatter she felt him watching her, sizing her up.

"Are you afraid your wife will object?" she asked.

"You ought to be able to look at me," he said, "and tell that I ain't got a wife."

She laughed. "So you're *not* married. I wonder if I should tell the girls in the office?"

"I don't care what you tell them," he said. Then: "How do you get along with them?"

"We get along fine," she said. "We don't have much to talk about except whether or not you're married, but that'll probably last until you *do* get married, and then we can talk about your wife."

But thinking for God's sake let's get off *this* subject, she added, before he could say anything: "You called me a country girl. Aren't you a country boy?"

"I am," he said, "but *I* didn't *change* my drinking habits when I come North. If bourbon was good enough for me down yonder, it's good enough for me up here."

"*I* didn't have any drinking habits to change, Mr. Davis," she told him. "I was too young to be drinking when I left home."

His eyes were slightly questioning, but he held his peace, while she wished that she had held hers. She concentrated on sipping her Martini, suddenly remembering that she was sitting opposite a man who knew more about why girls left home than could be learned from locker-room stories. She wondered if he had a sister and tried to be amused at finding herself still so incorrigibly old-fashioned. But he did not, really, seem to be much like her brother. She met his eyes again.

"Where I come from," he said, with a smile, "*nobody* was too young to be drinking. Toughened them up for later life," and he laughed.

By the time lunch was over she had learned that he was from a small town in Alabama, was the youngest of three sons (but had no sisters), had gone to college in Tennessee, was a reserve officer in the Air Force. He was thirty-two. His mother was living, his father was dead. He had lived in New York for two years but was beginning, now, to like it less than he had in the beginning.

"At first," he said, "I thought it would be fun to live in a city where didn't nobody know you and you didn't know nobody and where, look like, you could do just anything you was big and black enough to do. But you get tired not knowing nobody, and there ain't really that many things you want to do alone."

"Oh, but you must have friends," she said, "uptown."

"I don't live uptown. I live in Brooklyn. Ain't *nobody* in Brooklyn got friends."

She laughed with him but distrusted the turn the conversation was taking. They were walking back to the office. He walked slowly as though in deliberate opposition to the people around them, although they were already a little late —at least *she* was late, but since she was with one of her superiors, it possibly didn't matter.

"Where do you live?" he asked her. "Do you live uptown?"

"No," she said, "I live downtown on Bank Street." And after a moment: "That's in the Village, Greenwich Village."

He grinned. "Don't tell me you studying to be a writer or a dancer or something?"

"No. I just found myself there. It used to be cheap."

He scowled. "Ain't nothing cheap in this town no more, not even the necessities."

His tone made clear to which necessities he referred, and she would have loved to tease him a little, just to watch him laugh. But she was beginning, with every step they took, to be a little afraid of him. She was responding to him with parts of herself that had been buried so long she had forgotten they existed. In his office that morning, when he shook her hand, she had suddenly felt a warmth of affection, of nostalgia, of gratitude even—and again in the lobby —he had somehow made her feel safe. It was his friendliness that was so unsettling. She had grown used to unfriendly people.

Still, she did not *want* to be friends with him; still less did she desire that their friendship should ever become anything more. Sooner or later he would learn about Paul. He would look at her differently then. It would not be—so much—because of Paul as a man, perhaps not even Paul as a white man. But it would make him bitter, it would make her ashamed for him to see how she was letting herself be wasted—for Paul, who did not love her.

This was the reason she was ashamed and wished to avoid the scrutiny of Mr. Davis. She was doing something to herself—out of shame?—that he would be right in finding indefensible. She was punishing herself. For what? She looked sideways at his black Sambo profile under the handsome lightweight Dobbs hat and wished she could tell him about it, that he would turn his head, holding it slightly to one side, and watch her with those eyes that had seen and that had learned to hide so much. Eyes that had seen so many girls like her taken beyond the hope of rescue, while all the owner of the eyes could do—perhaps she wore Paul the way Mr. Davis wore his hat. And she looked away from him, half-smiling and yet near tears, over the furious streets on which, here and there, like a design, colored people also hurried, thinking, *And we were slaves here once*.

"Do you like music?" he asked her abruptly. "I don't necessarily mean Carnegie Hall."

Now was the time to stop him. She had only to say, "Mr. Davis, I'm living with someone." It would not be necessary to say anything more than that.

She met his eyes. "Of course I like music," she said faintly.

"Well, I know a place I'd like to take you one of these evenings after work. Not going to be easy, being *my* secretary."

His smile forced her to smile with him. But, "Mr. Davis," she said, and stopped. They were before the entrance to their office building.

"What's the matter?" he asked. "You forget something?"

"No." She looked down, feeling big, black, and foolish. "Mr. Davis," she said, "you don't know anything about me."

"You don't know anything about me, either," he said.

"That's not what I mean," she said.

He sounded slightly angry. "I ain't asked you nothing yet," he said. "Why can't you wait till you're asked?"

"Well," she stammered, "it may be too late by then."

They stared at each other for a moment. "Well," he said, "if it turns out to be too late, won't be nobody to blame but me, will it?"

She stared at him again, almost hating him. She blindly felt that he had no right to do this to her, to cause her to feel such a leap of hope, if he was only, in the end, going to give her back all of her shame.

"You know what they say down home," she said slowly. "If you don't know what you doing, you better ask somebody." There were tears in her eyes.

He took her arm. "Come on in this house, girl," he said. "We got insurance to sell."

They said nothing to each other in the elevator on the way upstairs. She wanted to laugh, and she wanted to cry. He, ostentatiously, did not watch her; he stood next to her, humming *Rocks In My Bed*.

She waited all afternoon for Paul to telephone, but although, perversely enough, the phone seemed never to cease ringing, it never rang for her. At five-fifteen, just before she left the office, she called the apartment. Paul was not there. She went downstairs to a nearby bar and ordered a drink and called again at a quarter to six. He was not there. She resolved to have one more drink and leave this bar, which she did, wandering a few blocks north to a bar frequented by theatre people. She sat in a booth and ordered a drink and at a quarter to seven called again. He was not there.

She was in a reckless, desperate state, like flight. She knew that she could not possibly go home and cook supper and wait in the empty apartment until his key turned in the lock. He would come in, breathless and contrite—or else, truculently, *not* contrite—probably a little drunk, probably quite hungry. He would tell her where he had been and what he had been doing. Whatever he told her would probably be true—there are so many ways of telling the truth! And whether it was true or not did not matter, and she would not be able to reproach him for the one thing that *did* matter: that he had left her sitting in the house alone. She could not make this reproach because, after all, leaving women sitting around in empty houses had been the specialty of all men for ages. And, for ages, when the men arrived, women bestirred themselves to cook supper—luckily, it was not yet common knowledge that many a woman had narrowly avoided committing murder by calmly breaking a few eggs.

She wondered where it had all gone to—the ease, the pleasure they had had together once. At one time their evenings together, sitting around the house, drinking beer or reading or simply laughing and talking, had been the best part of all their days. Paul, reading or walking about with a can of beer in his hand, talking, gesturing, scratching his chest; Paul, stretched out on the sofa, staring at the ceiling; Paul, cheerful, with that lowdown, cavernous chuckle and that foolish grin; Paul, grim, with his mouth turned down and his eyes burning; Paul doing anything whatever. Paul with his eyelids sealed in sleep, drooling and snoring. Paul lighting her cigarette, touching her elbow, talking, talking, talking, in his million ways, to her, had been the light that lighted up her world. Now it was all gone, it would never come again, and that face which was like the heavens was darkening against her.

These present days, after supper, when the chatter each used as a cover began to show dangerous signs of growing thinner, there would be no choice but sleep. She might, indeed, have preferred a late movie or a round of the bars, lights, noise, other people, but this would scarcely be Paul's desire, already tired from his day. Besides—after all, she had to face the office in the morning. Eventually, therefore, bed; perhaps he or she or both of them might read awhile; perhaps there would take place between them what had sometimes been described as the act of love. Then sleep, black and dreadful, like a drugged state, from which she would be rescued by the scream of the alarm clock or the realization that Paul was no longer in bed.

Ah. Her throat ached with tears of fury and despair. In the days before she had met Paul men had taken her out, she laughed a lot, she had been young. She had not wished to spend her life protecting herself, with laughter, against men she cared nothing about; but she could not go on like this, either, drinking in random bars because she was afraid to go home; neither could she guess what life might bring her when Paul was gone.

She wished that she had never met him. She wished that he, or she, or both of them were dead. And for a moment she really wished it, with a violence that frightened her. Perhaps there was always murder at the very heart of love; the strong desire to murder the beloved so that one could at last be assured of privacy and peace and be as safe and unchanging as the grave. Perhaps this was why disasters, thicker and more malevolent than bees, circled Paul's head whenever he was out of her sight. Perhaps in those moments when she had believed herself willing to lay down her life for him she had not only been presenting herself with a metaphor for her peace, his death; death, which would be an inadequate revenge for the color of his skin, for his failure, by not loving her, to release her from the prison of her own.

The waitress passed her table, and Ruth ordered another drink. After this drink she would go. The bar was beginning to fill up, mostly, as she judged, with theatre people, some of them, possibly, on their way to work, most of them drawn here by habit and hope. For the past few moments, without realizing it, she had been watching a lean, pale boy at the bar, whose curly hair leaned electrically over his forehead like a living, awry crown. Something about him, his stance, his profile, or his grin, prodded painfully at her attention. But it was not that he reminded her of Paul. He reminded her of a boy she had known briefly a few years ago, a very lonely boy who was now a merchant seaman, probably, wherever he might be on the globe at this moment, whoring his unbearably unrealized, mysteriously painful life away. She had been fond of him, but loneliness in him had been like a cancer, it had really unfitted him for human intercourse, and she had not been sorry to see him go. She had not thought of him for years; yet, now, this stranger at the bar, whom she was beginning to recognize as an actor of brief but growing reputation, abruptly brought him back to her; brought him back encrusted, as it were, with the anguish of the intervening years. She remembered things she had forgotten and wished that she had been wiser then—then she smiled at herself, wishing she were wiser now.

Once, when he had done something to hurt her, she told him, trying to be calm but choked and trembling with rage: "Look. This is the twentieth century. We're not down on a plantation, you're not the master's son, and I'm not the black girl you can just sleep with when you want to and kick about as you please!"

His face, then, had held something, held many things— bitterness, amusement, fury; but the startling element was pain, his pain, with which she now invested the face of the actor at the bar. It made her wish that she had held her tongue.

"Well," he said at last, "I guess I'll get on back to the big house and leave you down here with the pickaninnies."

They had seen each other a few times thereafter, but that was really the evening on which everything had ended between them.

She wondered if that boy had ever found a home.

The actor at the bar looked toward her briefly, but she knew he was not seeing her. He looked at his watch, frowned, she saw that he was not as young as he looked; he ordered another drink and looked downward, leaning both elbows on the bar. The dim lights played on the crown of his hair. He moved his head slightly, with impatience, upward, his mouth slightly open, and in that instant, some-how, his profile was burned into her mind. He reminded her then of Paul, of the vanished boy, of others she had seen and never touched, of an army of boys—boys forever! —an army she feared and hated and loved. In that gesture, that look upward, with the light so briefly on his face, she saw the bones that held his face together and the sorrow beginning to corrode his brow, the blood beating like but-terfly wings against the cage of his heavy neck. But there was no name for something blind, cruel, lustful, lost, intol-erably vulnerable in his eyes and mouth. She knew that in spite of everything, his color, his power, or his coming fame, he was lost. He did not know what had happened to his life. And never would. This was the pain she had seen on the face of that boy so long ago, and it was this that had driven Paul into her arms, and now away. The sons of the masters were roaming the world, looking for arms to hold them. And the arms that might have held them—could not forgive.

A sound escaped her; she was astonished to realize it was a sob. The waitress looked at her sharply. Ruth put some money on the table and hurried out. It was dark now, and the rain that had been falling intermittently all day span-gled the air and glittered all over the street. It fell against her face and mingled with her tears and she walked briskly through the crowds to hide from them and from herself the fact that she did not know where she was going.

The Game

Woodie King

Woodie King, Jr., born in Detroit thirty-four years ago, attended Wayne State University and Will-O-Way School of Theatre. He also attended Detroit's Arts and Craft Society. He was drama critic for the Detroit Tribune *for four years. His short stories and articles appeared in* Best Short Stories By Negro Writers *edited by Langston Hughes; Margarett Walker's* Black Theatre Anthology; Big City Stories; Rappi and Stylin Out: Communication in Urban Black America; Variety *Magazine,* Liberator Magazine, Black World, Tulane Drama Review, Black Theatre Magazine, New York Times, Rockefeller Foundation Quarterly, *and* The Association for the Study of Negro Life and History. *He is the editor of* Black Drama Anthology, Poets and Prophets, Black Spirits *(new black poets). As theatrical producer and actor, Mr. King has presented and appeared in some of the works of America's most respected Black writers. He currently works for Henry Street Settlement in New York.*

"Someone is always waiting for him," a hipster says to me.

"He is always doing something unusual," says another.

Both describes Sweet Mac to a tee.

I first met Sweet Mac two years ago officially; had heard of him all over town, though, especially down Hastings way. You see, Mac was going with Glorie, a babe that lived next door to me. Fact is, everybody was going with her—to her bed or the Foggy Night Hotel (everybody calls it the Foggy Day, though). No secret at all, everybody was laying Glorie. And since I was there, Sweet Mac musta been hip to the fact that I was one of the "everybody." Fact is, the most difficult part to making the broad wasn't the shoot-down, but getting there when no one else was around; which was in no way easy. Some of them squares waited for hours. It's a bitch if a stud ain't got nothing else going for him! But me, I was in a mellow position. Had a joint next to her pad; could dig out the window. On this occasion, after I had dug out the window, thinking it safe, I gets high and goes over.

And Sweet Mac was there; legs crossed, showing his Stacies and two-fifty sox. Together! Looking drugged 'cause I done blew his fast cop. He musta got there two-three seconds before I did 'cause it don't take too long to cop Glorie.

Glorie went through a few changes: pretending we were just visitors who were strung out over her; and kinda scared to show too much favoritism, making meaningless chit-chat, you know, like she had both our noses open.

I was getting drugged; Mac sat quiet most of the time, grunting now and then, as though in reply to Glorie's bogue chatter. So I started going through the same changes, hoping Mac would split. Sitting nodding; trying to outwait each other; grunts of conversation. We did this grunting—with Glorie's meaningless yarding between—until three-four A.M., at which time I went unwisely to sleep, and Sweet Mac musta wisely went for that action.

When I woke, Sweet Mac done copped and is almost outa his mind; laying on the couch panting like a mad dog. Between the pants, he is laughing like Wallace Berry. Fact is, he looks like him.

I was disgusted and pretty damn mad. If you ever missed that A-train, you know what I mean. I had just lost six hours to which I could have applied to making four-five other broads.

But from those short grunts Mac and me became good friends until this particular Saturday night. Did lots of partying together. The stud is a maniac for broads, doesn't matter if they are fat, ugly, skinny; let them come, Mac'll make them quicker than Speedy Gonzales. And they knock him out. I ain't jiving. I mean he passes out after a bust. Out. O-U-T. Like Liston when Cassius hit him up side the head. But this don't stop Sweet Mac. He takes care of business three hundred and sixty-five times a year! (Twice on his birthday, I hear.) That's how he got that name. Naturally, all the fellows would hate a cat like Sweet Mac. But anybody like Mac ain't Mac 'cause he knows how to stay friends with studs, too. I think it's because of that weird laugh.

Add to this: He also was a booster downtown a little time back. Could steal ten-twelve vines in one go 'round. Sometimes he'd let me cop a V or a Benny for nothing. We became even better friends because of his generosity.

Now, about this particular Saturday night. I was suppose to meet him at Joe's Bar B Que to get a hot number. I was told earlier by Sweet Mac: "If you don't, Monday night you will be very hot, too."

"But Mac," I said, "I am bare as the cupboard."

"This digit is going to keel over Monday evening before five o'clock," he said. "All the hippies got a bag open."

I got out of bed that Saturday night about midnight. Come Monday, if Mac was right, I would have my bag open, too. Musta been about twelve-thirty when I arrived at Joe's. Knew I was too early for Sweet Mac—he is one of them night people, you dig, a hipster at that; he don't show at night anywhere until somewhere near two A.M. (all the bars close at two A.M., you know, and most of the hip whoes around the city eat at Joe's).

While I'm standing outside of Joe's, onto the scene strode Logan X. A stone cynic, refuses to have a last name.

"Some stiff-ass farmer tossed me and my brothers a tag long time ago with a heap others doing same," he says. "And I ain't gonna buy that Jones, Smith, and Williams bull."

This particular Saturday night Logan was very neat indeed. Wearing a 3G; leather benny with a marino lining was laying on his arm, new do; hair laid snug and pretty to that big head of his. Sweet Mac calls him water head because Mac says it's like a tank. Looking at Logan's head, you can't help but to agree with Sweet Mac one hundred percent. Lo immediately pushed out his hand and spouts, *"As Salaam Alaikum,* Brother Pierre?"

Slapped his hand as I replied, *"Wa Alaikum Salaam,* waiting for Sweet Mac, Brother Lo." Called him "brother" because he supposed to be a member of this Muslim thing (though I know he ain't 'cause the cat eats pork, chitterlings, hog maws, and anything else he can sink his teeth into) and because I had intentions to hit on him for a pork-sausage sandwich. But he interrupts me as I was about to open my mouth. Cat must be psychic as well as cynic.

"Pierre, man, Mac is the cat I'm here to meet myself. Gonna git into something tonight, brother."

"Well," I said, "Mac is where it's at, brother."

By now, two-three other hipsters have also eased in, all

planning to cop a beg, since it was evident that Logan X was pretty clean and just might be open to said beg.

"Come mere, Brother Lo," I said. "Got something I want to run down to you."

We walked off a foot or two.

"Let me cop a Benny Franklin until my whoe brings me some dough," I said. "You can slip it to me while ain't nobody digging us, brother."

"I'm dead, brother," he said. "I need a dime to get some Lipton."

"Jive nigguh! Ain't got a half dollar? Get on way from me, nigguh!"

Herman started giggling. Stone junky! Giggles all the time. And always wears them black sunglasses. Another Sweet Mac waiter. Very neat, too, not to have a day job.

Herm had a funny-looking little book called *The white negro:*

"I was running from the Man," he giggled. "Hauling ass, man; goes into this gigantic bookstore, hiding and high, too; funny as hell, man. Looks up and see this funny-looking little book. Ain't that a bitch! So I stole the m. . . . .f."

Herman sticks out his hand.

Logan slaps it.

"Dig Lo," Herman continued, "if this ofay cat is so set on running down the Rocks, he forgets to mention your movement. If he forgets this, he ain't so hip."

"Told you," Logan X replied, "them cats don't know what they talking about most of the time; always running down them spooks who ain't into anything. Always forget to mention that the Rocks have hippies such as Sweet Mac."

Herman laid open his hand.

Logan X slapped it.

"Still it is strange that this gray cat can know so much about the spook," I said, reading a few lines from the book.

"But his knowledge of Sweet Mac's role is truly N.G.," Logan X said.

"Mac," Herman yawned, "is into something."

"Sweet Mac is never in a hurry," I said, remembering his many escapades, especially the Glorie affair.

Two stacked broads approached.

Everyone attained a hip position. It consisted of pulling pants high, rolling the Hi-Lo collar, taking silk handkerchief in hand, wetting the lips, getting the body limber, and the natural expressionless face. In his hip position, Herman says:

"Hey mamma, you putty thang . . . shorr look foine.

Come mere, let Hoim give you this buzz. Unnnnn Uhh!"

The broads continued on their way expressionless as we gazed wantingly at their big beautiful—

"You sho got a niaz box, baby," Logan X shouted. "The broad got her eyes on you, Pierre. See how she shakes that thang?"

"Dig that thang! Dig man! Broad stacked!! Damn! Dig it man!!" Herman said, jumping up and down, hitting the taps on his Stacies on the concrete, like he was about to wee wee in his pants.

"Yeah," I said, "broad is like that. Knows how to use that weapon."

"Business!" Logan X interrupted. "Mac is supposed to meet me here tonight and turn me on to a number."

"I'm supposed to cop myself," I said. "Mac's copping me a number from hell for a nickel!"

Herman, Logan X, and yours truly had this in common: we all had put a nickel in the hand of Sweet Mac to cop a hot number from a homo prophet. The prophet balls and blasts every Sunday night on a local radio station. One of them Sunday night preachers, you dig. But I hear the numbers he lets out of that gold-tooth mouth are sure to keel over. We had no beliefs that Sweet Mac would, in any way, try to beat us for our loot.

"Sweet Mac is on my shit list," a square standing near me thundered to everyone's amazement. "Sweet Mac was supposed to cop me a bag three nights back. I waited all that night in front of Little Sam's for the nigguh to show. I waited last night. And I'm waiting here tonight to get my bag of reefer."

"Dan, baby, you been on Mac's list for years," I said, knowing how Sweet Mac feels about Square Dan. Fact is, Mac don't feel nothing for Dan. Ever since Dan and Mac were in the kindergarten together, Mac been putting game on him.

"You a trick, Dan—a stiffy," Herman said. "You so square Little Orphan Annie could put game on you."

Dan told us we were some stupid Rocks; he also told all of us to kiss his black —. Square Dan has a nasty mouth, always had one ever since he was a kid at Moore School for boys.

It was nearing two A.M. I knew this because Joe's began filling. Stacked broads rushed in on the arms of stiffies straight from the cornfields; you know—them cats with the cowboy hats and ice-cream suits. Stone stiffs. I looked through the bug-infested window, broads were laughing everywhere. All them broads with their mouths wide, grinning, barbecue hanging in their teeth, arms greasy to the elbow; them tricks for that night were drinking Lipton Tea only. Takes a weird cat to spend all his dough on a broad while he goes without. Half them dizzy broads make more dough than us studs.

I turned from the window.

Sweet Mac!

Hurrying across Mr. Elliott Street to get to Joe's; walking kinda weird like he had to go to the john.

"Rip Van, my man," he said. He called me Van Winkle because of that incident when I fell asleep while he laid the aforementioned Glorie.

"My man," I said. "Everybody got a man and you my man, jive nigguh."

Mac gave that laugh like Wallace Berry when he did the Long John Silver thing. "You o.k., Van Winkley."

Sweet Mac was very dap that night. Sharper than Logan X because he was wearing more jewels; his benny and sunglasses were special made, his lid a stingy Dobbs. And though I believe his feet were hurting because of the narrowness of the Stetsons, he was neat from toe to stingy.

Without a doubt, Sweet Mac was carrying more loot in his pockets than all of us had had that week. And I was about to hit on him for my number so that come Tuesday I could have loot, too, but before I could inquire, he said, "Come on in, fellows. I got news on something just went down that'll knock you out."

We followed him in and seated ourselves in the back where the money people sit.

"Your orders, please," the waitress said.

"I'd like to have you, sugar," Logan X said. "You foxy thang."

She put her hands on her hips, waited. I visualized her naked.

"Yeah!" I said. "Three coffees."

To which Sweet Mac said, "Give us four pork-sausage sandwiches, momma." He turned to me. "Van Winkley, my man, never order Maxwell House when you with Sweet Mac. Get yourself some pork, baby!" Mac's pork is "poke."

"Mellow," we said in unison. I also noted a "mellow" from Logan X.

Then, through the yak-yak, Mac began to tell us the "unusual something" that he had just recently done.

"Dig," he said. "I'm with this Edith broad I been trying to lay on sheets for the past half month."

We puzzled because the broad was definitely unknown to us.

"Edith is the 'saved' broad who can't marry out of her religion," Mac says, "or do anything else out of her religion for that matter, especially what I wanted her to do. A bogue religion, man! So dig, for the last couple a weeks I been quoting the Good Book and all that stuff to her; telling her I am now saved myself, you dig."

"Four pork sandwiches," she interrupted, bending over the table, letting us get a gander at the big June Wilkerson action. Blew some hot air on them, she grinned. Sweet Mac gave her rear a light pat when she turned to leave, she continued to grin.

"*Alaikum-wa-salaam*," Logan X said. Just goes to show, regarding this Muslim thing, he doesn't know if he is coming or departing.

"Mac? You read this book?" Herman asked.

"Naw, man!" he said, only glancing at the title, "but I'd like to read the Black Caucasian, though."

"I ain't hip to that one, Mac," I said.

"Baby," he said shocked, "you ain't hip to the Black Caucasian? All them nigguh politicians is in that bag. Lots of them entertainer cats, too. Take that Belafonte cat. Ever hear him sing the Ledbelly songs? Sing 'em like a cat done just left Harvard. Ledbelly never seen the inside of a school. Dig this: Went to see this Belafonte cat at the Fisher, had my number one—six dollar seats, baby! Afterwards I went backstage to get the nigguh's name in his handwriting. He was back there grinning in them ofay broads' faces, speaking hipper than Oliver in Hamlet, not even looking in a brother's direction. Ain't that a bitch, man?"

"Told you, Allah is right," Logan X said.

"But my story is more important," Mac continued. "So tonight I says to her—"

"Where is my loot, Sweet Mac?" Square Dan interrupted.

"Dan, baby!" Sweet Mac shot back, turning a little red in the face. "Sit down, get a pork sandwich, baby."

"You got my loot, jive nigguh," Dan said. "My pocket is dead except for my blade."

Mac grinned like Wallace Berry when he plays a crook. "Gimme my dough," Dan said.

"The pocket's what—?" Mac said, giving Dan a Benny Franklin. "Here, baby. Go on cop yourself a pig sandwich."

"I gave you two for a cent pack, Mac," Dan said.

Sweet Mac frowned.

"Wait a minute, Dan; I'll give you two dollars, baby.

You think I'd put game on you for two cent? I got busted, the Man got me. Let me run this broad down, and I'll give you the cakes."

Dan took the half; sat at a table across from us, drugged. Couldn't argue. 'Cause when a cat gives a bagman dough, he loses everything if the bagman gets copped. Lately, every time you give a bagman dough, he gets copped.

"So what went down with the broad?" I asked.

Sweet Mac ordered two more pork sausages.

"I says to her," he continued with greasy mouth, eating as he talked, "Edith, baby, we can't go on like this. I dig you BUT—baby I'm one hundred percent man: And baby, from looking at you, you are one hundred percent woman (the broad went for this evaluation). Do you agree momma? I asked. The broad whimpered, yes Sweet Mac. So, I says, if that is the case, something or someone is trying to keep us—two pure American religious people of the same order—apart. At this point, I drop a quote or two from the Good Book on her; *thou shall not covet thy neighbor's wife;* and baby since you're not anybody's wife, I pleaded, *do unto others as you would have them do unto you.* I got the broad wiggling her legs! Next, I whisper to her secretly, doing the ear bit with the tongue, baby only something like that no-good Satan would want to stop something as mellow as laying naked in the Foggy Night with MJQ or Ravel on the Hi-Fi, me there playing with you, only Satan, I says. He trying to put game on us, momma. The broad is looking dazed like she done seen the handwriting on the wall. And I think I got the broad. But I'm still uncertain until the broad screams dead in my ear:

'IT'S TRUE. I been taught it is the Devil that tries to keep good things from us religious people.' Her legs are going like a washing machine; talking to me like she trying to shoot *me* down, breathing hard at the same time.

"I reply to her that *our* religion is definitely correct, many people go through life never realizing this important fact about that no-good Devil. I said this because the broad is definitely a dogmatist. Wasn't in no mood for any sudden disagreements, like the ones I had been getting for the past two-three weeks. We made a B-line from the oratory direct to the Foggy Night, into one of the most outstanding love sessions of my twenty-one years, starting when I was six years old."

Mac's story was very interesting. The introduction of the Good Book into the game is unique. There are so many religious folk nowadays. And if they listen to Prophet Jones and Sweet Daddy, I can dig why Edith dug Sweet Mac's rundown.

"This will knock you out. I told you this was an unusual session, but I forget to mention this doll is a champ on the sheets! She is brutal; death on sheets, man! Was out a my skull before we even finished the session. The whole room was spinning, twisting, and turning, and I'm telling the broad to take it easy; don't want to tell the broad I'm about to pass out, you dig. Then I faints, and she screams dead in my ear. That's the last thing I really remembered for a while. I wake up, and this fine devil is ready for another go 'round. Wants more! And I'm dizzy, all outta my head, in a hurry to split the Foggy Night and this brutal broad."

Then he clinched it, not embarrassed, either. "I was dizzy and in such a hurry to get out I put the broad's panties on, man."

I expected a Wallace Berry laugh, but instead the cat looked frightened.

We played it cool since we were eating off him; never can tell how a stud takes to being laughed at.

About that time, in comes the Edith broad—eyes glowing—like she done saved the world. Beautiful shape; cross between Tempest Storm and June Wilkerson, without make-up. I detected right away this was the action. Also noted she was walking kinda weird. She whispered something in Sweet Mac's ear. And at the same time she was rubbing Mac and kissing his ear and carrying on. Her eyes were almost closed like this Monroe doll in that flick *Some Like It Hot*. Could tell she was a natural-born champ.

"Baby, I thought you were dead," she whispered in Mac's ear, kissing him all on the neck and head. A born champ! Could make a ton of money off her!

We sat in complete expressionless silence.

The broad continued whispering while Mac destroyed the pig. I figured it was about the unusual mistake in drawers by, perhaps, both parties. Then, when Mac had finished the third pork, he broke into that uncontrollable Wallace Berry bag. And we broke our cool and joined.

Even Square Dan joined.

While we were in that cheerful bag, I heard Sweet Mac say: "I'm splittin' fellows. Later."

"Later," I said through hysteria; at the same time slapping Logan X's hand. I was so filled with laughter I forgot to cop my number.

The Poker Party*

William Melvin Kelly

William Melvin Kelly was born in New York City in 1937. He attended Harvard, where he studied under Archibald MacLeish and John Hawkes. His first novel, A Different Drummer, *won the Rosenthal Award. His other books are* Dancers on the Shore, A Drop of Patience, Dem, *and* Dunsford Travels Everywhere, *which won the fiction award of 1970 from the Black Academy of Arts and Letters.*

As I remember them, late-summer Saturdays were always hot, dry, and colored a deep green. I know now some Saturdays must have been gray; rain must have made water princesses dance in gutter puddles, as my grandmother assured me they did, each time a drop plunked down. But I will never really believe it rained on Saturdays, for I can remember only the sun playing with bits of broken glass in the vacant lot next to my house and myself running all day up and down the block like a heathen.

I never watched the sun when it was overhead, dragging the day after it. I saw it twice each day: in the morning outside the kitchen window, up the hill and behind the elevated subway, so close to the pillars they seemed crisp and flimsy like burnt match sticks, and later when it had hopped to the other side of the sky, when, as big as a saucer and the color of orange sherbet, it slid behind the stiff old monuments in Woodlawn Cemetery. I should have watched it glide overhead, for surely that was the way Indians told time, and I was an Indian most Saturdays.

But then I was not concerned with time, for time was the ticking of watches and clocks, and had nothing to do with the length of a day.

When the sun was gone, and car windshields reflected the sky and became pale blue, it would be dinner time. I

* Originally titled "Night Game."

311

would run to my house, prance up the porch steps, press the black button below the small window of thick glass through which I could see my father's name—THOMAS CAREY—and soon would come the buzz, somehow sweet, of my mother's answer on the second floor.

My mother always came to meet me. She knew it was I, for no one else pushed the bell so hard—grownups were usually not so urgent; they would thumb once lightly, stand and wait, tumbling hats in their hands. I would climb the stairs, and even before I had gained half of them, she would appear at the landing. She would wait, and as I hopped level with her, would touch my cheek or run her hand over my forehead, and if she found sweat, would march me to the bathroom and swab my face with a clean-smelling washcloth.

Some Saturday nights, the Poker Party was at my house. I would not be awake (bed-time was much earlier than the beginning of the party), but I would know it was at my house because my mother would boil and cut potatoes for salad and buy olives, and my father would come home those nights with five new decks of cards in cellophane as smooth as ice. I did not like the Poker Parties. They lasted very late, almost until I woke on Sunday morning, and my father would sleep all day and would not take me to the park like other fathers.

My father was a tall, very thin Negro. The bald skin on his head seemed also thin, for it was stretched until it shone brightly. He wore a white shirt in the daytime, and it was clean when he came home at night, except for the collar where oil from his neck gathered dust. My mother was small and very Spanish, being half that race. Her hair was black, straight, and soft as smoke. Her nose was sharp, her lips thin, her eyes deep-set and brown.

That Saturday, as usual, she sat on my left at dinner, my father on my right.

"Is everything ready?" he asked after he had swallowed.

"Yes." She did not look up.

"I told the fellows to come at ten—after he was asleep." He was speaking of me. "Will you have everything ready by then?" He seemed very excited and anxious.

My mother looked at him squarely, then glanced quickly at me. "I told you I had everything ready." We finished eating in silence, even I, although I liked to talk a great deal.

When dinner was over, I squatted on a small stool beside the radio. It was far bigger than I, bigger even than it had to be. It was mostly speaker in an ornate cabinet as large as a refrigerator. I listened until night pressed gently against the windows. Then it was time for me to go to bed. I crawled between sheets which had been warm that morning, but were now cold and unfamiliar. My mother sat with me and helped me say the prayers I could hardly understand, the words being too long, and the black outline of my father watched us from the doorway. They both kissed me, and I nestled down with my head under the covers.

I pretended I was in the cockpit of a plane carrying bombs to Burma, fighting the Japanese, who, being nearly the same color as I, seemed, no matter how I tried, more friends than enemies. And there, flying somewhere over Burma, I raced my plane straight to its destination to unload my bombs but never reached that destination, for sleep always rushed toward me faster than I, dawdling at my games, sped to my target and swept me into a tailspin where my game ended and my dreams began.

It may have been the cry of a star, netted like a snared white rabbit in the tree outside my window, that woke me. I blinked, and now the soft street lamp printed dark shadows on the walls of my room. I lay in bed, sleep stinging the corners of my eyes, and then came the low grumblings of joking men.

I had not heard the men come, had not heard them press the bell—much the same as I would have, without searching for the button, knowing where it was as well as I—had not heard them climb the stairs in shining heavy shoes, or the loud friendly greetings, or my father say, as I am sure he had, "Quiet, the boy's asleep," or the men tiptoe past my door to the back of the house and the kitchen.

But now I was awake, the darkness soft and as close around me as my one soft blanket. I was afraid; each shape was a man in a long coat coming with a silver knife.

Faintly above the rumble of their talk, I heard the sound of the chips my father never let me touch (they were plaster and easily broken) thudding on the kitchen table. I climbed from between my sheets and quietly opened the door.

The long narrow hall was dark, the walls straight on either side of me, moving up into a blackness so thick I was not certain there was a ceiling to stop them. I shuffled toward the kitchen, the hard wood floor warm beneath my bare feet. Ahead was the doorway, a tall rectangle of smoky yellow light. Jutting out from the black frame were the half hinges of the door which my father had removed because it opened into the kitchen and took up half its space. I could hear the men's words now but did not know what they meant. As I crept closer, I smelled something burning, not as if my mother had left food on the stove too long, not the rich smoke of fish or bacon, but more like the musty and ancient odor of dust in a cellar.

I stood in the doorway and watched them play a long while before they noticed me. My eyes smarted from sleep and the smoke, but still I recognized everyone at the table; I knew them all. My father sat with his back to me, his shoulders slightly hunched. Even from behind I knew that his eyes would be narrow, that he was annoyed. On his left was my mother's brother, whose last name was Cortez, and was therefore named Hernando after the *conquistador*. He was half Spanish like my mother. His face was kind and handsome; his hair was black and shiny. And then came Mister Bixby, small, almost as bald as my father, his remaining hair plastered to his scalp. A cigar poked out between yellow teeth. Heavy steel spectacles weighed on his nose and bent his ears forward. Next was my Aunt Petunia, Uncle Hernando's wife, who was West Indian and did not believe in false teeth. I did not like her very much because when she came to our house in the daytime, she always said, "Why don't you run along, child."

My mother sat next to her, clutching her cards almost desperately to her chest, looking very sleepy and not much like she was enjoying herself. Between her and my father was the table which I used on rainy days to cut pictures from magazines, covered now with liquor bottles.

Tossing her cards on the table, my mother looked up and saw me, and turned to my father. "We have a visitor." He had just slid two chips onto the table. He half turned, holding his cards close to him just below his chin, and looked at me, as did everybody else.

They all seemed surprised, even fugitive, as if they had been caught at something they were not supposed to be doing. My mother threw open her arms. "Come here." I ran to her, and she hoisted me into her lap, my back to her chest. "I'll put him to bed, Carey."

"You can't go until the hand's played out. And besides, he's up and probably hungry and might as well stay and watch. What say, son, you want to watch some?"

I nodded Yes. I had seen older boys playing cards in the corner of the school yard, had heard the ringing of their money on the pavement, but now, as I looked at the table covered with green felt softer even than my blanket, I was certain of two things: the chips were more valuable than money, and I wanted to stay.

My mother did not dispute my father, although I am sure she did not want me up. She wrapped her arms around me tightly and asked if I was cold. I shook my head, not knowing whether I was cold or not, too interested in watching the chips that were being thrown by my father, Mister Bixby, and by my uncle, who had more chips stacked in front of him than did anyone else.

My father clicked his tongue and spread his cards. Mister Bixby, smiling so broadly his cigar jounced ashes down the front of his white shirt, scooped the chips from the middle of the table with one dark hand as my mother might have gathered red beans into her apron.

"Say hello to everyone," my mother ordered quietly. Everyone smiled at me, and Aunt Petunia moved her lips and said something which I did not hear, for I was still watching Mister Bixby smile as he arranged his chips so high in front of him it seemed to me he might disappear behind them.

"How the child doing, Pablina?" my aunt fairly shouted. She would have known, had she not always shooed me along when she visited.

"He's been doing fine. Haven't you?" My mother tickled my stomach so I was forced to giggle a reply.

My father, who had hardly any chips, was irritated as if I had done something bad and without looking at me asked, "Who's dealing this hand?"

"Me." Uncle Hernando took the cards into his hands.

"I'm out. I might as well let Carey lose for both of us." My mother squeezed me and kissed my ear warmly. Everyone laughed except my father; Mister Bixby laughed the loudest.

My father waited for them to stop. "*That* is not very funny, Pablina."

Uncle Hernando winked at me and shuffled the cards, then began to throw them in front of everyone except my mother.

"Misdeal." My father clenched his fists. "You didn't have them cut."

Everyone looked at my father acidly and threw the cards back to Uncle Hernando, who took them up and burred them again, then planted them in front of my father as forcefully as he might have squashed a scampering bug. My father cut them; the deck looked the same to me. Uncle Hernando dealt them, some face down, others face up, and I saw the red and black figures, the numbers and the beautiful pictures. I watched him closely, watched the cards sliding and popping from his fingers as if they were being made within his fingers themselves.

He seemed to love the cards even more than the pile of chips in front of him (he never counted the chips) and enjoyed even more than the cards the gasps and sighs each card forced from the players.

Once the cards had been dealt, no one spoke. All I heard was the men blowing smoke heavily, Aunt Petunia whistling through the gaps in her teeth, and the thud of the chips on the blanketed table. My father's face was motionless, as if he had been photographed in the midst of boredom.

Uncle Hernando began to snap the cards once more and spin them across the table. Soon he and Mister Bixby turned theirs over and sat back in their chairs. Only Aunt Petunia and my father were playing. I hoped very much he would win, and stared at him, seeing small jewels of sweat slowly appearing on his forehead and running over his brows until he pulled a handkerchief from his back pocket and wiped them away.

"You ready to stop, Carey? I know I got you beat." My aunt spoke definitely, with such finality I was certain she was telling the truth and fully expected my father to admit defeat, but instead a slight smile crossed his face.

"I'll just call you, madam." He tossed two more chips onto the table.

One by one, tantalizing, she flipped over her cards: a red three, two jacks, and two queens, one red, one black.

My father grinned broadly and turned his cards over so we could see his three tens, a two, and a five. The men around the table gasped, then chuckled, drawing smoke deep into their lungs. My father laughed triumphantly, scraped in his chips, spread his arms wide, and bent slightly toward me. I took the two steps between us and hopped into his lap. "You brought me luck, offspring." The way he said it made me believe I really had.

He looked over my head at my mother. "Since you're not doing anything but heckling, why don't you get us some food."

She stood, nodded slightly, went to the refrigerator, and pulled out potato salad and cold cuts on huge frosted platters.

"Want to keep playing?" Mister Bixby had gathered the cards and was shuffling them loudly. His voice sounded like small-grained sandpaper on hard wood.

My father nodded, as did the rest, and Mister Bixby began to deal.

"Mis-*deal!*" My father leaned over me impatiently. I had expected him to say this, and I looked at Mister Bixby and wondered how silly he must be to forget the ritual of the game.

"Man!" Uncle Hernando shook his head. "Let's play and forget it this time. We ain't on no riverboat."

"Sure. Come on. Let's play." Mister Bixby continued to deal.

My father said nothing, but I could feel his body becoming stiff behind me. He had always told me to follow the rules. I knew he must have been disappointed with his friends.

Mister Bixby kept flipping cards onto the table. I counted four to each player. Then he turned over a card in the center. "This game, my friends, is *Spit in the Ocean.*" I thought they were playing Poker. No one seemed to notice he had changed the game.

My father reached around me and gathered his cards, pulled them just to my eye level, and made a small fan of them. His hands in front of me seemed my own, his arms seemed attached to my shoulders. I could see the cards very plainly. He had two queens. The card on the table was a queen, too, and I turned slightly on his lap and pointed at it. "Look."

He put his hand over my mouth and bent to me. "Now *you* be quiet. You want me to lose?"

I was silent, thinking perhaps I had already made him lose, and looked around the table. Mister Bixby was grinning at me. I knew then I had made a mistake and that my father *would* lose. I wished I would never be able to talk again.

I squirmed and looked over my father's shoulder. My mother was by the sink spooning potato salad into plates. She smiled at me warmly, as if to forgive me, as if she knew I meant no harm, and then turned back to her work.

Now chips almost buried the card on the table. Aunt Petunia was no longer playing. And then Uncle Hernando spun his cards down and stared at them. "This is too rich for my blood."

"All right, Bix. I'll raise you." My father's voice rumbled and shook me.

"You want to drop out now, Tom?" Mister Bixby was talking to my father, but smiling at me—as if we were great friends! "Well then, I'll just call you."

He tossed three chips into the middle of the table. My father spread out his hand, as did Mister Bixby, whose cards all had the same kind of markings and were in order, an eight, a nine, a ten, and a jack. I watched him rake in all the chips and snort a laugh as if he were cleaning his nose. Then he looked at me. "Thanks, little man."

I turned away.

"Now I know why you didn't want to re-deal." I could feel my father's body stiffen again; a warm fear shot over me.

Everybody stopped and looked at my father, and it seemed they were looking at me, too. Their faces were alike, as humorless as if they were relatives at a funeral and as accusing as my father's must have been.

"Come on, Carey," nagged my Uncle Hernando good-naturedly.

"That ain't funny at all to say, Tom," scolded Aunt Petunia, who had been collecting the cards.

My father grew even more rigid and grabbed my shoulders so tightly they hurt. "I simply said it was a misdeal. We all lost. Figure it out."

I twisted to face him. "But it was my fault. I made you lose," I blurted foolishly.

For an instant I did not know if he had heard me, and then I was certain he had, for he pushed me off his lap and turned to my mother. "Take *him* and put him to bed where he belongs." His voice was louder than it had to be.

He shoved me away from him, and I stumbled backwards, always facing the table, and finally my mother was behind me, her hands light on my shoulders. "Shhhh, don't cry. It wasn't your fault." It was then I realized I was tasting salt.

I paid no attention to that, watched my father with his back to me, his neck red above his stiff collar. "It was a misdeal. We should have stopped." *But it was my fault,* I yelled to myself, too afraid to utter it aloud.

"Maaaan, you're saying I cheated," Mister Bixby seemed almost to be pleading. "That ain't right."

My father breathed deeply. "I did not say you cheated. I just said we should have stopped after the misdeal."

Uncle Hernando leaned over and touched my father's arm. "Why don't you just forget it, Carey?" Before he had finished, my father pulled away.

"You may be rich enough to forget about nine dollars." His voice cracked and rose higher than normal. "But I can't."

"You want your money back?" chided Mister Bixby.

"No!" my father shouted. "I'm no poor sport. I just said it was a misdeal."

"Well then, don't yell."

"This is my house, and I'll yell if I want to."

"Okay, but you know damn well I didn't cheat."

"I don't know anything of the kind. And *watch* your language in front of the boy."

Both men rose slowly, as if by the same unheard signal, and glared at each other across the table. Uncle Hernando stood, too. "Come on, you guys. Sit down and forget it."

"Now you stay out of this," snapped my father; my aunt, too, began very slowly to get up, her empty mouth open.

"You've seen enough." My mother's hands tightened on my shoulders and navigated me in a circle so we both headed down the hall to my room.

"Now don't you act like a child, too. Don't you cry." But I was not thinking of tears, was not crying now because I felt I had made my father lose the game or the nine dollars but because, for the first time in my life I was afraid of grownups. I had never *seen* them argue; perhaps I had heard my father's voice raised to my mother, or hers to him, their voices seeping through my door at night, but I had never seen it or the anger in their eyes or their bodies bent and stiff like dogs fighting and snarling in the street. And even as my mother lifted me into bed, and I felt the sheets cold against my feet, and her hands through the mattress tucking me tightly, I heard my father arguing with Mister Bixby.

She sat with me, and when I stopped crying, put her warm hand high on my forehead so it was half on my skin and half on my hair and felt as if she were wearing half a soft glove. Then she kissed me and went out, closing the door behind her.

I listened intently as the guests gathered their coats from my parents' bed, then filed down the hall, one by one, without speaking. I heard my mother undress, cross the tile in the bathroom, heard the water travel explosively through the walls, and in the bedroom again, my mother brush her hair and climb into bed. After that the house was silent and dark except for the light in the kitchen which crept up the hall and under my door. I knew then my father was still sitting, alone now, at the kitchen table.

The Contraband

S. E. Anderson

*Sam (S. E.) Anderson was born in Bedford-Stuy-
vesant, New York. He attended Lincoln University
(Pa.), City College, and Hunter Graduate School.
He has published in* Black World, Viet Report, Blackfire Anthology, Black Scholar Magazine, Journal of
Black Poetry, New Black Poets Anthology *by C.
Major,* Black Seventies, Liberator Magazine, *etc. He
is editor of* New African *and co-editor of* Black
Dialogue Magazine. Muntu-Soul, *an anthology of
Pan-African Revolutionary short stories, will be published by Drum & Spear Press. His short story, "Con-
traband," was first published in* Black Arts; An Anthology of Black Creations.

His lungs filled his eyes with red swirling between searing howls. Lonnie Jo pressed his heart into the forest humus
for fear of its incessant pounding attracting the Hunters.
Baxer Creek was a couple of yards away . . . through briar
and over the knoll. He couldn't turn around, and there
was a cliff to his left and Mr. Hatter's house to his right.
The briar would cut Lonnie Jo's flesh and leave a trail of
blood, and the knoll was high and barren enough to expose
him. But he knew he could run over the knoll and into
Baxter Creek before the shooting started. He had gone
through this before—but only as a game with Mr. Hatter's
son Jeff. They played coon-catcher. Lonnie Jo was the
coon, and Jeff was the coon-catcher. At first Lonnie Jo
always got "killed" (hit with stones) so he began to find
escape paths that rabbits and possums always found. One
of them was the briar bush. He remembered how he would
slip in at one section and come out at another, leaving
Jeff to guess where he would come out. . . .
 . . . Lonnie Jo approached the other side of the briar.
Paused for just a second. To catch his breath. The cool

breeze of his swiftness stung his briar cuts as he leaped from the knoll and into Baxter Creek.

The creek was rapid, and it carried Lonnie Jo toward Carson's Bridge where he was sure of being greeted by the Hunters. But old Baxter Creek was filled with the silt that the spring thaw brought from the North—enough silt for Lonnie Jo not to be seen from the Bridge . . . unless he surfaced. He was hoping that he could hold his breath long enough . . . the water swirled and mud choked his lungs . . . he wanted to stay under longer but was too tired and too frightened. Lonnie Jo's head popped up gasping for air. He spun around searching for any signs or sounds of the Hunters. Carson's Bridge was a safe distance upstream. Soon he would be approaching Mr. Connor's north field where he would be able to see Sister Lillie's house.

His soaked body shivered from the chill of the creek. He no longer could feel the briar cuts: it was too cold; too Marchcold. Lonnie Jo crawled out onto the frost-covered bank and began waiting for sundown before making his move for Sister Lillie's.

He could hear the hounds and Hunters barking and shooting at shadows out of the frustration of losing the coon's trail. The sky reddened over the barren-brown fields while silhouettes in birdforms fluttered to their roosts.

No more redness. Silence but for the hollow gurgles of the creek. Darkness. Lonnie Jo had to listen for a pan to drop signaling him to come to Sister Lillie's house. There was a rustle. Where? Which way? Who? Lonnie Jo's body tensed in expectation of a gnawing houndbite or a piercing bursting bulletblow. Bulletblow memories clenched Lonnie Jo's fists: the whole year's explosion of bullets whizzing and careening around his body. The news of his wife's violent death so close to him . . . and yet so very very far: beyond Africa. But the Hunters continue their war. His son. What happened to Timmy? Was he castrated before he understood what the beastly act meant? Or did he die of shock as he watched the rape and shooting of his mother? Or did Timmy run and run and escape like his father is trying: escaping into the heat of the battle: facing the stark grin of Death for Future Lives?

Lonnie Jo passed out. Exhausted. Too much running and too much thinking about his lost family. He had run across Mr. Connor's north field and collapsed in front of Sister Lillie's porch. She had watched him as he fought for air with his mouth gaped going through the motions of gasping but not doing anything except making his arms swing wildly like a tossed ragged doll. The dust, as he fell, caught like tiny moths in the moonlight. Old Sister Lillie did her best to drag Lonnie Jo into her house. Sister Lillie had performed her magic many times before. She never lost a man in her station. They moved on within ten hours: rested and well prepared for the last but long trek. She smiled and hummed an ancient spiritual as she went about her chores. It was the same spiritual that her grandmother's grandmother hummed as she aided in the Resistance of the Hunters. She bathed Lonnie Jo. His dark rippling lean muscles brought tears and a smile to Sister Lillie's face.

The moonlight. The sharpsweet aroma of a man's freshly washed body; the strong black face; the hands: long, flowing with controlled power; the memories of her Man living and vibrant in Lonnie Jo. She: now gray-haired and curved with age; carved with the aged beauty of weathered mahogany. Not the sensual sepia-beauty that once captured her Man's soul. No. That beauty was for little brown babies growing into the future. Sister Lillie's beauty blooms another color—ancient—spreading a more spiritual fragrance.

A few hours later Lonnie Jo awakens refreshed and hungry. Sister Lillie has prepared his meal and packed some salt pork for the last leg of his journey. She warns Lonnie Jo that he must leave very soon so that he can arrive at Marshall's peak before dawn. After committing the directions to memory he kisses Sister Lillie. She replies with a tender motherly embrace and: "Go now, Son."

Once more Nature and the Hunter await him. For Nature he dressed warmly and wore heavy boots. For the Hunter a small pistol and dagger. The late Marchfrost crackled beneath his boots leaving telltale tracks. Lonnie Jo remembered Sister Lillie's moonlit face crying goodbye and good luck. He wanted to return and forget . . . and remember. But the peace would be personal and short-lived.

A sudden rustle of corn stalks brought Lonnie Jo back to the realities of his destiny. He stopped. He silently dropped to the hardened mud. Lonnie Jo knew what the rustling meant: it meant a man. A beast of a man: the Hunter. He sensed the Hunter to be about ten feet away and approaching him. By the rustling Lonnie Jo knew that the Hunter had no dog with him. Within a few seconds he saw the Hunter searching the top of the corn stalks. In the moonlight his face glimmered pale and tired. The Hunter taught Lonnie Jo how to kill a man without making a sound.

And Lonnie Jo did just that.

He took the dead Hunter's rifle and ammunition and moved cautiously listening and watching. He had to be fast and silent, for any minute the other Hunters might find the stabbed pallid corpse with eyes bulging at the heavens. Once again into Baxter Creek. This time waist-deep without a splash. For more than ten minutes Lonnie Jo waded downstream before crossing over to the other side using the exposed boulders. There were distant sounds of Hounds and Hunters once again frustrated by their game.

Did Timmy go this way, too? Or did he get this far? There would be heavy rains and no word from Timmy. It was winter then. Clara's eyes would sparkle as she bent over the balls of cotton. He would always see her from afar—always full of life—always his and nature's. . . .

The night was ending in deep frost and chirps of mockingbirds awaiting the yellow glow of the sun. Lonnie Jo walked on; sometimes trotting, sometimes running with the forest as his protector. He did not have much time left. He had a rendezvous exactly at dawn. . . .

Baxter Creek was still down in the valley to his right as Sister Lillie described. Soon he would start a steep climb to the plateau. Then to his left would be an open road heavily patrolled by Hunters. Sister Lillie said that they patrol in 4-man squads every minute. That whole area is wide open. Lonnie Jo would have to be careful and swift. Sister Lillie said in a full run it takes almost a minute to cover the open field and road. The climbing became steep. Soon Lonnie Jo was climbing with hands and feet. The rocks were slippery with moss and water. It was getting brighter. Lonnie Jo tried to climb faster but only resulted in loosening a few rocks. When he finally reached the top of the plateau, he peered over the edge to see if the patrol squad was nearby. Yes. They were just leaving. More birds were chirping, and there was a brightness to his right. The air was fresh and hinting of spring. He saw the forest . . . and the tall bent pine: the last marker.

Lonnie Jo's legs moved as fast as they could. His head high and arms pumping. Body tensed and tuned for thirty-one years for this moment. For this moment. The bent pine was not getting larger. The rifle becoming lead slowing his speed. But he must carry it. Every rifle counts. Once again his lungs filled his eyes with red. Lonnie Jo's boots pounded the ground as the sky yellowed. The tall bent pine grew slightly. In the forest ahead there was a dark face.

Timmy??!!

Time slowed. The sky blurred yellow with dots of birds.

Everything slowed down. The tall pine began to get smaller. Lonnie Jo felt something hot and searing cut into the back of his right shoulder. Then a rifle blast. A face.

Timmy??!!

No more air. Dawn. A Face: black and beckoning. A rifle blast. The tall bent pine tree looming encompassing everything—except the face black and beckoning.

A rifle blast. Then more. Lonnie Jo smashed to the ground exhausted and ducking bullets, feeling that his right shoulder was bleeding. The dark face fired toward the road.

. . . The dark face fired and was joined from behind by more rifles. The face turned and smiled with Lonnie Jo coolly saying:

"Now I know how them Viet Cong cats feel, Brother."

Liars Don't Qualify

Junius Edwards

Junius Edwards was born in Alexandria, Louisiana, forty-one years ago. He was educated at the University of Oslo in Norway. The short story in this anthology won first prize in the Writer's Digest Short Story Contest. In 1959 he won a Eugene F. Saxton Fellowship for Creative Writing. His short story, "Mother Dear and Daddy," is in John Williams' anthology The Angry Black. *Mr. Edwards is author of the novel* If We Must Die.

Will Harris sat on the bench in the waiting room for another hour. His pride was not the only thing that hurt. He wanted them to call him in and get him registered so he could get out of there. Twice, he started to go into the inner office and tell them, but he thought better of it. He had counted ninety-six cigarette butts on the floor when a fat man came out of the office and spoke to him.

"What you want, boy?"

Will Harris got to his feet.

"I came to register."

"Oh, you did, did you?"

"Yes sir."

The fat man stared at Will for a second, then turned his back to him.

As he turned his back, he said, "Come on in here."

Will went in.

It was a little office and dirty, but not so dirty as the waiting room. There were no cigarette butts on the floor here. Instead, there was paper. They looked like candy wrappers to Will. There were two desks jammed in there, and a bony little man sat at one of them, his head down, his fingers fumbling with some papers. The fat man went around the empty desk and pulled up a chair. The bony man did not look up.

Will stood in front of the empty desk and watched the fat man sit down behind it. The fat man swung his chair around until he faced the little man.

"Charlie," he said.

"Yeah, Sam," Charlie said, not looking up from his work.

"Charlie. This boy here says he come to register."

"You sure? You sure that's what he said, Sam?" Still not looking up. "You sure? You better ask him again, Sam."

"I'm sure, Charlie."

"You better be sure, Sam."

"All right, Charlie. All right. I'll ask him again," the fat man said. He looked up at Will. "Boy. What you come here for?"

"I came to register."

The fat man stared up at him. He didn't say anything. He just stared, his lips a thin line, his eyes wide open. His left hand searched behind him and came up with a handkerchief. He raised his left arm and mopped his face with the handkerchief, his eyes still on Will.

The odor from under his sweat-soaked arm made Will step back. Will held his breath until the fat man finished mopping his face. The fat man put his handkerchief away. He pulled a desk drawer open, and then he took his eyes off Will. He reached in the desk drawer and took out a bar of candy. He took the wrapper off the candy and threw the wrapper on the floor at Will's feet. He looked at Will and ate the candy.

Will stood there and tried to keep his face straight. He kept telling himself: I'll take anything. I'll take anything to get it done.

The fat man kept his eyes on Will and finished the candy. He took out his handkerchief and wiped his mouth. He grinned, then he put his handkerchief away.

"Charlie." The fat man turned to the little man.

"Yeah, Sam."

"He says he come to register."

"Sam, are you sure?"

"Pretty sure, Charlie."

"Well, explain to him what it's about." The bony man still had not looked up.

"All right, Charlie," Sam said, and looked up at Will. "Boy, when folks come here, they intend to vote, so they register first."

"That's what I want to do," Will said.

"What's that? Say that again."

"That's what I want to do. Register and vote."

The fat man turned his head to the bony man.

"Charlie."

"Yeah, Sam."

"He says . . . Charlie, this boy says that he wants to register and vote."

The bony man looked up from his desk for the first time. He looked at Sam, then both of them looked at Will.

Will looked from one of them to the other, one to the other. It was hot, and he wanted to sit down. *Anything. I'll take anything.*

The man called Charlie turned back to his work, and Sam swung his chair around until he faced Will.

"You got a job?" he asked.

"Yes, sir."

"Boy, you know what you're doing?"

"Yes, sir."

"All right," Sam said. "All right."

Just then, Will heard the door open behind him, and someone came in. It was a man.

"How you all? How about registering?"

Sam smiled. Charlie looked up and smiled.

"Take care of you right away," Sam said, and then to Will. "Boy. Wait outside."

As Will went out, he heard Sam's voice: "Take a seat, please. Take a seat. Have you fixed up in a little bit. Now, what's your name?"

"Thanks," the man said, and Will heard the scrape of a chair.

Will closed the door and went back to his bench.

Anything. Anything. Anything. I'll take it all.

Pretty soon the man came out smiling. Sam came out behind him, and he called Will and told him to come in. Will went in and stood before the desk. Sam told him he wanted to see his papers: Discharge, High School Diploma, Birth Certificate, Social Security Card, and some other papers. Will had them all. He felt good when he handed them to Sam.

"You belong to any organization?"

"No, sir."

"Pretty sure about that?"

"Yes, sir."

"You ever heard of the 15th Amendment?"

"Yes, sir."

"What does that one say?"

"It's the one that says all citizens can vote."

"You like that, don't you, boy? Don't you?"

"Yes, sir. I like them all."

Sam's eyes got big. He slammed his right fist down on his desk top. "I didn't ask you that. I asked you if you liked the 15th Amendment. Now, if you can't answer my questions . . ."

"I like it," Will put in, and watched Sam catch his breath.

Sam sat there looking up at Will. He opened and closed his desk-pounding fist. His mouth hung open.

"Charlie."

"Yeah, Sam." Not looking up.

"You hear that?" looking wide-eyed at Will. "You hear that?"

"I heard it, Sam."

Will had to work to keep his face straight.

"Boy," Sam said. "You born in this town?"

"You got my birth certificate right there in front of you. Yes, sir."

"You happy here?"

"Yes, sir."

"You got nothing against the way things go around here?"

"No, sir."

"Can you read?"

"Yes, sir."

"Are you smart?"

"No, sir."

"Where did you get that suit?"

"New York."

"New York?" Sam asked, and looked over at Charlie. Charlie's head was still down. Sam looked back to Will.

"Yes, sir," said Will.

"Boy, what you doing there?"

"I got out of the Army there."

"You believe in what them folks do in New York?"

"I don't know what you mean."

"You know what I mean. Boy, you know good and well what I mean. You know how folks carry on in New York. You believe in that?"

"No, sir," Will said, slowly.

"You pretty sure about that?"

"Yes, sir."

"What year did they make the 15th Amendment?"

". . . 18 . . . 70," said Will.

"Name a signer of the Declaration of Independence who became President."

". . . John Adams."

"Boy, what did you say?" Sam's eyes were wide again. Will thought for a second. Then he said, "John Adams."

Sam's eyes got wider. He looked to Charlie and spoke to a bowed head. "Now, too much is too much." Then he turned back to Will.

He didn't say anything to Will. He narrowed his eyes first, then spoke.

"Did you say *just* John Adams?"

"*Mister* John Adams," Will said, realizing his mistake.

"That's more like it," Sam smiled. "Now, why do you want to vote?"

"I want to vote because it is my duty as an American citizen to vote."

"Hah," Sam said, real loud. "Hah," again, and pushed back from his desk and turned to the bony man.

"Charlie."

"Yeah, Sam."

"Hear that?"

"I heard, Sam."

Sam leaned back in his chair, keeping his eyes on Charlie. He locked his hands across his round stomach and sat there.

"Charlie."

"Yeah, Sam."

"Think you and Elnora be coming over tonight?"

"Don't know, Sam," said the bony man, not looking up. "You know Elnora."

"Well, you welcome if you can."

"Don't know, Sam."

"You ought to, if you can. Drop in, if you can. Come on over and we'll split a corn whisky."

The bony man looked up.

"Now, that's different, Sam."

"Thought it would be."

"Can't turn down corn if it's good."

"You know my corn."

"Sure do. I'll drag Elnora. I'll drag her by the hair if I have to."

The bony man went back to work.

Sam turned his chair around to his desk. He opened a desk drawer and took out a package of cigarettes. He tore it open and put a cigarette in his mouth. He looked up at Will, then he lit the cigarette and took a long drag, and then he blew the smoke, very slowly, up toward Will's face.

The smoke floated up toward Will's face. It came up in

front of his eyes and nose and hung there, then it danced and played around his face, and disappeared.

Will didn't move, but he was glad he hadn't been asked to sit down.

"You have a car?"

"No, sir."

"Don't you have a job?"

"Yes, sir."

"You like that job?"

"Yes, sir."

"You like it, but you don't want it."

"What do you mean?" Will asked.

"Don't get smart, boy," Sam said, wide-eyed. "I'm asking the questions here. You understand that?"

"Yes, sir."

"All right. All right. Be sure you do."

"I understand it."

"You a Communist?"

"No, sir."

"What party do you want to vote for?"

"I wouldn't go by parties. I'd read about the men and vote for a man, not a party."

"Hah," Sam said, and looked over at Charlie's bowed head. "Hah," he said again, and turned back to Will.

"Boy, you pretty sure you can read?"

"Yes, sir."

"All right. All right. We'll see about that." Sam took a book out of his desk and flipped some pages. He gave the book to Will.

"Read that loud," he said.

"Yes, sir," Will said, and began: " 'When in the course of human events, it becomes necessary for one people to dissolve the political bands which have connected them with another, and to assume among the powers of the earth the separate and equal station to which the Laws of Nature and of Nature's God entitle them, a decent respect to the opinions of mankind requires that they should declare the causes which impel them to the separation.' "

Will cleared his throat and read on. He tried to be distinct with each syllable. He didn't need the book. He could have recited the whole thing without the book.

" 'We hold these truths to be self-evident, that all men are created equal, that they . . .' "

"Wait a minute, boy," Sam said. "Wait a minute. You believe that? You believe that about 'created equal'?"

"Yes, sir," Will said, knowing that was the wrong answer.

"You really believe that?"

"Yes, sir." Will couldn't make himself say the answer Sam wanted to hear.

Sam stuck out his right hand, and Will put the book in it. Then Sam turned to the other man.

"Charlie."

"Yeah, Sam."

"Charlie, did you hear that?"

"What was it, Sam?"

"This boy, here, Charlie. He says he really believes it."

"Believes what, Sam? What you talking about?"

"This boy, here . . . believes that all men are equal, like it says in The Declaration."

"Now, Sam. Now you know that's not right. You know good and well that's not right. You heard him wrong. Ask him again, Sam. Ask him again, will you?"

"I didn't hear him wrong, Charlie," said Sam, and turned to Will. "Did I, boy? Did I hear you wrong?"

"No, sir."

"I didn't hear you wrong?"

"No, sir."

Sam turned to Charlie.

"Charlie."

"Yeah, Sam."

"Charlie. You think this boy trying to be smart?"

"Sam. I think he might be. Just might be. He looks like one of them that don't know his place."

Sam narrowed his eyes.

"Boy," he said. "You know your place?"

"I don't know what you mean."

"Boy, you know good and well what I mean."

"What do you mean?"

"Boy, who's . . ." Sam leaned forward, on his desk. "Just who's asking questions, here?"

"You are, sir."

"Charlie. You think he really is trying to be smart?"

"Sam, I think you better ask him."

"Boy."

"Yes, sir."

"Boy. You trying to be smart with me?"

"No, sir."

"Sam."

"Yeah, Charlie."

"Sam. Ask him if he thinks he's good as you and me."

"Now, Charlie. Now, you heard what he said about The Declaration."

"Ask, anyway, Sam."

"All right," Sam said. "Boy. You think you good as me and Mister Charlie?"

"No, sir," Will said.

They smiled, and Charlie turned away.

Will wanted to take off his jacket. It was hot, and he felt a drop of sweat roll down his right side. He pressed his right arm against his side to wipe out the sweat. He thought he had it, but it rolled again, and he felt another drop come behind that one. He pressed his arm in again. It was no use. He gave it up.

"How many stars did the first flag have?"

". . . Thirteen."

"What's the name of the mayor of this town?"

". . . Mister Roger Phillip Thornedyke Jones."

"Spell Thornedyke."

". . . Capital T-h-o-r-n-e-d-y-k-e, Thornedyke."

"How long has he been mayor?"

". . . Seventeen years."

"Who was the biggest hero in the War Between the States?"

". . . General Robert E. Lee."

"What does that 'E' stand for?"

". . . Edward."

"Think you pretty smart, don't you?"

"No, sir."

"Well, boy, you have been giving these answers too slow. I want them fast. Understand? Fast."

"Yes, sir."

"What's your favorite song?"

"*Dixie,*" Will said, and prayed Sam would not ask him to sing it.

"Do you like your job?"

"Yes, sir."

"What year did Arizona come into the States?"

"1912."

"There was another state in 1912."

"New Mexico, it came in January and Arizona in February."

"You think you smart, don't you?"

"No, sir."

"Don't you think you smart? Don't you?"

"No, sir."

"Oh, yes, you do, boy."

Will said nothing.

"Boy, you make good money on your job?"

"I make enough."

"Oh. Oh, you not satisfied with it?"

"Yes, sir. I am."

"You don't act like it, boy. You know that? You don't act like it."

"What do you mean?"

"You getting smart again, boy. Just who's asking questions here?"

"You are, sir."

"That's right. That's right."

The bony man made a noise with his lips and slammed his pencil down on his desk. He looked at Will, then at Sam.

"Sam," he said. "Sam, you having trouble with that boy? Don't you let that boy give you no trouble, now, Sam. Don't you do it."

"Charlie," Sam said. "Now, Charlie, you know better than that. You know better. This boy here knows better than that, too."

"You sure about that, Sam? You sure?"

"I better be sure if this boy here knows what's good for him."

"Does he know, Sam?"

"Do you know, boy?" Sam asked Will.

"Yes, sir."

Charlie turned back to his work.

"Boy," Sam said. "You sure you're not a member of any organization?"

"Yes, sir. I'm sure."

Sam gathered up all Will's papers, and he stacked them very neatly and placed them in the center of his desk. He took the cigarette out of his mouth and put it out in the full ash tray. He picked up Will's papers and gave them to him.

"You've been in the Army. That right?"

"Yes, sir."

"You served two years. That right?"

"Yes, sir."

"You have to do six years in the Reserve. That right?"

"Yes, sir."

"You're in the Reserve now. That right?"

"Yes, sir."

"You lied to me here, today. That right?"

"No, sir."

"Boy, I said you lied to me here today. That right?"

"No, sir."

"Oh, yes, you did, boy. Oh, yes, you did. You told me you wasn't in any organization. That right?"

"Yes, sir."

"Then you lied, boy. You lied to me because you're in the Army Reserve. That right?"

"Yes, sir. I'm in the Reserve, but I didn't think you meant that. I'm just in it, and don't have to go to meetings or anything like that. I thought you meant some kind of civilian organization."

"When you said you wasn't in an organization, that was a lie. Now, wasn't it, boy?"

He had Will there. When Sam had asked him about organizations, the first thing to pop in Will's mind had been the communists, or something like them.

"Now, wasn't it a lie?"

"No, sir."

Sam narrowed his eyes.

Will went on.

"No, sir, it wasn't a lie. There's nothing wrong with the Army Reserve. Everybody has to be in it. I'm not in it because I want to be in it."

"I know there's nothing wrong with it," Sam said. "Point is, you lied to me here, today."

"I didn't lie. I just didn't understand the question," Will said.

"You understood the question, boy. You understood good and well, and you lied to me. Now, wasn't it a lie?"

"No, sir."

"Boy. You going to stand right there in front of me big as anything and tell me it wasn't a lie?" Sam almost shouted. "Now, wasn't it a lie?"

"Yes, sir," Will said, and put his papers in his jacket pocket.

"You right, it was," Sam said.

Sam pushed back from his desk.

"That's it, boy. You can't register. You don't qualify. Liars don't qualify."

"But . . ."

"That's it." Sam spat the words out and looked at Will hard for a second, and then he swung his chair around until he faced Charlie.

"Charlie."

"Yeah, Sam."

"Charlie. You want to go out to eat first today?"

Will opened the door and went out. As he walked down the stairs, he took off his jacket and his tie and opened his collar and rolled up his shirt sleeves. He stood on the court-house steps and took a deep breath and heard a noise come from his throat as he breathed out and looked at the flag in the court yard. The flag hung from its staff, still and quiet, the way he hated to see it; but it was there, waiting, and he hoped that a little push from the right breeze would lift it and send it flying and waving and whipping from its staff, proud, the way he liked to see it.

He took out a cigarette and lit it and took a slow deep drag. He blew the smoke out. He saw the cigarette burning in his right hand, turned it between his thumb and forefinger, made a face, and let the cigarette drop to the court-house steps.

He threw his jacket over his left shoulder and walked on down to the bus stop, swinging his arms.

Like a Piece of Blues

George Davis

George Davis has served as a staff writer for the
Washington Post *and with the* New York Times *Sunday Department. He is also a member of the John O.
Killens Writers Workshop at Columbia University.
He was a pilot in the U.S. Air Force and flew more
than forty combat missions in 1967 and 1968. He is
the author of the novel* Coming Home.

It was not until Rashman X, the little Black Muslim,
began talking to us, my friend Teddy Crawford and me,
that I began to notice. For him the teasing seemed all for
fun, but I was 15, living through a very serious, vulnerable
summer, so there was something deeper than fun in it for
me.

Rashman was a small man, four inches shorter than I,
and though I was skinny then, Rashman was skinnier. He
was a neat, taut man with skin the color of pitch. His neatness and his dignity prevented his looking scrawny even
with his knees and elbows coming to points as they did
when he bent them beneath his starched, white barber's uniform. His hair was pepper-gray and always neat and parted,
and I never saw him once when he needed a shave.

That Saturday morning when Teddy Crawford and I
entered his barbershop, the bums off Ninth Street followed
us, bringing with them their usual odor of tobacco, filth,
and wine to mix with the odor of talc and after-shave lotion inside. They took seats along the wall to wait for the
teasing that always followed when Rashman and I got
together.

Rashman's wit was as sharp as the razor he shaved himself with, and I was foolish enough to challenge him. He
had a clever way making small things seem significant;
thus leaving them no longer small. For example, that Saturday while I was in the chair he brought to my attention

339

that of all the women in my father's church's Woman's Society for Christian Service none were even as dark as Teddy
Crawford and I, and we were only medium brown.

Yes, and I remember how Rashman had stopped me
when I said "only medium brown," thus succeeding cleverly
at making the bums think that I had said that we had fallen
away from grace by only that much, that at least we were
not black.

"I didn't say that," I challenged quickly, but Rashman
was already laughing what I called then his little wickerwire laugh way back in the roof of his mouth. He cut me
off so I would not have a chance to explain myself. "Don't
let folks brainwash you, son," he said.

Whenever we faced off like this and he scored first, he
always spoke rapidly so I wouldn't be able to score back.
"I guess the Christians taught you that black is the color
of evil." He laughed deliciously. "Be careful, son. Be careful . . . Then of course brainwashing is seldom very painful, and if it's done subtly you never know it's happened.
I knew a fellow once who went his entire life brainwashed.
Died happy, though." He winked at the bums and bent
over to pump my chair up a little higher. The bums smiled.
A few of them cleared their throats, and there I was de-
fenseless sitting in the middle of the shop with the silly
barber's cloth tied around my neck.

"Wait. You're trying to make these gentlemen think that
I . . ."

"No. I'm not criticizing you. No-o-o. I don't blame you
one little bit. It's very hard to stand against the entire
Christian civilization. It's no fun having to make up everything from scratch. . . . better a servant in the house of
the Lord than a king among the unholy, huh? Is that the
way the Bible says it?" He laughed again. "I don't blame
you one iota. Why . . . why enter the woods if you're
not sure you can find your way out?"

The bums laughed partly at me and partly with me.
"We all have to enter the woods sometime," I said.

"Oh sure, yes, yes, it's not bad to come in. Just don't
come too deep. Come in, look around, then scat back." He
spun my chair.

"You jump to conclusions too fast," I said, but this was
not one of my good answers. It did not get a rise out of
the bums as some of my cracks used to do.

"Yes I do. I do. I shouldn't blame you for . . ."

"Give me a chance to talk."

"Oh! yes, all right."

I got down out of the chair talking, trying to hit on something that would swing the bums to my side, but Rashman had me too far down. He could afford to smile complacently while I argued. Someone else got in the chair and he began pumping the chair up again.

After much grumbling from Teddy Crawford, we left, but only after I declared that I would be back as soon as I got myself together. He sent me out onto the sidewalk with laughter and catcalls following me. I laughed myself. I liked Rashman, and I knew that he and the bums liked me. But the only bad thing was he had been defeating me too soundly and too often ever since back in May when too much seriousness began to creep into my mood.

Rashman's barber shop was the cleanest business on Ninth Street. However, my father warned me many times not to go there and listen to Rashman's bile; but Teddy Crawford and I, with our money in our pockets, would go down to Ninth Street on Saturday morning and wander around until I could talk Teddy into going to Rashman's shop instead of to one of the others.

I always had to promise him that afterwards I would go with him up to Maxine Green's apartment over the Tom Thumb Tailor Shop. Maxine's mother was never home on Saturday mornings, so I kept Maxine's three younger brothers outside while Teddy slipped the meat to her in the bedroom.

"Okay," Teddy said on the first Saturday in July, only one week after he had promised never to go with me again. "I'll go if you promise not to waste all day arguing with that nut."

"Okay, to hell with Rashman," I said as we were coming down from Teddy's house toward the upper end of Ninth Street.

"Now you're talking, baby," Teddy said, walking wide-legged, filling his lungs with air, obviously thinking about Maxine Green.

"Hey, looka here," Rashman said as I pushed his front door open. "My little friends from the hill have come back." The heavy glass door sucked close behind us. "I thought I scared you children away last time, making light of your Lord and Saviour Jesus Christ like I did." He spoke loud enough for everyone in the shop to hear. At least ten men had followed us in. Two of them had to stand because there were not enough seats. Teddy and I took our seats along the wall under the row of gleaming mirrors to wait our turns in the chairs. Rashman's assistant, a lean, quiet boy who came in from St. Louis each weekend to work at Rashman's Mosque #6 Barber Shop, always cut Teddy's hair. He liked to cut close, and that was the way Teddy's mother liked it.

Rashman did not say anything more to me until I got in the chair. This was a tactic of his. Then: "How are things up home?" he said as I sat down. "Did you tell the reverend what I said last week?"

"Yeah," I lied. "He said one of these days a bolt of lightning's going to hit your vilifying soul."

Shaderow, who had just sat down in the seat I had vacated, laughed and repronounced my word. Rashman laughed and shook out the large pin-striped cover cloth. He waved it in front of me like a magician.

Teddy got into the chair next to mine. The two men who had been playing checkers back near the shoe-shine stand turned around to watch.

The bums seemed out of place with their tattered clothing and dirty bodies in the gleaming tile, glass, and porcelain shop. The bright July sunlight passing thru the large, clean front windows highlighted their filth. It showed clearly the spittle in the mouth of one toothless one who was smiling as Rashman spun me around.

Rashman began by combing my hair briskly. It was kinky because with all the reading I was doing I didn't have time to care for it. He made it pop and made the dust fly to put me further at a disadvantage. By now all the bums were smiling, waiting for the argument between me and Rashman X, the only Negro in town who had courage enough to turn his back completely on Christianity.

"What words of wisdom do you have for us today, my young man?" Rashman asked.

"None," I answered, and looked over at Teddy Crawford.

"Still believe in the saving grace of Jesus Christ?" he asked, biblically, knowing that I was going to say, "yes." "Doesn't it frighten you being in here where lightning might strike, then?"

"No."

"How about you, young man?" Rashman asked, spinning Teddy's chair so abruptly that the other barber had to jerk his clippers back.

Teddy smiled fawningly. His oily, peanut-smooth complexion reddened. His fat slick cheeks and round slick head seemed to fill up with blood. "No, sir."

Rashman let him go. Teddy was not the one he wanted.

He wanted me. I was the outspoken one. Besides, I had secretly been considering following my father into the Christian ministry. I suspected that Rashman knew this, and this was why he taunted me more than Teddy.

We argued, but every time I was about to make a good point, Rashman would spin me away from my audience. I would be facing myself, self-consciously, in the mirror behind the chair, the image of the row of bums bouncing back and forth between the mirrors on the opposite walls. Then Rashman would pop my hair, and the bums would roar.

I stood up when he was done and let him brush the hair off my green and yellow polo shirt. Teddy was finished long before I was. He was in a hurry to get up to Maxine's.

"Christianity is dead. That's a fact, and it makes you a necrophiliac," Rashman sang.

The bums broke up over this word. They smacked their thighs and laughed: "Amen," "Yea," "Tell it like it is."

I waved Rashman away as I followed Teddy toward the door. I had to laugh, too, when Shaderow almost choked trying to repronounce, "necrophiliac." But my laughter was not deep. Too much of what Rashman said was too important.

II

The next Sunday was a bright, hot day. I got up early, let the sun into my room, dressed carelessly, and went outside thinking about Rashman. I wanted to skip church, but I knew that I would not be able to tell my father why. I walked around for a long time trying to decide what to do.

Our church was the largest Negro Methodist church in the district, and there were only three or four white churches larger—all of them city churches up in St. Louis. It was a natural stone building like the parsonage in which we lived. They both sat on a grassy plot a block and a half from the Negro college.

The neighborhood was not at all like you would picture a Negro ghetto. The houses and lawns were all well cared for. Most of the houses were brick or stone, and the few of them that were wood frame were in good repair. The vacant lots around the campus and the church were all well cared for. The streets were all paved. Sidewalks ran on both sides all the way up from Ninth Street back past

Carson Avenue and laterally on all sides from Bullock to Canterberry (except for the two blocks where the wall and the iron fence of the community cemetery precluded sidewalks).

Nearly everyone in the entire neighborhood was a member of my father's church.

Most of them were teachers at H. L. Single High School or over at the college. Ours was a world of secure jobs and easy living. The bigotry and injustice which menaced the lives of so many black people during these years was closed out of it. I walked down toward Mason Street thinking about that. When I got down almost to where Teddy Crawford lived, younger children started to come out of the houses dressed for Sunday School. I thought it best that I beat it back and get ready to teach my Sunday School class.

All during the hour I was hot with anxiety in the air-conditioned building. The lesson was about David the Shepherd. What, I wondered, did that have to do with anything.

Obviously, Rashman had a way of getting weekly bulletins from the church, for just as he said this was installation Sunday for the new officers of the Woman's Society for Christian Service. I watched them as they filed past me toward the front of the church.

"Ah! and you watch them," Rashman had said. "Everyone of them past the age thirty has to wear glasses because their eyes are weak. Mongrelization's done it. And you watch, every one of them will be fat from overindulgence and lack of discipline."

On Sunday, as I watched the women, I hated their stuffy, sanctimonious smiles. All of them were light-skinned, plump, and slightly bent. All except two wore glasses. I wondered if this was just a coincidence that Rashman had noticed and decided to use against me, or whether, however silly scientifically it might seem, his statement about mongrelization had some truth to it. I thought for a moment, then I shook my head, no. I could picture him behind his chair, his image in the mirror showing his scissors poised above my unkempt hair, his face caught for one static moment between smiles, his own eyes aided by thin, rimless glasses. As I sat there in church, I thought that I could hear his brief, wickerwire laughter.

Old Mrs. Turner, my high school civics teacher, was standing two down from the end. She had been called forward as the new recording secretary. I focused my attention on her. She used to call me her little preacher. I shook with fear at the prospect that Rashman might find out and tell it in the crowded barber shop.

As I looked at Mrs. Turner, I filled up with anger because even now I was arguing with Rashman and losing. Mrs. Turner was too much for me to explain to someone like the bums. Rashman would get the better of me.

Mrs. Turner was a big butter-colored woman who wore heavy coke bottle-bottom glasses. She hated her job, and she hated the kids she had to teach. All she taught for was the money in it; that was plain from the way she acted. I knew how much Rashman would make of the contempt she had for the poorer kids from over in Chambers who came to school poorly dressed and often a little dirty. These kids were either timid and backward or too manish or womanish for their ages to suit Mrs. Turner. The one group she ignored as often as she could, and the others she expelled whenever she could get away with it. I knew how Rashman would tease me about the way Mrs. Turner complimented me for not being like them: "her little preacher." I shook my head again.

She did have the biggest tits on the faculty. I could score with the bums by mentioning that and by adding that I was sure they didn't grow because of heavy sexual activity. "She must play with them every night. And, boy, you ought to see them big yellow thighs when she sits up in the window sill at school," I would say to make the bums laugh, "I'd sure like to get some of that stuff." They would break up over that—little skinny me and big Mrs. Turner. Still I would lose the argument with Rashman because he knew me too well to be sidetracked.

But I was beginning to know Rashman, too. He was wrong. His science was screwed up. Shaderow and the others knew he was wrong, too. They were Christians. I had heard how groups of them would get juiced up on Saturday night and pile into Filbert's car and go over to Elder Nash's church and sing and cry about whatever they had lost—a mother or father or something.

But Rashman was right about them in a way. Christianity would never do more for them than make them feel a little better for a little while, like a piece of blues.

III

For a month I did not go back to see Rashman. I was not ready to face him. He was wrong; but I did not know how to convince him.

His house sat across a vacant lot from his shop. It was one of only three or four neat houses amid the squalor that was Ninth Street. The house seemed very small sitting by itself behind a very straight, wire fence. Unlike most of the houses around it, it was freshly painted and all the boards were in place. The house sat on piles and back under it the dirt was raked as level as concrete. Usually after eight o'clock in the evening the windows in his house would darken. I would see them as I passed taking Nancy Adkins home to Chambers. As far as I knew, the lean boy from St. Louis was the only non-relative who had ever entered Rashman's house. Shaderow and Filbert never had, even the insurance man left him alone. Often I wanted to stop by. Nancy would say that it was all right with her, but I was always a little too afraid. I knew that Rashman would be different without the bums to show off for— different and deeper. Often as I passed the house I would comment on how lonely it must get for Rashman in there because at heart he was a talker. The windows in the little old house would seem like half-closed, darkened eyes looking out on this dumping ground of Christian civilization.

I went for six weeks without seeing Rashman. When my mother made what seemed her final threat, I went to Mr. Granison's barber shop to get my hair cut. But the Sunday after father let the man from the State Fish and Game Board mealy-mouth the morning service, I decided to go down to see Rashman.

I was met at the door by his wife. She was a small black woman who looked ten or twelve years older than Rashman. "My husband is not home," she said, "but do come in." She did not wait to see if I was going to follow but simply turned and walked ahead of me down the hallway into the living room. The house had a stale odor inside, like the odor inside the houses of very old people. No sunlight came through the windows, which were heavily draped. The living room that we entered was small. The heavy, old-fashioned chair and sofa were covered with matching, faded, flowery slipcovers. The rug was of a hard weave. On the wall was a picture of Rashman receiving his diploma from a high school in St. Louis. This made me wonder how old Rashman really was. He had many gray hairs, but his skin was very smooth. He could be any age. I examined the picture for a date but found none. When I turned away from the wall, Mrs. X motioned for me to sit in the chair under the picture. She sat on the sofa across the room. "Rashman has gone to

St. Louis now for a little while," she said. "He was very discontented here . . . He told me a lot about you. Said you were the smartest youngster he had seen in a while."

"Not really," I said, and waved her comment away.

She looked at me and smiled. "He said when you get out of college you will be a great asset to the race. The masses of our people need so much. It always must be hoped that your generation will do much better than ours." She examined me again with that curious look of hers.

Two barefooted, bald-headed boys of about four or five ran to the living room door and peeped in. She laughed and called them forward. "Pharoah and Benda, this is Mr. Billy Aaron." She pushed them forward to meet me.

The bigger one took his fingers out of his mouth and gave me his wet hand to shake. I was glad for their presence because I felt that their mother was very sad about something, and I was not sure that I would know how to respond to it if she would decide to tell me what it was.

I took the smaller boy and tossed him toward the ceiling. The bigger one pushed into my arms for some of the same treatment. While I was engaged with them, their mother slipped out of the room and brought back a glass of iced tea. The two boys sat on my knees while I drank.

Then I heard their sister come downstairs. I knew that it was Shera because I remembered that she was a very slow walker. At home she was a much more imposing girl than at school. She wore no make-up, and her hair had been cut very short and had not been hot combed in a long time.

"How was church this morning?" she asked. She did not call me "Billy" as she did at school but "Mr. Aaron" as her mother called me when she asked, "Shera, you do know Mr. Aaron, do you not?"

"Yes, mother, Mr. Aaron is the best athlete in the tenth grade."

"Well," her mother said rather sage-like, "Rashman told me that."

"How was church?" Shera asked and smiled.

"Good," I said, and shrugged. She must have known about the man from the Fish and Game Board. I did not know if she were going to tell Rashman. I did not know if I really cared.

"We were Christians once, even Shera was," Mrs. X said. "We were Church of God in Christ." She waited for a moment. She seemed happy remembering. "You don't sing spirituals in your church, do you?"

The Enemy

J. E. Franklin

J. E. Franklin is a native of Texas. She is the author of the highly successful off-Broadway play Black Girl. *Other plays by Miss Franklin have been performed by Mobilization for Youth Theatre, The New Feminist Theatre, and The Negro Ensemble Company. She is a lecturer in the Department of Education at Lehman College.*

After they wheeled Old Man Gaston away, the children were afraid to go near the place. Even some of the grown folks began crossing to the other side of the street after the fig trees and hedge bushes and weeds started spacing out like they owned the place. And then it didn't take much of anything from the wind and rain to suck the rest of the life right out of Old Man Gaston's little gunshot house.

From my house all I could see was the sunken, mildewed roof, but I knew full well of the things I couldn't see, too. Every child in the neighborhood knew of the snakes, black widow spiders, and scorpions which crawled among the weeds by day, and of the demons and haints which lived in the house at night. The reason Old Man Gaston's ghost was hanging around to watch over the place was because his body had hung around so long before it was discovered.

"Wouldn't nobody but the devil live in that house now."

That's what I heard my mother say, that only the devil, himself, would live in Old Man Gaston's house. So what were we children to think when the men came with the bulldozers and the lumber that day, shoved the weeds off their territory, and, in almost no time at all, made the place say "maybe" to life? What were we to think, with all the grown folks whispering back and forth, ducking and darting in and out of each other's houses, shooing us children away whenever we got within hearing range, with the women coming in from their porches and peeping from the

window shades whenever "she" passed their houses? What
were we to think? Why, we thought the devil surely had
moved into Old Man Gaston's house, that's what.

"Ain't no devil living in that house," one of the children
disputed us. "That's a lady name Miss Ella Greene."

"She dip snuff."

We all giggled.

"My mama say when you start dippin' snuff befo' you
old, you'll turn into a witch."

Our disputer did not dispute that.

It did not take us long, eavesdropping from under beds
and in closets, to piece together our portrait of who the
"witch" was.

She was no stranger. Some years before, she had lived
in the neighborhood with her four boys.

"Them was sho'nuff the devil's chillun'."

"Each one of 'em by a different man."

"Ain't no way in the world for none of 'em to be no
good with a chippy for a mother."

"God don't like ugly."

The boys had bullied little children, stolen tires from
cars and anything else that wasn't nailed down. They threw
rocks at houses and at people, and no one would forget
what waited for them that Sunday morning after the boys
had made a paste from their bowels and painted a message
to the preacher on the church's sidewalk. Because they had
never been caught in the act, they lied their way out of
everything, until the day they tied eleven-year-old Nora
Kingsley to a tree in the woods and left her there. It did
them no good to deny that they had "fooled" with her, for
she claimed that they had, and straight to the pen they
went.

"If she make one false move, she gonna' wish they had-a
put her in the pen with them bastards of hers."

"She got her nerve coming back here!"

"She must have her insurance paid up."

The women kept the "witch" in check. Each morning
when she left her house, some of the women would sweep
trash from their sidewalks into little piles, and pretending
they did not see the woman, scattered the debris in her
direction, or they shook thick clouds of dust from their
rugs. The old women, too tired to go in from their porches,
spat their contempt into their snuff cans and rocked themselves in their chairs. Not once did the "witch" break her
proud, youthful stride; not once did her eyes even turn
to acknowledge the women's presence. We children were

told that should the "witch" breathe on us, we would turn to ashes; and we would abandon our play and flee in terror whenever she approached. Always some small child had to be calmed down and comforted whenever the larger and faster children had left them behind. Soon we made a contest to see who could reach the safety zone first after someone had yelled "witch!" We had never had so much fun.

I began to come early into the yard. I would play in the big gulley and do nothing but watch the house. One morning, quite early, as I was looking in that direction, I saw a tiny figure move cautiously across the witch's yard and drag a garbage can to the rear of the house. Some force lifted me from the gulley and made me bolt into the house. The importance of my news I measured by the intensity of my mother's reaction.

"What's this? Where? When? You sure, Addie? Oh, Jesus, have mercy! Let me tell Hadley this!"

She shoved her feet into her slippers, grabbed me by the hand, and hurried from the house.

"Sho'nuff, Katie?!"

"Aw, naw, girl!"

"Jesus Lord!"

"Is it a boy young'un or a gal young'un?"

In my haste the image had not registered.

"He was moving real fast, Mama, like he didn't want nobody to see him."

"It was a boy, then?"

"I couldn't see too good way down yonder."

"But you said 'he,' Addie. You shore you saw somebody?"

"The child can't see through fog like Superman, Katie. If she seen anything at all, she seen more'n that hussy wanted us to see. Why she hidin' whatever she hidin'? That's what we wanna' find out."

"A man."

I was sent outside, but I knew I had done good. The story spread and my name with it. The women came to pat me on the head, planting wet, snuff-box kisses on me and smiling down at me their approval.

"Bless your little heart."

"You take after your daddy with that sense you got." I blushed with embarrassment and pride.

They waited for her this time like a delegation. With hands propped on their hips and standing with their feet wide apart and planted on the earth, there was no sweeping or rug-shaking this time.

"Say, you!" one woman yelled. "We wants to have a word with you."

The straight, tall figure, with her thick hair combed back and twisted into a bun, the stiffly starched and ironed uniform fitting her neatly, moved on past the delegation. Even in her work clothes the other women looked old next to her, though they all said she was every bit of forty. Someone threw a stone with such force it lifted the hem of her maid's uniform and left it folded upward. She stopped without turning, then proceeded.

"We know what you hiding, and one-a these days you gonna' come back and find that shack *and* that bastard burnt up."

The "witch" whipped around as if she had been stung. "You goddamn bitches!" she let loose.

"Fight, fight!" some child yelled, but the women backed away from the wild force that was advancing toward them.

"You a *damn* lie! You better pray-God ain't non-a you crazy enough to do no shit like that. If you're trying to get to hell quick, you shore know what to do, 'cause I'll kill every last one-a you bitches before God get the news. I mean, you better not bother my child. I wish she would tell me you come anywhere near my yard. Who the hell do you think you are? You done did enough dirt. Just kept on and kept on till you got my other chillun' locked up for something they didn't do, but this is one time the graveyard won't have enough room to hold all-a you if you mess with *that* child. Naw, I ain't gonna' hide her no'mo, and she gonna' be goin' to school next week, too. Put that in your pipe and smoke it. Cows! Puff on that good. Cockroaches!" And she went on down the street mumbling more epithets to herself as if she had just lost her mind. As the "witch" stormed away, I thought the rocks would fly after her, but the women just stood looking helplessly after her, exchanging impotent growls.

"Had nerve enough to use God's name in vain."

"I'm gonna' wash the Lord's name out with disinfect 'fore I use it again."

"That uniform wasn't even ironed good."

During the days before school the woman began letting the "witch girl" come out into the yard to play. At first she stood on the porch with her hands on her hips and guarded the child while she played hopscotch, dug with her hoe in the garden, weeded grass from her flower bed, and turned somersaults. What she seemed to enjoy most was gathering the leaves which floated from the big tree in Mrs. Rose's yard next door. She would gather piles of them and then arrange them as if she were performing a religious ritual. What she saw in a dumb leaf was beyond my comprehension, and everyone believed the girl was crazy. But she looked happy to me, and I felt myself growing envious. What right had she to be as happy as she was? I longed to come face to face with her to tell her what I could only scribble on sidewalks, dirt trails, trees, and old bits of paper: "Addie vs. the 'witch girl.' I goin to git you."

My desire to maim her was nurtured in my dreams, as night after night I would waylay her, and despite her pleas for mercy, I would rip her apart. But dreams were not enough. And it was not enough for me to hear people boasting of the traps they had set in case she came into their yard: "traps that'll kill man, woman, or pig." And it was not enough to see her chased away by Mrs. Rose whenever she got too close to her hedge bushes with her leaf-picking, sending the stupid leaves scattering in the air. No. I wanted her all to myself, to torture her until she was no longer happier than I.

My mother warned me to keep away from her should I see her at school. All us children were warned, lest the "witch girl" teach us bad things. But the fact that she was delivered into my hands the very first day was testimony to the existence of a plan by God to have us thrown together. After all, it was I who discovered her, and therefore it was meet that I should have the power to say "yes" or "no" to her right to be. Of course, not having ever seen the "witch girl" close up, I did not know who she was when she first entered the room. But the teacher did something that made us all know. She waved her over to a seat near the window, close to the front of the room.

"Over there, Greene," she ordered, taking no trouble to hide her displeasure. The "witch girl" kept her head hung so low I could not see her evil eyes. The children began whispering and giggling.

"Here, here!" the teacher yelled, rapping her puffy, yellow knuckles on the desk. "You children must not know whose class you're in. I'm not the teacher you had last year."

In the silence I studied my enemy. How odd she looked! There it was the first day of school and she didn't even have a new dress. She wore it short, almost up to her panties, and it had been washed so many times it had almost lost its original color. Her hair was short, too, not long like mine, and a dozen of those little twig-plaits tucked under and pinned looked like knots rising on her noggin. She would not lift her head to look at anyone. Every now and then her guilty eyes would dart quickly over the room and then back to the tablet which lay open on her desk.

The teacher watched her all day from the corner of her eyes, made sure she was not left alone in the room when children went to recess, locked even her paper clips and rubber bands in her closet and desk, checking and recheck-ing the locks to make sure they were secure.

During recess the children played kick-ball, tag, and other games. The "witch girl," of course, was excluded. Filing in from recess, she was pushed to the back of the line. No one would allow her to get or stay in front. It was easy for me to fire the children into a spirit of war. I egged the boys on to copping spitballs at her in class. Her body would give a little jerk, her face would register a flash of pain, and then she would quickly compose herself and go back to reading. She always kept her head buried in a book whether she was reading or not. In the morning and from lunch or recess we brought dead frogs, worms, and small snakes to hide in her desk before she would arrive. She took to peering into the dark hole with her large, scared eyes before sitting down. We would hide her books and tablets whenever she left them alone, and she soon began taking every article with her.

One day the teacher inquired, "What's the big idea tak-ing your books to the rest room with you, Greene? You think somebody in this room is a thief?" She hung her head and did not answer. "Put them back and get out of here."

We muffled our giggles behind our books. I knew my classmates enjoyed the fun I had created for them. They hardly ever missed a day from school for fear they would be left out of some trick played on the "witch girl."

What I think we all waited for was the day she would break down and cry or complain to the teacher, but she bore it all, head downcast, without a murmur. It was this strength she portrayed that mystified me, caused an angry storm of impatience to gather inside me. Even more in-furiating was when she would outshine me in class. She was no dummy, this Dawn, and I could see that she was smarter than I in every way. Even the teacher could not wear her down for me. One day she hammered away at my enemy's wit until the girl emerged victorious. "What is the capital of Iowa?"

"The capital of Iowa is Des Moines."

"New Hampshire?"

"The capital of New Hampshire is Concord."

"Wyoming?"

"The capital of Wyoming is Cheye . . ."

My ally came back like a whip-crack. "What would you do to find out how many apples John started with if John now has sixty apples after giving Joe fifty?"

"I would add John's apples and Joe's apples."

She answered in that rapid speech of hers, so fast that one barely saw the even row of tiny, white teeth that flashed from her round, black face. Each time I felt her drawing respect from the other children because of her smartness, I reinforced my war on her. I told my pals of the time the Greene woman used to go to the city dump to look for old canned food the big stores could not sell, and that the odor I smelled on the "witch girl" was probably because they were going to the dump again.

"A bad smell? On who?"

"On Greene? On the 'witch girl'?"

"You better not get too close to her!" I yelled to one girl who was on her way to check. The little girl fell back clamping her nose, positive that even from that distance she had smelled it. I could see my chance was ripe, and I seized it.

"I got a good idea. See, I make this sign, see? Now, this what we gonna' do, see? I been noticing her watching us play kick-ball. She mad 'cause we won't let her play. So. We'll let her on our team, see?"

"For real?"

"Not for real, just play-like. Just so we can slap this sign on her. You know how when we make a score we slap each other on the back? Well, when she make a score or something . . . I bet this will make her bathe."

In crooked lettering the sign read:

> Oh, gabbage pail
> Oh, gabbage pail
> Your B.O. wont forsake you

"We need a fielder to stop the balls that go 'way out yonder," I told her. Her eyes lit up, and her mouth broke into a smile. She shifted shyly from one foot to the other and did not hesitate.

She caught the very first ball that come her way for an out. Those that were not within her reach she tore after with the swiftness of a deer. Once a ball soared through the air and headed over a clump of bushes. She leaped into the air and was swept back over the bushes by the impact of the ball, but presently she bobbed up again and threw the ball with such force, players were held at their bases and prevented from scoring. She played with a vigor that shamed us all in our fumbling and error-making. At the end of the game we went into our back-slapping act, leaving the sticky sign dangling from her back.

"Who taught you how to play like that?" I asked.

"I just learned myself." She shifted herself from one foot to another and tried to catch up with her breathing.

"Keep up the good work and we'll make you a regular on the team." And then we all moved away, hardly able to hold in our laughter. The "witch girl," sure of the friends she had just made after her performance and unsuspecting of any bad faith, joined us in the laughter even though she did not know the joke. We could not cut off the laughter and giggling after we moved back into class, and our teacher, peering over the top of her glasses, barked, "Here, here! Have you children gone crazy?"

We snapped to attention and set our tickle-box right-side-up until time came to file out for lunch.

"What's that thing you're wearing, Greene?" the teacher snapped, pleased that her sharp eyes had discovered the cause of the disturbance.

"Ma'am?"

"You heard me. What's that thing on your back?"

She screwed her moist eyes around over her shoulder as if she expected some animal to leap up. Teacher spun her around and snatched the note from her back. She read it, comprehended right away, and trying to rescue herself from embarrassment and disappointment over the loss of her victory, halfheartedly reproofed us. "You children know better than this." Then, thrusting the paper in the "witch girl's" face, said, "Put this thing in the wastebasket. Couldn't you feel that thing hanging on you? If it had-a been a snake, it would've bitten you. You children get on to lunch and stop this nonsense."

The long, dark hallway echoed with our laughter. Congratulations were poured over me like grain. How clever and proud I felt of myself! My new name became "Champ." The "witch girl's" name became "B.O." She withdrew into herself after that, casting furtive glances or simply gazing off into space. Whenever she answered in class, she was beginning to stutter, and she did not display that love-of-knowledge spirit she had once flaunted before me. At recess she went as far away from us as she could. Each day I watched her go to sit beneath the big tree that stood near the edge of the school yard. She took to playing her old leaf game again, arranging the leaves on the ground in the shapes of children. Watching her involved in her leaf game aroused my old feelings of envy. She is not suffering, I told myself, and I grew uneasy. Vaguely, I felt that some sinister twist of fate would soon wrest from me the victory I had won over my enemy. The thought that she might bounce back gnawed at me every minute of the day. I knew that I had done all I could to defeat her. What else could I do? The problem so completely absorbed me that I did not realize, when chasing after the ball during one recess, that I had headed in the direction of the enemy's tree. The sound of a strange song floated in the air and seemed to be coming right out of the tree's trunk. I stopped short. My feet were inclined to run away, but I could not move from the spot. I stood there, turning my ears around in search of the source. The voice was light and unstrained, like some bird, and with a melancholy, human note. Only the sounds of the frantic children screaming for me to hurry with the ball moved me from the spot. My heart drummed fiercely, and a heaviness was in my feet as I ran back to my team. I dared not look back, for I felt some unknown force close behind me.

Moments later, when my eyes were pulled in that direction, I saw what I had feared all along. I could see her clearly now, and I felt tricked. And yet, all day long I thought about the song. Was it the tune or the words which troubled me, repeating itself over and over?

> Nobody's fault but mine.
> Nobody's fault but mine.
> If I die and my soul be lost,
> Nobody's fault but mine.
>
> I got a Bible in my home.
> I got a Bible in my home.
> So if I die and my soul be lost,
> Nobody's fault but mine.
>
> My mother taught me how to pray.
> My mother taught me how to pray.
> So if I die and my soul be lost,
> Nobody's fault but mine.

What did it all mean? The expressions "evil blood, bad, and devil," used so often when referring to the Greenes, had impressed themselves on my memory, and I could not believe that such people prayed or read the Bible. The whole matter completely baffled me; and when I could stand it no longer, I told my mother what I had heard.

"A Bible?! Praying?!" My mother let out a loud, derisive hoot. "Baby, God don't even listen to people like that, prayin' or not. He oughta strike 'em down for dirtyin' His Book. Prayin'! If that don't beat all!"

And, of course, Mother was right. God did not favor such people. The Greenes had fallen from His grace, and it was meet that everyone should scorn them. As for the song, it was a deliberate trick played by the girl to cast some witch spell on me. And, presently, my belief in the truth of the stories I had heard about the Greenes came back to me.

But at night, when I was left alone with myself, I would shut my eyes tightly and see a meek, little girl with gentle, troubled eyes waiting for me in my dreams; and when I awoke, I knew I could not go again to the school or come face to face with her at all.

My mother stuck her head into my room to arouse me, and I feigned illness.

"What you mean you don't feel good? Where it hurt at? All over? Addie, don't nobody hurt no all over, it got to be in one spot somewhere. You don't feel like you got no fever. Here, stick this thing up in you . . . you know how to take your temperature. What the . . . ! Girl, ain't I told you not to be sleeping in your drawers, what the devil's the matter with you? You losing your mind? Ain't no telling how many mornings you leave outta here with the same drawers you had on the day before. Look at this, see? Normal. I knew you was lying . . . ain't nothing wrong with you. First you said it's your stomach, then you say it's all over, then you say your head. You know I got to go to town today, and I ain't leaving you here by yourself. It's something you wanna hang around here to do . . . you ain't fooling me. Here, take these aspirin and get outta here."

My heart became hot within me. I was aware that violent feelings were trying to disobey my command to play dead and stay at that place where I had buried them so long ago. I hardened myself to all of it. So what if in a few minutes I would see the girl? So what? But simultaneously with that thought I caught sight of the schoolhouse, and my heart suddenly broke loose and beat fitfully against the armor I had constructed to shut out that voice whispering, "For shame, for shame." Then, with all the mean fury they could gather, burning tears burst past my tight eye gates. And I had not meant to cry at all. I had not meant to surrender to anything.

Loimos

Edgar White

*Edgar White is a native of the West Indies. He was
raised in Harlem. His plays have been performed at
the New York Shakespeare Festival Public Theatre
and the Eugene O'Neill Foundation, and in Boston
by the New African Company. Both his fiction and
his drama have been published in* Liberator Magazine.
He is represented in Mel Watkin's Black Review *and
in his own collection,* Underground.

Part 1

Tonight, as yesterday, I am alone. Sitting here, sitting,
sitting, under partly colored skies, under plastered ceilings.

Something important has happened, though I forget
exactly what.

A new noise is upon this place. Or a new silence. Today
I did not go out. I went out yesterday, though. Stepped over
certain prostrate bodies, passed others.

There is a cat which has chosen my room for lounging.
He or it does not mind my presence here. Dogs howl in
yards, ashcans clatter.

The same dogs, the same ashcans. I do not travel at
night. They say it is not safe, though there are nocturnal
guards almost everywhere. Their voices can be heard sometimes amidst the other noises, moving beneath windows,
commenting on the bodies.

At first everyone was frightened, but then those who had
something to lose were only half-frightened; the ritual of
order kept them going. The media gave out information
saying only that it was but a temporary affliction of the
city caused by a series of freak accidents in several vital
sewers. The result was a pestilential increase, and though
but few actually saw signs of rats, rumor was fast about.

I was quite amazed to hear those I knew speak of it. The

wise spoke wisely, the foolish foolishly—such is the boring way of life—but now even the foolish saw things I thought them quite incapable of. Many knew before they died (which you will have to admit was quite something).

In the beginning I heard the more learned of them say, "This pestilence will be a good thing because the rich will be hurt by this; it will bring them to reality." I heard them speaking in small cafés or outside of school buildings holding paperback books in gloved hands. But later, when the rich efficiently left the city, being followed quickly by the bourgeoisie and the friends of the bourgeoisie (comprised mainly of the aforementioned learned people), I heard nothing. Now among the dying there are only the poor, the artists, the scavengers, and the various police and guardsmen who have volunteered (for a laudable sum) to oversee us in our peculiar stages of frenzy.

Strangely enough, though, this affliction upon the city has caused little change in the various exigencies. For did I not upon the early part of the morning experience with more than a little dread the metacarpal knocking of my landlady upon my door? She, staring into my sunken and myopic brown eyes, asked with hostility for the rent. Then myself, speaking as one afraid, saying, "Mrs. Mortmain, I regret not having the rent, but my grandmother died three days ago. She raised me, you see."

For, in truth, I had gone out upon the streets some three days before, walking awkwardly through streets which had never seemed so narrow toward the hospital to acquire the false teeth, the small mirror, the slippers, and the one or two pieces of effluvia which were to be membered among her remains.

My landlady, who was clad in some gray garments to hide her now-withered and childlike sex, looked from behind her eyes, unspeaking. She told me to state the particulars of my grandmother's death. This I did successfully, I think. I ushered her in from the doorway, saying, "You see, Mrs. Mortmain, several days ago my grandmother, having reached the latter part of seventy, suffered an inroad in her health, culminating a few days after, when her heart reached the maximal point of disease and perished. They believe it to be an affliction of the heart, though it may have been the plague."

Whereupon Mrs. Mortmain stopped me and let out a series of jeremiads regarding the difficulties of maintaining Topeth House, our domicile. I wanted to say something clever but didn't (or couldn't). She paused a moment, involved herself in various fiscal machinations, and then said in a voice not altogether foreign, "I'll give you one more week. Next Monday, the money or you're out!"

She exited by the door, leaving death behind in the hallway. Mrs. Mortmain is a woman of unusual cruelty.

It is winter now, so if my grandmother died several days ago, she died in winter. It's better to die in winter than summer, I think, though perhaps not. I left the funeral home along with the body and the pollinctor. I entered the funeral car, which seemed sufficiently real to be entered. En route to the graveyard, we passed many young people, and older people, some on their way home, some leaving from home. I saw also several women who moved me to think of pussy. This, however, I dismissed, as I feared some might judge my action of fornication in a public streetway, or atop a hearse amid day-laborers, to be asocial. Later, however, as I walked upon the too soft earth of the graveyard ground, I had great difficulty keeping myself from thinking of the many times Jill and I had made love in dark afternoons. Making love on couches and beds and creaking floors, and her small strong thighs swelling, quivering, and myself breathing into her quite open woman's body. I like the smell of the room after we've made love. The fish smell, craven warm smell of aftersex. Then out of the window night would come.

There being no priest, the pollinctor spoke the comfortable words; the trees stood up for death. Shadows which were our shadows walking away. Some had thrown what I believe to be flowers upon the grave. Having gathered for death we departed, fingers of branches downturned. The wind backward moving.

"They say when people are buried their bones turn to snakes."

"To snakes?"

"Yes, to snakes."

"Large snakes?"

"Yes, large snakes that slither along the earth."

Part 2

Perhaps at this point it would not be amiss to speak on the matter of my youth: my youth was an unfortunate one.

Part 3

Perhaps it is the asymmetry of my house which causes everything here to seem so warped. There are so many mirror angles, so very much unevenness here.

When I am thrown out of sleep and wake to a lower earth, I brush my teeth with the bristles of a pig. I wash away the visible pain of the yesterday and prepare a quick identity for today. A clean body at least gives you the illusion of control.

Sitting at what I shall call a table, I note that a bit of burnt toast tastes better if dipped in lukewarm coffee. Should I use one or two teaspoons of sugar? There is a plague on, in times of extreme poverty such as these it is best to conserve resources, think of tomorrow. Fuck tomorrow, there will be no tomorrow. Even the plunderers of my food have stopped coming. I must teach myself to wait. Perhaps look at television for many hours and watch one white man's face dissolve into another. In times of plague comedy is always requisite. Perhaps if I watch some blonde bitch figure out new ways to take her husband's balls on T.V., I'll forget that I'm dying. I sometimes see black faces on the screen, but none of them seem as tortured as mine for some reason. They are all happily floating into brightly lit apartments and celebrating each other's existence. The blacks of television land, people such as I've never met. Perhaps if you keep a myth constant enough it will become real. Perhaps if I stare at this television screen long enough I will become what I see. How nice.

I notice I am having more trouble with the spacing of time these days. Ellen was here some darknesses ago. It was not such a huge space of time. Taller than Jill, more desperate with her hands. I can't remember what her nails feel like on my back. If it was two weeks ago that would be less than a month. There is something which I try to get from her which I can't get. I don't have to be careful of hurting her, thank God. She is stronger than Jill. I don't know how not to damage what I touch anymore.

With Jill I have to be slow. Slower of speech even than of action. Words slip out. Words like: "kill," "plague," and "nigger." She doesn't want to deal with any of that. She comes to visit me in my lean house, she makes love with me and returns to a less vicious part of the city.

Ellen is high yellow and carries Georgia in her head and mouth. When we make love, we bring four hundred years of white-hot hate to bed with us.

She blames me for every white man that has control of
life. She blames me for the sequestrated death which is
New York City. She is right. Her eyes ask: "Amid the slave
ships, why did you not kill them on the way? If you could
not kill the masters, why did you not kill me and then
yourself?" And because I will not answer, her fingers take
more skin from my back. It was some space of time ago
that Ellen was here.

Part 4

I have a neighbor named Dave, he plays music on a
willing piano. Every day his fingers grow stronger. You
can measure the extent of the plague by how much music
he plays. Perhaps he will show me the way. He is angry at
me for not making my own music instead of living off his.
There will come a time to play, but first I must learn to
listen better. The music is the mother. The rhythms are
the poles of life which you must live between. The rhythms
are unavoidable as the beating of the heart. As when my
mother breathed over me with a naturalness which allowed
me silence.

My mother was immense and black. She had warmness
running through her which is why I was so disappointed
leaving the womb. That much I remember clearly.

I do not dream much these days, usually it is the same
dream. Something about myself entering a strange city.
Snow falling very carefully, laying itself down on its ap-
pointed piece of ground.

And into this town which I enter strangely, various
people place themselves. I ask them the way, but they can
not understand my language, and one by one they disappear into various houses, leaving footprints only upon
the snow.

I remember the way Carolyn slept. She would entwine
herself in her hands or sometimes just one long thin
African arm making a pillow for herself.

My room has colors now. It must be the reflection of the
traffic lights on the rain wet windows.

The infra luminescence of the outside world. The sound
of garbage cans being overturned. Someone is searching.
The voices of the ARABBIATI. Is that noise in the street
perhaps God? No, it is just a noise in the street.

I can't travel today. The subways are catacombs. That

woman came again seeking her rent. I sat in silence and
listened to her breathing behind the door. It was a long
time, and then her smell went away. I'm going to have to
kill this woman, she interrupts my quiet. What is it that
white people have with money, this necromancy which
they have with lucre? I thought that at least now when the
end is so ridiculously visible they would get away from that
foolishness. I should have realized that this is all they have
left, the only thing, which defines them. The bitchhound
which drives them to hell and causes them to string atrocities together as beads later to be called history.

Part 5

Jill penned the following note on an immaculate pink
sheet of paper and slipped it under my door:

Dear Blackamoor,
Came to see you today. You were not at home. I need
to see you. Are you all right? Are you missing me?
                                        Yours Jill.

Jill is madness and two minute breasts with nipples hard
and glad and the nose of a rich girl.

Jill does not know, as she did not know, as she will not
know, what's happening. She does not see the plague, she
will not ever let herself.

If the world goes on at all, she will continue to slip in
and out of silk panties in front of silent dead antiques. I'm
willing to concede now finally that people are far better off
in ignorance.

Jill floats through the streets of the lower east side; she
is unaware of the predatory buildings and the low conspiratorial sky over her. She passes the vacant churches with all
their desperate bells and odors. She passes the store-shops
of the Jews who flee like bandits when the sun gives up the
sky, the sounds of their iron gates giving off the screetch
of animals. Jill passes it all and doesn't see. Her eyes look
only for my broken building with its hallway narrow as an
asylum's.

I remember taking Jill with me up to Harlem, on a hundred sixteenth street and eighth ave. And I put her in a
restaurant to wait as I went in desperate search for a con-
nection. The drizzle of the sky and the junkie-whores dying

all around us. The twenty-year-old tired and aged woman
who coughed into a mysterious paperbag; and her knees
giving out beneath her. And Jill standing amid all those
pox-marked women, completely distant as if this was
merely someone else's dream wherein she was but an
incident.

When I was small, I followed my grandmother through
the chimera of the New York streets. Her arms were strong
and had many veins, which always made me think of
plants. She would pull me along by centripetal force as
she shipped around corners. She moved strong through
dangerous streets and defended me against dreadful metallic beasts which were called cars. When I was small, I
believed that anyone who bent over me was doing so to
kiss me, and I always turned my face upwards to receive it.

As I grew older the image that was always in my mind
was of pursuit. It seemed that I and everyone I knew were
running through backyards or over rooftops, always being
chased. Preparation for the plague.

This much I know. Black bodies long and angular, asses
upturned, limbs always moving. These bodies were not
made for cities. Eyes which were fashioned for sunlight,
eyes made easy at the sight of green. Bodies designed to
outline before the moon. Have no business with concrete
and do no trade with brick.

Black women turned into office girls taught to perfect a
vacancy of expression. A dementia of thighs, skirts, and
commerce. Men with warrior bodies carrying envelopes
and pushing buttons until finally they develop that look of
irrelevancy. Until there is no separation between the black
bodies and the garbage in the streets. A heavy plague
through the city.

Part 6

The newspapers now say that it is not safe to walk the
streets even in daytime in sections which have been named:
"desperate." They mean of course my section of the city.
They have made this place into an armed camp. It seems
that it should be evident, even to them, that it is impossible
to lock me out without locking themselves in. These fools
have made a perfect prison for themselves. Perhaps the
gates and locks give them some comfort at night. They

seem so fearful, though. Where do they think they can go without me? Wherever they need cheap labor I am. Don't they see me driving the subways, cooking their food? I'm at every hospital in the city, and if not me, then my woman is. My woman operates their telephone, overhears everything. Anywhere in the city they can't escape us. The more frightened the city the more they need the music, our music.

And you can tell the mood of the times by the bodies you meet. The bodies have become androgynous. The women have become like men, hard, cold bodies incapable of being held. They have made the flesh into wax, into greedy capable machines. Stiff arms culminating into hands held clenched. The corpulent senility of isolation. But I have seen all this before. It is part of a total re-remembrance of another city, another plague.

Days which I have walked before. Perhaps in Europe where, too, the signs were evident. The Dutch with their grotesque faces, Holland which gave off a reek of colonialism and diamonds.

I advance on a level ground, the sun as equal before me as behind. The screams which I hear are only more constant now because I focus on them. Screams never leave the earth, they merely take up the spaces between past, present, and future, they incorporate themselves in continuity.

The androgynous bodies move on. The Ukrainians along seventh street, dying in their dark clothes.

The Chinese who find themselves placed in a labyrinth of ghetto streets seem more somnambular.

There is a chaos even to the process of putrefaction.

Ten thousand years to get from the cave to the tenement house, they shall have to call that progress. It's strange, though, for even these people lay at night impaled upon a pillow. As they lay awake awaiting the momentary cessation of pain from the body's engine, yet they are not willing to give up any power. They want it until the end. I can not understand these people.

They have to maintain property which is the remnant of the large dream. Property is a device of remembrance, a kind of feeble way of continuing a presence which was possibly warm, possibly loving. Finally they find themselves in a closed house filled with pictures of barren properties, and the penalty is infinite time in which they must think on themselves.

Rockefeller has land upon which he has never walked and may never walk. Houses into which he has never entered.

But let me say it another way. I live in a city which was not built for me, a city which never noted my existence. Everything in this place was built either from my flesh or the flesh of others who do not matter. I look out from a window unto Gomorrah. I note faces darkly contorted, ashen. Men halfmen, sidle graveward in the streets.

The lower east side quivers, utters up a smell like the shit of diseased animals. The almost dead of the Bowery stumble toward the Red Cross shelter to sell their polluted blood for wine.

The liquor stores are little beacons of death all run by white men who flee the city in the night. The artists move with dead eyes. The women all have one body. These are the women of the field. The women are the only light down here. Black women, black Puerto Rican women, silver cross between their thighs.

All the houses are boarded and mute. Queer toy houses filled with screams. The police who scatter darkness. They wait for us to go mad. Unnatural colors, unnatural taste, unnatural sleep.

Footsteps going directionless. Eyes which dare not look up.

Gentlemen, coxcombical daywalkers in finery and emptiness. Some who walk with the staff of the druids.

Faces sometimes encountered which were once familiar and now are aged and crumbling. Young men who turn the plague inward upon themselves. The same streets which Leroi walked hating himself. And with the passing of the day the passing out of the white powder which is dope. You sprinkle heroin in the palm of the hand, and a cross is always visible, which always whispers death.

The catholic priests when they walk go straight as the church steeples. Their collars betray a bit of public filth. They do not see me as they walk. The church is one of the last strongholds. It hopes to outlast the plague.

Then the night falls down covering up even the harlotry of the stars. A time for vagaries and inquietudes. A time which God must have put aside for men to steal and run into the swamps which are the backyards or over rooftops.

Those who are afraid always sit behind the locked door in expectation of something from outside. But what defense have they from all that which is within? They would like the old lies in a new way. They do not want to hear the word plague, they would rather hear music. There will be a time when they will come to learn survival even from us. They who have the frames but no homes, power and no life flow of culture. And I will wait watching. And everywhere and so loudly the plague. And tonight as yesterday I am alone.

The Flogging

Ron Milner

Cleve sat on the bench in front of his locker, slowly buttoning the white jacket on before clamping the black bow tie to its oriental collar. (It was too hot for the white shirt that officially completed the Detroit-Horton Hotel's busboy uniform.) He stared into the mirror facing him; noting in his dark face the grim, lifeless expression that came to his eyes and mouth the moment he entered the doors upstairs; how, even sitting, his shoulders slumped to appear to lose a couple inches from the 5/8″ on his draft card. He smirked at the slightly elongated shape of his head and chin.

At the locker just to the left of the mirror, Jack stood changing from his street clothes, his short, squat body bare to his waist, sweat already showing on the bridge of his wide nose, above his huge lips. Jim could be heard running water in the small, shower-room toilet used by them and the (Negro) porters.

"Dig this! Look at this!" Jim came rushing with a frown out of the shower room angrily waving a *Jet* magazine that one of the Porters had probably left. "—On one page! The same page!—" he declared, accenting his words with short, indignant nods of his marcelled head. "In Alabama they drug a colored stud outta' his house and *flogged* him! With clubs and whips! Right in fronta' his family! What you think of that, huh!? . . . And in Mississippi they givin' a cat life, man! *Life!* 'cause he stole some God-damn money! A fuckin' seventy-five cents! From a fuckin' newsstand! And in—" he stopped, shaking his head with his legs pressed together, his narrow shoulders hunched upward in exasperated fury—his tall, thin body seeming a human exclamation mark signifying rage.

"I'm sure glad I ain't down there in that shit," Jack grumbled, sitting down next to Cleve on the bench; dressed for the job now, his black bow tie clamped to the collar of his jacket.

371

"You ain't the only one, man! I couldn't take it! I'd probably be hung by now—or on the most-wanted list! 'cause I'd kill me onea' them hillbillysonofabitches! Pushin' me aroun'! Tellin' me what to do! Like a damn dog or somethin'! I just wouldn't take it!—" Jim cussed again, and threw the *Jet* on the floor.

The three of them stared at it lying there with its pages exposed. Cleve had the strange, wearying feeling that he had lived or dreamed this before; the three of them staring down at the *Jet* with the exact same expressions, saying the exact same things they were saying now.

"What do all them books you read say about that stuff down there, college boy?" Jim asked him with smirking sarcasm.

"I ain't a college boy, yet; trying to save enough dough to be one," Cleve answered after staring at him a moment; feeling that he had somehow known Jim was going to ask him that in just that tone, had even known that when he asked it, he would pull up his pants like he was getting ready to fight somebody.

"Might as well be in college, all them books you read."

"Uh-huh," Cleve sighed, getting to his feet. "What time is it? Maybe we better get up there. When I came in, Miss Pritchard said somethin' about us startin' at *two o'clock*— not a quarter after."

"It's five to," Jack mumbled, looking at his watch.

"To hell wit' her," Jim said, sitting down on the opposite bench. "Too hot to be runnin' aroun' wit' them damn trays. Be smellin' like mules in a hour."

"Why don't we go 'round to the other locker room an' take a shower tonight after work?" Jack suggested, giving them both a challenging glance.

"Hell! Why don't they fix this one, like they said?" Jim evaded, then answered him. "You know why—I don't feel like hearin' all that noise."

"I don't see no signs sayin' we can't go 'roun' there."

Cleve sat back down heavily, sure that he knew every coming word before they said it.

"Naw, ain't no signs, but what happen everytime we go 'roun' there, huh?" Jim looked at Jack derisively. "I'll tell you what happen: Miss Bitchard or Mr. Gordon will come to us tomorrow with this—" he pursed his lips putting on his prim "white" voices. 'Now there has been complaints about you boys dirtyin' up the other employees' locker room; so to avoid any difficulties and misunderstandings

I think it's best that you don't go in there anymore.' That's what'll happen."

"Yeh. Like the time they claimed somebody had stole somethin' from over there."

"Stole or dirtyin' up means the same thing: Stay Out!"

"Yeh, well, I don't give a damn—if I feel like it I'm goin' 'roun' there, anyhow! Any time I feel like it!"

"Go 'head. Where you want me to send yo' last check?"

Cleve had listened to this old replay long enough, he got up again.

"I'm tellin' you," he sighed, "Miss Pritchard's actin' like it's her time of the month. We better make it."

"Hell wit' that ol' bitch," Jack declared, but nevertheless stood up to go. "She bet' not start no shit wit' me today. Man, that ol' broad made me so mad las' night I coulda' just picked her up and broke her 'cross my knee like a damned twig!"

They laughed at the picture of Miss Pritchard cracking in two across Jack's knee.

"Damn, she musta' really got nex' to you, man. What she do?!"

"That's right, y'all wasn't in there. Well, I was standin' way back in the back, you dig, and some customers came in up front; started to one a' the front tables, saw it was all messed up, tablecloths and everything, so they turned around and walked out, man. I saw 'em leave, but I didn't know what was wrong. You know them waitresses won't let us touch them tables until they through wit' em; scared we might cop they little tips. But Miss Pritchard come runnin' up to *me*, man! Stickin' her bony finger in *my* face! Hollerin' at *me* in fronta' all those people. Screamin' I shoulda' been watchin' and shoulda' changed the table 'immediately.' Knew damn well it was them lazy-ass waitresses' fault, but didn't say a word to them. I was so mad, I couldn't talk. Went up there an' changed it, feelin' all them white bastards laughin' at me. Coulda' broke her in half."

Along with Jim, Cleve grunted his understanding, then opened the door and started out. Jim and Jack followed.

"Say? What about Ralph? Where is he?" Jack asked as they went down the corridor toward the stairs.

"I told you, he's goin' to see about that other job today. Think he got it, too," Cleve said.

"Crazy. Wish it was me."

"One college boy made it, anyhow," Jim cracked.

"If you keep yo' mouth shut, Jim, man, nobody would know you're jealous," Cleve smiled at him.

"Shiit," Jim smirked. Jack laughed, slapping an arm around both of them.

They went on up to the hotel's coffee shop.

As he hustled the trays back and forth (covering both his and Ralph's work stations), Cleve couldn't get away from the feeling that everyone and everything around him formed a droning, driving repetition, constantly increasing in vividness and relentlessness, while he himself grew smaller, lighter, more blurred in his own eyes with each sliding moment. He took salt tablets to guard against the heat of the kitchen. But didn't feel really physically sick. It was a half-sensed, half-thought something that had a grip on him. Actually, it wasn't unusual having one of these days making him feel as if he were trying to go up a long, inclined treadmill with a concrete block on his back and the waitresses and chefs and Miss Pritchard and the room-service waiters all throwing oil and lit matches beneath his plodding feet. Wasn't unusual seeing how they (the busboys) were at the bottom of a pile of sweaty, hard-worked, underpaid people who had to feed the semi-rich every day and find somebody to take their envy, resentment, and frustration other than their sweet families at home—caught down at the bottom he and the other "boys" caught it all as it drained on down. So it wasn't unusual, this sense of being overwhelmed by four-pronged harassment. And it wasn't strange knowing what was coming or going to be said next when about the same things were done and said every day. What was different, strange, was the sense of himself sliding slowly away from himself as well as away from the rest of it: not knowing where he had been standing or what he had been thinking, feeling, the past moment; having no definite or recognizable stance or response—just drifting along, fading, like a shadow into darkness.

Maybe it was because Ralph wasn't there to talk to. (Ralph, two years older, and married with a year-old daughter; finishing up his six-month plan in "this hole," that made it possible to carry a full, daytime load of classes at the City University, the small salary added to his wife's keeping his in-law landlords quiet as he sweated through his first year of accounting.) Sometimes he and Ralph would get on an idea, a discussion, and lift each other right on out of this crab-pile.

All Jim and Jack talked about, besides each other, was some funny-looking Jew's big nose, or Cadillacs, Buicks, and Pontiacs, or alpaca sweaters, or hip shoes. They reminded him of two kids going through a picture magazine: "—and I'm going have this, and that, and—"

He was thinking that Ralph was twenty with a wife and a daughter and on his way to being an accountant, wondering when two years had passed what *he* would have and be doing; when, backing into it with a tray full of dirty dishes, he pushed the door open into the back of a waitress who was leaning there polishing her nails. Angry, she continued to block the door, glaring. Tired, he told her to get the hell out the way. Insulted, she screamed that he couldn't talk to her like that and that she would tell Miss Pritchard. She did.

All he really heard of Miss Pritchard's tirade was the constant repeating of her favorite line, "—you're not indispensable—you're not . . ." Flushing with awareness of all the staring white faces, he watched her jabbing, bony white finger going up and down; thought of his long-gone father, his two younger sisters, his mother saying she couldn't help him much with money but sure hoped he would go ahead and better himself—and hoped that Ralph would hurry and come on to work before he lost his damned mind.

They were taking their break downstairs in the tiny, combination (Negro) lunchroom-loafing-room, two hours later, when Ralph finally did come.

Jim was standing outside the doorway, talking to some girl on the payphone. He nodded to Ralph as he passed, tapped his arm. His six-foot even athlete's body seemingly slanted forward at his square shoulders, his black eyes just slits in his deep red-brown face, Ralph didn't even glance at Jim; came on into the room, grunted to Cleve and Jack, sat down on the wall bench and put his feet in a chair.

Cleve had checked his eyes, seen the tie clamped awry to only one collar of the jacket (inviting trouble from Miss Bitchard), the tensed shoulders, the hands jammed into the pockets; and didn't want to see or hear anymore about it.

But, in grinning innocence, Jack asked him, "Well, big shot, get the gig? When you puttin' us down?"

There was a pause in which Cleve kept his eyes away from Ralph's but knew Ralph was looking at him. Then Ralph sighed, chuckled, and got out a half a laugh. "They told me to keep my black behind away from Jolsey Dept. Stores' clerk-accountant's trainee program! That's what! What did you expect, huh? . . ."

"Aw, man, I'm sorry to hear that," Jack intoned sympathetically.

"But not *surprised!* I hope, for your own sake."

Cleve couldn't help turning to watch him as he lit a cigarette. Ralph looked up, glared almost hostilely for a moment, then seemed to relax.

"It ain't that bad, man," he smiled. "It's just that—that —Cleve, man, that letter, that damned notification, said I *had it*, man. Had the damned job. You know? Sheila told her folks. They was happy as hell, too—thought we was gon' finally move out, you know. Hmmph. And I go down there and—and—Yeh, maybe, I better tell you about it, man. So you'll know just how—how—*real* it all is! Cool? ... Okay. This is how it went ..."

Cleve nodded because he knew Ralph wanted to tell it, maybe needed to, but he stared down at the floor and resolved not to look at him, not to really listen, because, again, he knew everything that was coming.

As Ralph told him and Jack, "This receptionist thought I had come about a stock-boy job, you dig," he wondered what Ralph would say if he interrupted him to ask him if he ever had the feeling that he was returning again and again to the same situations, with the situations and the other people involved being more ominous and powerful each time, while he and his reactions were each time weaker?

And as Ralph went on—about the bespectacled, blond executive stumbling to get at his lie about the *re*-notification to the effect that they had decided not to add another trainee at this time being evidently lost in the mail—Cleve, hearing what he knew he would hear, in that chuckling but despairing tone, kept visualizing something someone had told him or maybe he had dreamed: Someone, maybe himself, being hemmed in a corner by a grotesque blind man who, his useless ravished eyes straining obscenely, kept shrieking, "I'm blind, boy! I can't see! I'm blind, and you can't help me! I'm blind, boy! I'm—" All the while Ralph was telling it, Cleve kept seeing that and squirming inside.

"But the kicker was," Ralph finished it, "was when the receptionist called me back when I was leaving, man, and gave me my application and told me that in the future I should fill them out completely. Yeh. You know those two little squares down at the bottom somewhere? One for nationality? And the other for race? Well I overlooked them. And that's really where the mistake they kept talking about came in. If I'd marked my N like a good little nigguh, they woulda' let my black butt lay in the first place. There wouldn't have been any notification, and lies about re-notification. That was the whole thing. Those two little coffins down at the bottom of the page." A warm nauseous resentment passed through Cleve at "coffins," but he didn't even look up; just let it slide on through—a sense of merely wanting to spit.

Jim hung up the phone and came in grinning. "Damn, what you all lookin' so serious about?"

They were all wondering whether, and how, to tell him, when the ominously familiar sound of rigidly tapping high heels on concrete made them all tense and turn toward the corridor.

Miss Pritchard appeared; her dyed, unswept black hair showing its bluish tints under the harsh, close light in the hallway; her rhinestone necklace and silky midnight-blue hostess gown flaring in their eyes; her tiny, grim-veined hands clenched at her sides.

"What are you boys doing?! You've been down here much longer than the time allotted you!" Her nasal yet gritty tone seeming an echoing stone thrown into the cave of their silence.

"We'll be up in a minute, Miss Pritchard," Jim finally told her when they had all swallowed what they really wanted to say.

"See to it. And where's Ralph? I thought I saw him come in. Is he back there?"

"He'll be up when he gets dressed," Cleve told her when Ralph didn't answer.

"See that he does. He's paid extra to keep the rest of you in line," she said, and turned and left quickly.

"I couldn't trust myself to talk to her, not right this minute," Ralph said as they got ready to go up.

It was another hectic, sweaty night (with Ralph not saying four words). When their half-hour dinner break came around, no one had to tell them. Jim and Jack got the rolling-table ready with the tablecloth, the ice-full glasses, and the utensils. All four went into the kitchen.

As they approached the hot-food counter, a room-service waiter walked away munching a piece of celery and carrying a tray on which there were two large lamb chops, butter- and gravy-covered mashed potatoes, side plates of peas and whole kernel corn, a soup, and a pie à la mode. Watching the waiter dip his celery in gravy, Jim grinned, "Well, all right. Looka' here. Fill 'er up." He shoved his plate across the counter.

"You boys kinda' early tonight, ain't 'cha'," Clyde, the beefy-jowled chef showed his tobacco-stained teeth.

"Yeh," Jim muttered, craning his neck to see his helping. His lips slowly formed the half smirk, half smile of those accustomed to being dissatisfied as he saw: SPLAP! a large scoop of leftover Spanish rice, thickly sauced; PLOPP! PLOPP! two tiny hamburger patties, thickly greased; SPLIP! a scoop of pale, dry lima beans.

"Hope you boys enjoy it," Clyde smiled.

"Yeh, hope you boys enjoy it," Jim repeated bitterly, letting the others see his plate.

Cleve looked from the plate to Ralph, who stared first at the plate, then at Clyde.

"Shit!" Jack protested. "We had that mess yesterday! Give us what he got!" pointing at the room-service waiter busy with his lamb chops.

"What who got? Oh, you mean him?" Clyde said, his eyes wide and innocent. "Why that's an order there. Ain't that right, buddy?" The waiter looked up, and stuffing the last piece of gravy dripping celery into his mouth, nodded and grinned.

"An order for the boys in the basement," Jim muttered, putting his plate on the table.

"You sure is some wrong—" Jack started feebly.

"Forget it, man, le's go," Cleve broke in, taking Jack's plate and reaching for Ralph's.

Ralph held on to his plate. *"How come* we can't have what he has?" He confronted Clyde with a tone that made everybody in the kitchen stop and look at him. For the first time that day Cleve heard something unexpected. He stared at Ralph, blinking rapidly, trying to place that tone.

"Listen, boy," Clyde finally answered Ralph, "this is all you gon' get. If you want it, eat it, if not, don't."

Ralph's eyes narrowed to two dark lines; the hand holding the plate tensed, then lowered. Certain he was going to throw it, Cleve grabbed the plate, pleading, "Come on Ralph, man. Come on now."

"I don't want it," Ralph said after a moment, releasing the plate and moving away.

Then Clyde said it was no skin off his ass. Ralph told him not to say "nothin' else to me, man. Hear?" Clyde told him, "Don't tell me what to do, boy." Ralph told him he had his boy in his pants and started over to the counter. Jim and Jack got him turned around. Cleve took the filled plates over to the table. It seemed all over.

But while they were waiting for the elevator, Clyde cracked that he didn't see what they were "raising such a fuss about. They don't eat that good at home." And Ralph reached and whirled around and glass and ice splattered against the aluminum oven just above Clyde's head, one split second before he had to dodge a plate that sailed flying-saucer-like back into the stove, bursting into frantic pieces.

"Told you don't say nothin' else to me? Never! Not a goddamn thing!" Ralph shouted, his body still bent with his throwing motion, "I'll kill onea' you red-faced bastards!"

A knife suddenly in his hand, Clyde started around the counter; the two other chefs grabbed him.

"Let him go! Let him go!" Ralph shouted. "Come on, dammit. Come on—"

"Boy, I'm gon' slit you like a bull in a slaughter house," Clyde hissed with spit on his lips.

"Well come on and do it, then, dammit! Come on!" Crouched there in the center of the floor Ralph near-pleaded. " 'Cause that's all you can do to me from now on! Kill me! Kill me! But the rest of that shit ain't goin'! Goddammit! No more!" In his voice was an ugly writhing.

Cleve and Jim rushed to him and tried to grab him. He knocked their hands away.

"Get away from me! Don't touch me! You gon' keep takin' this—this shit till it kills you! But not me! No more, dammit! Get away from me!" Shocked by his scalding eyes, Cleve and Jack moved back. Cleve hearing what he had said. "Till it kills you . . . Till it kills you." Through with them, Ralph turned back to Clyde, still held by the other two. "You bad back there! Bring yo' fat ass out here an' we'll see! Hillbilly mothuh-fuckuh!"

Cyde flared red, flung one of the men away from him, struggled with the other one. "Lemme' go. Lemme go. Gon' run this knife so fuckin' deep . . ."

"Yeh! Yeh, you got a knife! Well I ain't got one!" Ralph cried, seemingly looking at some point above Clyde's head, like on through the walls, ceilings, roof, on out over the whole city, whole world. "So come on out! I'll fight you with my bare *hands*!"

At "hands" his voice trembled and crumpled to a shattering sob. And Cleve was suddenly aware of how many people (waitresses, porters, waiters, dishwashers) had come into the kitchen to look. A ring of varied expressions standing there watching Ralph cry. He wanted to destroy them, or Clyde, or Ralph, or himself. He moved to Ralph, gripped his trembling shoulders, saying gently, "Come on, Ralph. Let's go, man. Le's go."

Ralph's face was dark, sweating, grimacing pain as he looked at Cleve. "Man—man—" he whispered, his fingers gripping Cleve's forearm. "They better leave—leave me—I'm a father!" he forced tensely through his teeth, his face brushing Cleve's. "A husband! A man!" He shook his head to cool his intensity. "—What—Busboy?—What does that mean? Huh?—If this is it, I can't—can't—"

"I know, man, I know—" Cleve led him away, feeling a terrible heat in his chest as Clyde shouted they'd better get him out of there.

"Jus' take it easy, man, we got you," Jack came up to help. They could feel him relax, slump, stifle a sob. But then Miss Pritchard was suddenly there at the front of the crowd behind them.

"What's the matter with *him*? Is he *sick*? . . ." she asked, making the word sound obscene.

Ralph stiffened at her voice. He pushed away from Jack and Cleve, tugging at his collar.

"Yeh, I'm sick! Sick to death of all of you!" he shouted, and before anyone could catch what was happening his black tie sailed into her face. "Take the mothu-fu—"

She let out a shriek and ducked behind her hands. The crowd pressed toward Ralph: "Hey, there, now!" "Say, boy?!" "What're you—" Cleve, Jim, Jack, and two of the old porters moved Ralph through them to the corridor and down the stairs. They could hear behind them talk of the police.

In the locker room the three others stood back watching as Ralph got his locker unlocked, flung his jacket inside, then just leaned there on his hands, his head down. Cleve looked away from his sweating, trembling back. The *Jet* magazine was still there on the floor. Seeing it, Cleve remembered what Jim had read: ". . . In—— they drug a colored—and flogged him!" He looked at Ralph leaning there, his head down, his trembling back bared; and what he had said upstairs, "till it kills you!" came back and struck him again, hitting home this time, forcing something inside him to give way, leaving him weak and trembling. He slumped down on the bench opposite Ralph, breathing deep with his mouth open, his head down.

"Now what the hell's wrong with you?" Jim asked.

Cleve just looked at him and shook his head. It would be too long and hard a job to make Jim and Jack understand about being slowly, relentlessly driven out of yourself and into a chained image without even being aware of the whips or resentful of the commands.

Ralph turned and stared at him.

"You had enough, too?" he asked him.

Cleve nodded, "Yeh, cut me down, too, man. I'll be dead in a minute."

"Le's go, then."

"What, Cleve, man?!" Jack exclaimed as they both started putting their clothes back on. "You goin', too? Gon' leave us with all this work?"

"Aw, jive-ass college boys," Jim sneered. "Where the hell you think you gon' go? All the jobs just as jive as this one."

"Maybe. But we'll go in different this time," Cleve said, zipping his pants.

"Yeh, and leave quicker if we have to," Ralph grinned at him, buttoning his shirt.

They got their stuff and went out, leaving Jim and Jack cussing incredulously in the doorway. They only hesitated a half-beat when Miss Pritchard came through the archway in her midnight blue hostess's gown, flanked by two policemen in their blue uniforms.

"That one, the tall one."

"Was the other one with him?"

"Yeh, I'm with him."

Their smiles were only slightly nervous as they went to meet them. Now this was better, more real. Those guns and clubs. They could get ready for this. The way they were doing it upstairs you wouldn't even know until they started honing the wood and driving in the nails.

"What's the charges?"

Yeh. Dig. Should have known that's what they'd call it —disturbing the peace. Yeh . . .

Other SIGNET and MENTOR Books
of Special Interest

☐ **THE CONFESSIONS OF NAT TURNER by William Styron.**
The record-breaking bestseller and Pulitzer Prize-winning
novel about the devoutly religious, well-educated Negro
preacher who led a violent revolt against slavery.
(#Y3596—$1.25)

☐ **A RAISIN IN THE SUN AND THE SIGN IN SIDNEY BRU-
STEIN'S WINDOW by Lorraine Hansberry.** Two outstanding
plays: one, winner of the New York Drama Critics Award,
about a young Negro father's struggle to break free from
the barriers of prejudice, the other, portraying a modern-
day intellectual's challenge of the negation and detachment of his fellow intellectuals. With a Foreword by John
Braine and an Introduction by Robert Nemiroff.
(#Q4111—95¢)

☐ **THE BLACK WOMAN An Anthology edited by Toni Cade.**
This volume presents the eloquent writings of Abbey Lincoln, Joanne Grant, Kay Lindsay and others—all discussing
such topics as politics, the Black Man, sex, child-raising
in the ghetto and much more. (#Q4317—95¢)

☐ **THE CHRONOLOGICAL HISTORY OF THE NEGRO IN
AMERICA edited by Mort Bergman.** Events, people, ideas,
laws, legislation and literature—all that constitutes the
history of the black man in the western hemisphere from
colonial times to "Brown vs. the Board of Education."
(#MW937—$1.50)

**THE NEW AMERICAN LIBRARY, INC., P.O. Box 999, Bergenfield,
New Jersey 07621**

Please send me the SIGNET and MENTOR BOOKS I have checked
above. I am enclosing $_____(check or money order
—no currency or C.O.D's). Please include the list price plus 15¢ a
copy to cover handling and mailing costs. (Prices and numbers are
subject to change without notice.)

Name_____

Address_____

City_____State_____Zip Code_____
Allow at least 3 weeks for delivery